Dream Knights

By Paul Kev Hudson

Cover Art by the amazing Tullius Heuer

This is dedicated to Maurice, the father I could almost claim, the mentor I could enjoy for a brief time, a warm glow of generous insight in this world of harsh glare.

Chapter 1

Sounds reverberate louder like eerie echoes playing in reverse. Swelling noise and confusion draw me in. As I concentrate, her face snaps into focus.

"Please," she pleads with me, "keep this safe—don't let them recover it, whatever you do. I'll get it later. *Please*." Solid, confident, aloof Mandy, our third floor manager who never stays long at gatherings, whose smile never reaches her lovely green eyes… Never have I seen her so flushed and desperate, and this makes me mumble in worry. "Go!" She gives me a firm push and the weighted business satchel comes away in my hands.

This isn't good. This isn't what I planned for the day—not at all! But my stumble turns into a spin, and I'm hurrying for the sliding doors of the elevators. No, too slow. I veer toward the stairs, feeling Mandy's anxiety at my back, still pushing me.

Instinctively, I know what swings at my side as I hurry down toward the parking garage. Inside are project details from our corporate back campus, work none of us in the front building ever know about except it's unhealthy to discuss. Yet, we sometimes speculate about it in hushed whispers among those we trust most. Somehow, Mandy dared to find out and then did something unbelievably heroic: she stole it!

Ms. Prissy, what have you gotten me into? She must know they're suspicious, coming for her but not for me, and she has trusted me with everything. Not the bold or the confident or the athletic in our office, but me. And that is enough, to be judged worthy. I won't let her down.

I burst into the quiet garage and then slow my manic pace. Our cars are tracked; of course everyone's is, for their own safety. The gate guard would stop me and ask why I'm leaving at an odd time. Probably even call my superior, who's hopefully doing her best at this moment to avoid trouble. So, not my car. I must do something they'll never expect.

Wandering up to the garage railing, I gaze across the manicured, colorful side gardens. Beyond that, in stark contrast, is a ragged wall of trees and bramble. The pitiful remnant of cleared forest hides a security fence and would also hide me. And in the back floorboard of my car there happens to be expensive garden sheers I have yet to use...

Once I cut just enough of the fence to push through, I pick my way around the undergrowth and hatch a plan. It will be a simple matter to follow the creek to the side highway leading to our residential area—oh, thank my lucky stars her building is close to mine! I can hitch rides anonymously, act normal, lay low, and then hand over this burden once she returns. Yeah, simple—

I'm blindsided by wafted stench that breaks my self-pep talk. Glancing down into the tributary, I see a macabre carpet of bovine corpses so numerous that they obstruct the flow and pile up against the company fence. Apparently, someone's idea of disposal was to mostly cover the bodies with a white powder, as if that would prevent the decay or the smell!

Can this cover-up be related to information I now safeguard? It hardly seems dastardly enough for this level of risk since pollution and death might be the least of the problems coming from the company's secretive operations. And this is probably the end of my corporate life, the beginning of *my* problems. Regardless, I must press on—I make myself press on. I just hope nothing else drinks the water.

When I reach the housing complex, my anxiety level jumps. Two company cars sit like dread sentinels in front of her building. Already! This can't be coincidence no matter how fervently I wish it so. My courage is sputtering in the face of what might become a very hostile encounter. Do they know about me already? If so, they'll be waiting at my place too. I *must* remain hidden.

Gazing down at the satchel, part of me wishes I dropped it in the creek with the cattle and forgot all about it. That urge is faint but still it shames me. Even with security here, probably waiting for her, or waiting for me, I need to deliver this information safely where she can retrieve it without them finding out.

Using every precaution, I creep around to the backyard area of her building. If anyone comes out now, I'm screwed. They'll act like I'm the bad guy betraying their trust, all the while preparing to disappear me... My courage wavers again, but then I see the top edge of an old black tarp poking up through the overgrowth along the edge of the building, remnants of an aspiring garden planned during happier times. With a final check to make certain no one is watching me, I pry up the thick mesh, wedge the satchel underneath, and pat down any signs of disturbance. There. It's ten strides away from a domicile that is surely getting ransacked and safe from the weather until I can tell her of my clever deed.

Now I can return to normal: "No, no, C-man, I was just sent home by my boss and have no idea what you're talking about. Satchel, what satchel?" If only I could be as convincing as Mandy, because I'm sure no one suspected a thing until the very moment she made her move. I just hope I helped and that the result will be worth the stress. But mostly, I think it's past time I vacation somewhere far away.

My door looks undisturbed, and I open it ready to give fervent denials and excuses. Breathing a sigh of relief at the familiar stillness, I immediately go to the kitchen sink and wash the dirt from under my fingernails. *The evidence of my part is now down the drain*, I think in a giddy rush before slumping down at my table and pouring a strong drink. But any celebration sours at the thought of the company on the trail, pressing my boss. She will still be there, inside the gates, with our very angry employers. She's good, tough, but is she that good?

I raise the mug to my lips but can't take a drink. Please be okay, Mandy. If only I could be sure...

I feel my hold *loosen*, my perspective drift, my vision blur...

Instantly I'm hovering over a shock-bright room. Mandy is sitting in a chair, straight back, straight face, even breaths, but I can sense the fear she suppresses. Pacing in between her and the door is a stocky, cocky man who leers at her with each turn he makes. A two-way speaker on the far wall crackles, and suddenly I know this room. On the first floor in the back of the building is series of rooms no one wants to visit because they are the disciplining area of Human Resources. Shielded, isolated, and a disturbing reminder of the power of the company.

"Nothing at her place," reports the static-filled and impersonal voice. "You may proceed."

"Gordon," Mandy calls out quickly, "you're making a mistake, whatever you think I've done. I've been exemplary for over two years—you know that because you hired me. I can bring many more productive years but you have to clear up this misunderstanding and let me get back to my job."

There is only a momentary pause before the speaker crackles again. "Proceed."

"Gordon!" This time it's her voice that cracks, and the brute's intimidating leer widens into a pleased grin. My heartbeat is her heartbeat, racing wildly despite her best efforts.

"We know more than you think we know," he intones and looms over her. "Three of your staff are no longer in the building. All others have been questioned while we waited for H.R.'s verdict. Did you give our information to each or only one?" Leaning in close, his voice is an urgent whisper. "Tell us who left with it. They will get your punishment, and you will walk free. This need not get ugly."

I feel her consider, that tiny craven in us yearning for release from responsibility, but the force with which she stamps out that lying wisp of hope impresses me more than anything else I know of her. Under no circumstances would she betray him...me...no, him. I grow dizzy at my disjointed understanding but refocus just in time to see the big man's hand shoot out to grip her by the throat.

In a fluid motion, he lifts her from the chair by her neck, into the air, and then slams her onto the nearby table. Mandy whimpers and tries to cough, but her resolve doesn't waver. She's heroic, no doubt. However, the man leans into her face, and his leer seems even more threatening. Wicked.

"Long before I'm done, you will want to tell me everything," he states in an excited rumble. "You will beg me to stop. But I won't. Long after you want to faint to escape I won't stop. Because I gave you a fair chance..."

The thought of damage done to this brave woman is too much, and I almost flee, but *please, please let me help her*. I focus our blossoming pain and my desperation and anger, and *reach* down into the offending hand and *wrench*.

With a cry of pain, he jerks back, staggers a step and glares at her. "What did you do?" he yells. Mandy is all confusion and fear and temporary relief, with a returning whisper of hope. Encouraged, I gather again, build a desperate pressure, and *reach* into his brain. Eyes rolling up, he slumps into a large pile of unresponsive muscle.

"*Run!*" I send at her, but she merely rises to a quivering elbow, waiting for her world to make sense. "*Run!*" I repeat, and I feel like I'm making her twist herself to her feet. It's my turn to give her the motivational push. *"Backyard tarp."* I shove that one last image at her and feel…completion.

* * *

Doug lay in bed with a smile on his face, even though jumbled emotions and his racing heartbeat were slow to fade. Mostly, he felt like he had accomplished something wonderful, made a difference that would matter. Did she—Mandy—make it out? He wished he could dive back into sleep and find out, and he let his heavy eyelids drop closed just in case the answers would come. But he knew full well that once these kinds of intense dreams were finished, they were gone forever. That wouldn't stop him from drowsing happily with the notion she would succeed against the corporation she had infiltrated. He was left with nothing but vague impressions about the company and the odd environment but knew it wasn't a happy place, and it seemed so foreign to his waking mind. Not a place he'd ever voluntarily visit. Besides, it was like he could still smell those cow bodies, or maybe that was his underarm too close to his nose.

He gave a confirming sniff and a groan and rolled out of bed even though it was at least an hour before any self-respecting college student began their day. After a hot shower, he used his excess time to stare out the dorm window at the waking world. Familiar environs cast in this unfamiliar light of early dawn reminded him of the dream setting, both real and unreal, normal and yet so skewed.

The man from the dream—and Doug decided once and for all this wasn't just some strange future portrayal of himself for there were too many differences—had needed help to rise to the challenge of the unforeseeable emergency, a task he wouldn't have completed on his own. As the student lingered on this baffling experience, he wondered if the man would make it to a better place. Only if he had gotten off his ass and hurried. Concern crept into Doug's reflections, for he felt the dream man had little motivation once he was sitting in his own place. They might come for him there, and his capture would probably mean failure after all that crazy effort.

Doug looked down at an archaic gift from his parents, a subject notebook on his desk, and considered writing down each detail before they faded. He fingered the top corner, considering the urge to open the cover. But how to begin? Who else would even care about shared moments that had made him care? Motivation was a strange thing, he mused, much like that man sitting in his own dark place after his wild surprise and desperate flight. Now here he was, sharing Doug's headspace, staring at the still-closed notebook and looming effort, and unsure it really mattered.

Sounds of his suitemate stirring broke the trance, and the mumbling in low tones to his girlfriend meant, as usual, she had spent the night here instead of her own dorm room. And since Doug didn't feel like dealing with the awkwardness, he roused himself, grabbed his pack, and headed for the cafeteria. The dream echoes, so out of place amid the bright bustle of campus life, stuck with him, mainly because he wasn't ready to let go. It made him less sociable and distracted him in classes. One moment he was twirling his pen around his thumb and the next he was watching the pen drop, as if his fingers had forgotten how to work right.

It'd been a long time since that had happened, and Doug felt a lingering connection to the dropped satchel. What secrets were really in the bag? What had that corporation—?

"I'm glad you find my lecture so entertaining, Doug," the professor called in a louder-than-usual tone, and the relatively small class snickered when that sudden change made the guilty student's head jerk up.

"Uh, sorry, Mr. Weisinger. I'm trying to focus."

"But what else could be so distracting? Big plans for the upcoming weekend? Do share."

"Just a dream…uh, remnants… Never mind."

"Ah, I see, I see," the professor said in deep understanding. "So was she hot?" As classmates tittered and Doug sunk into his seat, the teacher knew it was time to return to his important pre-Civil War analysis.

The day lumbered along and slowly regained clarity for Doug, and yet the unease of the unresolved clung to that mystified part of his mind. Back in his dorm, he again considered the notebook, but this time it was brief because he knew he'd already forgotten too many details which had seemed so vital in the early morning hours. Instead of the notebook, Doug opened his laptop and navigated to the campus intranet, following a vague urge to an off-topic chat board and the new topic button. "I dream super freaky!" he typed. "Real and yet not, but it clings even though everything else is so normal. What a wild sensation, like a new memory about an impossibly far off place! Do you dream like this, too? Need to talk about it before my head explodes!"

Chapter 2

Part of Doug wished for a continuance or some kind of closure the next time he fell asleep. Just the thought of being able to dip into that adventure again was both exciting and disquieting. Was this how blockbuster movie ideas formed? This dream experience faded much faster than memory, and yet it felt so similar to actual memory, like a distant relation.

Just then the adjoining suite door opened and Donna popped her head in to catch him stretched out on the bed. Grinning when Doug started, she commented, "Heard you early this morning, and then here you are. On a Friday night. I thought you were a night owl."

"Yeah, well..." He shrugged. His suitemate, Tim, poked his head in above hers, creating an intrusive totem pole.

"Bro," Tim said, "come clubbing with us. Unless, you're—" His teasing look was a challenge. "—studying?"

"Nah. Thanks, but it's been a weird day. And we have the intramural match tomorrow."

"Weird alright," Donna said with heavy sarcasm. "It's barely nine."

Tim applied the pressure: "Are you old, or are you full of *life*? Get your ass into party mode and let's go *live*."

"Fine, okay," Doug conceded, a smile growing to match theirs. As he hopped up and grabbed his jacket off the back of the chair, he added, "But only for an hour."

"Or two," Tim agreed.

Bright lights and loud music snapped Doug out of his mood, and the fun release helped him sleep more peacefully that night. Still, he wished he'd moved off campus for his junior year. He'd wanted to minimize the expense for his parents since apartment life was more costly, but it sure would have been more private than having a "bonus" suitemate who seemed determined to include him in their activities.

The next day after returning home from their flag football game, Doug could hear Tim throw his equipment bag to the floor and flop onto his bed. *Man*, that sucked," Tim called through the open suite doors, and it was like he could hear Doug's shrug when he continued. "I know, I know, it's just a game, but we weren't even *close* to prepared for their cheating."

Doug preferred not to dwell on it. "So we'll get better prepared next practice, maybe try out some of their tricks."

"Cheaters," Tim grumped. "Besides, Kevin kept throwing the ball like I was an Olympic sprinter, and their Q.B. was nailing his receiver."

"Yep. Not much we could do with those long routes—except maybe steal their quarterback. First dibs on the shower." While Doug washed away the sweat and sting of the loss, Tim came to the adjoining doorway and continued to sulk.

"I mean, we have a good time at practice, but when we're up against a tough team, we have no ability to step up our game."

"Well, we might have won if you hadn't made us go dancing last night," Doug teased, causing Tim to snort and lay all the blame on his girlfriend. "So where is Donna this afternoon? Someone I know needs comforting."

"Eh, she's hanging with her girls, probably shopping or some shit. I say we take out our anger on aliens. Slag-fest, Halo style. So hurry up in there."

Unlike their flag football opponents, even big scary aliens were no match for the soldier team that raced through the levels with wild abandon. Every disappointment was forgotten under the twin influences of Dew and pew-pew. When Donna showed up around dinner time wearing one of her dancing dresses, Doug already had his excuses cemented.

"No, and don't look at me that way," he lightly scolded when Donna began pouting. "I'm still feeling that game, and I need to get some studying done. You know? The reason we're here?"

Tim chuckled and patted Donna's rump. "That's not why I'm here."

"Well, whatever. Enjoy. A full fifteen-hour semester, remember? And I refuse to fall behind." Into the night, Doug struggled to focus on his homework, even switching subjects to relieve the feeling of dissatisfaction. Finally he gave up and dragged his problems into dreamland. He vaguely remembered his roommate's return and Donna's giggles, and he wondered if he'd ever be able to ignore them.

The next morning while Doug was stirring, his mind chased slippery thoughts. There was a jumble, some meaningful yet frustrating event that faded with each passing heartbeat. When he cracked an eyelid to gauge the sunlight beyond his window blinds, tidbits vanished, leaving him with a sense of failure or a vague lack of fulfillment. He felt he should be able to figure out why it affected him like this, but had no starting point, no anchor. Why the emptiness when there was so much happening in his life? Was it an unfulfilled wish within the mystery of sleep, or did it belong to waking issues?

Then a thought made him freeze in the act of sitting up: could this have to do with Friday's dream, the one he had the longing to dive back into? The final remnants of dream discordance gave him no answers. But he remembered his good-funk from that dream and his post after Friday classes. With purpose, he slid into his desk chair and navigated to the thread.

"Har har," he muttered, reading the first couple of posts claiming to have dreamed of Doug's mother. Though he would never respond, he mentally saluted the reaction post asking how ten-year-olds could access a college intranet. The only other public poster admitted to having strange and indescribable dreams while offering no details or proof. These initial posts were unsurprising and totally unsatisfying.

Then he opened his one private message entitled: You definitely aren't alone.

"I was standing upon strange grassland, like an African savannah. Thick grass and weird trees…but that was nothing compared to the herd of grazers. Huge balls of fluffy white hair the size of Volkswagens, kind of like living cotton balls but with spiky hair. Above them circled what I thought were vultures, but then I saw them clearly. They were some kind of flying elephant, not at all like Dumbo. They had long matted fur, all grungy. Nasty.

"All the sudden I wanted to warn the big cotton balls, because they were nothing compared to what lurked above them, but they were clueless, and I could only watch as one elephant made a large swooping curve to line up on one and…dove at it. I can't even say if it meant to hit the cotton ball or just land close, whether it meant to land on its feet or roll, but it slammed into the ground and rolled with such force that the ground vibrated—and I swear to you—it was me feeling that ground impact that woke me up.

"So, you definitely aren't alone. Nolan."

Doug leaned back in his chair and laughed, partly at the bizarre visuals but also in relief at his first real response. His own bad feelings were gone, replaced by amusement and curiosity. He knew he had to return the favor, so he hit the reply button.

"Nolan, thanks for the great response. I needed that and promise to return the favor. I hear my roommate and his bubbly girlfriend getting up, and they're going to drag me to the cafeteria. But when I get a chance, I promise to tell you all about my epic adventure in some far off land."

Every Sunday, Doug's dorm hosted a matinee movie-watching party in the TV lounges on each floor. Normally, he would take a pass, but one of the movies playing struck him as relevant. So when he returned to his room after watching *Inception*, he was in a pensive yet creative mood. Friday's dream wasn't nearly so over-the-top, yet it had an undeniably similar undercurrent: a struggle in an altered reality that resonated of important consequences, with perhaps a matching dose of corporate dystopia.

Doug pondered the idea of his dream being set in the future rather than merely some exotic location, though neither felt like the answer. Maybe it had been both. When he settled on this conclusion and began the task of telling Nolan about it, he was surprised to find much of it came back to him with the responsiveness of a recent memory. He felt especially reconnected when he recalled the brave woman's name, Mandy. Even though it had been a dream, he sent her a mental cheer and well wishes.

While detailing the story, Doug found he could think of the possibilities and consequences, the fates of players and the information, without becoming upset. His telling the story for Nolan was cathartic. He felt productive, having shared, even unburdened. After finishing the tale, he closed the reply by mentioning how good it felt to talk about it. "Maybe things like this, these rare or even funny dreams, are meant to be shared," Doug concluded. "If you agree and want to hear more, let's talk the next time we have something freaky."

It didn't take long for Nolan to answer. "I'm game," he wrote. "I enjoyed your mess and can only imagine how mind-blowing it seemed. Yes, it was also good to write mine out, though it took a long time to find the right words. This way, the dream made more sense to me."

Doug encouraged the few half-hearted posters to share details but wasn't disappointed when he got no takers. He and Nolan had found their outlet, and they traded speculation over the following week. When Nolan had a dream that left him agitated, they agreed to try a face-to-face. He lived off campus and was in his final year. Pizza and Ramen noodles were his normal fare, but he was willing to visit Doug's regular cafeteria.

"Mom would be happy I'm getting some greens," Nolan said, toying with the last of his broccoli. After a flurry of introductions, they had taken a break to wolf down lunch, and now Nolan seemed reluctant to recall the dream that had brought them there.

"Gonna grab a chocolate." Doug motioned to the ice cream freezers lining one wall. "Want one?" After Nolan had bussed his tray and accepted an ice cream cup, Doug leaned forward. "You're keeping me in suspense."

"Not sure where to start."

With a reassuring gesture, Doug said, "Just launch into it and let's have fun."

"Well, the 'dream-me' knew how to fly. The wheel stick, the gauges, the knobs. Based on my memory of the experience, I searched the web and I think it was some kind of Cessna, which seems a common small airplane. And—get this—it was eerie seeing the cockpit pictures and getting a hit of recognition."

"Nice." Doug grinned and pointed out, "It's like Matrix learning, so when you need to fly us somewhere you'll already know how."

"Ha! Don't know about that. So, I was flying in to visit friends—no idea who—but they lived outside of any town. Funny enough, I used the roads to land and parked in their front yard. So far so good, right? I had a nice visit and when it came time to return home, I loaded into my plane and got rolling.

"But now the roads had traffic, enough that I couldn't find the right cleared hill or free stretch to act as a runway. My wings were high enough that any car could pass under them, but to avoid some trucks I'd have to dangerously hug the shoulder or ditch. Then, I tried a larger four-lane road, and it was almost a traffic jam, with cars honking impatiently, crowding me rudely, and me trying to avoid hitting anything with wings *or* propeller. So, I turned off another small road and had the same damn problem as before."

Nolan paused and leaned forward. "With the constant cars and trees and power lines, I just couldn't find enough room. I only needed a couple hundred meters clearance to gain the speed for lift. It was maddening.

"The road eventually turned to gravel and led to a huge construction yard, with stacked crates and junk machinery all around. I knew I could dodge those things if only the ground were smooth. But it was slightly muddy and so rough that I was certain I'd damage my landing gear before gaining enough speed. That frustration, that being denied, was what I woke up to." Nolan blew out a breath and then visibly relaxed.

"Telling it makes it seem like no big deal," he finished lamely.

"Telling it, sure," Doug said, "but I know what it is to experience something like that, to *be* in the thick of that problem. In the dreams, it's like we're there, living it."

"Yeah."

"Maybe the dream-you should have used the place they invented for such an occasion," Doug teased. "You know, an airport."

Nolan chuckled. "Yeah. So, funny thing: I *knew* I shouldn't have been on the roads, even in the dream, but I felt like it was necessary. Like that's how it had to be? Like a strange dream disconnect, for some reason I don't know or can't remember."

"Huh. So, have you ever flown a little plane or been in one?"

"Nope. And no desire to; not after that dream."

"And it wasn't a house or people you recognized?"

Nolan shook his head. "Though that construction yard was similar—maybe the same—to one I knew from my previous internships. My dad was an army man who knew many contractors," Nolan explained. "So when I was finishing high school and considering engineering, he helped get me temp work at this engineering firm his base uses."

"Nice to be connected," Doug commented. "Are you getting a job with them when you graduate?"

"Maybe, though I didn't work for them this past summer. I might do a bit of traveling first, and see what else is out there."

After a comfortable silence, Doug mused, "I wonder if the dream was telling you to 'land' there at the job or stay away from it?"

"No clue," Nolan said after snorting. "I just know I need more ice cream." As they were returning with second helpings, Nolan asked, "So what about you? Any new whoppers?"

"Sadly, no. Just flickers I can't remember or those that are instantly lost in the ordinary noise."

Nolan understood. "Yeah, white noise. That's most of my dreams."

"And a good thing or they might drive us bonkers." After sharing a grin, Doug said, "Fun times."

"This definitely helps."

Doug was struck with an idea. "I wonder if we can talk a few more into joining so we have more dreams to poke at. With the right group, I could see it being highly amusing."

"Maybe, with the right people."

"I think I'll ask on the thread. We can always ignore them if they won't play ball." Glancing at his watch, Doug continued, "Speaking of playing ball, I need to get ready for intramural practice. Our flag football team needs all the practice we can get." They parted with a promise to continue communicating, and to see if they could find a few others to add to the fun.

Since he had already spent the effort to detail his epic dream for Nolan, Doug further refined it and posted it on his thread, hoping to inspire more participation. "You can use private messages if you want," he encouraged. "We already shared interesting and fun examples and would like to see more. Even dreams that sting tend to have less of a hold when you talk about them."

Over the weekend, Nolan also posted his dream stories into the public thread, and still they didn't get any activity. Doug even toyed with the idea of bribing his roommate to post encouragement so it might prompt others to participate, but quickly decided against it. He'd already turned down Tim and his girlfriend when they tried dragging him to a music concert, and when the socialite suitemate wanted to attend a binge gaming session down the hall. Doug knew that owing him a favor would make it harder to resist the constant invitations, and he already felt spread thin.

He was about to give up on the thread when he received a new private message late on a Monday night: "I really enjoyed your dream. It would make a good story or even a movie! My name is Cathy, and our freshmen group adviser just so happens to be a grad student in psychology with a special interest and training in dream stuff. I saw your thread and asked him if he would host another group for those of us interested in dreaming, and he said yes! During our group, we agreed on Wednesdays at seven-to-eight or whenever. I hope this isn't too short of notice, but I just got it to happen. PM me back if you want in, and I'll give you the building and room number we're using."

The relief Doug felt made his response a no-brainer. "Finally," Doug murmured as he copied the message to Nolan. Outlet or amusement or both, it would be worth giving it a spin.

Chapter 3

    For support, Doug and Nolan met outside the hall before locating the meeting room, which was already filled with animated conversations. Pushing past his moment of awkwardness when the smiles turned toward them, Doug waved, and they gave their names. The unassuming adviser rose from where he was reclining on a couch to shake their hands and introduce himself as Mark.

    "I think we're all here," Mark said once everyone settled onto the chairs that had been arranged in a loose circle. He glanced to a girl with curly black hair for confirmation before opening their first meeting with an expansive gesture. "Think on this:

Hello, Darkness, my old friend.

I've come to speak with you again,

because a vision softly creeping

left its seeds while I was sleeping.

And the vision that was planted in my brain…

still remains.

    "A moving bit of poetry put to music," Mark intoned after a moment's silence, "sung and re-sung by so many who know *exactly* what this feels like. And in this group we'll delve into dreams, coming away with more insight and—for sure—more entertainment.

"For those who don't already know, I'm nearing the end of my doctorate studies in psychology. Just the grand finale to go: my dissertation. I'm pleased Cathy came to me with this idea, because I've always taken a special interest in dreams and how they affect us. Appropriately enough, some friends and I used to trade dreams, so I know well the need to share and how fun it can be. But before we truly begin, let's share a brief introduction to get to know each other better."

He motioned to the curly-haired girl on his left, who, with an energetic bounce, introduced herself as Cathy. "I'm studying web design," she continued, "front-end graphics if I get lucky, but I'd take anything—backend, webvertising—as long as it's a part of the world's greatest show-and-tell." Her bright grin highlighted her buoyant personality. "And when I read your shared dreams, I knew this kind of meeting would be a perfect way to see just how crazy dreams can get."

By contrast, the blonde sitting next to Cathy was cool and composed. "I'm Kris," she said, waving manicured fingers and exuding stylishness. "Journalism major."

When she offered nothing more, Mark prompted with a supportive smile. "That's it? So why journalism?"

"Because finding out and communicating the truth is how we all grow," Kris replied matter-of-factly.

"Is it?" Mark's question was lighthearted and comfortable, owing to the fact most of the group had spent the first six weeks of the semester getting to know each other. "Isn't truth subjective to the receiver?" When Kris shook her head, Mark added, "Dreams might just test that theory."

The slender boy lounging next to Kris had a face that belonged more in high school than college, and it wouldn't take long for his complementary attitude to show. "Will, here," he said with a lazy salute. "Biology's my thing; it makes the world go round."

"Actually, that's celestial physics," corrected Cathy with a raised brow.

The challenge was immediately matched by Will. "Oh, how little ye know. Physics accounts only for the rock, not the partying upon it. *That* is what makes it all spin. My dreams have confirmed this," he concluded with an exaggerated nod of confidence.

Rolling her eyes without a hint of a smile, the girl next to Will leaned forward in her chair to introduce herself. "My name is Gabriella."

"Call her Gabi—she loves that," Will interjected.

"No," Gabriella said firmly, "because that is not my name."

Before Will could poke her further, Mark said, "Will," in a referee tone, though he was wearing a partly suppressed smile.

"Anyway," the ruffled girl said, "I'm a psychology major, so I have a special interest in all things dealing with the mind."

"Which is why we keep Will around," commented Cathy, and shared chuckles finally got Gabriella to smile. Next to Gabriella was a meek girl who hugged her spiral notebook to her chest and introduced herself as Quani.

"I don't dream much and don't remember them, but I am curious. And since I'm here to learn about many things…" Quani shrugged as if that were explanation enough, and since everyone turned their attention to Doug, it was clear that was all the others expected to get out of her.

"I'm in my junior year, though still living the dorm life," Doug explained. "It's less costly, but sometimes my suitemate makes me regret my decision." To understanding nods, he continued, "I'm a poli-sci major and until this year I was on a law track, but…" He waved it off yet tried to find a diplomatic way to explain his change. "I don't fit that mold, so I'm leaning toward philosophy and writing."

Mark pointed out: "Your training shows in your detailed dream recall, which was very interesting—both of yours." His gesture included the two newcomers, letting them know he'd done some homework of his own. "It's good to have you join us."

The final member of this small circle cleared his throat. "Nolan. I'm a senior in civil engineering, and like Doug, I'm here because my dreams are freaky."

"Thanks to Cathy pointing them out, we have seen that," Mark agreed with a disarming smile. "So mind if we begin with them?" Doug and Nolan nodded, but Mark interrupted his own thoughts by saying, "Oh, and before we dive in, let me reinforce that dreams are individual and can be hopelessly inscrutable. Yet, it's fun to try, and *fun* is our operative word, always. We'll poke and prod the dreams but never make it personal. Even the nicest person can have ugly dreams, and talking about them is soothing if nothing else."

"I think we both began talking about ours to take the oddness or sting out of them," Doug said in support.

Scanning around the group, Mark emphasized that point by poking at the air in between them. "Exactly! Let's always keep that in mind. Now, let's start with Doug's magnificent example. I can only imagine the potent emotions it evoked."

Nodding self-consciously, Doug said, "So strong it made my waking world seem unreal. I felt lingering anxiety, and yet at the same time I was satisfied I helped in some way, if that makes sense. And the details stuck with me for a long time. Things like climbing through the brush then getting blindsided by the smells and sight of the dead cows seem more like a normal memory, as if I had actually been there."

"In that sense," Mark stated, "dreams have direct access to all the emotions of our mind, and by mixing thoughts and feelings in certain combinations, they can even make us feel like we're experiencing something completely new. Just know that it's a perfectly healthy and normal way our resting-state brain processes memories as well as ideas."

Nolan snorted. "Pretty sure I've never experienced anything like my dreams. In real life, that is."

"But as we look deeper," Mark countered, "you might find things that tie into what you know or are experiencing or thinking. That's one of the ways we can have fun: trying to connect the dots, so to speak. For example, your dream of that field might have been your creativity pondering what large furry bunny-things would look like, or flying elephants. If you aren't familiar with Dumbo, I suggest looking it up later and seeing if that cartoon might have been inspiration."

"Or maybe the creator had a similar dream that inspired the cartoon," Will guessed from where he slouched, crossed feet jutting into the middle of the circle.

"No telling how much of our creativity—books, plays, movies, even music—is inspired by dreams," Mark said.

"Safe to guess most of them," Cathy commented and Will snickered.

"That or hallucinogens, *heavy* drug use." They continued discussing Doug's and Nolan's dreams until they had a lag, and Mark asked for others to tell of their dreams.

"Anything?" he prompted. "Cathy, the way you brought up this good idea surely means you have something juicy."

She shrugged. "Mine are mostly about not being able to find classes or showing up to them only to realize I have no clothes on."

"That'd be fun to watch." Will prodded her using his boyish grin.

"Yeah, right." With a rolling of her eyes, she continued, "I think I'm processing the typical fears of college, this new lifestyle of spread-out buildings and tricky schedules."

"More common than most would admit to," Mark confirmed. "Can you zero in on an example to share?"

Cathy again shrugged and pondered before bouncing in her chair. "Oh! I barely remember one where I'm, uh, *swimming* to class. The sidewalks were long swim lanes like in the campus pool, complete with turns and intersections."

With a giggle, she said, "The only problem was when I finally reached class—late of course—I was still dripping water everywhere, in a one-piece swim suit, and without my backpack. I shrugged that dream off as fast as I could, but since you asked, it came back to me."

"Do you remember when you dreamed it?" Mark asked. "Any other details?"

"I'm not sure. Maybe it was early last week, but definitely within this month. I think," she added, laughing at her foggy memory.

"That's how it often is," Mark told the students, "hazy details, uncertain timing, but..." He held up a finger for emphasis. "This can all be improved upon. There are tricks we can employ, using them in much the same way we learn anything: repetition.

"Every night as you fall asleep, tell yourself over and over that you want to remember your dreams. This will raise the awareness in your mind and keep your dreams closer to your memory so you can pull them with you into the waking world. Be sure to have something by your bed to record what you remember while it's still fresh, before you even get up to shower or eat. This trains you to have better recall. Our minds are always active, pseudo-dreaming, whether or not we remember. By understanding this, the dreams will open up to you.

"So, did anyone else remember a dream to share?" Mark asked. When he got no other volunteers, he straightened. "All right. Before next week, let's search for quotes about dreams, famous or otherwise, and each share one quote that resonates with us. And remember to keep a notepad or something handy to record as many dream details as you can. The more you do this, the easier it gets.

"Feel free to hang around and chat for the rest of the hour, and thanks to Cathy for instigating this."

As some were gathering backpacks and purses, Cathy replied to Mark, "Thanks for agreeing to lead it. This is going to be loads of fun."

* * *

Smells of rich earth and the hum of grand expectations. Not a single straight line on huts or walk paths, but the village seems functional, a true home built from hard labor rather than skill, and fierce love. Despite the situation.

Shabby clothes, unkempt hair and smudges, yet bright smiles. The rains had been perfect and the harvest a success. And now, two of the village's finest youngsters, beautiful lovers of matching hearts and minds, pledge themselves to each other for all time. A celebration to be remembered with fondness on even the coldest of nights.

Soon, there will be plenty of mead and loud laughter, and even the transient carpenters who toil ceaselessly for the nobility in the land will pause to enjoy this custom and soak in the moment. The lounging nobles and their guards are like a dark cloud threatening to block the warmth of the sun, but the villagers are determined to let nothing spoil this special time. And the lovers have eyes for only each other.

Their love is pure, unspoiled, and a testament to what all people desire, even if that longing is buried deep. Many in the crowd yearn for it, or smile fondly at their own lover while remembering their first time together. But, there is one who feels unbearable envy.

"I will *not* bless this," the fancy young man stands and calls amid muted gasps. The father, the lord, scowls and says nothing, so his son continues. "We were playmates when we were young, before we felt the duty and burden of class." Feeling his father's considering stare, the young man turns to him. "There is none more beautiful, more perfect for *me*, in all the lands. Had we not been separated, she would be up here with me now."

The uncomfortable rustle among the nobility is drowned out by the outrage of the peasants; loudest among them is a blind-sided groom. The girl is a frozen statue, the very image of mortification. "How *dare* you!" the father of the bride bellows, while the mother and groom close ranks to protect their cherished one. "We do not toil for you so you can make fun of the sacred."

"*Peace*, peace," the lord commands, rising to his full height. Only the son dares press his advantage.

"Look at her, Father. See the perfection—there's no way her blood is merely peasant, despite what we thought. I claim nobility runs through her, and so this…" Having moved as close as he dared to the defensive knot, he gestures in disdain to the quivering, red-faced groom. "This…union cannot be right."

The crowd erupts again, buying me a precious moment.

I realize I've been hovering, watching this scene unfold like a drama that has me clenching my teeth. I also know the wounded groom is about to explode and cross a very dangerous line. So I *ghost* into him, settle into the tornado of violent emotions, and bring calm and confidence. Just enough to prevent the cry for blood.

I bite my tongue, draw a deep breath, and say, "Let us be. You have no right."

"I have *every* right," the grossly spoiled boy counters. Pinning the girl with his challenge, he asks, "Would you rather be a dirty farmhand's woman, or mother to future rulers, *decision*-makers? Possibly kings?"

I wave dismissively at him. "Your very question proves you know nothing of our love. Leave. Us. Be." My sudden change in manner and speech catches notice, especially from the lord who is now eyeing both boys warily. The token guards are also alert.

"*I* cannot accept this strife," the lord mutters, shaking his head. "This must resolve. We *must* find resolution."

"We all believe and trust in God," the lord's son declares and holds aloft something that glints in the sunlight. "Let Him decide through this toss of a coin, for He will not choose wrong." Capitalizing on his moment of opportunity, he glares around. "Does anyone dare say otherwise?"

The father quickly holds out his palm for the coin. "Let God decide, then, as the highest authority, who she will marry."

With a tiny smirk, the noble boy adds: "Heads and I leave them in peace with my blessing; tails, I get *her* tail."

This twist unfolds quicker than my shock can handle. I witness the exchange of nods, the coin pass, the drop of the arm, bend of the knees, and *plink*...the metallic pop as the coin flips skyward.

I feel sick.

Time slows the coin's trajectory until it is doing slow-motion summersaults into the air. I know something is wrong; I know *right* or *choice* has nothing to do with this moment. And I know what will show on the coin, even as I strain to see each side when it flashes into view. I feel the boy already straining against the injustice, so he knows it, too.

"Wait, *wait!*" The girl shrieks, popping time like a bubble. The coin falls and is caught in the lord's fist, and he stares at her with raised eyebrow. "Please," she adds belatedly in a voice that trembles so much I'm surprised she is still able to stand, but now I know that the girl also perceives her fate. *No,* I silently scream, but I am helpless to stop her. "I will give your son my wedding night and *only* my wedding night if he leaves us alone after that."

The crowd remembers it has a voice, and the uproar drives me skyward like the scoundrel's coin. "I want to see that mark," the boy yells to be heard. The lord scowls and tucks it into his vest, and I'm now positive. "It was rigged," the boy screams and is drowned out by others. "They tricked her!"

Again, I am the sickened observer, knowing without a doubt that if the girl goes with them she will be forever changed, the joyful, innocent part of her love forever broken. A spoiling incapable of being undone. The boy will get a broken love and be forever trapped by his hatred of the deed. I float further away, and wish they would run for it, flee. That surely the fate of an outlaw is preferable, but I am drifting out of range, unable to tell what is happening.

Chapter 4

Nolan was in distress, as much as the mild-mannered senior could be, so the group set aside the opening plans to hear him out. "This felt like I was witnessing the very beginning—the wicked roots—of 'right of the first night' medieval custom. I looked it up to make certain it wasn't just all in my head."

Scowling, he continued to vent, "Small comfort that the boy didn't throw his life away and challenge the lord right then and there. Calming his rage meant so little in the big picture, with their helplessness to the whims of the nobility punk." Nolan blew out a breath. "I'm not even sure he had any desire except to disrupt the couple's happiness. And if the girl went with them to avoid further conflict… Well, she would have never been the same."

"Disturbing," Kris muttered with a shiver of empathy.

"Yeah, and I was playing out scenarios of escape or revenge—I didn't even realize I was already awake until there was no context. The crowds and the nobles and the awful situation were just…gone. And it was only my mind stewing on the what-ifs, feeling like I had just *been there*."

When Nolan relaxed back into his chair, Mark leaned forward. "This is a great example of how dreams can have unhindered access to our emotions, and how those emotional memories bleed through into our waking life. Do you feel as if this were a personal truth experience or that it's merely a dream, unimportant?" When Nolan shrugged in discomfort, Mark tried a different angle. "Better yet, would you recognize a similar injustice in real life and maybe react differently because you've had this dream?"

"Maybe…probably."

"*Pfft*, I definitely would," Cathy said, "and I only heard about the dream!"

With a satisfied look, Mark straightened. "Conventional studies suggest our minds process memories and work on problems while we're dreaming. Pioneers like Freud and Jung focused on dreams as a result, an aftermath of something already on our minds. But get this," Mark emphasized with a raised finger, "recent studies connect dreams to our learning process. Some researchers see links to support the theory that dreams can actually teach us. If we try to understand our dreams, we can grow even more than just forgetting or ignoring them. I think Nolan's need to discuss this and his reaction to it would add a data point supporting their conclusions."

With a small clearing of his throat, Nolan mumbled, "Sorry for blurting it out."

Mark assured him with a placating gesture yet addressed them all. "This is what our group is primarily for: bringing those powerful dreams out into the open, blowing off steam. It helps, right?" Nolan smiled and nodded, so Mark continued, "Anyone else have an urgent one they need to share before we continue?" He scanned the circle of expectant looks.

"If not, let's share quotes and discuss them. I'll go first with one from my old friend Carl Jung. It has always resonated with me and fits nicely into the point I was making. He said, 'Who looks outside, dreams; who looks inside, awakes.'" Mark paused a moment before repeating the quote and asking, "Any comments on what you think he meant?"

"Was he talking about meditation?" Cathy asked.

"More like study," Gabriella corrected.

"Humph. He was probably talking about daydreaming out the window." Will imitated the thousand-yard stare, while Mark wore an indulgent smile.

"Daydreaming, probably not, and maybe in a way he was talking about meditation. Meditation encompasses self-reflection, right? And an important way to reflect would be dwelling on and analyzing why we dream what we do, and how we use those understandings." When no one else offered analysis, Mark continued.

"I think he's making a distinction between having dreams and doing something valuable with them, because what we do and consider in the waking world builds up food for thought, so to speak. Ammunition for our dreams to work with. But to truly awaken to ourselves, who we are, we must dwell on what those dreams mean to us. Perhaps," Mark emphasized as he motioned to Nolan, "what our dreams have to teach us."

When Mark turned and asked Cathy what quote she had found, she gave a self-deprecating laugh and said,

"Don't expect mine to be so deep. Anyway, no one is sure who said this, apparently, but I can't see how someone could say something this beautiful and not be known. Anyway…" She giggled again and straightened her back before reciting. "'Keep your heart open to dreams. For as long as there's a dream, there is hope, and as long as there is hope, there is joy in living.'"

Will snickered. "Some flower child said that."

"Oh, you!" Cathy returned fire by sticking out her tongue.

"Inspirational," Gabriella commented as a way to support her friend.

"Hope can drive us, keep us going, for sure," Mark added, "though the use of dreams here could be better stated as aspirations, don't you think?"

"Sleeping-dreams can still fill us with hope," Doug said, "especially ones like the dream where I helped that woman escape interrogation."

Mark nodded. "True. Perhaps certain dreams can even motivate us or show us goals." He paused for a moment to await further comments before motioning for Kris to take her turn.

Without preamble, Kris quoted, "'A dream you dream alone is only a dream. A dream you dream together is reality.' John Lennon said that."

"Again, talking about goals," Will pointed out, "so doesn't count." He grinned as Kris gave him a "you brat!" stare, but she was far more willing to defend her choice.

"What Lennon says is truly important, about sharing. Whether those are goals or ideals or 'real' dreams," she argued while sending Will a subtle smirk, "they are all *more* real when shared, and pretty worthless, I say, when not shared."

"And that sums up sharing nicely," Mark played moderator before Will could voice the retort everyone could see was coming. "Your turn, Will."

"Oh, so you want me to share," Will said with a warning undertone to match his mischievous look.

Kris arched an eyebrow. "Now we're not so sure..."

Ignoring her, Will continued, "My quote is also from a genius named Will, though I suspect they removed the ending 'ed' from his last name, Dement. He knew this truth: 'Dreaming permits each and every one of us to be quietly and safely insane every night of our lives.'" Amid the outburst of laughter, Will stood and made a mock-formal bow before flopping back into his chair.

"Oh," Cathy said, wiping at the corner of her eye, "figures that would resonate with you."

"How appropriate," Kris agreed.

"At least I'm not the only one," Nolan said, sharing a grin with the other boys.

"And more fortunate than most," Mark added while still chuckling, "we can share the insanity of our dreams with each other."

With Gabriella's turn, the group returned to its original track. "The great Leonardo da Vinci once said, 'Why does the eye see a thing more clearly in dreams than the imagination when awake?' It's like for all his creative skill and great mind, his dreams were even greater."

"Or dreams inspired his waking imagination," Doug offered, and Mark agreed.

"That must surely be the case, and his quote is telling. Imagine dreaming about the possibility of man flying—*feeling* that—and then obsessing, driven to make that a reality, to...reconcile that dream-feeling with reality."

"He couldn't have been the only one to dream of flying," Gabriella said before amending, "well, the *first* one."

Cathy said, "I thought we all dreamed of flying."

"Yeah, look at Superman," Will added.

"Yes, probably wasn't the first," said Mark, "but it was da Vinci's labor, his attempt to make it practical that drove the eventual reality. That invention could have been one entirely created by dreams." When no one else added anything, Mark thanked Gabriella for the quote and motioned to Quani.

The shy girl had looked nervous all during Gabriella's turn, and now she looked down at her notebook long enough for some to wonder if she was going to participate.

"'Nothing happens unless we first dream' is a quote from American writer and poet Carl Sandburg," she said in a quiet voice.

"Nice," Mark commented. "And why did you choose this one?"

"You might think it is about goals…" Quani glanced toward Will for a moment. "But it's more than that. Without dreams of being more, we don't push, and if we don't take the risk, nothing good ever happens. I know this well. I am the first of my family to see so much of the world and come to college."

Encouraging murmurs drifted to her from around the room. Gabriella rubbed Quani's shoulder, and the two exchanged rare smiles. "Great meaning," Mark commented, "and here you are with us, because of your dreaming. It is possible that *visualizing* is the very first step. It shows you the possible, and so you push toward that." He nodded in satisfaction before shifting his prompting gaze. "Doug?"

"The quote I chose speaks to me after my recent powerful dreams—or maybe I relate better now. Edgar Allen Poe wrote, 'All that we see or seem, is but a dream within a dream.'"

Tilting his head, Mark encouraged Doug to repeat it. "All that we see or *seem*," Doug quoted, following the unspoken request to emphasize the strangeness, "is but a dream *within* a dream."

"Now there is a man who's unsure of reality," Will joked, but this time his joking drew nods from others.

"Another creative man driven by his dreams," Mark speculated before turning again to Doug. "So what did you get out of that?"

"Well…" Doug shrugged. "I know that reality can seem less real after some powerful dreams. When you're deep in them, they can feel every bit like reality. And here's this famous writer telling me that all we experience is much like a dream, or maybe he thought it was *only* a dream. Who can say with certainty that he isn't on to something?"

"I can," Gabriella stated. "I have vibrant dreams, but they're just dreams, some fun, some annoying, but nothing at all like my *real* life."

"For one thing," Mark said with a smile, "dreams tend to cut out all the boring, ordinary parts. But this is a great quote. So many ways you could take it."

"I think Poe could fill my dreams with sadness and nightmares, if I let him," Cathy stated with a shake of her head.

"It'd give us more fodder besides you swimming to class," Will teased, earning another sassy stuck-out tongue.

"Just remember that we aim to understand or take any sting out of dreams, replace discomfort with fascination," Mark reminded them. "But before we get to any of those, Nolan, do you have a quote for us?"

Nodding, Nolan glanced down to reference his note. "An old self-help guy named Napoleon Hill said, 'Man, alone, can dream and make his dream come true.'" Shrugging, Nolan added, "He might have been talking about the hope thing, but we also have the ability to dream something and make it happen like our mention of flying. Or they can make us go crazy."

"And have fun doing it," Will agreed, sharing another grin.

"With a self-help focus, he probably was talking about aspirations," Mark said.

Nolan shrugged again. "Yeah, but it could fit that we are the only ones who can make our dreams come true."

"I don't know about that," Gabriella argued. "Who is it to say that cats don't have dreams that teach them they are able to climb trees or leap fast enough to catch birds? Or show a dog what it feels like to chase cars? Many animals can act like they're running in their sleep."

"But that's not really the same."

Mark held up a hand. "We can all agree there are differences in degree, at least. Dreams could have paved the way for us travelling beyond the earth and other fantastical accomplishments. And let's not forget, on the other end of the scale, that some early people were said to have visions that set them apart. The ability to see long-ranging effects or give unconventional advice...to see gods or hear divine will. This might very well have come from dreams, too."

The group was quiet, in thought or in agreement, so Mark gestured around the circle. "Speaking of, who has had a vision or other fun dream to share? Cathy? Did you have any more?"

She tossed her hand flippantly and snorted. "Most of the ones I remember are the normal ones about finding class—or not!"

"Can you recall details of any of them?" asked Mark before teasing her lightly. "These meetings will be short if no one pays careful attention to their dreams."

Laughing at herself, Cathy replied, "I doubt you want to hear that I recited my shopping list or wove through a crowded mall to get to a sale."

"I had an interesting one," Kris volunteered, and the group's interest turned to her. "I mean, it's no epic, but I think it's interesting."

Mark gave an encouraging smile. "Go on, Kris."

"Okay," she said as she smoothed imaginary wrinkles from her slacks. "First, you need to know that I took several years of piano lessons, mostly in elementary and junior high. Now I'm in a music appreciation class. And these had to strongly influence this dream.

"So, I was sitting at a piano in a decent sized room, though most of the room was dark, the lights dimmed or only on the piano. And I was—now don't laugh." She shot a warning glance at Will before continuing. "I was teaching some unseen people about music, specifically the beautiful shifting tones of major chords to minor and back again. It was like they were trying to figure out music and I was explaining it to them, chord progressions, I mean.

"I played them an example—and here's the really strange thing: I was playing a *country* song. Not classical or modern music, but a song I would never know or play in real life. Yet I heard it clearly and *remembered* it even after I woke up. My dream-self had called the song 'Dancing in the Dark.' I went down to the piano in my dorm and hammered it out to be sure I wasn't just confused. Then I began searching YouTube for the song that got loaded into my head. Took me an hour, but I finally found it." Kris involuntarily shook her head.

"It was the exact same chords from my dream: D-major, G-major, E-minor, to A-major. *Same* chords and timing I played as an example in my dream, and I don't listen to country music. It was 'Fishin' in the Dark' by Nitty Gritty Dirt Band, if you're curious, and it alludes to dancing so I wasn't far off on the title. But I've never heard the song before having that dream, I think."

"Really?" Mark leaned forward with keen interest. "Sure you hadn't heard it somewhere?"

Shrugging, she answered, "None of my friends or family listen to that kind of music, but maybe in passing in a store or at school? Nothing I would remember, I'm quite sure."

"And now would you listen to country music?" Mark asked.

"No," Kris said, giving another shake of her head, "but—God help me—I really like that catchy song now that I played it in my dream. Repeated it on YouTube again and again until I made myself stop."

"Huh." Mark leaned back in his chair and rubbed the stubble on his chin. "Fascinating, and a clear exercising of your musical talent."

Will smirked. "And now we know dreams can make us like bad music."

"You wouldn't think it was bad if you had my dream," she retorted. "It's not a bad song at all."

"Exactly my point."

Kris rolled her eyes but was smiling. "Maybe so."

"Do *you* have a dream to add, Will?" And Mark's challenge was answered.

"Indeed I do, and a confusing one." It was Will's turn to shake his head at the memory. "Well, I was being offered superpowers."

"Yikes!" Cathy commented.

"I know, right?" Will favored her with a grin before continuing. "Don't know if those abilities were going to come naturally or some powerful being like God would inject them...or something." He strained to capture the fleeting, to make sense of the incomprehensible. "I just know I considered them carefully. In the dream, I could fully visualize what they were and how I *could* use them and the terrible possibilities—what it could lead to and the huge burden that would be. It felt like it would be a constant struggle and, I don't know...*repression* of myself. Or maybe not repression but..." He frowned at the lingering confusion.

"So anyway, I rejected the powers. Hell, for the life of me I can't remember what they were or what they would allow me to do. Maybe it was like the act of drawing away was me *forcibly* forgetting most of the dream. And even though it was my choice, what I remember most is feeling loss like a deep, scarring missed opportunity, if that makes any sense." With a shrug, he relaxed and chuckled. "Heh, stupid dreams."

"So," Mark analyzed, "the choice was a clear one, but still very difficult to make?"

"More like an easy decision to make but…" Will scratched behind his ear and then shrugged again. "Even that choice had a high cost now that I fully understood the power I had rejected."

"Glad you chose to remain human," Gabriella commented dryly which prompted a retort.

"Well, next chance I get I'll accept the powers just to spite—"

At that moment the door opened. A guy with thick glasses and a scraggly beard stuck his head into the room. "Oh," he said when curious stares met his.

"Can I help you?" Mark said in reflex. "This is a private discussion group."

"We have the room after you, I guess," he explained while giving a small wave with his free hand. "I just thought maybe we could set up early."

"For?" Mark glanced at his watch. "The room is reserved for at least another 30 minutes."

"Ah, a gaming group," the guy said, raising and tapping his Dungeon Master's Guide. "Could we wait here while you finish up?"

Mark shook his head. "I don't think that's a good idea. Please give us the full time." Once the door had clicked shut, he tried to shift gears. "Sorry about that. Where were we?"

"I think the groups have more in common than you think," Will joked. "They could learn a thing or two from our dreams."

Gabriella smirked at Will. "We have enough disruptions inside the room."

"Agreed," Mark said though he was smiling. "Going forward, I'll make sure we have this room for the entire evening. Even if I have to pull some strings."

Chapter 5

College life is so vibrant, like a dream of rollercoaster-shaped hallways lined with a daunting array of colorful doors. And behind each door exists a new activity that can lead to even more colorful opportunities. The explorer will find no lack of paths and choices, which is good. Unless the subconscious is warping and mystifying those choices, turning experiences upside down and inside out— with the dreamscape growing louder and more demanding.

Then, college life can feel hectic, with too many opposing forces and not enough time or energy to deal with them.

Doug's flag football team lost again, despite finding time for a practice that had encouraged them. They had gorged on pizza and gaming to commiserate, but then Doug needed to get back to schoolwork, which was slowly piling up on him. He skipped the matinee movie and missed another concert his roommates raved about.

When Doug passed on the "midweek madness dancing frenzy," as his roommate called it, Tim threw up his hands in disgust. "Seriously, man, you're letting the work *own* you. This isn't at all how life's supposed to turn out— growing old and shriveling before you even know what's what!"

Chuckling at the wide-eyed antics, Doug shook his head. "It's not about studying this time. Remember? I have the dream discussion group tonight."

"Oh! Fine, so dance now and dream later," Tim teased. "Anyway, how's that going? Anything I'd be interested in?"

"Not unless you have a hidden reserve of crazy dreams or spare time."

"I dream some," Tim said in mock-offense before adding, "but they're all X-rated."

"Heh, yeah that'd not go over too well. This group is fun, but you really have to be fascinated with dreaming."

"Ah, well..." Tim shrugged. "Any freaky-hot girls in your group?"

Doug gave a disbelieving laugh. "What? Are you greedy? Is Donna not enough for you?" That earned him a pulled punch to the shoulder.

"Punk! I mean for you! Get you something to *really* dream about."

Doug shrugged. "Not that kind of group. Not everything is a meat market, you know."

"It is if you got the right stuff." Tim began strutting in the doorway, and Doug used a shooing motion.

"Get out of here. Save it for the dance floor."

* * *

Doug reached the meeting room ten minutes early. Most were already chatting about roommates, looming midterms and the possibility of having to drop a class to keep from drowning. He chuckled when he heard that Will's roommate was also curious about the group, but Will asked if it would be okay for him to participate. "Sure," Mark replied before adding, "just have him bring his own quote and any dream for us to discuss."

As soon as Nolan and Gabriella arrived and settled in, the students dove enthusiastically into dream recounting. This time it was Gabriella's turn to urgently unload her experience.

"You are not going to believe this," she began, "I wasn't asleep for long—it was barely after midnight—when I had a clear impression of a woman with shoulder-length bob-style hair standing over me as I was sleeping. She wore light makeup, had brown hair and wore a blouse that looked nice without being too fancy, like business casual. She leaned over me with an intent manner, interest or concern or whatever. It creeped me out because she shouldn't have been there so my eyes flew open—*and she was still there*! I swear to God, she was still there, in my room, for a long couple of seconds. In reflex, my leg flew out from under the covers to try and push her away but hit nothing because by that time she had vanished.

"You know how someone can come up behind you and you just know they are there? You can't see them but you can hear them or feel them and so you *know*. Well, I knew—or felt—her there *and* on top of that I saw her clearly with my eyes after they were open. She was *in* my room so I freaked out, gasped, kicked out with my heart lurching. Then that moment later she wasn't there."

"Maybe an alien in disguise coming to probe—"

"This is serious, Will," Gabriella interrupted with a scowl. "I *saw* what I couldn't have seen. Or at least what felt real," she finished lamely. "Anyone else have this happen to them?"

When others only shook their heads, Mark said, "You aren't alone, in that many have had strong visions that seemed more real than waking sight, like an echo that carries a sound or smell or sight over to a waking moment. Remember the lyric: '...and the seed that was planted in my brain, still remains.'"

"Well, I was barely able to sleep the rest of the night—this was two nights ago—and I worry that it isn't normal. And everything I found while researching only made me worry more, with plenty of wild speculation and no one *knowing* anything."

"Remember that dreams have unfettered access to our emotions," Mark soothed, "even the complicated emotions of feeling watched. And the research you need to check out is about brain activity during sleep, where often the visual cortex is highly active. So it's entirely possible for you to see something clearly before you open your eyes— remember that the brain is what does the visual processing. I can send you the links to the studies where they scanned brains of active dreamers in an attempt to pinpoint where the dreams were originating.

"I think maybe what made your experience so interesting and unusual is how quickly you were awake after experiencing that strong imagery, before your mind could fully transition to its aware state."

"Well, I was hyperaware, if anything."

Smiling, Mark said, "That has to be one of the essential parts of a strong dream, because awareness is so perfectly modeled. You respond to it as if it were real, but the feeling faded, right?"

"I guess…yeah. Been nothing since then."

"Try this exercise," Mark encouraged. "Focus on something, that light fixture or any other distinct item. Fix that image in your mind and then snap your eyes shut. Can you still see that image for a second or two? I think what you experienced was the opposite of how it typically works."

"At any rate, it was creepy," Gabriella stated after opening her eyes again, though she looked more relaxed.

"But creepy-*cool*," a grinning Will amended.

"If you say so," Gabriella retorted. "Next time I'll send her to bother *you*."

After sharing the mirth, Mark asked who was next, and Cathy popped up. "Me!" she said before giggling at her own exuberance. "My recent one was an adventure in hiding. You know those dreams where you're in trouble but don't really know why?

"Well, in this case, I was in serious trouble with the authorities but it was for something silly though I don't remember what. I managed lots of evading and hiding as they kept looking for me, even used some cave in the woods, but I knew I'd get caught unless I did something unpredictable." Cathy laughed. "So I went home to my parents, hid in my old room, right next to the bed, under a tree log and a pile of dirty clothes—I have no clue what the log was doing there but it was pretty big and covered with moss! I remember hearing them knocking and then talking to my parents, and I was trying to make myself smaller and smaller under the pile of clothes. I think I was going to get caught anyway. That's when I woke up."

"But your plan was so brilliant," Will teased.

"Shaddup, you!" Cathy laughed again, saying, "I swear I felt I had outwitted them, that I would be completely safe at my parents' house."

Grinning, Mark added, "That is perhaps a great illustration of how you cannot run from your problems. They will always find you until you solve them. Do you remember anything else, about the situation or environment or what your parents were doing?"

When she shook her head, Mark leaned forward. "So, remember to push yourselves, both in recalling and describing every detail of your adventures to us. Make up or twist words if you need to—anything to help us truly understand them. That's a valuable exercise in communication, in its own right."

"Do you have an example for us?" Doug asked.

"Yeah." Cathy motioned to Mark with a bright smile. "We have yet to hear one from you, and you're the one with all the experience."

Mark made a dismissive gesture. "I'm mainly here for you, to help increase your experiences..." Twisting his mouth, he seemed to be wrestling with a decision. "But it so happens I had one this week that's still on my mind. Would you all like to hear it?" When he got an instant chorus of confirmations, he settled back into his sofa and turned his gaze upward and inward.

"I was attending a psychology conference when two men approached me and identified themselves as FBI agents. Somehow they knew I would be taking my daughter (who might have been around 8 years old) to a retreat directly after the conference, and they pressed an important task upon me. Of course I don't truly have a child and so haven't honed fatherly protective instincts, but it's still troubling that in the dream I felt perfectly comfortable risking my daughter for this covert work.

"Turns out, a devious criminal, a mobster with only a love for crime and family, was going to be at the retreat with his son, who happened to be the same age as my daughter. Using my daughter to befriend the boy and then getting close to the father, I was to do a full evaluation on him. Naturally I said I would help so they could gain valuable information. You know, anything to discover his weaknesses and put him behind bars."

Cathy gasped, and Mark smiled. "I know. I'm daring in my dreams.

"My daughter and I arrive at the retreat, which featured a series of small cottages alongside a pleasant lake with lots of playgrounds and a few large meeting areas. I find out where the boy is and make sure my daughter joins the same activities. Then I encourage them to play together and take snacks together while being the doting father. I encourage the boy as well, which makes him happy and so it's only a matter of time before the excited boy involves his father.

"Now I've created the natural opening to converse with him about fatherhood. This leads to talk of responsibilities and how we try and juggle them with our other lives. I assumed I could get to know him and begin figuring out what made him the way he was. I even entertained the idea of helping him become better, if only for his family's sake.

"However, the more we talked and the more carefully I dug, the more puzzled I became. On the surface, he was a normal guy, and played the doting father like he truly meant it. But as I analyzed, I began encountering an...emptiness that was frightening. This wasn't a tough guy act, or even a calloused nature from long years of repression; this guy was off-the-charts psychopath. And I could feel his lack of humanity like the kind of blackness inhabited by the most monstrous of things, things that are all the more terrible because you cannot see them.

"He knew how everything worked, what games to play. But the man was only filled with the screams of his victims. He could suck anything good into his void and make it disappear forever, which I assure you is a complex dread that nobody—not even a psychologist—wants to believe exists. And I *felt* it, so disturbing that I awoke with the pressing urge to save his son before the black hole of a father swallowed up that innocence."

To prevent the silence from stretching any further, Cathy muttered, "Wow."

"Heavy," Will agreed.

"Now you see not all my dreams are pleasant, either," Mark said bearing an easy smile at odds with the intensity of his retelling, "but I always try to learn from them even though some take a while to digest. Would I really have taken that risk for the greater good, for the chance to help? Probably. And what would I actually do once I discovered the truth of the monster? Probably slip away, grab my daughter and make a run for it. Tell the FBI that the man is more dangerous than I or anyone can handle, more damaging to everyone than they suspected."

Catching Doug mid-yawn, Mark teased him. "I see I bored some of you."

"No, no." Doug looked embarrassed. "It's just I've been dreaming a lot, sometimes two or three times a night, and the yawn just slipped out."

"Ah, which reminds me," Mark said, turning serious. "It's possible to wear yourself down with too many vivid dreams, so you might need to reverse the trick we use to explore our dreams. Different tricks work for different people, but it's helpful to avoid or reduce caffeine intake for a few days, make sure your room is as dark and quiet as it can be, and that you're very drowsy before getting into bed. Then as you drift off, try relaxing all your muscles starting from the top of your head and drifting down through your toes while repeating to yourself 'calm, deep sleep.'

"This forgetting process will lower the frequency of strong dreams, or at least bring them under control. It's a balancing act we all must find. You look to be the one who needs it most, Doug. I'm guessing you have another dream for us."

"I guess, though many of mine are too bizarre to make sense of, or just too..." Doug searched for the right word. "...tedious. For example, one I had last night had a strange atmosphere to the whole thing. I had been away for a long while, maybe a couple years on a tour of some kind, cross-training or something of the sort.

"When I finally returned home, our once cozy village now looked more like a bleak fortress. My close friends and family had grown into a huge clan—I suppose by merging with others for protection. I still knew other leaders, elders and veterans, but so many of the people were strangers, even though they acted like they knew me. They were industrious, almost militant, as if preparing for a war. And I do remember the surrounding countryside feeling hostile, that vague sense of being unsafe. Again, everyone was busy except for me. I kept trying to apply my skills, find where I was needed and prove myself, but no luck.

"I even visited an outpost that had been founded during my absence, which felt more like the smaller home I once had. So naturally I wanted to help them, train newer members, work on logistics, or whatever. However, the elders kept insisting I was needed at home though I could never figure out what I was supposed to do there. The entire dream was a fruitless search for a way to fit in and be useful, and it left me quite irritated once I woke up. I wrote it down anyway, since at least it made a certain kind of sense."

Mark nodded in empathy. "Dreams of struggling to fit in and not-quite-belonging are common, especially among college students, as you might suspect. So many new experiences and new people, stretching boundaries, and sometimes it's tough to find just the right group."

"Well, I'm not having that problem here," Doug said with a smile, which drew murmurs of agreement and fondness from the others.

"I agree," Mark said, "and I feel this group is only going to get better." After the mental group hug, Mark cast around for the next dream.

Kris held up a hand and said, "Speaking of bizarre, I've had another one, and I can totally empathize with the frustration of not being able to help. This time instead of music, I was treated to extreme visuals.

"So in the dream I was most definitely somewhere exotic, a completely different planet of lush life and glowing skies. Everywhere were colors so bright I could practically feel them vibrating through me, enveloping me. No matter how I try I'll never be able to express the extreme beauty of the place.

"The skies radiated health with an almost blinding blue-white, like the brightness when you look right next to the sun on a perfectly clear day—that was the color of the *entire* sky. The vegetation glowed bright greens and reds and rich purples and a million shades in between, but every shade seemed to glow. The people—oh!

"Some of them radiated a deep yet bright red that slowly pulsed, like a sleepy heartbeat. Some shone with a constant, magnificent blue, clearer, cleaner than anything I could show you. Others had an erratic feel, swirling like the color—if you can call it that—of the sky. Their bodies were vague shadows within each powerful color. So, it was like these...beings...embodied powerful elemental forces that seemed both natural and magical at the same time, and most definitely a product of this exotic world.

"But somehow I knew the entire planet was coming under attack. Something from space—fleets of ships, giant technological terrors—I'm not entirely sure what because I spent all my time on the planet. I knew each type of being would try in their own limited way to fight off the attackers, and it wouldn't be enough. I went back and forth to each type, pleading with them to combine their abilities into something powerful enough to save their precious home, but they were too proud, too short-sighted, and too damn stubborn to listen." Kris shivered at the memory and reached down to pull her laptop out from under her chair. Everyone else in the room was completely silent.

"I was so sad," she continued once the computer was safely on her lap, "way more than sad. Because I knew those people would lose if they refused to work together. And I brought that intense sadness into our dull, normal world. I wanted to forget the problems and remember only the colors, of course, so I spent some time on my laptop trying to figure out how I could dream in such marvelous colors—what my waking eyes could never see."

"Ultraviolet?" Mark guessed and Kris nodded, opening her laptop to the images and passing it around for all to see.

"My research led me to Getty Images and enhanced photos that give us an idea what we might be able to see *if* our eyes could see outside of our slim red/green/blue spectrum. The best of these photos I stored, and they're pale examples of the vision range I had during my dream. Finding these pictures brought back the entire thing, like the frustrations and failures are tied to that beauty. I can't remember one without the other."

"Fascinating," a moved Doug stated, getting an eyeful of the pictures before passing the laptop to Nolan. "If only we could have made more of a difference, been able to somehow alter our dreams."

"Why not?" Will challenged. "We're delving into dreams, remembering much more of them, so why shouldn't we focus on better outcomes?"

"Like stacking the deck?" Cathy asked.

With a shake of his head, Will said, "More like guiding, steering a powerful dream that we're taking an active part in, having more control than just feeling helpless. Like when I actively *chose* to give up those powers."

"I doubt that's actually possible despite what it feels like," Mark said. "It's remarkable to *feel* conscious, but to make conscious choices means you're not really dreaming, i.e., unconscious."

Eyes alight, Will wouldn't be deterred. "Why not push it further than being only observers in our own head? Inject that *need* for it to be better. What if she could have pushed harder and *made* those things fight for their home, or if Doug could have been able to *choose* his role and follow that instead of feeling aimless?"

Quani flipped back in her notebook and muttered, "Like Doug did when he saved Mandy." When Will gave her a blank look, surprised to hear her comment, Quani cleared her throat and reminded him: "When he was floating above the interrogation and made that man release her. Mandy was her name."

"Oh! Exactly!" Will exclaimed. "Great recall. I, for one, am going to push for more control and better results."

"Me too," Cathy stated, nodding enthusiastically.

Mark wore a humoring smile, but as he looked around at the range from interest to excitement, he began to wonder. "I will be fascinated to hear the results of your own research." Like a whispered hint, his wondering grew into inspiration. "In fact," Mark suggested, "I think we should all try this and report any improvements or success. Let us embrace this possibility and see where it takes us."

Chapter 6

Like the soft yet radiant glow of distant heavens brought close, she is *here*. As I lie prone upon my bed staring up at her, so she hovers above me like a reflection, though infinitely more divine. Flowing long hair stirred by ether's movements, flowing gown nebulous. Gentle, curious expression considering me. I wait with breath, heartbeat, soul held still.

A slight smile touches her lips. Amusement? Understanding at my wonder? Fondness? With grace, she opens her arms and her gown grows with her reach, unfurling like a ship's sail in some long forgotten silent film. Then, my existence *tilts*.

Disoriented near to panic, I struggle to understand: is the entirety of my world rotating or only the two of us? It matters not. She settles onto my bed, arms still spread, glowing hair fanned across my pillow. Now I am hovering above her, and it is her turn to wait.

Slowly, I sink toward her, toward her expectant smile. I long to curl up and nestle, to rest upon her bosom. Though as my skin touches hers, something far more profound happens. I drift to her and then *into* her, and into new awareness. I *feel* her, her welcome and her confidence, thoughts coming like a soothing heartbeat. And underneath those, her hopes. And her love.

If awaking means leaving this moment, then please let me never wake.

* * *

"The dream was mind-blowing, totally unexpected and…I don't know…precious," Will explained, uncharacteristically serious.

"Uh *huh*." Cathy clicked her tongue. "Did you have to change your sheets?"

Nolan answered for him: "Only if he's a typical guy."

"I thought we agreed to keep this PG," Gabriella complained, the first words she had spoken since the group convened, and she continued to wear a look like she had a bad taste in her mouth that she couldn't get rid of.

"Hey, it wasn't like that," Will defended his dream with unexpected ardor before relaxing into his usual grin. "It was so much more, but you can believe whatever you need to."

Mark wore a considering look, pursing his lips and then leaning forward. "Any thoughts on what it meant?" he asked Will.

"Nope, only that I was lost when I first woke up. And in mourning like I was missing something. From now on, I'll take dreams more seriously!"

"I presume we've all been practicing remembering every detail and trying to steer our dreams like we discussed last week." Mark motioned to Doug, adding, "All except those who need the break. Do you feel like that had anything to do with your dream sequence, Will?"

"I might have been able to choose…maybe," Will answered and shook his head. "But I'm happier with the thought that all of it was included." He cocked an eyebrow at Gabriella. "If that was the woman from your dream, I thank you for sending her to me." Gabriella scowled but said nothing, and Will turned serious again. "If I can feel more, *learn* more, I would welcome her return any time. Honestly, I think I passed out before she could show me all she wanted to."

An amused Doug pointed out the contradiction: "Passed out? Inside your dream?"

"Best way I can describe it—being totally overwhelmed and losing the connection. I can't put it into words how amazing the whole experience was, like a once in a lifetime experience."

"We can tell it made a grand impression on you," Mark said. "Thanks for sharing. Who's next?"

Nolan raised his hand and then motioned across their circle to Will. "Speaking of steering and learning, I have one, though not nearly as exciting. This dream started out great: I was very successful in the engineering world, making lots of money. Don't know how many years but I remember being confident. Definitely no problems there, so I decide to reward—"

The meeting room's door swung open and a guy stuck his head in. "Ah, there you are, Will! Hi. Sorry I'm late but his directions were crap."

"Right," Will answered with a quirky smile. "This is my roomie, Nerron, who either can't find a simple building and room number, or lost track of time."

Mark ignored Nerron's casual shrug that said, "You got me," and moved to shake his hand. "Welcome, Nerron. Pull up a chair from the back of the room and we'll make a spot." Mark prompted them to make quick introductions while Nerron grabbed a folding chair, shooed Will to move over the opposite way he was headed, and wedged himself between Will and Kris. When Nerron had settled and the name exchanges were done, Mark motioned for Nolan to continue. "So, you were telling of your future success."

"Yeah," Nolan said, recovering from the interruption. "Things were going so well at work that I considered buying a supercar. I've always loved the curves and engineering of most Ferraris and that carried over into the dream. I went to a dealership, they verified my finances and signed me up for a loan program. I clearly remember going to the showroom floor, and of course there was the perfect model in red."

"Where can I buy a dream like that?" Nerron snickered.

"I remember bending down to eyeball along the lines, putting my hand close but not touching the shiny paint job. The act of tracing those red curves is burned into my memory, the feeling was so real. Like I was actually there, admiring this beautiful car that would be mine.

"But I drove it slowly out of the showroom and to my house—and I mean slowly, because I was afraid I'd hit something or someone would hit me. Even as I was awed by the perfectly tuned engine, I was worried. I remember avoiding driving it, and instead taking the bus to work." Nolan laughed at what surely felt like a foolish notion now that he was awake. "I remember when it rained I would go out of my way to stay dry and avoid puddles because I didn't want anything to mess up the interior. And this snowballed, getting worse and worse, until I dared not use the Ferrari at all. So in the end I felt like I had no choice but to return it."

Mark considered and then said, "Perhaps you felt more like it owned you rather than the other way around."

"I know! The pressure of needing to preserve this crazy-expensive perfection literally stole all the fun, and that was the entire reason I wanted it to begin with. And here's the thing: I would have never considered that angle before my dream. While I'm sure I wouldn't be that neurotic about it, I'm not going to buy something that fine, no matter how much money I end up making."

"Come on," Nerron prompted. "No matter how much money?"

"Well, I'm going to be an engineer, not a Wall Street shark or tech founder," Nolan answered defensively.

"It's that feeling, the understanding, that's important to focus on," Mark stated. "The consequence of *how* a dream uses those powerful emotions, perhaps teaching you something about yourself."

"The feelings I experienced basically cured me of ever wanting a car like that. And I felt like I could have kept the car in the dream, but me—the real me—knew that would be a mistake."

Mark nodded in encouragement. "Alright, that's something. Let's recap for Nerron that we're attempting to remember and detail as much as we can about our most influential dreams and even try to steer them in a way, to alter them rather than being a mere observer.”

“Is that really possible?” Nerron asked in a tone that said he already thought he knew the answer. “I mean it’s more like you make up changes or additions as you’re waking up.”

“Yes,” Mark agreed, “that’s likely, but if anyone can actively control their dreams, it’s this group. There’s no harm in trying.” When no one had any further comments on Nolan’s dream, Mark returned focus to the newcomer. “So, Nerron, did you bring a quote and dream to share? Oh, and tell us more about yourself.”

With an aura of confidence, he said, “I’m a sophomore in finance, working toward an MBA. After that, I’ll start my own business—don’t know what yet, but it’ll be big.” Nerron tapped Will’s shoulder. “I know this joker from high school. We were both on the mile-relay team, so when I found out he was coming here, it was a no-brainer to room together.”

He cast about for something else to mention. “I’ve made some friends on the track team here, even a few on our football team though I’m nowhere near collegiate level in sports. Fun guys, though,” Nerron added before realizing he needed to switch gears. “A great quote I found from Lord Tennyson goes like this: ‘Dreams are true while they last, and do we not live in dreams?’”

“Nice,” Mark commented. “What do you think he meant?”

"Well, clearly he was promoting drugs." Nerron chuckled at his own joke. "I mean, some dreams might seem true while we're dreaming them, and they blurred his connection to reality. Or something."

"Perhaps that's part of the mystique of dreams, and Tennyson was acknowledging it," Mark suggested before pausing a moment to give it more consideration. "Given much of Tennyson's philosophy and writings, it's a safe guess that he's highlighting the strange and finite qualities of our lives here. A subtle way, by asking the question, of comparing our waking lives to the type of dreams which seem real. I know he was a deep thinker with a talent for twisting and loading words, so who really knows? Anyone else have thoughts on the quote?"

Doug said, "It feels very similar to the Poe quote about this being a dream within a dream. Like they were thinking about the same idea."

"Hmm," Mark mused before pulling his laptop from his satchel and opening it up. "I think they were from similar times, around mid-1800s." After a flurry of typing: "So, 1809 birth for Poe, who died just before the midpoint of the century, October 1849. And…" More pecking at the keyboard. "Yeah, get this. Tennyson was born in the same year, so definitely contemporaries. And of course they were influenced by enlightenment thinkers, a time when we began a return to questioning ourselves and our establishments." He glanced around the circle before motioning to Nerron. "Did you have a dream to share?"

"I don't remember many dreams," Nerron began with a shrug, "but I had a goofy one last night. In it I was a small-time farmer, I guess, because my plot was small. I remember hating what I did, and I'd been forced into doing it." Nerron laughed. "Maybe a glimpse of post-apocalyptic drudgery without any Hollywood gloss.

"Anyway, my mother was there, standing with hands on hips, nagging me about my poor work and small crops. I remember looking over them—and it was a pitifully small plot—and trying to convince her I was doing a good job even though I knew my plants were not as healthy as they should be. I needed to convince her everything was fine so she'd leave me alone.

"I should have planted more crops, but the existing ones also needed watering and I couldn't do both at once, especially not with those hawkish eyes watching me." Nerron snickered again. "So I took up a hose and began watering the plants, and I remember consoling myself that at least I wouldn't have to dig around in the dirt while it was wet." Crossing his arms, Nerron summarized, "Told you it was goofy."

"Clear mommy issues," Will teased, earning a retort regarding his own mother.

Mark was grinning while clearing his throat. "Does anyone have a *serious* comment or question? Nerron, did you see any other details about why you were there tending crops or what that might signify? Any tie-ins to your current situations?"

"It was just a dream." Motioning across to Nolan, Nerron laughed and said, "I'll trade you my crops for your Ferrari."

Mark conceded with a nod. "Alright. Just remember, the more details we can remember, the more we have to play around with. Anything we learn, even if it's just in good fun, will make this experience better, especially when you're looking back on this time, this epic freshman year for most of you." He scanned the faces, before asking, "Anyone else have something? Cathy?"

"Nah," she said with a self-deprecating flip of her hand. "Most of mine aren't worth sharing—I'm just getting so many. I really don't want to shut off the creativity tap, but I'm feeling tired, more than usual and it's beginning to hurt my focus in class."

"Yeah, me too," Nolan admitted. "Feels like I'm getting only a few hours of sleep even when I get seven or eight."

Mark encouraged, "Yes, take breaks whenever you need. It is a matter of learning how to pace yourselves. Ideally, it's better to have fewer, more meaningful or fun dreams, than an overload of jumbled ones. But that takes time and training."

"I can assure you the tricks work, though," Doug added. "Have to start early and stick with the mantra, because it takes a while. I just had my first truly restful night three nights ago. Slept like a baby and remembered nothing. And nothing intense since then. Now I just have to hope I can turn it back on."

Mark chuckled. "You won't find that to be any challenge." Turning to Kris, he raised an eyebrow. "Kris? Any more grand tales from dreamland?" When she replied,

"Nothing worthy," Mark continued to sweep the circle. "Gabriella? Quani?"

"I've had some bad ones," Gabriella admitted, still looking dissatisfied. "I don't think they're fit to discuss, and I need to make more sense of them or just turn them off."

"Well, bring them out in the open," Mark prompted with a fond smile, "into the light. We promise not to poke, right Will?" Sending the stern look ensured Will would behave.

"They just aren't any fun," Gabriella said with a shake of her head. "And...I don't remember much about them anyway. Just another visitation one that's really...bothersome."

"Bothersome how?" Mark probed gently. "Like the one of the woman standing over you?"

"I'd rather not talk about it."

"Okay," Mark relented, relaxing back into the couch. "Just let us know when you change your mind. Anything for us, Quani?" When the shy girl shook her head again, Mark wrapped up the meeting. "Well, I guess it looks like we finish early tonight. It will make up for the nights when we can't stop. Have a good week of classes, and remember to hunt for those special dreams, just not to the point of exhaustion."

As they rose and gathered their things, Nerron turned to Kris. "It's great meeting you, Kris. I'd really like to hear about your grand adventures, maybe over coffee?"

With a tight smile, she said, "Should have been here when they were fresh. I really don't remember them now."

Nerron chortled. "Maybe I'll dream up a time machine and do just that."

Kris adjusted her purse and clutched her pack to her chest. "I'm sure more will show up at some point. Excuse me, but I need to get back to studying."

Cathy had walked over to Gabriella, talking in a low voice and offering to be a sounding board if needed. The girls walked out together, and Mark noticed Nerron watching Kris as she hurried to catch up.

Chapter 7

The girls of the group clustered together, whispering. When the last member entered the room, there was a final flurry of encouragement, and then Gabriella announced: "I'm ready to share an important dream."

Mark, who had been watching with curiosity from his normal spot on the couch, said, "This is good news. We're all ears."

"But this is serious," Gabriella said by way of warning. "They talked me into it." Once everyone was settled in their seats, she cleared her throat dramatically. "This wasn't about me. The woman wasn't Asian, for starters. And she was tall, shapely, wavy blonde hair, dressed in an exotic gown that glistened in the lights which shown down on her. She was a performer, on stage, and yet..." Pausing, Gabriella screwed up her face, twisting her mouth as if still locked in an internal debate. "*I wasn't part of the audience, nor was I floating above or anything like that. I was the woman, or a part of her, and yet there's no way I was her*—if that makes any sense."

Sensing she was derailing her own story, she made a flippant gesture. "Anyway, I...this woman raised one hand, slowly, with great purpose, and everyone was holding their breath. As she leveled her palm, flashing images showed above it, like from a television screen she was holding up. Yet there was no screen, only the bright images.

"They were fascinating and pleasant images, though I can't remember details. In the dream, I strained to see them. And even though I couldn't see any of the audience because of the stage lights in my eyes, I knew they were all captivated by the enticements shown in those images.

"But…" Gabriella drew a shaking breath, and when she faltered, Cathy gave her an encouraging nod. "The *real* show was playing out in the woman's other palm, the one she held behind her back. Dark images, vitally *important* things, information or understanding or something that desperately needed to be shared. I remember feeling so terrible that I kept the truth from them, like I was somehow responsible or in control of that hidden hand." Gabriella glared from the remembered frustrations and inability to recall details that felt so important to her. "I *wanted* to bring out that truth, to reveal the palm with the answers on it and put away the distracting flashes they were seeing. But then the hidden hand snaps closed into a fist and the dream abruptly ends. There," she ended with a grunt. "I did it."

"We have an intense group here," Mark said with a grin to lighten the mood. "Anything else you remember or want to add?"

"No. Even as I woke up I struggled to recall what I had seen or understood about those images on the hidden hand. What would be so important that it filled me with guilt? I felt that if I could just remember those things, then I could get relief. But of course, that's silly because nothing I do in the real world connects back to that strange guilt." Gabriella's tone spoke of the unfairness she felt, and Mark made a soothing gesture.

"I think I know how you felt about your connection to the woman. This is a dream type—and I've certainly had my share of them—where you gain experiences as someone else. It isn't just that you look differently, but the dream persona makes decisions you would not make if that were *you*. However, the level of familiarity is confusing since you normally only experience it with yourself. Because of this interesting mechanic, you can understand and feel what it's like to make a certain choice, like pure, vicarious learning. For example: being able to fully experience a tragic mistake and its consequences without actually having made that mistake."

"Yeah, maybe," Gabriella said with a considering tilt of her head, "but what does it mean?"

"Echoes of internal conflicts, the mind teaching itself, flickers of past lives, alternative reality...the speculation for this runs the gambit, but what is similar in this highly uncommon experience is that the person dreaming it feels more than just being there. They can sometimes access history like a backstory, motivations, and other emotions that would not be possible to a mere observer. It's like they gain knowledge by being someone else for a moment." Chuckling, Mark added, "I dare any real life experience or simulation to match what a dream can give us."

"Speaking from experience, sounds like," Cathy commented with a giggle.

Mark favored her with a smile while also including Gabriella. "Very much so. The dream study group I was in as an undergrad never thought up the idea of steering, but we were well versed in dreams like Gabriella described. For special dreams, we'd do what we called 'deep diving' where we analyzed every aspect of a dream, teased out every detail. What could each piece mean, was it tied to any real world experience, what could we learn from it, and so on. We could spend hours talking about a single dream, if it was rich enough.

"If no one else has more to add or an urgent dream to share...?" Mark let that question hang in the air as he scanned around the circle. "I feel it's time to try the deep dive technique with this group, and I'd like to offer an example, if no one objects." Once he had murmurs of consent, he opened his laptop and continued, "Now, I don't want to spend time prefacing this, except to say when I had the dream, I spent the entire day dwelling on it and on this new person I had grown to know. Because of him, I wrote this in a story format." Mark refocused on his screen, and with another pause to prepare himself, he began:

"When they ask me if I'm sorry, I'll say I'm very sorry. For one final time, I'll say I'm so very sorry. But sorry won't bring him back. There's no doubt I must pay.

"When we left her, she was crying, begging us not to go. Those blue eyes.

"Remembering the rest of her gracious and loving spirit, I'm transported once more to that rainy morning in November. She was normally so vibrant, so fun...the last time I saw her, she was slumped in defeat and it almost ruined our mood. But what can compete with the brash energy, the invulnerable mischievousness, of youth?

"We met in the golden years of college during a creative writing class. We'd traded papers to peer-edit and

when I got mine back, her note said, 'Meet me after class!'
It was underlined three times—that I can see clearly as if it's
sitting in front of me now instead of this gunmetal gray desk,
'safe' pen and three sheets of paper. But these three sheets
are enough, just like that note had been.

"She had challenged me with intent blue eyes.
Under the scrutiny, I cocked an eyebrow at her causing her
face to explode in a wide grin. So enchanting. No doubt I
was as hooked as I was curious. Once we left class and to
break the ice, I commented, 'Interesting note.'

"She flashed me one of those soon-to-be-famous
smiles and shot back, 'Interesting story.' Such a small
comment, but it made me flush and realize we were flirting.
'What do you plan to do with it?' She cocked her head
slightly to the side, letting me know how intently she was
studying me.

"'Turn it in for a grade, I suppose.' This earned an
endearing bark while she pushed and then captured my arm,
making me stroll alongside her out of the building. 'No,
goofy,' she drawled. 'What are you going to do with your
enormous talent?'

"'You can tell all that from a few hundred words?'
And she had nodded, so serious, so sure of herself and of
me. 'Of course! You could light up the world with your kind
of talent.'

"I chuckled, warmed by her earnest presence yet
savoring my own game. 'Really? With words? I enjoy
writing as much as the next guy, I guess, but I love *doing*
even more.'

"'Oh, don't pretend to be self-effacing,' she shot back, tugging on my arm and slowing our pace. Only another writer…

"'No seriously,' I insisted playfully, before seizing the moment to stop and turn. 'I guess I just lack the inspiration.' I was only halfway surprised when she pulled me into a deep kiss.

"'You're looking at your inspiration, mister,' she said breathily, blue eyes piercing my soul."

Mark paused for a moment in his reading before continuing to channel the man from his dream. "If I linger in the glow of what we'd found together, I won't have enough time or paper to finish what must be said. After a few weeks and parties, we were an item, a love taking root amid the swirling chaos of college life. And she was right: she inspired me.

"But then so did the parties and dreams of eternal youth. I was twenty at the time, and she was barely six months younger, and we fervently wished for this never-ending lifestyle. Yet we were growing all the same; my buddies and I certainly felt the impetus to become men. Sometimes women caused those feelings, sometimes it was each other, pushing, pacing restlessly, hungry to prove ourselves. And underneath that was the nagging doubt, the sickening uncertainty of earning a place in the world, of striking it rich.

"The world's a much smaller place when you're on top of it looking down, and smaller must be easier to handle, right? That's what we figured.

"Through the haze in the apartment, my friend Dixon suggested we get a jump on life, a head start. Seemed to make sense. Even good material for a bestseller, I remember saying. They all laughed, all except my blue eyes. Those were pissed.

"'Don't be stupid!' she spat, dropping her cigarette into the cup like the idea had killed her buzz.

"'Puh-*leez*,' Dixon said in a droll tone, asserting his dominance. 'It's simple enough and we'll be careful, smarter than anyone there.'

"'And you know this how?' she countered, standing up and tugging at my arm. 'Come on.'

"'You're gonna take that from her?' he asked me, making me scoff as I rose.

"'Don't play that,' I told him, deftly defending her and my macho status. 'I know what's good for me.' I'd pinched her hard on the ass, causing a squeal and laughter before wrapping my arm around her waist and heading for the door.

"But as it turns out, I didn't know what was good for me. I let Dixon talk us into doing it—no pretending it was an impulse. We planned it. She'd found out at the last minute and had been livid, shouting that I was throwing my life away, even punching me in desperate fury. I pinned her against the wall and kissed her almost hard enough to bruise us.

"'Love me?' I asked.

"'You know I do,' she replied and began crying. 'Please don't do this,' she whispered one last time, changing tactics to one I'd never encountered before, and that selfless love almost swayed me. 'I'll do anything to keep you here.'

"But my friends were waiting, honking the horn. I simply said, 'Then wait for me to get back.' I released her, grabbed my long coat, and tried to brush off her anguish. Attempting to lighten the mood, I joked, 'You can tell me how stupid I am again, and next time I'll probably listen.' She followed me into the early morning November rain, and stood there hugging herself as we drove away.

"The plan was simple: hit the bank right as it opened. The masks and gloves and guns would be enough. They'd never suspect college kids, and ones living so close. We'd just grab what we could easily get and be off. We knew a deserted place to abandon the old, stolen car and our outer clothes, and we'd be back in heaven before the news hit the TV. That's not how it went.

"Memories alone cause this sore heart to beat in a frenzy.

"The forced entry went fine; almost no one was there or awake yet. And they were smart enough to lay low. Then the hero... I now believe there are enough small bits of hero in humans to balance the bad, but back then he was merely a wannabe trying to spoil our easy plan.

"Write his name. Allen McConnell.

"He came in low from a side room as we collected the few bags. Had his gun out, shouting for us to drop the money. Three of us, and he stares us down. Dixon dropped his bag, all right, but only to get a good shot at him. The duty cop dropped like a sack after the second shot, and that was a clear sign for us to flee, never mind the growing sirens.

"*Easy*. I mull over the bitter irony of that word as I have many times since, the sheer volume of forced ignorance it takes to think something like that will ever be easy. And that first time, in the dimness of a sleepy sun, the sentiment was loaded with adrenaline and terror. An unfamiliar car on slick streets has a zero chance of outrunning cops, but we certainly tried. We already knew we were so wrong, so *stupid*, and the accident knocked the flight out of us—I don't mind acknowledging I pissed myself, sorry piece of crap that I was.

"Dixon got shot trying to run, and I was too dazed from the crash to register anything until cuffs were crushing my wrists. I must breathe, even if it's one of my last.

"Breathe." In empathy, Mark took a long, trembling breath in a bid to calm his emotions before finishing.

"I never saw her again, never got to hear her say how stupid I was, and dear God, I know how right she would have been. I've agreed every day for the past *fifteen years*.

"So, in a while when they come to collect me and ask me if I'm sorry, I'll say I'm so very sorry. Sorry for our actions and sorry for the McConnells' loss. I'll add that I know it doesn't change a thing, but my regret knows no bottom.

"Those blues eyes... I'm so very sorry."

The group sat in silence. Some not believing the story was over, and others not trusting themselves to speak, so after a long moment, Mark said, "I call this dream inspiration 'Blue Eyes Crying' after the old Willie Nelson song, though the songwriter didn't mean it the way my dream did."

With big eyes, Cathy exclaimed, "Oh my gosh! And you said *we* were intense!"

"If you haven't already, you should publish it," said Kris.

Mark shook his head. "Nah, I needed to trust you and have a good reason to share. It's too intensely personal, even though it wasn't me. Does that make more sense now, Gabriella?" She nodded while staying pensive. "If you can feel what inspired me to write this, imagine experiencing it as the man on death row."

Though the others were still stunned, Mark continued calmly, "Happily, my group had already learned to trust each other as we analyzed dreams, or else sharing this—even with them—would have been difficult for me. I think I remember many of the conclusions we came to about this dream.

"First and foremost was the experience of a crushing loss of potential, and not just with the young man who I remembered as if he were my own lost self. The older man was reformed in every sense of the word, in that the mistake which ruined their lives had also been channeled into the kind of corrective regret that changes you, that grows you in a way which makes similar mistakes impossible. I felt he could have helped others avoid their own terrible mistakes, just as surely as I knew that he was going to be put to death for that armed robbery."

"But," Gabriella sputtered, "he didn't shoot the police. The chances are he would have been paroled."

"Our group debated that very thing and decided that the situation in the dream was a wider representation of the kind of mistake that you can never undo, that you have to live—or die—with. Sometimes you are in a situation where you pay the full penalty because you are a part of that wrong. The law could have easily decided to make an example of him."

"I guess," Gabriella said with an unhappy look.

"It helps to focus on the lessons the dream portrayed, but before I get to that, consider the girl in the dream. It was most painful to me to dwell on, partly because I shared the regret of the older man. She had invested all of her emotional energy when she saw his talent. She *committed* herself to him, and he destroyed that, too. I never saw or felt what became of her, but I get the impression that her idealistic energy would be shattered by his choice—and it was clear to me that she had great potential of her own. Would that also have been lost? I felt like it would be."

"Those blue eyes," Doug mused, ignoring Nerron when he interjected a comparison of Kris' eyes to those in the story. "That was a repeated theme in the dream as well?"

"Good catch," Mark answered. "Our group decided they were always present, especially in his memory—and therefore mine—like a clear window to the spirit. When he was doing right, they showed that force for good, the nurturing. And they were piercing, cutting him to the core, when he was doing wrong. They went from being the symbol of his inspiration to the symbol of his regret."

"Is that why you chose the title?" Gabriella asked.

Chuckling, Mark said, "Nothing so planned. That came a while after, when I browsed the web and ran into Willy's song. It fit my experience so closely that I had to borrow it.

"The lesson I most took to heart involved the risk in choosing your friends. Initially, I rejected the notion I could ever make that kind of mistake. But as we played with the idea in group, I began to realize that I was armored against it only because I had felt the mistake and its consequences and that I didn't have a charismatic friend like Dixon to talk me into it.

"But here's the thing: I *did* have a similar friend, one my mind might have even patterned Dixon after. He could be reckless, just on the dangerous side of impulsive. Wild, hilarious and impossible not to like."

"Did you tell him about his bad dream self?" Will teased.

"It was hard not to," Mark replied and shared the grin. "He was in the dream group."

"Ohhh!" Will and Nerron crowed at the same time, laughing at the thought of how awkward that must have been.

"Of course he was annoyed when I shared the insight, but I wouldn't have bothered if I hadn't cared so much about him and our friendship. I swear he took the experience to heart enough to add a protective layer of judgment to his impulsiveness."

Nerron snickered. "No longer friends?"

"Actually, we've remained close—well, as much as we can since he lives out in California near LA. Also, the dream made me yearn to prevent that type of horrific waste of potential, to help in whatever way I could. I was more certain that I was on the right career path. And here I am," Mark said in summary as he leaned back and motioned around the circle, "enjoying this time with you, one step away from my own practice."

Chapter 8

Doug arrived early to the next "dream meet," as they had taken to calling these evenings, and decided to pull a chair out into the hall to wait on the others. When Nolan showed up, they gave each other a high five. "See I'm not the only one who's eager to dive in," Doug greeted, motioning for Nolan to join him.

"Good dreams, good times," Nolan stated in satisfaction, and he slouched into the chair he dragged to the other side of the doorframe.

"Yep, and I'm still happy you joined our flag football team." Doug rolled his eyes at himself. "I mean, I'd love to think we could have finally won a match on our own, but since that was our first win... I can only say thanks."

"Your team wasn't complete yet."

"Ha! True enough. True enough."

When Cathy and Quani strolled up, they talked Cathy into joining them, and Quani settled for leaning up against the wall a few feet from them. Naturally, they asked if the girls had any new dreams.

"I'm not telling early," Cathy scolded, but she was beaming, and Quani did her standard head shake, replying, "Just normal ones."

"Someday, you're going to have to share what 'normal' is to you," Doug teased.

"In my dreams, I organize," Quani admitted with a sheepish grin. "It doesn't matter what. That's all. I group and I categorize."

Nolan chuckled. "Orderly, even in sleep."

Nerron's boisterous laugh announced their arrival before he and Will were even in sight. "'S'up," Nerron hailed. When he looked like he was about to call them crazy, Doug explained, "We're guarding the room to make sure only the worthy enter."

Will snickered. "That rules out this punk." Narrowly dodging a shoulder punch, he ducked into the room to grab a chair with a grousing Nerron following suit.

Nerron was reciting his weekend adventures at a fraternity party and talking up the new friends he made when Kris rounded the corner. "Hey, Beautiful," Nerron called out to her. Slowing her pace, she raised an eyebrow at the odd gathering.

"Seriously, man," Will told Nerron with a shake of his head, "give it a rest."

"What?" Nerron asked defensively. "Nothing wrong with calling it how it is."

"I pity the woman you catch," Cathy said, though she wore the amused look of someone who had dealt with her fair share of cluelessness and survived with humor intact. Kris joined Quani against the wall without comment, and they resumed small talk until Mark and Gabriella approached.

"Sorry, I'm running a little behind…" Mark registered the situation and asked, "We having meetings in the hall now?"

"We're hall monitors," Nolan improvised.

Cathy added, "Making sure no one is running with scissors."

"Or if we don't like them," Will joined the silliness, "we hand them scissors and send them on their way."

After sharing a laugh, Mark motioned to the doorway. "Alright, come on, you jokers. I hope we all had successful weeks, both in classes and in dreamland."

"It's great being able to turn back on the creativity faucet and still do well in school," Doug commented and traded grins with Nolan as the group reformed inside the room, "and it seems like we're able to steer some dreams."

"Oh, really?" Mark dropped onto the couch and then leaned forward with interest.

"At first, trying would just wake me up quicker," Doug explained. "But then I had a really powerful dream—I was immersed in it and yet I felt I could control what I said and did. Nolan had some success, too."

"And I think I did," Cathy added with a bounce in her chair.

"Great! So where do we begin?" Mark asked. When Cathy and then Nolan pointed to Doug, Mark motioned that Doug had the floor. "Looks like you've been nominated."

"I had the dream four days ago, so glad I wrote it down." Doug flipped through the notebook. "It began normal enough. I was out for a run along a country road—and this would be realistic because I ran cross-country in high school, but I dislike running through neighborhoods, mostly because of noisy dogs.

"When I stopped at a small corner store to rest and buy a drink, my step-father—at least I *think* it was him—pulled up in his truck towing an empty trailer and offered to drive me home. While I was making up my mind, something truly crazy began to happen. I heard what sounded like distant thunder, and so I accepted the ride because I certainly didn't want to get caught outside in a lightning storm.

"But this wasn't normal sounding. Thunder rolls around, you know? You can hear the vastness of it. But this felt very close, tight, personal. And I swear I could hear crackling, like extremely loud static electricity. I hopped in the passenger seat, asking my step-dad if he could hear the bizarre noises.

"He didn't answer and moved slowly, exaggerated like trying to prove he was calm. As the strange sounds got louder, crisper, I remember saying something like, 'It's probably a good time to hurry home.' But he never drives fast, and as he was putting the truck into gear and slowly accelerating, I glanced over my shoulder through the back window.

"A small black cloud floated maybe ten or fifteen feet above the road, pulsing and crackling with energy, and—get this—I could now hear very annoyed grumbling coming from it. Again I asked if he could hear it, and told him, 'I see it, like a cloud about the size of a large person.'" Looking up at the group, Doug chuckled. "I think I was trying to involve him so I could confirm this wasn't just me losing it.

"Thanks to our snail's pace, the thing flew past us and was now ahead, hovering over the road. Of course *this* is when my grim step-dad decided to speed up. We were drawing alarmingly close. In an attempt to get him to change his behavior, I pointed and commented that it didn't look healthy to be so close to it.

"And that small recognition—or maybe it was because I knew what to look for now—opened the floodgates of what I can only describe as paranormal activity. So many shapes, and shades from dark black-green to barely visible sky blue. But they all crackled with energy of varying intensity and they were all floating around like localized, sentient clouds.

"Swerving to narrowly miss a car, my step-dad aimed for the shoulder below an overpass where he came to a halt and abruptly killed the engine. I think he was fervently praying, because his head was down, eyes squeezed shut and his lips were moving. Since he didn't set the parking brake and had the gear in neutral *and* we were on an incline, we began to roll toward a guardrail and concrete bridge support."

Doug looked up from his notes. "Now at this point in the dream, I'm positive I could have freaked out in some way, following his example as his fake calm began cracking. And I think the dream would have turned out way differently, maybe devolved into a typical fleeing-hiding scenario or whatever."

"But you didn't?" Mark prompted, clearly intent upon the example.

"Nope. I pointed out that we were drifting. And though he seemed annoyed that I interrupted his praying, he noticed we were about to hit the rail, and slammed on the brakes. This final lurch popped the trailer off the ball hitch. I could hear the impact and crunching gravel as it dropped onto its retracted foot and yanked on the safety chains, which made us lurch again like an aftershock of his overreaction.

"I could have been irritated at his incompetence during such an emergency. I felt the urge, but I *chose* to control my temper. I told him, 'Don't worry about whatever these things are and just focus on being safe. We have to focus on practical matters.' I could see his hands were shaking, so I reached over and shifted the truck into park. Then opening my door, I offered to reattach the trailer and drive the rest of the way home.

"I have no clue how I intended to realign a 3,000-lb trailer by myself, but as I neared the tail, a cloud solidified on the very back of the trailer, looking strangely like some chaotic pile of junk. 'I'm sorry,' said this rumbling junk. 'Let me help.' And pressing down on the back of the trailer—I guess that's how it happened—it *lifted* the tongue and set it back onto the ball hitch with only a minor thud.

"By this time, I had clearly accepted this craziness. When this thing wanted to continue chatting, I thanked it as I latched down the trailer, but pointed out it wasn't helping since my step-father, who had barely managed to slide across to the passenger side, was nearing total breakdown. I guess in response to that, the thing faded away as I rounded the truck. Opening the door and sliding behind the wheel, I said in soothing tones, 'We must accept this new reality. We must move forward.' And to take my own advice, I started the truck, eased back onto the road, and headed for home."

When Doug closed his notebook, Nerron snorted. "That was weird."

"Probably stranger than mine," Cathy said a little laugh, "but just barely."

"So, steering," Mark prompted them to stay on track. "It might feel like you made choices, but are you sure you changed the dream?"

Despite shrugging, Doug replied, "It certainly felt that way as I was waking up. I didn't want to freak out, so I made myself remain calm. I was curious about the bizarre things, but I focused on the small things, the practical things. I felt annoyance but knew that getting angry would be as bad as freaking out, so again I forced myself to be cool. To just accept what was happening and deal with it."

"So what were those things?" Gabriella asked shifting uncomfortably in her chair, and even Quani was tapping her pen against her bottom lip as she considered the possibilities.

"Could they have been spirits of the recently dead?" Kris speculated.

"I wondered that, too, though I really have no idea." Doug scrunched up his face before a thought caused his boyish grin. "Maybe my dad was afraid he was missing out on the rapture."

Mark made a musing sound. "Certainly strong symbolism with those entities. Not only did they alter your dream into the completely bizarre, they interacted directly with you. They weren't just a part of the scenery but something that forced you to react. Like an x-factor that makes you cancel plans or change something about yourself. But they might also be a specific reference to something you haven't thought of yet."

"Watch any horror movies lately?" Will teased.

"That's the thing," Doug said with a shake of his head. "Maybe it wasn't a creepy dream *because* I reacted so calmly. Bizarre...you bet, but it's like my acceptance level kept it from playing out as a horror movie."

"Fascinating," Mark admitted. "So a certain mindset—an open attitude—injected into the dream might very well change the entire tone and contents of the dream. We need more data points." Rubbing his hands together in his exuberance, he asked Doug, "Anything else you remember about how you felt inside the dream or emotions you remember coming out of the dream?"

"No," said Doug while double-checking his notes. "I wrote this the same morning, everything I remembered and felt. It's just that I had the sense it all turned out okay because I remained calm."

Gabriella muttered, "I could use that in my dreams."

"If only we could all be so controlled," Mark agreed with a smile before broadening his attention to the rest of the group. "Okay, who's next?"

"Oh, me, me," Cathy piped up before laughing at her own antics. "I just want to add that I'm dreaming again without feeling the drag, like I'm getting used to it."

"Gaining stamina," Will insinuated with a wink.

"Oh, you," Cathy said, slapping the air in his direction and laughing again. "More like a second wind. Isn't it weird that dreams can bleed over and affect how we feel during the day?"

A couple members agreed, and Mark said, "No denying they affect us, as if dreams sit on that metaphorical bridge between our minds and our bodies. That gives them plenty of leverage."

After an energetic hop in her chair, Cathy launched into her dream tale: "So my latest is like some strange pre-history lesson. Our ancient matrons thought in terms of clans, nurturing our family and our land. We took care to farm and hunt as well as tend our relationships. Simple times, dealing smartly with whatever each day brought.

"But when our area became more crowded, neighboring tribes began squabbling over resources. Our matrons tried various things to avoid conflict. I remember being a part of those meetings—or maybe just hearing about them—and oddly enough, I specifically remember helping pull weeds that were a part of the other clan's struggling

crop problems. But these efforts were always temporary.
Real, dangerous conflict was always just one mistake away.

"So the matrons called me in and told of a plan to tie
the tribes together through marriage, with the idea that the
danger of war would be fixed once we were all family. I
remember being shocked by what they told me, the newness
and suddenness of it: they wanted me to marry a son of the
other tribe. For the sake of peace, I would need to commit
my life to this man I didn't know—maybe I didn't even like
him.

"But people needed an example that this would
work, and it was up to me to make it happen, no matter
what. Ugh, no matter what! I remember thinking that I'd
have never chosen the man if it had been my choice and that
for all time I was sacrificing my right to choose—and it was
completely common that women chose their own mates.
Except for now, with me."

Cathy shivered at the memory and then laughed at
herself. "I was scared and upset but also determined to
make this alliance work. I knew it was important to keep this
man—who probably didn't want this either—to keep him
loyal to me, to our alliance." Holding up her hands, Cathy
said, "Now don't laugh because I swear this happened in my
dream: a narrator's voice said that this is how it all began,
'not with lots of drama and vast armies like in Hollywood
movies.' I remember him saying that specifically." She
tittered before adding, "Bizarre, right?"

"I think Freud would have heaps to say about that
one," Will suggested, wagging a mischievous eyebrow.

"Oh, here we go," Mark suddenly changed his moderator tact now that Will had put himself in the spotlight. "I would be very interested to know how you think Freud would analyze this—as long as you keep it PG."

After casting a shocked glance at Mark, Cathy caught on and turned back to Will. "Yeah," she challenged. "Play Freud on me."

"Well, this is clearly an echo of a past life." Will waved a hand dismissively, but Mark chuckled and didn't let him off the hook.

"No, reincarnation echoes more of modern psychologists like Stevenson. Remember that Freud was all about repression and unresolved issues in the part of the mind we cannot consciously access. Come on. Channel Freud." Will straightened and cleared his throat, then pantomimed bringing a pipe to his mouth as he contemplated, much to the group's amusement. "Except it was a cigar habit," Mark prompted, and Will smoothly changed to puffing on a fat stogie.

"You *see*," Will explained, assuming a thick German accent and taking a confident last puff on his imaginary cigar, "zees iz clearly a matter of deep seated need for the young miss...a need to defy convention and be liberated—all the while creating justification by seeing marriage originally az a forced contract."

"Hey, not bad," Mark praised before adding a belated, "Doctor Freud." Amid chuckles, he said, "So let me see if I understand: the patient's unconscious mind invented this dream of an arranged marriage because she doesn't want to be in one—or perhaps because she secretly desires to be in one?"

"Indeed, indeed," said a satisfied "Freud" pointing the imaginary cigar at Mark. "You know, you would make a good student of my psychology." The group burst out laughing, and Cathy led a round of applause for the play acting. Will acknowledged the ovation with prim nods, before relaxing back into his normal slouched posture and grin.

Once the antics had run their course, Mark nudged the conversation back on topic. "So now that is established, how did you feel you had control over the dream?"

Cathy shrugged and looked at the ceiling. "Well, I never considered marriage to be like an alliance before having the dream. And you used the perfect term: arranged marriage. It was like the very first time it had been tried. And I didn't have to be the one setting the example—I think. But it was a compromise to solve a dangerous problem, and I knew I would stick with it no matter what and make it work for us. That was a choice no one else made for me."

Nerron made a derisive sound. "But what choice was there, really? The dream sequence would have been the same even if you could have refused."

Cathy flipped her hand at the speculation. "Maybe. It just felt very real to me, and before making this choice, I knew it had been different. Women bonded based on a carefully considered need."

"No way that'd work," he argued. "Marriage and family have only ever worked as it is."

Gabriella jumped to Cathy's defense. "Other support structures work fine even in modern situations."

"It's true more of our history has been lost than recorded," Mark said as a way of moderating without taking a side. "Who can know for certain? But does anyone have more to add about the dream itself?"

"At least in my dream I didn't have an ex-boyfriend who still wants to 'hang out' even though he married some other girl." Cathy shivered.

"What a creep!" Gabriella commented, turning back to Nerron while still in her defensive mode. "Sometimes marriage can be *less* stable."

"Not to get derailed," Mark said before Nerron could retort, "but let's stick with interesting dream analysis, though perhaps our resident Freud covered most of it." After a tension-relieving chuckle, Mark again asked for more speculation before motioning to his right. "Nolan?"

With the current group mood, Nolan seemed uncertain. "Not sure I should tell mine."

"It's good, man," Doug encouraged. "Tell them about it."

"Well in my dream, I developed an online friendship with a girl from the other side of the world," Nolan began. "We really enjoyed hanging out, gaming, chatting. The more we learned about each other, the closer we became.

"Though I know next to nothing about radio, it was one of her hobbies, and she introduced me to a very special kind, like shortwave I think. Anyway, it would allow us to stay connected even when offline. So of course I bought equipment and we spent late nights playing around with it and talking about things like who would visit who. As our longing to visit each other grew, we began experimenting with our radios.

"Late one night, she found she could concentrate on my signal as long as we both tuned to a special off-frequency, maybe like the space between frequencies. I don't know, but it was a surprising discovery. By focusing on me, she could slip along that connection and appear in my apartment."

"Oh, it was one of *those* dreams?" Cathy teased, and Will responded, "That's like asking if he has a heartbeat."

"Guys," Mark warned, "let him describe it."

Nolan made a face at Cathy before continuing, "So this discovery threatened to change everything. Of course, I wanted her to stay quiet about it. But she had a friend in radio research who also hosted a show, webcast or something. I was very uncomfortable when she involved him, 'cause I knew it could complicate what felt like a private gift. It could change travel forever, but was that for the best?

"Of course he didn't take her seriously, but she offered to do a live test on his show. He was streaming with both of us on the phone—or maybe webcam. I don't remember the details about the test, only that as she slipped through and showed up on my end, her friend began freaking out, making excuses, talking about reasons, making plans maybe.

"I worried about her friend and others who would find out, but only a little since I was busy—distracted—staring at her, standing there with me in my room, beaming proudly. I could have just accepted it all, but I didn't want anything invading our personal time. I reached over, turned off the radio and whatever else was linking us to that live test. I wanted to focus on only her. When I went to touch her face, my hand passed through her, which jerked me awake." Nolan ended with a resigned grimace.

"Bummer," said Nerron.

"Yeah, talk about a disappointment," Doug empathized.

Mark rubbed his chin. "How did the ending make you feel?"

"At a loss," Nolan answered. "Or maybe afterward, because my first thought was wishing I had chosen to leave the connection open. Maybe the different choice would have kept her with me."

"Or maybe it was just your time to wake up," Gabriella speculated.

"At five in the morning?" They shared matching shrugs that eased Nolan's frown. "No idea, really. I just know how I felt about it, and I *felt* like I'd done the wrong thing."

"And what would Freud say?" Mark prompted Will.

Grinning, Will said, "I don't need to channel Freud to know he needs a girlfriend."

"But only the right one," Nolan qualified with an embarrassed chortle.

"Choosing the right one is important," Mark said, "but if she has to shift between radio signals, your bar might be set too high." After the group shared a laugh, he glanced at the wall clock and said, "If anyone else has an urgent dream or comment, now's the time."

Cathy wore a satisfied look. "Well, I think we've been getting more experienced at dreaming."

"Yeah definitely," Will agreed. "At the beginning of the semester I could barely remember any details, much less share in a coherent way."

"Does that mean you also have one to share?" asked Mark.

"Oh, not this week," Will replied before adding, "at least, none that I *should* share."

"Oh ho!" Mark raised an eyebrow. "And what might Freud say about that?"

Will sighed dramatically. "Probably that I also need a girlfriend."

Chapter 9

College life begins in overwhelming chaos. Yet, as students adjust expectations, understand new patterns, and set new priorities, they begin to find a rhythm that works for them. What before was only turbulence and uncertainty solidifies into resolve and then confidence. With practice comes skill, an urge to *fly* and test limits. The quick adjustments, the thrill, the success and satisfaction, the soothing whisper of sleepiness, and contented letting go. Satisfaction drifting…drifting off…drifting like gleaming clouds, a peaceful hum like gentle breezes after a storm, a vibrant treat to all the senses.

I know this place!

Above, stars twinkle in the vast distance, near space is now empty. Below, colors riot as trees sway and grasses dance in morning light. Even without understanding the singing, celebration is an obvious unifying force. Beings cluster together, harmonizing like never before. The swirling ones are easiest to identify, their quick motion and patterns a joyous, raucous prancing, blustering. Interspersed are the aching-pure blues, calm beings to rival the beauty of their flashy fellows.

At the heart of the gathering, slowly circling, is one of each type. They dance to each other's rhythms, close and then away, flirting, playful. And where they brush, energy *crackles*. A promise of magic. Each one tempts their partner, each time more lingering, each pulse more intense.

Their desire is its own gravity. They draw together, their color-merge becoming blinding white.

I quickly divert my view and heat up—I would blush if I were able to.

There and there, long swathes of devastation. Sinister charcoal-black valleys run like sacrilege through the chorus of colors. The browns and grays and blacks have no business being here! They are clearly all that remains of previous life. But around the edges are glints of red.

I must look closer.

Here the slow-pulsing-red beings are at work, pushing in debris and stimulating the raw edges. It will be slow work, but they will heal, renew. The loss is heartrending, but they have learned in time to survive the invaders and regrow and strengthen their resolve. A deep red being looks up, separates from the others, *sees me*. With gratitude that shows in every brightening pulse, its arms cross and it bows.

I have trouble breathing and tears well up. I weep out of relief and joy—despite my worry, they saved themselves.

* * *

Fall had almost turned to winter, bringing out the dark orange tints on both leaves and sweaters. Even with Thanksgiving two days away, the group was enthusiastic about meeting. Mark postponed his travel plans for a day to accommodate them, though the grinning Will told him they would have found a way to meet regardless. Part of their insistence had been news already rippling through the group: Kris had a dream where she returned to her colorful world.

Now, Mark glanced around the circle as Kris told her emotional tale and ended with the admission that she'd awoken crying and smiling and hugging her pillow. He could see he wasn't the only one who would cancel all plans just to spend more time delving into dreams. "About the differences," he prompted. "Are you certain this was the same place?"

Her nod was easy and confident. "As familiar as my parents' home. That night, I was in my bed getting drowsy and thinking about how soon the semester will be over. Seems like we had midterms last week, and yet we're less than three weeks until finals? It's like the second half is way shorter than the first half." This sentiment drew a few assents while she continued.

"And then I was floating and recognizing unmistakable colors, even before I saw the celebration and the people. Any change had been from whatever battles took place—which I'm so glad I didn't witness. Even in the first dream, I had worried." Kris' voice trembled a tiny bit as she stated, "It's like I was given closure."

Looking to Mark, Gabriella asked, "How's that possible?"

"I don't know," he admitted, marveling and thinking aloud. "Reoccurring dreams, of a sort, are fairly common, but continuance? With such high level of detail? My guess: it's rare, like once-in-a-lifetime rare."

"Yeah." Will was nodding and absently picking at a chipped fingernail. "And only because we're focusing on them, training, do we remember the details and see patterns."

Doug agreed: "So many would easily dismiss their dreams as unimportant, and forget."

"Speaking of pattern…" The room went still and all eyes swung to Quani. She cleared her throat and ducked her head in apology, though she continued while tapping her open notepad. "There is so much more than randomness here."

Mark smiled and motioned for her to expound. "What do you mean?"

"You talk about the experience dreams, and how some people study, even learn from them. But among our group's dreams is a pattern of… I don't know the right word—like solving, but not like a math problem or how to find a class, but something completely foreign. Like Doug's guiding actions with the stolen information and helping Mandy escape."

"One doesn't make a pattern," Nerron commented with a touch of ridicule.

Unfazed, Quani flipped back through her notes. "Nolan also tried to warn those grazing creatures right before we began our dream meets, and helped the young man with the noble when they were doing the coin toss over the girl, the bride. Will guided the karma of the villagers who had been mistreated. Kris, when she was teaching music and then trying to warn the colorful people against the invaders."

When she looked up for support, Will grinned. "You're like a human recorder. So you're talking about this pattern where we're all awesome?"

"Within our experiences," Cathy said with a couple of slow nods, "are dreams where we guide or boost someone, like when I helped with the arranged marriage or helped the girls flee the witch hunters—oh! And like when Mark did the mobster profiling for the FBI."

"Well, aren't you guys the little dream helpers," Nerron teased.

Smiling, Mark said in a humoring tone, "Well, we do tend to like helping others, so it makes sense we might take that with us to dreamland."

"Could some of our dreams be feeding the others?" Gabriella asked.

"Sure," Mark agreed with the speculation. "Dreams seem to use anything and everything as influence. We can make patterns from everything we experience. After all, our brains are complex problem solvers, and even helping a fictitious entity is solving a problem, in the sense that we rehearse or practice for a real situation."

"But I see what she's saying," Will argued. "It feels like more than that. We're *going* somewhere, slipping into some situation and trying to fix it."

"While extraordinary, wouldn't that be a fine example of what I said, of our minds practicing solving problems?"

"Seriously strange training," Doug pondered that possibility slowly. "I kind of feel more prepared after studying all the wild dreams we've had."

"More prepared to dream bigger and better," an exuberant Will agreed, flashing his boyish grin. "We're conquering levels and advancing to the next tier of difficulty!"

"You boys!" Gabriella groused, which only amused them further.

Cathy wondered, "Couldn't it be the case where the more we get used to the idea, the more success we have?"

"Discussing possible interconnections will be a fun way to speculate about dreams," Mark said diplomatically. "We can chase data points of vicarious learning and special helper versions, all the while seeing if and how they are tied to each other…if perhaps our dream group is stimulating or prompting certain dreams among us."

Nolan motioned to Cathy and mused, "Like our historical ones. I kind of wondered if my dream of the coin-flip marriage was related to your one of the arranged marriage."

Cathy shrugged and began to reply when Nerron interjected, "Well you haven't helped me dream of my Ferrari yet, so I'm feeling gypped."

"Okay, back to Kris' extraordinary experience," Mark said. "Any more speculations or questions?"

Doug leaned forward. "I don't have a question, but I like thinking Kris' follow-up dream helped complete the story. Truly special. How I'd love to know what happened to Mandy and the company through another dream."

"I wish I got your complete story," Nerron said, aiming a smile at Kris. "Such a vivid imagination!"

An awkward silence stretched and Cathy drawled, "Oh-*kay*."

"I guess it's time to move on," Mark said. "Anyone else have one to share?"

Nolan raised a hand and chuckled. "Speaking of an epic interrupted... I had the most annoying dream—well, not the dream itself but the fact that a 6:30 A.M. car horn stopped me from seeing where it was leading."

"*Oofa*," Cathy empathized.

"Time to move to a quieter neighborhood," Will advised before changing his mind. "Or a noisier one, so you learn to tune it all out."

"Something," Nolan agreed with chagrin. "This had the makings of an epic. I was somewhere completely foreign, a fancy boat or even a starship—I don't remember looking out any windows. But I had the feeling it was somewhere exotic. There were narrow pathways and close-together sleeping or lounging pods, but they had privacy screens and nothing struck me as cramped. It was all finely made, just practical. I remember analyzing the construction and making no sense of it before moving on, meeting the closest passengers and looking around.

"The showers and restrooms were centralized and shared, but again it didn't strike me as odd. I think I remember clean corridors with sliding doors to separate the sections, so I might have borrowed that from Star Trek. I remember finding the swimming and lounging pools—the really important stuff," Nolan interrupted himself with a grin. "I even began meeting others and flirting a little, but then that rude horn tapping yanked me out. But I swear, the environment lingered and felt important, like the setup was done and the story was about to begin."

"Serious bummer," Doug commented once Nolan finished and crossed his arms.

Nodding, Mark added, "As disheartening as the interruption can be, I think it shows you didn't travel farther than your own mind."

"Unless the travel is instantaneous," Will argued.

"Like in his dream about the radio waves?" Quani half-asked.

"Right," Gabriella said in tone of mild derision. "What comes from our heads is freaky enough without it having to be an actual destination."

"Oh, and you're the expert," Will countered with a wink. "So tell us your latest."

She grimaced. "Just another upsetting visitation."

"A *third* one?" Cathy asked, incredulous. "That has to be a record."

"Hardly a record," Mark assured them with a soothing tone and smile, "but fascinating none-the-less. Did your visitor say or do anything?"

"Nah," Gabriella said. "Still that same flash of awareness and vanishing act, but I did beg her to leave me alone," she admitted sheepishly. "It always feels like an invasion of *me*."

"Try not to think of it as such," Mark counseled. "Remember it's your mind playing tricks. Then look for patterns or insights. I highly recommend being curious rather than affronted."

"I know, I know. But it's hard to control how it makes me *feel*."

"You can control that," Doug urged as others nodded in support. Gabriella only shrugged and motioned for them to move on.

"Okay, any others?" Mark asked, looking around the circle. When nothing was offered, he shifted gears. "Okay, so anyone besides me going anywhere for Thanksgiving? My older brother is having us all over, so I must endure the cooking and be thankful I have family who gets along well. It should be pleasant, though my seven-year-old niece will probably run me ragged."

"I think I'll eat a TV dinner with turkey in it," Nolan stated, and Cathy teased, "Classy!"

"No one else excited about the big homecoming game?" Nerron asked. "Gonna be a big game and lots of partying over the weekend."

"I'm pretty sure none of you except Nolan and maybe Doug are legal yet," Mark said with knowing grin, "so try to keep the craziness to a minimum."

"Not until next year," Doug said, confirming his age.

Undeterred from his objective, Nerron turned to Kris. "How about joining me for the game? I have the best seats."

Cathy pointed out, "I thought the seats were free."

"The best seat is next to me," Nerron replied, "and free to you, Kris." A ripple of amusement went around the circle and Will guffawed.

"No thanks," she said politely.

"You have plans? We could attend one of the parties I'm invited to or whatever makes you feel alive."

With a twist of her mouth, Kris replied, "I don't need your help to feel alive, but thanks for the offer." She let her annoyance slip, but clamped down on her tongue when Nerron mentioned how she'd be missing out. "Excessive noise does not make me feel more alive."

"Okay, so give me a clue what you want," Nerron prompted.

"I charge extra for that—for hints. I mean, for hints..." Reddening as she realized the implication and possible reason for the round of chuckles, she wagged a finger at Will. "And don't you dare run with that." The group laughed over his protestations of innocence, and then Kris noticed Doug and his look of admiration. And it struck her like a bolt of lightning: *that*! *That* was the kind of cool attention she wanted.

"Okay, okay," Mark said as the laughter died down. "Before it gets crazier, we should call it an evening. Enjoy the extra days and be safe." After they stirred, gathered up their things and began leaving, Mark caught Nerron's attention. "A quick word, Nerron?"

"Sure," the boy said as he lingered. "What's up?"

Lowering his voice so he was sure the last ones out the door wouldn't hear, Mark said, "I realize this is more of a fun activity rather than a support group, but remember some are still new to college and we want to nurture a safe environment here for sharing. I need your help keeping it light fun and focused mainly on the dreams."

"Sure."

"And I think your extra attention on Kris is making her uncomfortable, which risks the safe environment."

"She's too hot, though."

"But I can promise you that you'll stand more of a chance making her comfortable, not uncomfortable. Think on this: yes, she's beautiful, but that's on top of all the other things she is and will become. She is clever, thoughtful, independent, and a very inventive dreamer."

"Maybe I'll dream about her."

"Whatever it takes to get a better plan," Mark said with another light suggestive push encouraging Nerron to change his behavior. He was afraid, though, that the only hint Nerron could understand would be the "N-O" written on the palm that Kris slapped him with. "Just keep your efforts toward her outside the dream meets, okay?"

"I hear you," Nerron said nonchalantly and finished with, "her loss for this weekend. Speaking of, I need to get busy preparing."

Mark gave him a small wave. "Stay safe, then—while maximizing your fun, of course."

Chapter 10

Quani forced herself to breathe easy, trying to unravel the knot in her gut as she navigated to the administration page. This was it: her first university course completed, and the professor had promised the final exam would be graded and posted by the weekend. And from her point of view, this grade mattered more than any other.

Finding the link, she inputted her student ID number when prompted and stared at the screen while it refreshed. 92! A relieved laugh burst through her restraint. She would maintain her top grade—in American History, when others were grumbling about harsh grades! She might be a curve buster, as other students termed it, but this was important to her.

In a class where memorization met careful reasoning in essay format, she had proven something important to herself. And she could show her parents that their trust wasn't misplaced. Flopping back on her bed, she giggled at the ceiling, the sky beyond, and any ancestor who might be watching. And that night, she dreamed of smiling ones who were pleased with the results of her struggles.

* * *

Whether celebratory, consoling or indifferent, campus activity increased to an almost frantic pace during finals time as if trying to make up for the upcoming few weeks' lull between semesters. The university's football team had won their homecoming and then eked out another two wins to qualify for a bowl game, a strong season finisher that gave all the fans reason to revel. Nerron dragged Will around to several parties and sacrificed a letter grade on at least one test. But Nerron had met frat "brothers" who made him feel a part of the inner circle, and this feeling was addictive.

Doug had to balance the last push of schoolwork with the seriousness of an impromptu gaming tournament for his hall. The chosen game wasn't one Doug had mastered, and so while Tim grumbled a bit that it wasn't Halo, they both ended up losing with grace. "All in the name of amusement and blowing off steam," Doug reminded him.

The culmination of their intramural flag-football league was the truly challenging tournament, which dominated most of the weekend before finals began. Thanks to their practicing and improved teamwork, they won their first round only to fall to a superior team in the following round. No one could be displeased with the result, though, and it was another good reason to celebrate.

The girls of the group had taken to meeting for lunch or dinner at a central café, and by the last meeting, Quani had gone from being a smiling observer to an active participant. Their chats ranged from dreams to grades to roommates, and planning for the future led to the spontaneous agreement that Cathy and Kris would become roommates for the spring semester, maybe even beyond. This decision was celebrated by excited hugging and yet more planning.

These activities and their energy carried over into the final dream meet of the semester. Conversation bounced across the spectrum until Mark urged them on topic. "Before we use up all of our remaining time," Mark prompted with a grin, "let's see who had interesting dreams they want to share."

Doug held up a finger. "I had a powerful dream last weekend, but I had so much going on and was feeling the drag again that I had to turn them off. If I hadn't written it down, I would've forgotten it completely."

Amid nods of understanding, Cathy admitted the same had happened to her within the past couple of days. Will said, "That begs the question: Can our minds ever get tough enough—in shape enough—to be able to dream every night without tiring?"

"Research says no," Mark answered with a shake of his head. "Potent dreams are disruptive. We are often restless during those, and what sleep we get isn't recuperative. We have plenty of proof that without enough restful sleep, even a healthy mind begins to malfunction."

"Hey, then that's another data point to support our working theory that some dreams are actual journeys."

Rolling her eyes at Will, Gabriella groused, "Not this again. More like it proves you haven't been allowing yourself enough recuperative sleep."

Nerron snickered and Will playfully challenged, "Just wait until you've heard my latest. We'll make a believer of you yet!"

Gabriella snorted, and Mark motioned to Doug, suggesting, "Let's hear them in the order they were mentioned."

Doug said with a wry smile, "Mine doesn't have any steering—unless you count fleeing, maybe."

"Think we've all had those," Cathy said agreeably.

"Well, this wasn't a fun one, but it *was* interesting," Doug prefaced. "While the dream had plenty of nasty details, I mostly remember the feelings, the lesson. Also, I have no idea of the where or when, only that we'd just settled into a new area. Our settlement was still mostly make-shift, with small huts and hastily built fences, trenches and two lookout towers—for some reason, I remember the lookout towers clearly.

"All would be well, except some invaders wanted to claim the fruits of our labor. I'm sure we could have fled, moved on, but we chose to stay and defend our home. We committed to it. Most of the details are gone, but it was truly brutal: the fear and struggle to cope, the costly defenses against attackers who I knew would *not* give up just because we bloodied their nose.

"I *remember* the horror of having to kill people and suppress that feeling so I could manage to go on. At one point, I had to deal with a fellow guard. He was so scared that he wouldn't fight anymore. He stayed crouched, trying to shrink into himself, and I had the task of constantly trying to rouse and motivate him to face this madness.

"If we didn't fight, we faced a fate even worse. Needless to say, it didn't turn out well for him, like he knew if he fought again, he'd be killed, which was exactly what I made him do." Doug shrugged helplessly before continuing. "I remember fervently wishing we had chosen to flee, that none of this compounded pain was worth it, even if we had felt justified in the beginning or had to swallow our pride and leave behind our accomplishments." Doug paused before repeating, "We should have fled, and before the dream was finished with me, that's exactly what I did."

"Daaamn," Nerron drawled after a moment.

Nodding in agreement, Mark suggested, "Sometimes we have to protect what's precious to us, even at a high cost."

"Do we?" Doug questioned that statement with sudden conviction. "I know the terror you can face by standing up to a terrible wrong. The result's just another...terribleness. Nothing you'd lose by fleeing compares to the intense fear, pain and death of combat. Well, that's what it feels like because of this dream, if that makes sense."

Kris offered him a supportive smile. "I feel the truth of that. Regardless of the justification, warring is the *opposite* of living."

"Yeah." Doug looked relieved. "Better to suck it up than deal with the nightmare-made-real."

Squinting, Mark said, "Hmm, something to ponder in depth, for sure. You mentioned the towers and that has me curious. Why do you think they stuck out? What might they represent?"

Doug considered it before shaking his head. "Maybe the dream-me had built them? Or they struck me by their complete lack of usefulness. They sure didn't help us avoid the fighting."

"In another time, vigilance might have helped," Mark added to the speculation. "In any case, I've found that many dreams have icons, things that stick out to represent an important consideration or some other aspect. They are always fun to try and decipher.

"If you don't have anything more to add or any questions..." Mark glanced around the group before motioning to Cathy.

"Funny enough, I left this dream early, too," Cathy said, "but for an entirely different reason. And after this, you guys are going to call me super sleuth." She laughed and made sure she had their undivided attention.

"So, in this dream I was a nosey local, a well-connected busybody—big stretch, I know!" She shared grins with Kris and got an amused chortle from Nerron. "These nice brothers moved into the area and took over a failed business, remodeling it into a classy place. It was like a cute tea parlor and coffee shop combo, but more clever than that. I just can't remember exactly why I thought that.

"Anyway, not long after they opened, there was a murder of a local troublemaker, like a gangster-wannabe. He was shot down behind their shop, and the rumor mill was churning like crazy even though the police just seemed to blow it off. Well!" Cathy laughed. "This didn't sit right with me—the nosey me—because all this conflicting information was flying around, some of it about the police corruption or revenge or even a plot to ruin the good name of the fledgling business.

"I wasn't going to stand for the brothers being hassled by this event just because the thug got himself killed behind their place! So I made it my job to set everything right! I put on my detective hat, went to the scene of the crime, viewed every stain and every corner. I talked to all the nearby people, who of course I knew so I could tell if they were hiding something.

"I went to the police station and applied my same skill set. They were surprisingly helpful, basically letting me have the run of what little they had collected. This is how I knew they had truly given up. They weren't bothering to see this through and were content to let it simmer before eventually cooling off—but this might be after my new friends and their business suffered!

"No way, I thought to myself. So I redoubled my efforts." Cathy had to pause and laugh again at her antics, both in telling the story and remembering the silly dream. "I remember walking to the library, despite there being a heavy storm that made me clutch my coat and lean into it. Following my intuition, I even went to the county records office—or whatever passed for that in this dream—because an unexpected angle presented itself.

"The dots connected there. So, the place had originally been owned—or maybe originally shut down—by the very thug who'd been murdered!

"By piecing new evidence and matching with the gossip, I realized he had buried bodies at the run-down place. He knew once the place was remodeled, the brothers had to have found the bodies and just kept the secret, in essence, reburying them. So of course being the scum opportunist he was, he hassled the brothers for 'protection' money. Their shared secret would stay secret and he could skim from their profits.

"But he'd made a fatal underestimation." Caught up in her storytelling, Cathy let the conclusion hang in the air for a long moment.

"Carefully, so very carefully, I approached the brothers with my collection of clues. I was stunned at my having misjudged them. And yet, politely, they admitted their dilemma: tangle with the local connected gangster, involve the police, which would more likely destroy their new cafe, or simply get rid of the source of the problem, one who'd given himself away by coming to them. Not only was he a crook trying to harass them, they told me, he'd already gotten away with much worse.

"So here I sat, having cracked the case, doing the opposite of what I thought I *wanted* to accomplish in clearing the air so their reputation and cute shop wouldn't suffer. I was miserable. I needed to turn them in as murderers of a murderer, or choose what I had never done before—being the consummate nosey busybody I was—and turn a blind eye to all the crimes."

This time Cathy paused long enough for Nolan to prompt, "So what did you do?"

Laughing again, she said, "I told you, I woke myself up. I refused to make that choice."

"And by doing so, you clearly made that choice," Will pointed out with a smirk.

Cathy returned his sass. "Oh, you!"

"It was just time for you to wake?" This time Gabriella didn't sound as sure.

Shaking her head, Cathy said, "It was still early, like 6:30, though at least it gave me a head start on writing the story. But I was in full control of the ending, even if some of the previous stages felt automatic. I've never experienced a dream like this!"

"Such a good story," an admiring Kris praised. "I like the twist and the style, like you channeled a little old Miss Know-Everybody."

"Super sleuth, indeed," Mark added with a smile, and Cathy gave a pleased giggle, blushing from the compliments. "So let's apply our own skills to this dream. Are you by chance a fan of mystery books?"

"Only if they're on my computer screen, though I remember my mom liking Agatha Christie." Cathy shrugged to show she thought that fact irrelevant to the dream.

"So I didn't feel any control over mine—thank goodness," Doug said, "but I'm curious to know where you felt an active role."

"Well, let's see... Being nosey was just part of the experience, but I might've made the choice to get involved in the sleuthing. I feel like much of the fact-finding just happened, but I remember considering going back to the police once I had done their job for them. However, I felt betrayed by the brothers not being straight with me—though I know they'd have no interest in confessing to the local busybody!" Cathy tittered at the silly notion of them confessing right away to their new "friend," the meddlesome local. "It definitely felt like my idea to confront them. And here's the thing: As the complete reveal happened and I saw their motivation, I was truly torn. I sat there in their shop wondering what I should do, and then I thought, I'm not making this choice! And I swear that's when I woke myself up."

"Or possibly fled back to your reality from wherever it was happening," Will suggested.

"Maybe." Cathy shrugged.

"Oh, please," Gabriella said. "Can't we just focus on the fun without chasing this insanity?"

Cathy smiled and shrugged again. "It *did* feel so very strange, and fleeing—actual fleeing—is the most apt description of what I did."

"Maybe she was experiencing this with another, through another's eyes," Will said, partly to poke at Gabriella's discomfort.

"That's nonsense," Gabriella huffed. "I don't want to be in anyone else's head and I certainly don't want them in *mine*."

"Just relax and enjoy the show," Will insisted with a wink. "Remember my quote about being safely insane?"

Gabriella scoffed while others chuckled, and Mark said, "If no one has other input, then let's chase Will's crazy."

"Anyone else feel like the dreams are getting clearer, more definitive?"

"You all are becoming more practiced, to be sure," Mark agreed without accepting Will's innuendo.

"True, but I see this trend coming through all the normal dream static," Will insisted. "My latest one might seem weird to you, even disjointed, but it's all about perspective. I viewed—or better yet, understood—the incredible experience in whatever way made sense to me, like experiencing something completely alien but only being able to describe it in the familiar. So in some ways, the reality of it was amazing, and in other ways, it was baffling. But I was definitely fully aware, actively choosing what to do."

Will rubbed his hands together. "First of all, I now know what working in the weightlessness of space feels like. *Thrilling* doesn't even begin to describe it. I became aware that I was inside of a highly sophisticated suit: self-monitoring, informative heads-up displays, not bulky and yet very protective. Looking out over the vast, brightly twinkling star field was disorienting, and I spent a while doing that until I spotted a satellite's flickering lights and knew that was my destination.

"No idea if I was standing at a spaceship hatch or one of the hubs I visited later—I never looked back—but I sprung off toward the satellite with wild abandon. As long as I kept my target in the reticle of my helmet display, the suit I was in sped me up, correcting course and then slowing as I reached my target. My first impact was a little jarring, but I instinctively knew I could finesse it so that I'd barely feel the contact through the pads of my gloves as I met with and latched onto each satellite.

"Oh! And did I mention I was wearing tools? On my front and outer thighs, stomach and lower back, with smaller tools attached to my upper arms. The thing was, they were locked onto my suit somehow. I had zero worry of losing them, because they would only come away when I grabbed them, and then they were locked to my palm until I opened my grip against my suit. All very intuitive, and obviously I was doing some kind of repair work, or tweaking, upgrading the satellites.

"I sprung from satellite to satellite making various adjustments, like playing tag with them in and among their orbital patterns. And what were they orbiting, you might wonder—not something as mundane as a planet. It was a badass space station, but not like one from any science fiction movie. It looked more like a normal city center, but more on that strangeness in a bit.

"There were *so* many of these space hubs spread so far apart that the glow from them nearly blended into the backdrop of stars. After finishing my tasks, I made a jump to another hub, maybe heading home. For covering this great a distance, there was some kind of baffling quick-jump system built into the suit, I guess, that made the stars blur a bit. It made me woozy for those few moments until I slowed down and the star field regained its sharp clarity.

"And here's where it got strange." Seeing Gabriella's look, Will amended, "Okay, *more* strange. As I reached the hub and settled onto the normal gravity and began walking, it was like there existed an *overlay*. So it was like two people, two experiences, in vastly different places yet doing the same thing: walking down a normal street to a typical pub. A familiar-feeling place with all the usual amenities like pool tables, darts, hang-out booths, and of course a long bar. This double perspective was truly disorienting—I couldn't figure out where I was. Was I on a space station, or was I in a city on some planet doing the exact same thing? I can only explain it like double-vision déjà vu dizziness." As he slouched back in his chair, he concluded, "Intensely strange, yet cool."

Gabriella made a face. "I think you might be freaking yourself out within your own mind."

"Ah, but what a trip it is!" Will countered her ridicule with mirth. "I can promise it was an exceptional experience."

"So that was the complete dream?" Mark asked to see if Will had finished.

"That was the long and short of it, though I can't do justice to the feeling of spacewalking or the twin perspective confusion."

"What about others?" Kris asked. "Could you see any people, or otherwise?"

"Yeah, like alien hotties," Nerron added helpfully.

"Around the hub, surely—I'd have noticed if it was abandoned but I couldn't tell you a thing about them. I think I was too mind-blown." Will chuckled at the thought. "Or maybe I was experiencing some alien form of preoccupation."

"Maybe you were sleepwalking," Doug teased.

"Well I didn't wake up naked on a park bench or in a jail cell, so that's a bonus."

Mark was tapping his lower lip. "So the dream was focused around the space walk and repairs and then the confusing trip to the bar, though disorientation usually happens *after* you visit a bar. What about steering? It seems a pretty clear and powerful experience dream."

"True I didn't select anything about the environment," Will admitted, "but I felt like I was controlling the travel to each satellite—granted, it was much like riding a bike equipped with very intelligent training wheels. I knew there was a risk of mishap in space, in the unforgiving vacuum, but it was like that was a daily thing, minimized and accepted."

Gabriella interrupted, "Surely you all aren't taking his dream seriously!"

"In what way? What do you mean?" Mark asked in a soothing voice.

"I *mean*, like it's real or whatever."

Will twisted to give her his full attention. "In all these weeks, can't you see it, this emerging pattern? We improve, and these kinds of dreams get clearer, more frequent, more amazing." There were murmurs of agreement from Doug and Nolan and then Kris and then Cathy, while Gabriella wore an incredulous look. "These journeys, experiences," Will pressed, "are like prep work or training."

"But for *what*?" the agitated girl demanded.

Smiling, Mark reflected the question back to her. "Does it have to be for anything specific other than what it is, the growing experience of the dream?"

"That makes no sense!"

Countering Gabriella, Will said, "But it makes perfect sense, and it can be so much more. In these powerful dreams, there's some kind of bleed-over effect with reality—I don't understand how, but it's *a* reality even if it isn't our waking reality. It's the only thing that makes sense in all our wide range of dreams."

Even Quani piped up, tapping her notepad, "This is worth pursuing, if only to—"

"No, no," Gabriella blurted while shaking her head, "not if you have *my* dreams." Looking around and seeing no support for her growing distress, she stated, "This obsession can't be healthy—you know what? I'm done." Yanking her books and purse from under her chair, she repeated in a quivering voice, "I'm done."

Shocked onlookers watched her launch from her chair and hurry from the room. Cathy was the first to react. "Wait, Gabriella, wait," she called as she raced to catch up.

Mark looked concerned. "I didn't see that coming. Thought we were all having fun with it."

"She'll be back," Kris assured them, but she was wrong.

Chapter 11

"I don't know," came the voice over the phone, and Cathy patiently waited through the long pause. "Maybe I can talk about it...should talk about it. If you're absolutely sure you want to hear it."

"Of course, Gabriella," Cathy softly encouraged. It had been almost two weeks since she raced into the hallway to catch the fleeing Gabriella and had a brief talk which left them both in tears. Now that each was back at their parent's home in more comfortable environments, Cathy figured Gabriella might be willing to talk about her nightmares. "Come on, it's me. No judgments."

"It's not that," Gabriella began to deny before sighing and making up her mind. "Of course I told you about the creepy visitations, but then I had something *much* worse. *So* much worse!"

Cathy could hear another shaky breath. "It's okay," she soothed.

"Well, it's definitely *not* okay! Imagine you're all alone, exposed, defenseless, in the middle of nowhere. And coming at you is this huge, dark, threatening *thing*! It's not a human or a cloud or...or a shadow, but it most definitely is *alive* and wants to cover you, ooze in everywhere, eating you—dissolving you—until there's nothing of you left...

"You'd have to feel it to understand the terror of being *unmade*. I screamed to wake myself up. And I swear to you, Cathy, the threat still lingered like an aftershock of something you *know* wants you erased. If I hadn't run to the toilet, I'd have peed myself!"

"Sheesh!" Cathy tittered nervously before stopping herself. "You sure have the scary ones. I don't—"

"And you are all thinking they're real—trying to convince me they're real, and I can't...*can't* take that. Yeah, maybe school isn't going quite like I want it to and it's giving me dream fits, but I swear to you that dwelling on them in group is making them worse." In a pleading voice, Gabriella continued, "Any worse and they make me lose my mind. So please don't talk me into coming back. When I said I was done, I meant it."

"If you're sure," Cathy said, resigned to losing this emotional tug-of-war.

"Oh, I'm sure! I've had to beg my mind every night to leave me in peace. Mental conditioning, and it's working, for now."

"Good."

"But there's no way I should do the group thing."

It was Cathy's turn to sigh. "Okay, I'd probably do the same thing. So... How is your family time going? Anything juicy?"

As soon as their call ended, Cathy rang Kris and scowled at her phone when it didn't reach the real person. After rejecting the idea of leaving a long and confusing voicemail, Cathy settled for the brief and mysterious: "Hey, you. We were so wrong about Gabriella. Call me!"

Then Cathy flopped back on her bed, chewed at a fingernail, and considered Gabriella's problem. How could the group and dream experience be so different between them? Would Cathy flee the same way if her dreams were as terrifying? And more importantly, was there anything left to do or say to help? Her musings were interrupted by her door opening and her four-year-old nephew's head appearing.

"Boo!" said the mock-childish voice of the sister who held him up in full view. Then the sister came into view, bouncing the giggling boy on her hip and saying, "Me and the little man are going to a movie tonight, and he wanted to know if Aunt Cathy would come too."

"Not sure, Tina. I'm waiting on a callback."

Tina pouted, which grew exaggerated when she turned it on her son. "Oh. Now Miss College Girl is too good for us, Little Man. See what happens when you let them leave home?"

The baby's imitation of his mother's scowl made Cathy laugh. "You're teaching him to be a brat."

"But it works, doesn't it?"

"Someday it might just backfire on you."

Tina made a rude noise of disagreement. "Anyway, latest animated movie, and the admission price is right!" Since she worked at the only theatre in town, she didn't have to pay for any show that wasn't near capacity. And it turned out singing fish didn't bring in the crowds.

Cathy knew her sister was going to push until she got her way, as usual, so with resignation, she agreed. "Alright, alright. But I might get a return call from my new roommate, and I expect privacy."

"*Privacy*," Tina mocked before closing the door.

Cathy needn't have worried, though, because Kris didn't return the call until the following morning. "Hi, girl. Sorry I didn't get your message last night. I was dining with my mom and dad, and then we were stargazing on the deck until late. I always leave my phone in my room when socializing. It convinces my parents that I'm maturing."

"Ooo," Cathy responded with a giggle. "Good strat! I'll need to remember that one. So, yeah. I had a heart-to-heart with Gabriella yesterday. No way she's coming back to the group—she even begged me to not talk her into returning. She feels like the more we delve, the worse her dreams get. Like it's torture."

"Sad to hear, but I think it would be the exact opposite." Cathy could hear the shrug in Kris' tone. "It isn't for everyone. Frankly, the group would be pretty lame without the huge dramas that come up so often. Except for Nerron drama, of course, who hit on me yet again!"

"Uh oh," Cathy said in a tone that meant, "Do tell!"

"Yeah, he ran up after and asked for my phone number. Said we should try a formal date over the break." Kris mimicked in a rough, low voice: "'I don't care how far I have to drive.'"

"So what did you tell him?"

"I replied he could get in his car and keep driving in the opposite direction."

Cathy laughed. "Ouch!"

"Yeah, well, if I have to show my fangs to make him back off, then it's for the best. I'm just glad he didn't do it in front of the group this time."

"Yeah," Cathy agreed. "He has some bad timing—to say the least! Speaking of..."

"Oh?"

"I told you about my long-time boyfriend who knocked-up and married another girl," Cathy recapped. "So, I run into him last night at the movies, my bitchy sister *leaves* me alone with him, and this time he suggests we should spend more time together 'for old time's sake'. Meaning, he wants me on the side."

"Ugh! We both know a thing or two about pesty boys... So what happened?"

"I just told him that wasn't going to happen." Cathy laughed. "I wish I'd had your line and told him to drive off in the opposite direction. I swear they become even worse when they're married!"

"Show them fangs when you need to, girl." They shared another laugh and promised to stay in touch, especially as the next semester drew close.

Shortly after Christmas, Nolan had an amusing dream which prompted him to email the group: "Mark encouraged us to practice and stay alert for the next blockbuster. Anyone else get one that must be discussed sooner rather than later? I dreamed of our group, in our circle all talking and laughing. The camera slow-pans around and when it gets to Mark's couch, it isn't Mark at all, but Santa, complete with bright red suit and curly white beard! Who else knew that Mark was really Santa?!"

Almost immediately, Doug replied, "Haha! Well in a way, Mark gifted us with this group. I can't match your blockbuster, but I'm game."

Cathy responded shortly after: "Aww, you also miss us. Of course, I'm game! Maybe we can use Facetime to make it more like the real thing."

"No blockbusters and I can't do Facetime," Quani wrote, "but I am good for support."

To which Will joked, "A support line for crazy... I'm in! Any time before New Year's works for me, if given enough notice."

Kris simply wrote, "Sure. What time works for everyone?"

"Don't you guys have better things to do during this time of freedom?" Nerron razzed. "Not like you get extra credit..."

Will quickly responded with a scolding, "Seriously, man, play right or lay off. Don't make me regret inviting you."

Nerron went quiet after that, and though Gabriella was copied into the flurry of emails, no one heard from her.

In private, the other group members exchanged numbers so they could create a conference call but struggled to find a time everyone could be available. After two days of misses, the dejected organizers gave up and settled for an email chain though it dampened the creativity and interaction they all craved. "If only we had a website," Cathy lamented in one email, "we could have coordinated better and even chatted real time. Anything would be better than this."

Will replied: "Even snail mail?"

"You see my tongue sticking out at you, don't you?" she shot back, but jousting over email just wasn't the same.

With registration for the new semester less than two weeks away, Cathy and Kris used Facetime to better approximate the upcoming, real event. They talked excitedly of new semester plans and details, but they really just missed hearing and seeing each other's excitement.

Cathy leaned back in her chair and grinned to Kris' image. "Get this," she said. "I had yet another run-in with my ex at the local coffee shop this afternoon, and now he's playing it all cool. He tipped his hat at me! Like he was some gentleman and I was his lady interest!"

Kris rolled her eyes in empathized exasperation. "I hope you showed him your fangs."

"In public?" Cathy giggled at the thought before adding, "The yocals probably would have taken his side."

Wearing a mischievous grin, Kris said, "Yeah well, we can fantasize about the public shaming, anyway." Then suddenly, Kris turned pensive, almost uncertain.

"What's on your mind?" prompted Cathy.

"To completely switch gears...sort of..."

"Yes?"

"Ah, never mind."

"No 'never mind', you tease!" Cathy laughed when Kris hid her face. "Show me your face, roomie. What? You need to get used to telling me these kinds of things."

"Okay then, so what do you think of Doug—just curious what you make of him." Kris wore a guarded look.

"You mean Doug from the dream meet? Of course you do, silly me! Hmm, a little intense for my taste, but I'd do him." Cathy's fishing had the intended effect, and she saw Kris blush before hiding her face from the camera again. "Oh. Oh!" She laughed and coaxed, "Come on back—I'm just teasing. So, you're interested..." Cathy let that hang in the air just long enough to see Kris' tentative nod. "You could make it work, or rather make him work for you."

"But do you think it'd mess up anything?"

Cathy intuited both angles being asked simultaneously, and retorted, "Why would it? Kris, you're always careful—and smart. If you work your magic, nothing will be different." On a whim, Cathy leaned in close to the camera, raising an eyebrow and whispering, "Except for you two sweet things. It could be our very own inner circle fiery romance."

With her pensive look, Kris murmured, "Or more than that."

Leaning back, Cathy let the implication sink in. "Yeah," she said slowly, matching her friend's consideration. "Yes, it could be more than that."

Chapter 12

Beginning a new semester can be a complicated juggling act. While campus activities stir to life like an awakening party animal, students are often stressed by new living arrangements piled on top of the unknowns of new class schedules. To add another layer of tension, some professors act like they should be the student's only focus, assigning qualifiers or homework before the first class. This message broadcasts: "Expect to learn far more than a mere semester can support."

Social organizations add their own kinds of chaos as they compete for the remainder of attention. If they don't jump in front of others, they risk losing the best fits to another activity. Marketing madness abounds, including pre-rush events, gaudy banners, costumed hawkers, a blizzard of pamphlets, and other inventive attention-grabbers.

In short, the semester opens with a test of discipline. Can students navigate the multiple competing distractions while deciding what works best for them? Because variety will often compete with the reality of limited time, do they neglect something of interest or skip sleep? Details might vary with each individual, but the overall feel of this time has no equal.

Despite the whirlwind, the group couldn't wait for the first scheduled dream meet. They quickly settled on lunch at a café, and despite short notice, most showed up early. Squeals of delight followed multiple rounds of hugs.

Like an arrow shot, Kris rushed to Doug as he walked through the door and lingered in the hug, just long enough to give him something extra to think about.

A flurry of questions bounced around the group even before they had settled down with trays of food. "Nerron sends his best," Will reported, before revealing the truth with a chuckle. "Actually, what he said was, 'Have fun in La La Land while I do real things.' So, I say good riddance. And I might need a new roommate if he gets into the fraternity he's going to rush with."

"I think we're better off," Nolan stated, matching Will's grin.

"Here's to him driving in the opposite direction," Cathy toasted while raising her glass of sweet tea toward Kris.

"Driving? What?" a perceptive Doug asked, splitting his attention between the two giggling new roommates.

"Oh, nothing," Kris said quickly before Cathy could elaborate. "Just an inside joke." Cathy almost choked on her tea while Kris hurried to change the subject. "Also, Gabriella won't return. We confirmed over the break, and she was adamant. Which is why we didn't copy her in on planning for this meeting."

Quani frowned. "That's sad."

"Yeah," Cathy said as she sobered. "She's in a really bad place, but there's always hope for later."

"Maybe as a group we should send our best wishes," Doug suggested, but Cathy shook her head.

"Nah. It'd just make her feel worse."

"I see." He sighed. "Guess we just have to hope she knows, then."

Kris reached across to light-touch his shoulder for the time it took her to say, "That's a sweet thought, Doug. She knows we care."

Will shrugged. "Gabi has to find her own way. I, for one, am running down this path, full sprint." Amid nods of agreement, he chuckled and revealed, "I had another superpowers dream that stood out from the noise of normal crazy."

"You, always wanting to be superman," Cathy teased with a happy laugh. It felt so good to be back together!

"Well, if you remember the last one... This was also more of a warning rather than me indulging a superiority complex."

Using his dry humor, Nolan pointed out, "You've yet to prove to us you don't have a superiority complex."

"Hey now, I never claimed I didn't." Will grinned and then leaned into the table intently. "But get this: it was like heroes had very limited powers, but no one could figure out how they worked or where they came from.

"Abilities passed and morphed seemingly at random—not through birth or training but like a contagion, or some other mysterious means of unlocking them. And because of all the negative attention they caused—envy, mistrust, government probing—these random powers were more of a burden than anything else. Or at least that's how it could be."

Doug mused, "What an odd twist."

"Yeah," Will agreed with a wry turn of his lips. "I mean, in the beginning of the dream, *I* was normal but I had a friend with the powers and they caused him no end of trouble. Like he was shunned, outcast, even though they made him stronger or better or something. The details were so frustratingly vague!"

He cleared his throat. "Anyway, I began feeling changes or seeing little manifestations, and I felt this...awkwardness. Despite the positive changes, all I remember was needing to conceal it from others, to safeguard myself from their overreactions. I guess I felt put out, wondering if the trouble I 'caught' was because of my friend or through some other random occurrence." Will chuckled and leaned back. "Trying to figure out how I was going to cope with them was what I remember clearest, especially once they became noticeable—not that I was frightened of them, more like wary."

"What was that initial quote you brought to group," Cathy teased, "about quietly going crazy?"

Will snorted. "Yeah, tell me about it! Had I only known how true it is!"

"It's a crap world when even having superpowers is a negative," Nolan said. "Remind me not to vacation there."

"Oh, you'd be fine. Just don't do anything super."

"Speaking of standing out," came Quani's soft voice, "I finally had a big dream." Everything at their table froze, all except for widening eyes and turning heads. Hunching her shoulders, Quani giggled and said, "Well, it's not that big."

"Do tell!" Will urged.

Kris held up a finger. "Shouldn't we save the rest for the actual dream meet?"

"We can always give Mark a quick recap," Cathy piped in, obviously keen on the here and now.

"Hell, the once per week meeting isn't enough anymore—at least not for me," Will added. "If we hadn't met today, I'd probably have had another dream making me forget this one." He tapped the side of his head. "A memory like a small cup, it only holds so much."

Cathy gave a small noise of inspiration and bounced in her chair. "If only we had a shared space like on a website where we could at least vent our dreams until the actual meeting..." When she saw Kris' subtle nod toward Quani, Cathy instantly switched gears. "Oh! Sorry, sorry, I got carried away," she said though there were only knowing grins. "Please continue, Quani." Then she couldn't resist a final silliness: "I blame Will. But please continue."

"Well, I am no story teller but I am glad I can finally contribute," Quani began haltingly.

"Hey," Will objected, "you're such an important part of our group. You make up for my terrible memory."

Smiling at the compliment, she added, "It's just that now I know the feeling of a truly special dream, may it inspire me." Quani unconsciously began straightening the fork and knife on her tray, making sure they aligned perfectly to her plate before clearing her throat.

"In this dream, I had just moved into an apartment. Since I could not afford much, the area did not feel safe. I kept to myself and in the shadows as much as I could. I focused on what little I could control. I bought cute things for my apartment and arranged everything to my liking.

"But a group of...rough girls noticed me, and when I tried to avoid them they only noticed more. They would stand in my way and make me change my path. They would sniff at me like I smelled bad. And when I didn't react, one even poked me with a pin. It was just a prick, but it hurt! I tried fleeing back to my apartment but they followed me. They surrounded me at the door and my hands were shaking." Caught up in the dream memory, Quani became even more expressive.

"But in a flash of insight, I decided I had brought this on myself by making assumptions against them. This time I looked clearly and saw they needed attention. They wanted me to *see* them, so I asked them if they wanted to come in and see my new home.

"They followed me inside and made jokes about my decorations. One of them was viewing a set of the pictures I had arranged in a diagonal pattern, and she tilted the bottom one out of alignment. I knew this was a test, so I laughed and tilted the top one in the opposite direction and said, 'Now it's perfect.' They giggled up a storm.

"Though I was silently making plans to find a new home, I offered them tea. They said that was fancy and uppity, but I told them it just flavors the water so it doesn't taste so bad. I could use the same tea leaves all day and never have to taste the awful tap water. This made them curious and after sipping the tea, their attitudes also began to change. I think they began to understand more about me, maybe actually *see me* in return.

"The girls relaxed and began having fun with each other. Caught up in this goodness, this sharing, I told them they could visit anytime. And you know what? They began to protect me from the worst elements of the neighborhood, to make sure I was safe and one of them, sort of."

"One time when we were sitting around my tiny living room sipping tea, one girl began humming. Another followed in perfect harmony, though they weren't singing the same thing. Each would join in and make the music more complex and each of them sounded perfect together. It was astonishing. I was awed and inspired.

"After their little impromptu song, I was moved to tears. I said they were amazing, a rare talent they should share with the world. They didn't believe me at first, but I definitely knew talent, and I was also good at arranging and coordinating. Now, I had no thoughts of moving away because I was focused on helping them use their talent. And I knew I had the skills to help them unlock their gifts and share. And…then I awoke.” Seeming to deflate a little, Quani glanced to the others in the group for support.

"So nice,” Cathy said, impulsively getting up to draw her into a hug with Kris following the next instant.

"I didn't know you were musical,” Kris marveled while returning to her seat and Quani gave a small laugh.

"Oh, I am not. But when the talent is so…good, even I can notice. In the dream, I could *do* important things: help them with presentation, use my influence or connections to gain notice for them. It was like my reward for kindness.”

A smiling Doug commented, "I know that feeling exactly. I'm guessing we all do.”

"A shame we have to return to our non-inspired selves,” Will said before brightening. "But then there's always the next dream.” They shared the laughter of knowing and belonging.

* * *

These paths are dusty, filled with debris from both man and nature, and yet the crowd makes everything seem dirtier. They are noisy, rowdy, jostling each other in the way that makes most festivities a bother, yet there's also an undertone, something ugly. I try ignoring them all, only noting they are making my errand more difficult. When the anticipation rises to a new level, they pack together tighter.

I'm curious, but then again, the idle and dispossessed are always flocking together. My choice of paths today seems a poor decision. Resigned to cross regardless of obstacles, I point my shoulder and use it like a wedge. I catch a glimpse of the intersection and am relieved. At least it's not also packed solid.

Then the crowd's tone changes, their jeering and taunting roll like black waves among faint cries of sorrow. I know I must press harder if I'm to make my appointments. With a last push, I pop into the intersection—and freeze.

Amid bright uniforms, the lurching catches my eye. I see a healthy body, stumbling, bowing beneath the weight of abuse, both physical and emotional. My gut clenches painfully at the sight. A barked order and a laugh, even as the abused man struggles to comply. It's clear, even to the guards, that he needs time to regain the strength to heft himself and the large beam he's lashed to.

This cannot stand! Before asking myself what should be done, I am moving forward, around the amused guard. I'm uncorking my water pouch and kneeling. The tortured man sees my action and then looks up at me, into me. Time shimmers and insight is an icy fist around my pounding heart. He is passed living, resigned to his awful fate. But I know of no other way so I offer my water.

"Please, drink," I urge. Even as I raise the skin for him to sip, I am struck with realization. Rather than me relieving him, gifting him, it is the other way around. He accepts my water because I beg him, because he understands that *I* need to reject this horrific treatment.

Injustice hammers me. I long to cry out, to reach out and shame those gathered to add to his suffering. I envision *prying* open their understanding.

But Jesus gives me a warning look, a small shake of his head as I stand. This isn't my burden or my right. I'm responsible for myself and fulfilling my own potential, and that must be enough.

A barked order in their cold tongue makes me realize only a few labored breaths have passed. "Get out of his way or take his place!"

Jesus has already yanked himself to his feet. I'm pushed against others along the edge, and the appalling procession is moving beyond me. I stare at their backs until the crowd closes, hiding him from sight. In those few breaths, I am crushed and yet I am inspired beyond all understanding.

Chapter 13

"Quite the religious experience," Mark mused into the stillness of the room.

Nolan shrugged and used his sleeves to prevent tears from falling. "Nah, it was something more than that. It was so detailed, I *lived* that moment." He paused in an effort to control his shaking voice. "I considered—but only for a moment—not sharing the dream because it was so intensely personal." He looked around at attentive faces as if searching for proof of his trust. "But if anyone can understand, it'd be you guys."

The group exchanged warm smiles, and then Kris asked, "So…what *do* you think it meant?"

"I just absorb the experience, let it wash over me…I don't know. It's been two days since the dream, and I keep coming back to that essence: sticking to the facts as I experienced them, not adding what I want or guessing about it."

"And learning whatever you can from the actual impressions," Will added with a nod.

"Exactly."

Mark leaned forward and gestured around the circle. "So let's see what we can all learn from this. By feeling the crowd's reaction, I can see how it could taint your view of other humans in the story, the mob mentality."

Nolan pondered this while sniffling. "I didn't think of that because I was focused on my brief meeting with Jesus and all it meant, but of course I was outraged at the crowd." His eyes rolled slightly while searching for some way to express himself. "It feels like they were symbolic, maybe. They were in my way, some blockage and then...this wall of hate, but it wasn't directed at me. More like they were blank injustice, if that makes sense, which was completely different from what Jesus felt like. He was right *there*...yet apart from what was being hurled at him and focusing on me as soon as he noticed me kneeling.

"His gift to me, the moment of attention and...counseling was exactly what I needed—that I'm sure of—and then keeping me focused on him rather than turning on the crowd."

"I'm sure that would have ended well for you," Will quipped. "Might have been an extra cross."

Nolan smiled without humor. "Nah, I'd have fought with a fury until they killed me. But then I wouldn't have made any difference or understood what I needed to, wouldn't have had those few precious moments bouncing around inside my head. You see, even as Jesus moved away and the crowd hid him, those realizations were washing over me. Waves of...*importance*.

"And I woke up amazed at just how much he'd helped me—or maybe the dream experience itself. Attached to the mind-blowing meeting was the understanding of what I should and shouldn't do. It feels *meaningful* that he prevented me from turning on the crowd." With wonder in his voice, Nolan added, "And he did it so effortlessly while involved in his own horror."

"Hmm…" Mark considered Nolan's takeaway for a long moment before speculating, "Like perhaps a lesson of personal responsibility, the line we must find and walk in our life journeys." When he noticed the questioning looks, he qualified: "Our own lives should be a balancing act, focused on our goals and trials without being too self-centered or ignoring others and their plights. Yet not too invasive, not too much pushing into others' lives in ways they don't welcome or need."

"So not at *all* like shrinks," Will said with flippant sarcasm, causing a ripple of tension-breaking mirth and earning a look of amused exasperation from Mark.

Not to be derailed, Doug turned back to Mark for clarification. "So, you mean like in-between selfish and nosey?"

"Yeah, in essence." Then Mark pointed out, "Many psychological burdens come from an oversized sense of responsibility. I agree with you, Nolan, that it's a valuable lesson to gain from your dream. Thanks for sharing. Did anyone have anything else to add?" He looked around at the pensive group and then cracked a grin. "Anyone have one that's perhaps a little less intense?"

Amid chuckles, Cathy raised her hand. "I've had a great dream that I think further proves our speculation, but before we get too far, we must come clean. We couldn't wait on the meet, so we've already discussed a few dreams.

Like," she said as she shifted to fully face Mark, "did you know you're really Santa?"

Mark arched an eyebrow while they watched him handle the blindside. "Is that so?"

"It came right around Christmas," Nolan explained unnecessarily. "I guess I was missing this group. So, I was witnessing us talking and laughing in this room, and it was like a camera was slowly panning around to each of us, smiling, laughing. When it got to you, you were in a Santa costume."

As the circle cracked up again, Mark replied in good humor, "Okay, that's a little creepy. I hope you weren't viewing my future, one of scaring babies and having them pee on my lap."

"I speculated that the costume might have been included because in a way you gifted us with this group," Doug said.

"Huh. That's thoughtful, and I am so happy to help make this possible, but we'd not be here without you all and your dreams." Then Mark's warm smile turned boyish. "Besides, whenever a dream is baffling, we can always poke at the symbolism. But, me as Santa..."

"I have some symbolism for you," Will announced and quickly recounted his dream of contagious superpowers.

A perceptive Mark said, "It seems like your impression of superheroes doesn't fit. You sure you weren't seeing it from a villain's point of view? You remember nothing about what you could do?"

"It's all so vague, even at the time," Will admitted, "but it wasn't forceful or megalomaniacal. It felt more like we were victims, or *could* be victims to our surroundings. Like the abilities should have been appreciated but weren't."

Mark explained, "Feeling underappreciated is common, even in dream sentiments. In fact, many variations—or even the vague sense of injustice—play out in dreams. Researchers are seeing how the brain processes and stores those feelings even as it processes memories."

"That doesn't make much sense," Doug disagreed, "because many dreams can be hopelessly jumbled and yet our real memories are clear, factual—even if some feelings are similar between a real event and a dream."

"You sure of those clear memories?" Mark teased before pulling himself back. "That's a dark trail to follow, so we better not get sidetracked. But let's just leave it at this: Once, I was convinced my shower drain was clogged, and I'd have to go buy stuff to take care of it. It wasn't until I checked and saw it drain fine that I realized my impression, my 'memory' of the drain problem, came from a short, mundane dream *masquerading* as a memory."

"That's bizarre," Cathy commented.

"Hey, at least the clog repaired itself," Will joked, causing more laughter.

The group sobered and listened intently while Quani recounted her epic dream. When she finished, Mark smiled encouragement and said, "Perhaps your dream is inspiring you to become a music producer." She demurred and shook off the notion, and he added, "I imagine some got their start because they found they were gifted at helping other musicians organize and promote."

"But I'm no musician," she stated.

"Are you sure about that—have you tried?" he asked.

She shook her head, but considered and brightened. "Not yet."

"Great answer," Kris praised. "You might feel drawn to it if you give it a chance. I love that now you can share with me what it feels like to have a powerful musical dream. I just wish I'd get another great one."

"The point was about the attitude adjustment and the girls' reactions," Quani reminded them. "I had a shift in thinking and then felt the benefits. I know what it's like to really see them and help them succeed."

"That's a remarkable feeling to have, and worth dwelling on," Mark emphasized, not wanting her to pull back into her shell. "Did you recognize anything familiar in the dream, about the girls or the place?"

Quani shook her head. "Nothing was familiar about it."

"You sure it really was you in the dream?" Will asked with a teasing undertone.

"I wasn't floating above or hearing a narrator or sinking into someone else's body, if that is what you ask. It was just me, as I am...well, except for having contacts in the music world and maybe being good with music."

Mark shifted on the couch and rubbed his chin. "I find it interesting to consider how the dream atmosphere might have differed had another of us dreamt it. I might have floated above it all, analyzing the positive psychological boost, the healing. Or like Kris might have focused more around the music, dreamed more details of that, perhaps."

Cathy flipped a hand in Will's direction. "If it had been Will, he'd have merged into the girls in some completely inappropriate way."

"Oh, I'd make them sing alright!"

"Oh, brother..." As Cathy rolled her eyes, Will pointed out that she had brought it up.

"You did kind of ask for that one," Nolan said and then held up placating hands when she rounded on him with a look of exaggerated shock.

"Boys!" Kris sassed. "Thinking they have to stick together."

Doug laughed and said, "Don't paint me with that broad brush."

"I stand corrected." Kris shared a special smile with Doug, adding, "Here's to the exceptions." She tilted her head in recognition and then smoothed the material of her stylish leggings.

Mark looked around the circle of grins and noted, "The friendliness of you guys makes this group very special. I can tell we've made great progress over the break. This meeting highlights how far we have come. Were there any other dreams you shared before we cover new ones?"

"That was it, I think," Cathy said and then gave one of her snort-laughs. "My newest can't wait any longer—sorry to those also anxious to share." In the moment it took to get murmured permission, she wagged in her chair and held up a finger. "The dream convinced me, more than any other I've had, that there's something different, special, about these helper dreams. At least, I *feel* certain we make a real difference, even if it's only to our self." After indulging in a short, self-deprecating laugh, she continued with her telling.

"There were four girls—three sisters and a friend—at a movie theatre. Disappointing movie and all, and they go to leave. They're in the lobby when the youngest, who was probably in high school, starts and realizes she forgot her purse. I remember the older girls frowning at her with their silent pressure to measure up.

"So, in a way I was there, maybe hovering, I don't know. I could feel the girl's quiet embarrassment without *being* her. As she returned to find her purse, I also felt a growing sense of dread even though she was clueless. She picked her way down the steps, trying to remember which row was theirs, and my awareness was my own, but very close to hers like we almost shared the same space but not quite. I knew she should get help from her sisters, but that idea would be rejected partly because of the scorn she'd have to endure.

"Just a simple snatch and run, right?" Cathy tittered, before straightening her posture and continuing. "I *knew* something bad was going to happen. The theatre had gone dark again, and there was almost no light from the strip lighting along the steps. She had to squint down at the floor in front of each row near the middle of the room. There it was, a small azure-and-silver clutch purse, her only one and so it was valuable to her.

"When she eased past a few chairs and bent to retrieve her purse, I heard a sinister shuffle and saw a creep rushing up to her in a burst of quiet movement. And I chose exactly that moment to merge with the girl—right as we were grabbed from behind and now I was sharing the same terrifying situation! He was dingy, smelly even, and he slapped his hand over our mouth, hard!

"I flailed with desperate strength, twisting and trying to break free, but he was stronger and only squeezed harder, and it was painful! I was having trouble getting enough breath. I remember the sliding of my heels on the theatre carpet as he dragged me backward, down the steps toward the emergency exit door near the screen.

"I tried going limp and pleading with him, at least with my tone since his hand was still clamped down on my mouth. I could feel the near paralyzing *grossness* of his body as he crushed me to him. So I began struggling again as he pushed us out the door into the night, biting at fingers and twisting. And..."

Cathy straightened in a realization and turned to Nolan. "You'll find this an interesting coincidence, because in my head I was singing the children's song 'Jesus Loves Me' over and over in an attempt to keep calm and focus on freeing us. Now that we were on pavement, the man was speeding up and I was stumbling, trying not to lose my shoes. I think a few people were witnessing this, but were too shocked or whatever to help.

"He slowed as we neared a big tree and I think he was parked behind it. And I knew my chance to help was now or never! I twisted so our backs were to the tree, pushed him against it and reared back with my head as hard as I could. I crushed his nose with the back of my head, which made him slam his head into the tree trunk! He was stunned and I was crazed. I kept slamming him against the tree as his hold on me—on us—weakened and then broke. I think he fell, but I was screaming, thinking, *run-run-run*!

"She stumbled away, clear of him, and the violence of that finally woke up an onlooker or two because I remember them with their phones out calling the cops. But the details of the scene were fading beneath this *rush* of adrenaline. It was a surge of triumph. The purse was forgotten, the terror and struggle were forgotten. There was only the sense of victory, and then I awoke thinking to myself, 'I won... I won against that attacker!'" In contrast to the intense tone of her storytelling, Cathy sighed happily.

"I lay in bed for a while, shaking the bad feelings and thinking about what just happened. I knew by being there and lending my support and perfect timing that I saved that girl from abduction. Those were *highly* conscious decisions in my dream—they were my own." With a self-conscious giggle, she concluded, "I don't think without this training in our group I would have been able to handle it. Only because I stayed calm and then acted at the right moment did the girl break free, and I dare anyone to prove otherwise."

Rather than rise to her dare, even Will was nodding, and Doug said, "I think we understand the feeling. These few special dreams are more...real, like they actually happen somewhere."

"That's quite the leap," Mark pointed out gently. "Where's the evidence to support a reality within the dream state?"

Will insisted, "They're definitely stronger than any figment of imagination. I mean, *I* have a wild imagination, and the experiences still blow my mind."

"No one's claiming the brain is simple," Mark answered. "It's the most powerful, layered processor we know of and can be creative beyond our own expectations. Much in a similar way people like long distance runners or soldiers can use mental exercises to push themselves far beyond normal."

"But it *is* different than some runner trance," Will said. "That's more like willpower, and this is somehow more...external."

In agreement, Kris added, "The special dreams are far more than a figment. The music I heard and played, the world I visited—twice..."

Cathy was bouncing in her chair again. "Yes, far more *real* than something just inside my head while I'm sleeping. I'm getting more aware of them and growing more capable within them!"

"But we have plenty of studies measuring brain activity during sleep," Mark protested this latest push in thinking. "We know areas like the visual cortex—which processes our light images from the eye into complete images—are active during dreaming. We have plenty of measurements showing how our brain is creating dreams, and we have plenty of evidence as to why it happens."

After a moment of silent contemplation, Doug asked, "As someone—Will maybe?—hinted at a while back, does that mean the brain is creating the dream, or just responding to it?"

Will held out his hands in front of his face to illustrate. "It makes sense that if I'm seeing something in my mind's eye, my brain reacts similarly to me seeing something right here." Unable to resist his silly impulses, he began wiggling his fingers and then making wave patterns with his hands.

"Guys..." Mark said, entreating them to get serious. "Feeling the reality of dreams is special, incredible learning experiences, but thinking they are actually real... How would that even work? Are we talking about alternate lives or alien abductions here?"

"Hey," Will joked, "even if I felt probed by aliens I wouldn't admit it." When all he got were eye-rolls, he turned back to Mark. "I'm curious: do you know if any of those studies actually *prove* that the brain is creating the dream? Wouldn't it react similarly for normal stimulation while we're awake? Which reminds me, do researchers even make a distinction between types of dreams? Sure, some are scrambled eggs, but some are crisp and every bit as powerful as anything we experience here!"

"I can freshen up on those studies," Mark offered. "Perhaps we should table it for the next time."

"I'm betting," Will continued, "you won't find any evidence showing the brain is specifically causing the dreams."

Mark made a bland gesture. "And yet that's the obvious conclusion, right?"

"Is it obvious," Doug pressed, "or only an assumption?"

Unable to stand the slight tension, the challenge hanging in the air, Cathy popped up from her chair and held out her arms. "Group hug," she announced. "Come on, group hug."

Smiles and grins came together into a ball in the middle of the circle. As they separated, Mark said, "I truly appreciate how close and brave this group is."

"We are explorers!" Cathy stated excitedly, noticing with amusement that Kris took the chance to give Doug an extra hug.

"And soon you'll appreciate how right we are," Will claimed with a smirk.

"Only if I take the red pill." Mark smiled before amending, "But we'll see, we'll see. I promise I'll dig through the research before the next meeting."

Chapter 14

Again Cathy teased her roommate as she hung her coat over an empty chair. "Ah, this beautiful weather, Kris. Perfect for a picnic—*or getting intimate*. It's a real shame you chickened out."

"Stop that," Kris said before settling in a seat around the café's outdoor table and defending herself. "I told you it just wasn't the right timing. And I don't want to be too forward. It's not my style." But if she were completely honest with herself, she would have to admit she did kind of chicken out.

After the last dream meet when she approached Doug to ask if they could get together, his small, amused smile had unnerved her. He seemed to know exactly what she was going to ask and why; it was like he knew she wanted to test him, to spend one-on-one time to measure him against her high standards. And so instead of carrying through with her carefully planned script, she switched tactics to include the entire group in the idea of a caffeine-inspired pre-meet.

Her smirking roommate was certainly getting the full mileage out of her dilemma. "Wipe that grin off your face and get my usual," Kris snapped, tilting her head to soak in a sun that seemed to forget it wasn't yet spring. It *was* perfect weather with an occasional gentle breeze to offset the strong rays. Maybe Doug would be the first one to show. She could make that work, as a start. Despite the friendly harassment, Cathy would keep her promise not to spoil Kris' plan.

Yet it was Will who showed first, hopping over the low decorative wall instead of using the walkway like a normal person. "I heard rumors of a party…"

Kris returned the banter, "Then you've come to the wrong place."

"Unless your idea of a party is dreaming and talking about them," Cathy added, raising her cup of coffee in a salute.

Will settled into a seat across the table. "As it so happens, I'm full of them."

"And full of it," Kris teased, with Cathy adding gleefully, "So you fit right in."

Next to arrive was Quani, who apologized even though she arrived a few minutes before the agreed upon time. "Class ran late," she explained while receiving quick hugs from Cathy and Kris.

Then Kris spotted Doug making his way to the crosswalk, and he got his first hug before he was even in the patio area. "Sheesh," Will commented as they strolled back to the table. "Where's my bear hug?"

Kris instead gave him a sassy face and her roommate covered for her by also giving Doug a hug and saying, "We've decided it's a great idea for group hugs every meeting."

"So we're warming up for when Nolan gets here," Doug half-asked, clueless yet amused. Glancing at his wristwatch, he added, "His class should have ended, but I think it's on the other side of campus. Though, I know he always goes for strong coffee, so I'll have it ready. Anyone else? Refills?"

"I only drink chai," Quani mentioned before realizing how that sounded. Rising though she had just sat down, she said, "I will get it, thanks for the offer." After the momentary you-go-first-no-you-go-first dance, Quani led Doug into the coffee shop.

"This day," Will commented, performing an impressive stretch before returning to his slouch, "is perfect, like we planned it."

"Yeah," Cathy said with a giggle and a glance at Kris. "We should have done a picnic."

Partly to deflect the attention, Kris asked Will, "So do you think Mark will have any evidence to shoot holes in your theory?"

"Hey, it's *our* theory," he corrected before shaking his head. "I doubt he'll come up with anything. I did some quick searches and we just don't have the experimental ability to do more than draw inferences about what's going on with dreams. Besides..." A well timed yawn interrupted him. "As you can tell, I've been doing a bunch of research of my own, and nothing in my best and wildest dreams tells me it's homegrown. I'm just—we're all—experiencing things *far* outside our ability."

Nodding, Cathy added, "And the more we look for it, the more purpose we find. Like it's all there, waiting to be found."

"Yep, we're homing in on it," Will agreed, unconsciously toying with a scraggly wannabe-mustache.

Once Nolan made it and each was hovered over their beverage of choice, the catching up and small talk shifted to their budding theory, though they agreed to save retellings for the upcoming dream meet.

"Some of mine are *so* very clear—especially since we got serious—that they rival reality!" Cathy held up her cup and tapped the side. "I mean, is this even real?"

"Well, let's not start doubting reality," countered Doug with a chuckle. "Not a rabbit hole we want to go down."

"No, that's not what I mean. But why would I take all this for granted, and then completely doubt dreams that in some way feel just as real? At least while they're happening."

Correcting his posture, Will nodded and gestured around him. "I see exactly what you mean. Since we accept this, it's like inconsistent to reject the other. In a way, that's kind of what we were doing before we began taking them seriously."

"And it's like they respond by getting more crisp, more clear, more *real*," Cathy continued with her enthusiastic head bob. "At least mine have." She made sure the others were in agreement, that they were all experiencing various degrees of dreaming growth.

Doug mused, "I've always had a few freaky-strong dreams, but they're more frequent now. And maybe more controlled? Less random? I don't know. But those in combination with my roomie and his girlfriend always pushing me to do stuff with them leaves me worn out."

"Yeah, my dreams are also more," Kris said, lightly touching his arm. "And yet so many don't fit any pattern. Still plenty of completely random ones to support the random brain activity theory."

"Hey, if they all fit neatly together it wouldn't be a pattern to find," Will pointed out. "It'd just be constant, obvious, which is boring."

"The good ones definitely seem like hidden gems, waiting to be discovered," Nolan said before upending his cup to get the last few drops. "And I'm going to need another liquid boost to keep my eyes pried open." His motion triggered a surge of refill requests, because much of the fun of exploring life is doing so while boosted with caffeine.

* * *

Mark seemed surprised when they all burst into the room at once, already laughing and talking animatedly. "I see this is going to be a good session," he commented, catching the contagious grins. "Glad to see everyone in such high spirits."

As they were getting seated, he opened by admitting, "As promised, I did more research, and of course there's enough to fill several semesters so I might have missed important points. But as you suspected, nothing we've yet found *proves* that dreams originate in the brain." Will chuckled, so Mark directed this at him: "You'll be amused to know that in a prominent paper, researchers basically said, 'tangible evidence remains elusive.'"

"A fancy way of admitting they don't really know," Will quipped while settling into his preferred slouch.

Mark continued, "Now there's plenty of research comparing scans and brain chemicals, surveys and pattern matching, but yeah, we cannot be certain of anything regarding dreams. We know REM sleep is a special buffer from the anxiety-causing Noradrenaline, and we can see that emotional and memory centers are activated so they can process in relative peace."

"Or better yet," Doug pointed out, "without interruption so that the experiences can play out. No reason it has to be an either/or."

"Yes, but we have indicators that this specific dreaming function is necessary in the storing and processing of memories. We know memory function can fail without solid sleep."

"But we can have strong dreams outside this REM sleep, right?" Kris asked, and Mark nodded.

"Yes, true. It seems to be rarer yet frequent enough that it prevents correlation of a predictable 'dream mode.' I know we can all agree dreams are important. Carl Jung went as far as to suggest they have an important impact on the development of personality, terming that idea 'individuation.' So, I say it's vital to embrace them and be content with…well, whatever they are."

Waving his hands in what could be considered concession of a point, Mark added, "Even Freud's theories were filled with a disruptive force he labelled the 'unconscious,' which could most certainly be interpreted as a force external to our normal, rational minds. Evidence that 'our minds have been elsewhere' is the exact phrasing in one report."

"This is great news for our dream journeys," Cathy stated happily.

"But good luck getting people to accept the mind trip," Mark teased in good humor. "It's…far out there."

"We know, right?" she replied with a bounce in her chair, and Nolan added with conviction, "There's pattern *and* purpose in what we're dreaming."

Will laughed with his admission: "And I'm hooked."

"I can see that," an amused Mark said. "So, shall we continue our own dream research? Who has a new one to share?"

"I've had an interesting one," Kris stated nonchalantly, yet everyone's focus snapped to her and the room seemed to hold its breath. That was an obvious enough sign to begin. With a small clearing of her throat and a settling in the seat while opening her laptop, Kris dove into her dream recall.

"The walls were white, doors, trim, ceiling squares, everything. Bright fluorescents were at precise intervals as I strolled down the hall, trying to get my bearings. All of it was supposed to present a clean, safe environment, but it was more sterile and lifeless, without happiness.

"I made this comment to my attendants because I knew my destination would be just as bad. I regretted not wearing something brighter and less professional. I told them warm colors were every bit as important as anything else we did, and a man in a lab coat promised to arrange more color.

"We halted outside a door that he unlocked with the swipe of a key card. Once I stepped inside, the door click shut behind me and I was alone, except for the child in the far corner of the sterile-looking bedroom. At that point, I knew what—who—this was, even though, strangely enough, I'd had no idea when I was walking down the hallway and into this room, if that makes sense?"

"Sure," Mark said easily. "It's common for you to have or make up information exactly when it's needed."

Running her hand over a knee, Kris said, "Maybe, maybe. In the dream, I was trying not to be creeped out by this new information, or scared. The child had glanced at me for a moment before returning to her book—and I somehow knew it was a girl despite the fact her head was shaved and the white gown she wore was just functional. In that glance, I knew she had measured me and understood everything about the situation. Effortlessly, dispassionately, inhumanly fast.

"Despite this, I paused only for another moment before casually asking, 'Hello, do you know why I'm here?'

"'Don't worry,' the girl said without looking up again—and she seemed maybe eight or ten years old. 'I know how to behave.'

"I forced myself to approach and settled cross-legged on the floor beside her. 'I'm sure you do,' I said softly and warmly, knowing I had only a very limited time to make a difference."

"Wait," Will interrupted as he stirred in his chair, "what did I miss? Who or what is she?"

"Don't rush me," Kris chided. "I'm trying to reveal it like the dream did to me."

"But you already said you knew—"

Cathy made a shushing noise and motion at Will before waving for Kris to continue.

"I told the girl, 'That's not what worries me. I'm worried that you don't know *you*.' I used a finger to gently turn her chin toward me. So she could really see me. So she could see I, too, was an open book and far more interesting than the one she buried her attention in. Again, I knew I had no time to play head games. Her focusing on me was disturbing, almost distracting. She was so intense, but regardless I laid it all in the open for her to see.

"'This is *me*, caring about *you*. Not some experiment results or whatever insights they can gain, but *you* as a living bundle of awesomeness.'

"Her response was immediate and challenging: 'But how can you?' In a flash of insight, I could tell she expected me to fail—to fail her—like they had. That she thought she knew all she needed to about us. I felt such deep sorrow at this judgment. I couldn't help myself; I began to cry, softly at first, but with big tears when she hurried to hug me.

"She squeezed me fiercely, promising that it would be better. There, in her snap decision, was her comforting maternal instinct, and that was her avenue of escape. She had to *feel* the necessity to care for us normal, slow humans for her to survive this experiment. Because you see, I'd been brought in to evaluate the mess: a project exploiting intelligence with results that had scared those in charge enough that they were on the verge of scrapping it. Her.

"With her mouth next to my ear, she whispered, 'They shouldn't have made me.' And I knew then she had no intention of living. This nearly panicked me, because what I felt from her was the possibility of...I don't know, call it survival, but something much more important. Like she could save us, if she wanted to enough, if I could somehow get her to change her mind.

"I drew her to arm's length and shook my head, saying, 'No, no, that makes less of a difference than you think. You are here and a miracle, but you have to want to truly become *you*. And despite any level of intelligence, that takes time.'

"I could tell she didn't believe me, didn't see any proof, because despite her staggering intelligence, she was still a child. And one stuck in an awful, sterile environment. I have no idea how the experimenters could think this was acceptable for a child, but then they weren't considering the human element. That's why I was here—I mean there.

"I explained, 'There are things you cannot see or feel from inside this room, or in there." I tapped her temple and then ran my palm across her smooth head in a way that made her eyelids droop. Inspired, I did it again and told her, 'It's easier for us because time just happens while we struggle along, and experience gets blended in with our meager understanding. Does that make sense?'

"I felt such relief when she nodded. 'I get this is much harder for you, but it's still vital and you cannot speed it up. So, please have patience with us and with yourself.'

I held out my arms to her and this time, she did the crying. It was in perfect imitation of what I had done, but I didn't really care because it would buy her some time, and that's what she needed more than anything else. And...that's where the dream faded."

After a moment of silence, Mark commented, "Ah, the power of perspective. Something only time and experience can buy." Taking a deep breath, he continued, "At least I think that's what the dream-counselor-you was alluding to."

"Maybe," Kris said with a shrug. "Some finer points were lost in that dream haze, of course, and maybe from me struggling to grasp the whole thing."

"So you dreamed of a test tube baby," Will quipped. "I knew those were dangerous—speaking of, how was the girl so scary to them?"

"Not sure. If I knew those details, I've forgotten them. Just that she scared them with her abilities."

A grinning Nolan asked, "Was her name Pandora, by chance?"

"She seemed too much for them to handle, so the name would fit," Mark agreed. "But speaking of handling well, Kris, you strike me as someone who would do well as a counselor, even in real life."

This earned a wry grin from her. "I think it might be better to dream about being one than to actually *be* one."

Doug snorted. "I think that can be said about most occupations."

"Nothing turns out as glamorous as we want it to," Mark agreed. "True."

Will wore a boyish grin as he amended this thought: "At least not in this reality, but in dreams..."

"Yeah," Cathy agreed with a sigh of contentment. "All the glamor you could want."

Chapter 15

I'm strolling through a brightly colored setting: fields of soft grasses, tiered flowerbeds and decorative trees separated by polished cobblestone walkways. It feels like I loaded into a game without any load time, but where is here? Scattered around the grounds are people lounging in fancy robes. For the most part, they are chatting or debating in small groups, though here and there are loners simply enjoying the solace, scenery and sunshine. We are also carefree and jovial, my friend and me, but we have a completely different reason for being here.

"Now *this* is a nice day to fight," he says with a crack of his knuckles. This close, I can feel joints releasing tension. I sense his calm, practiced excitement of a trial waiting to be overcome, and I grin at such a casually cheerful spirit. We're in sync, *grouped*, and looking for the fun kind of trouble. Which, given our rough and dirty clothes, will find us.

A couple nearby women in bright, delicate dresses gawk at us as we stroll by. My friend's return wink intimates: "Don't you wish you were with us." And sure enough, with more people arriving to enjoy the park activities, a group of fancy dandies saunter our way.

They're already sneering, assuming we're easy prey for their amusement. After all, they are five to our duo. Lanky boys freshly released from their studies and all without a clue, but that is my friend's specialty, his calling: to clue them in.

"You don't belong here," claims the leader standing in our way. "Who let you loose from the quarry?" Soft snickers from his wingmen encourage his foolishness.

"I belong where my feet lead me," my friend states with an aloofness guaranteed to offend. "Careful you don't get in the way." The bully-punch to his stomach comes sudden and predictable but lacking the desperate strength of a dangerous opponent. My friend always lets them throw the first punch.

Bending with the impact, he gracefully transitions into a leg sweep that sends the leader slamming to the ground. "Get them!" the scream erupts following the embarrassing flop, and the four others pile into the fight.

"Woo!" my friend taunts and laughs while taking some hits and dodging others. "You swing like babes. Barely from the cradle. Need practice. Before you're worth anything." He's toying with them, rarely returning a punch. He's a long way from needing my help, but I like to keep him at peak performance.

Little unobtrusive me shifts to stay close as the fight dances into the grass. I stretch my willpower, subtle motions of my hands: healing to his shoulders, nerve calming in the gut so it doesn't hinder, snuff the sting from his foot and shin. *Ouch!* A lucky and vicious hit lands on his jaw and I clamp down on the pain while dosing it with rejuvenation.

We can maintain this pace all day, scrapping until these punks are too tired to lift a limb. But I'm the impatient one. I send my friend a burst of adrenaline, increasing his reflexes and quickness so he can stop toying and begin the lesson already. One of the boys notices my input, yells in anger, and stumbles toward me, but a kick sends him sprawling before he takes three steps. As long as I'm behind my taunting whirlwind of fists and feet, they cannot touch me.

Hardly needed, I let my attention roam. Our brawl has collected a few amused onlookers, yet most of the park is filling with animated people absorbed in their own conversations and laughter. The festive atmosphere is distracting with so much to see—*ow*!

My friend's head reels as the combined mass of five maddened bullies sends him into a tree trunk. That would have scrambled my noodle, yet my friend barely feels it. Sometimes it pays to be thick. I clear the fog and boost his equilibrium just in time for him to avoid an elbow to the nose. Finally deciding to even the odds, my friend lays into one of the dandies until he collapses in defeat. Though now the remaining four are truly pissed, doubling down on their stupidity. And on and on it goes.

My gaze wanders again across the nearest field and glimpses a pitiful sight. A boy is curled up on the ground at the feet of two laughing punks, trying to protect himself from being kicked. No one else is moving to help so I'm drawn, leaving my friend to his playing, and hurrying to the unfolding scene.

As I near I see he's more of a runt than a boy, perhaps not so different than me, and with such admirable nerve! He clutches a kicking foot with desperate strength, riding it like a cowboy on a bucking bronco as the tormentor shouts and stomps and nearly falls. Sure, I can't fight but I can still help. I can work my own kind of magic.

"Roll into his legs," I send to the scraggly victim while giving him a burst of adrenaline. For a moment, he seems to freeze in confusion. But then he does just that, rolling with renewed vigor *into* the grasped foot, which is way more off-balance than even a ballerina can handle. On his way down, the staggering hulk screeches like a startled pig.

"Pivot!" I send again. *"Lash out at his head!"* The runt might be small, but he's full of spunk and a quick learner. Two enthusiastic kicks is all it takes to silence the fallen bully, but it also gives his buddy a clear shot. *"Roll!"* I send, but it's too late and the runt's head takes a vicious kick. I rush close enough—within arm's length now—to feel the stunning damage on top of the pile of bruises.

The looming brute stops to laugh and admire his handiwork, which gives me plenty of time. I pour health into the battered scrawny young man and boost his failing courage. *"Roll; get up!"* Instinctively, he complies and now I can lay a supportive hand on his heaving shoulder. "This is *your* fight," I say aloud, giving him both a physical and magical squeeze of encouragement. The bully is scowling at me now, but his former victim is grinning like a scrappy miniature version of my warrior friend, who…well, he's surely doing just fine on his own.

"I'm gonna beat you both stupid," the brute promises in a low growl.

"Hey, I'm just passing by," I respond with an infuriating level of innocence I must have learned from my friend. *"I'm with you,"* I send again to the nodding, grinning runt. *"Go get him!"*

The mean troublemaker has a reputation to uphold and cannot back down, even though his buddy is crawling off hoping no one is noticing. The victim-turned-tiger moves with sudden grace, stalking as the gap closes and they circle. Before he loses his nerve, the aggressor launches into the small guy.

Chaos erupts and spills into nearby areas. Loiterers hurry to stay out of the way, and spectators gather for the show. The brute is practiced, but the boosted boy is alight with new fire, with body singing and wounds a distant memory. The fight is epic: an increasingly desperate bully versus the increasingly nimble scrapper, whose bark now has bite!

My new friend begins experimenting, using the terrain like a springboard, throwing himself into the fight— literally! With cunning now directed toward the offense, his tricks and speed more than make up for his lack of strength. And even a dim-witted punk can feel the unrelenting force against him. After taking another swift kick to the backside, he limps off with one last hollered threat.

The happy victor bows for those who chuckle at the entertainment, throws up his arms in celebration, and even receives a few claps. "I'll never forget your help," he promises, saluting me with a fist to his heart.

I return his grin. "You have it in you now. Never play the victim; never be the bully. At least," I add with a chuckle, "make sure they underestimate you until it's too late." He gives a nod and a contented sigh. Never again will he be the loser.

With a final wave, he wanders off to find drink and food, which is now in great supply. There are vendors everywhere, hawking their wares from carts full of produce and beverages. The park has packed with people enjoying the pleasant weather in all manner of activities, and now the place truly resembles a fairground.

But that vibrant backdrop frustrates my search for my friend. As I look around, worry creeps in. I shouldn't have wandered off, but surely he's all right. I weave through a few crowds, listening—*feeling*—for the ruckus that would signal my friend and the dandies still going at each other.

Surely he didn't need me while I was gone… Oh, I'm a bad, bad friend. In my budding panic, I begin asking around and one man smiles, offers to help, offers his name. But it's such a long, crazy name that I can't even hold it in my head. I pull out my notebook and pen and ask him to repeat it so I can write it out, but everything is fading too fast…

* * *

"And now you know," Will admitted wryly, "I'm a bad friend, even in some bizarre gaming-type dream."

The group amusement turned into laughter and Doug quipped, "Remind me not to hire you as my healer."

"ADHD even in your dream," Cathy teased with a click of her tongue.

With mock offense, Will corrected her: "Hey, the kinder term is 'wanderlust-enabled.' But yeah, I guess I had issues." Suddenly earnest, he continued, "The craziest thing was that man's name, how it was so long and odd that it kept sliding from my mind. And I felt like I needed to remember it to—I don't know—be able to group with him and get his help. So, I whip out this little spiral notebook, which was where I kept my notes for my spells, or something. So freaky!"

"That's one sorry excuse of a spell book," Doug pointed out, and Will played along: "Well, my full-sized one doesn't fit in a pocket, of course."

Like the rest, Mark had been amused yet turned more considering. "Aside from the dream antics," he said, "what kind of lessons did you draw from it? You could feel that you let down your friend, and it seems much of your confusion came from this. Looking back on it, what would you have changed in the dream, given the chance?"

"I don't know. I still wouldn't let the little guy get picked on, but..." Will shrugged. "I probably should've let my friend in on the plan. Then maybe the dream triumph wouldn't have been spoiled. Or maybe the dream just needed to turn into one of those can't-find-shit dreams."

"Speaking of searching-frantically types," Doug said into the lull, "I had a confusingly powerful one I wasn't going to share because it might offend. But Will reminded me we can admit anything to each other, so please, ladies, don't take this the wrong way."

Tilting her head a little, Cathy furrowed her brow and said, "Okay, now I'm impossibly curious."

"Go ahead," Mark prompted when Doug hesitated a moment longer.

"It was my first day at a new job—well, more like the beginning of my career—and I was listening to instruction from various coworkers and looking around to find supplies I needed, like a pen to take notes. Of course, supplies are never around when you need them. But here's the twist..." Doug paused dramatically.

"I was a young *woman*! With all the extra worries, the extra level of awareness of my environment. Some might call it vulnerability. It sure felt that way at first! But it's not a weakness to understand, to *see*, all the subtle clues around you and ways others might exploit the situation. That was a constant consideration as this woman—as *I*— went through orientation and training.

"At a conference table, there was a man sitting next to me. Could he smell the tiny amount of perfume I used, and would he get the wrong idea? I used it for me, not for him, but he was sitting *way* too close so it felt like a mistake on my part.

"I remember the women across the table smirking at me. Were those friendly smirks that could mean possible friendship or at least some help in this foreign place, or dismissive ones that meant they were already judging me harshly? Was there a barrier I needed to overcome somehow?

"When the meeting ended and we split into various roles for training, did the manager who was very attentive to me only want to help with my job? When he leans over my shoulder to point out something in a report we were reviewing, do I shift to put distance and do it subtly enough not to risk offense?"

Giving a frustrated sigh, Doug continued, "It's tough now to give enough examples or explain what I was feeling and understanding, or remember all those subtle instances that could be distracting yet were just as important as what was happening on the visible level. The dream was realistic and had lots of details. But I think the most important thing to remember is the emotional work: the considerations, slight adjustments to compensate—that uncomfortable yet amazing awareness!

"I needed and wanted the job, and that also put me in a position to be taken advantage of. In fact, just being sweet and young opens up a chance for someone to take advantage. And at first I was deeply uncomfortable by this constant undercurrent.

"But it dawned on me: that's *not* a weakness. Those subtleties were playing out around me whether or not I noticed them. So, it felt...I don't know...*responsible* for me to account for everything. There were some decent people around me, but also men and women who viewed me as a victim—I could tell that from how they addressed me or their body language. These were understandings I used to navigate my way through my first day."

Leaning back and forcing himself to take a breath, Doug concluded, "It was exhausting, in a way, but I knew it was also the way to be. Again, by vulnerability, I don't mean it as some might think of it, but more a constant awareness of who might take advantage of what I—or she, rather—is all about, the goodness she represents. So..." Doug drew out the word, looking at the women in the circle. "Was the dream entirely made up or like a real experience?"

Quani pretended the question wasn't directed at her and said nothing. Cathy and Kris exchanged glances before replying. "More or less," was all Cathy said, giving a noncommittal shrug.

"See," Doug replied with enthusiasm, "I would've never noticed the little things, but since the dream, I see that silent communication as you decide who's going to reply and weighing what to say."

Smoothing her pants and then crossing her legs, Kris said, "It's a little creepy... I don't know, like you're accessing our secrets." She followed up on that with a sudden bright smile for Doug. "But let's all agree it was a fascinating dream for you to have."

"Indeed," Mark voiced his interest, "a perfect example we can dig deeper into."

With a shake of his head, Doug mused, "Can 'disturbing' and 'illuminating' even fit in the same sentence together?"

"Sure," Mark said. "Difficult or sudden growth could be considered disturbing. Insights and experiences aren't always pleasant, especially when they push us way out of our comfort zones. But arguably, those are the most important for us. It seems your dream certainly qualifies."

"Details fade with each day, but what sticks with me is the careful consideration, the...*anxiety* from that extra level of awareness." In earnest, Doug continued, "I feel it's important to have that level of consideration even if it's lots of work. I mean, how can someone be understanding if he is oblivious?"

"Hey, I prefer my oblivious life," Will protested with a cheeky grin.

Mark leaned toward him, elbows on his knees. "But do you, really? Consider an example we all know—not naming names—of someone who means well, but lacks the skills, the insight, to do so. As a result, that person blunders and makes others uncomfortable even though it's not intended."

Will made the mental leap. "Ah, my roommate."

"Not naming names," Mark repeated with a smile. "But again ask yourself: do you prefer being oblivious?"

"Okay," Will conceded. "Maybe I'll sign up for a little bit—but just a little bit—of that, what Doug got dosed with."

Tapping her pen against her chin, Quani asked, "But didn't that floating woman give you some of that last..." She flipped quickly through her notebook. "...October when you dreamed of merging into her?"

"Huh. Maybe." Struck by the notion, Will noticeably shifted gears, leaning back repeating his considering "huh".

Then he closed his eyes for a moment and shivered slightly. "I hadn't connected that. Thanks for having such an amazing memory." That drew a pleased smile from her.

"And I think…maybe she did. It was all so overwhelming, more than I could process at the time." Then realization struck him and he turned back to the rest of the group, saying, "These dreams are shaping us so much it's hard to remember myself before them! We took them seriously and now they are taking *us* seriously."

Chuckling at the burst of enthusiasm that rippled around the circle, Mark corrected, "More like you are taking full advantage of these exercises to grow. And grow we all have!"

Hopping up from her chair, Cathy stated, "This is a perfect time for a group hug. Come on."

Smiling, Doug rose and said, "Here's to changing for the better."

Chapter 16

From the first moment of the dream meet, the atmosphere was electric. Quani was flush with excitement, pacing even while others found their seats, wide eyes letting them know she had a major breakthrough. "I finally see the big picture—well, more of the big picture!" And with barely a pause for the others to recover from shock, she planted herself in the middle of their circle. "Last night I had the most incredible dream!"

Widening her stance, Quani began pantomiming. "I was standing like this, within swirling, milky-glowing surroundings the color of softest chocolates. And all around me were floating panels with—get this!—moving images of our dreams on them!" She slowly brought her hands together as if connecting floating puzzle pieces. "I could move them around, arrange them together and when they were related in some way, their touching edges would...blur into each other. I could pull in another dream and if the edges fit, they would become part of the greater whole. Soon I noticed this pattern as I collected more and more dreams together.

"They were forming a kind of tapestry. There was Nolan's airplane dream, and, and the fancy car and Cathy's swimming and Will's bear hunt and the space jumping and the music and the arrowhead injury—"

"Hold on, hold on," Mark said with a chuckle. "Be sure to breathe or you'll faint on us. No need to rush the description."

Smiling anxiously, she nodded but said, "There's just so much of it." In more of her quiet manner, she cleared her throat and continued. "This center of dreams, once all together, showed clear similarity. They support each other and increase our learning, allowing more, different dreams to happen." At this point, Quani's tone made it clear she was still seeking answers. "Or they are expanding on what we can learn? Like preparation for a test?" She spread her arms in a helpless gesture before her features cleared and she pushed onward.

"With enough support, we dream very powerful ones that touch us deeply and we *feel* them, or experience through them. Like Doug's dream of the woman in job training and Nolan's meeting Jesus." A thought occurred to her and she motioned to Mark. "Maybe yours about Blue Eyes was among them, but there were so many forming a border or connection points..." The room was still, but the silence wasn't awkward. More like awed. "I think I even remember Kris' dream of the artificial child connecting onto our music dreams.

"Anyway, that layer of dream grows our understanding, prepares us further." Quani paused to take a deep breath, though urgency was creeping back into her voice. "And then spiraling out into the distance in all directions came our dreams of travel and assisting people: my dream in the bad neighborhood with the singing girls connected to Cathy's dream in the theatre—I think that was the order. I saw the slow coin toss and thought of Nolan's terrible wedding dream. I saw a satchel being clutched and thought of the first dream Doug told us. At least these were the impressions I brought back with me, but..."

At this point, Quani faltered and looked around with uncertainty. No one, not even Mark, dared say anything to risk interrupting her internal struggle and reveal. Finally, she spoke again. "I thought I could see everything, understand each dream's place. Though, I knew some areas were bland like they were made of dreams waiting to happen, windows waiting to open.

"But then I got a glimpse of depth underneath. I must have reached out to tilt the huge tapestry, because what moved all around me—what I saw underneath ours— were layers and layers and *layers* of connected tapestries. Instead of being flat, there were more angles, all swirling patterns, and as I tried to hold onto the idea of millions and millions or more..." Quani shrugged and sighed, already returning to her seat. "Well, I failed because I woke up."

Mark expelled a breath and quickly corrected, "You didn't fail at all, Quani."

"Yeah, that was incredible!" Cathy added. "I would have awoken bawling my eyes out!"

All Will could do was whisper, "Jesus," as he watched Quani settle uncomfortably into her chair.

"Surely the queen of pattern recognition," Doug commented with a grin that eased the tension.

To prevent another silence from descending, Mark mused, "Where do we even begin to explore this one?"

Will leaned forward intently. "I *knew* there's something incredible going on here!"

"An incredible group, for sure," Mark said agreeably, but Will was shaking his head.

"No. This is larger than just us. Like we're just stumbling around on the edge of something…"

"Immense!" Cathy finished for him.

"Epic!" added Nolan.

"Profound," said Kris.

Several of them giggled at their word chain and Will summed it up. "All that and then some!"

"We keep getting confirmation that what we sense is *real*, somehow," Cathy added.

"Real, as in real-life real?" Mark couldn't keep the doubt from his voice. "These are incredible exercises—learning experiences, for sure, that touch our real life. But, there are limits to how deeply into speculation we should go."

Will challenged: "As we experience more, doesn't the idea that, 'Oh, they're just dreams,' seem more and more absurd?"

"And how do you account for the pattern?" Doug directed the question at Mark and then motioned toward Quani. "Then, we get confirmation this powerful."

Mildly, Mark explained, "We know dreams can tap into every part of our mind, seemingly without restriction, at least in some cases. When imaginations are as boundless as yours are…"

"But there's more to it," Quani insisted.

"It certainly can *seem* like that."

"And yet you want to deny the chance," Cathy said in an almost accusing tone.

"Alright, alright," Mark conceded with a chuckle. "All I ask is that you delve without leaping to conclusions. Use your reasoning to swim rather than drowning in the unreal."

Again leaning forward in his seat, Will asked, "What if instead of being unreal, it's more like hyper-real? Some realm outside or under or surrounding our own, but actually there?"

Mark shrugged in several small movements, at a loss for how to continue. Finally, he said, "Just keep talking it through. Keep exploring, but remember what happened to Gabriella and what she had to do. Pull back if you need to." Relaxing with a smile, Mark nodded to Quani. "Now, let's truly delve into your exceptional dream, which sounds like a magnificent example of connecting dots on a grand scale. The ultimate puzzle."

"I wonder where—or what—the murky place was," Kris pondered.

"Yeah." Cathy was nodding, motioning to Quani. "The way you describe it, I imagine it's both mysterious and recognizable at the same time."

Quani smiled and hesitantly added her feeling. "I think it was like the feeling of...unborn ideas."

"Like a creative soup," Nolan added helpfully.

"Something like that," Quani said without conviction, "where ideas or needs can become dreams. Maybe. It was so overwhelming that I can only guess. I could focus on our set of dreams, and when I saw more around them, I just lost it."

Cathy did her little chair dance. "Well, I think it's enough just to know it's all there. The largest of large pictures!"

Quani again smiled at the kind support. "Despite it all, it felt real. Well..." She ended the faltering thought with an apologetic shrug.

Giving his wild look, Will speculated, "Hey, maybe that's what 'the real' is made from."

"Okay, okay," Mark said with his moving-right-along tone. "Quani, what about the individual panels? What about them reminded you of specific dreams?"

She gave a small "how should I know" movement as the group waited for her reply. "Some of the ideas that made them... I could glimpse them in action, or...get that impression? But mostly I was seeing how they joined together."

Nodding, Mark commented, "Yes, that's a truly fascinating aspect of your dream."

Will couldn't stay silent any longer. "When you saw my healer dream, did I ever find my friend I lost?"

The group laughed as Quani shook her head, and Kris rolled her eyes, saying, "Don't expect her to finish your silly dreams for you."

"Did you see the dream of that goddess visiting me?" Will persisted. "I wonder if that was more of an experience dream or a feeling one?"

"They aren't boxes you can drop a dream into," Quani corrected gently.

"More like they drop onto me!"

Without being distracted by Will's quip, Quani continued. "Think of what I saw as pieces—no, that's not right. Like the different colors that make up the tapestry but with no definable lines. Not separated areas or categories but flowing into and around…"

Doug leaned forward earnestly when again Quani faltered. "Like a different percentage mix of elements? Where one dream might be all about the experience, but another might also have elements of the empathy or helper type?"

"Maybe," Quani said, at a loss to find a way to describe it. "But it was all so…organic, blended."

Kris offered an analogy. "Perhaps like no single shade of color can be used to paint a proper image. I remember trying to paint leaves and struggling, trying to mix and blend enough kinds of greens to make them look at least somewhat realistic."

"Yes, it seemed more like that," Quani agreed, motioning to two different imaginary spaces in front of her. "A subtle blend, with more of one pattern in this dream and less of it in that dream. But the patterns were there, helping them belong and support the dreams around them."

"I think this forever changes how we talk about our dreams," Nolan mused. "Such a powerful vision!" With others nodding in agreement, he drew on an example. "So like, my dream of the Ferrari was mostly about feeling how terrible it is to have something, no matter how beautiful, own you. But it also had a tiny amount of the travel experience element, and nothing about helping someone, unless you count it inadvertently helping me."

Amid group chuckles, Will joked, "Hey, it helped me. I was going to buy a gigantic fancy yacht to sail the seven seas, but now I think I'll stick to a cheap sailboat just to check that off my bucket list."

Doug leaned forward and said, "I agree this is a breakthrough, and I had an exhausting epic that—if no one objects—I think fits *all* the elements." When Quani sighed and flipped open her notebook, Doug caught himself. "Unless...did I interrupt?"

"No go on." Quani waved her pen and gave a self-conscious smile. "Sorry, that was my happy sigh."

*   *   *

All around our old dorm is commotion and anticipation and more than a little fear. And under that is personal urgency.

I have been tasked with making sure the kids are clean, hair in place, living areas spotless, all best-manners-or-else. Yesterday, I was informed that today's visitors are special; the stern scowl promised long hours of punishment if I fail to make it go smoothly. Rather than the infrequent shopper, a group of influential people will be considering patronage, more chances to be "adopted." Which means our worst and best chance.

"Will our parents finally show up this time?" asks my youngest charge, the ten-year-old Danny.

With a glare to cut off the anticipated snide remark from his older brother, I turn to Danny and smile. "Anything's possible, especially today. That's why we are going to be cute and pay attention to everything the adults do and say. No fidgeting or looking bored—remember the mind games I taught you to hide that. No picking noses or farting. Get that all out of your system right now."

With much giggling and fake farting sounds, the eleven boys under my care indulge in rare antics, while I try to remember what it's like to feel so carefree. "Today," I announce as the fun begins to run its course, "we will be more calm and clever and lovable than any other group. I'm sure of it. Remember the grand game: watch them, learn them, and get them to love you. Now I'm told the guests will be arriving for lunch, so make sure your area is clean, bed perfectly made. I'll be around soon to check with you."

Before they leave with the others, I hold back my chosen: Neil, because he's only two years younger than me and the one I trust the most; Tomas, because with his sullen spirit is the least likely to fit in; and finally, his younger brother, Danny, whose bubbly innocence couldn't survive this place without my protection. I would do this for my entire group—with the entire place—if I had any chance of success, but with such short notice these three are the best I can manage. Later, if we succeed, I will mourn the rest.

Once I see everyone else is busy, I lean close to tell them part of the plan. "Today, we've been given an extra special assignment," I say using my best secret-adventure voice. "This must stay among us and only us. Swear it before I go further." I look at each of them in turn and get their enthusiastic nods.

"Since our training is so close to being complete, we've been given a top-secret mission. This will test and prepare us for our future lives. It won't be easy but it's more important than anything you have ever done before. Can you hide this important mission? It can only be for us, at least for now. Okay?" Again they give nods, eager to share in what I am offering.

"Your first job is to pretend that nothing else is going on except for the visit. Got that? Because everything fails if you tell or even hint that you know." I make sure they understand this before going on. "Now, right when lunch is called, and everyone is headed for the main room, go to the back bathroom but instead of washing up, use the toilet—for real, if you can—and then stay in there until I come for you. It won't take long, but *no one* can see or hear you stay in the bathroom."

As expected, they look baffled, so I reiterate. "Got that? Stay casual, have fun, be clever, but when lunch is called, slip away to the back bathroom and then hide in the stalls. Keep your feet picked up so no one sees you and *stay quiet*. You have to be able to do all this before I tell you the next stage of the test."

"Simple enough," states my best friend. "I hope this gets harder."

"Keep an eye on each other, but don't be obvious," I say with a pointed look at Neil. "Only once we're successful can we get to the epic part."

Our morning instruction and chores and inspection will take up most of the time before the visitors arrive, and still I feel the waiting will kill me before the right time ever comes. Being casual is far harder to do than say, but as the leader I must also set the example. I throw myself into the preparation and even ask the headmaster if there is anything extra I can do to help prepare. He scowls at me, considering, before sending me to double-check the state of the other dorm areas.

Finally, the moment comes, and I hear the dinner call and see the augmented kitchen staff begin plating food. The visitors are arriving and being greeted, and lunch will begin right after. We have this single chance before the interviews begin. I slip into the kitchen and smile at the chef who seems to eat more than she cooks.

"I need servings for the three boys confined to the rooms," I explain, holding up a container for her to ladle in stew that is clearly more robust than usual. With a grunt, she complies, and then I'm off. The timer is counting down.

An unwitting accomplice would explain that I'm tending to boys who are sick with nerves, but the cover wouldn't last much past lunch. On my way to the back, I duck into my room and grab the carrying pack I took from the storeroom in the dead of night.   It isn't much preparation since the pack only contains a few changes of clothes and two bread loaves. But at least we have the hearty stew.

Now I'm committed, exposed, and soon the other boys will be too.

I stick my head into the bathroom by our rooms and though I can see feet swinging from beneath the stall walls, at least they are talking in whispers. *"Psst,"* I hiss to get their attention. "Follow me, and be completely silent." They come out with curious faces and when they see my anxiety, they hurry to obey. This would be what I count on for as long as they allow it.

Saying nothing, we slip out the exit at the end of our hall and I steer them toward the tool shed. We are never allowed to go there except with supervision, but my training as a gardener prepared me for what I must do next. And to their credit, the boys follow dutifully until I begin cutting the back fence wire with a tree cutting tool.

"No way is this okay," Neil claims with widened eyes.

"Trust me," I say, yet I know they need to hear more. "The lesson is stealth, cleverness, to see if we can leave without anyone noticing. This tests our systems and will be a grand adventure." Blades meant to trim tree limbs make short work of the fence. After replacing the cutters, I kneel to push open the edges and squirm through.

I turn to see their reluctance to leave the only home they remember. Being trapped in a small world makes the larger world intimidating, if not beyond imagining. "Trust me," I repeat, and Neil leads the others through while I hold the wire open. "So far we've passed every test." I give them a grin and a hug.

Danny begins dancing around as he looks up at the sky. Though my heart longs to indulge, I'm prompted to warn, "We still have a long adventure ahead, so save your energy. To win this game, we need to be smart."

I check the sun to make sure we head north and only change course to avoid houses and roads. When another question arises, I remind them to trust me and to remain careful. "The game is on by now," I tell them. "We win if we escape notice, and the team hunting us wins if we get caught. And we do *not* want to lose."

When we pause to rest, I make sure we eat sparingly. Telling bold stories distracts Danny from his tiredness, though how long can this last? I know Neil now understands how serious this is. I see him clenching his jaw to keep from adding accusations to their questions. "Please trust me," I beg him.

As the sun is setting, we drink our fill from a yard sprinkler, which is amusing and rejuvenates Danny's spirits. Even with a grin on my face, I remind them to keep quiet and watchful. Then I add water to the small amount of stew we have left and encourage them to press onward until the first stars are visible.

When Danny stumbles, I let the boys finish the last of the watery stew and hold Danny's hand for support. I wonder how far I can carry him if it comes to that, but the thought is interrupted by Neil's accusation.

Sullen, softly, he says, "You lied to us about the headmaster making us do this." I have never heard this tone from him, and realize we're all exhausted.

"In a way, he did," I insist even as my pace slows. "Those people he invited are even worse than he is. Remember all the times he beat you? Well, they'll do much worse."

"How can you know that?"

"I just do... Just—"

"Don't tell me again to just trust you!"

I sigh and glance at the dark sky to the east. Somehow, I know that if we cannot reach the border tonight, we never will. "You were too young to remember your home. Or the way a home is supposed to be. But I remember, and I know where we came from is just north of us somewhere, waiting for us to reach it."

"I'm ready for bed," Danny announces, tugging on my hand.

"Just a little further, tough man. We must make it to win our game."

Neil comments, "This is nuts. You don't even know where home is!"

"It's *way* back thataway," Danny says while motioning behind us.

"Just a little farther," I urge. "I know we can be together and safe, in a real home. With adults who love us."

Neil snorts but keeps dragging his feet by my side. When I think of failing, I remember last night's nightmare that forced me to take this desperate risk. Each time we teeter on the edge of giving up, I coax another long minute of walking.

As I begin to worry about the consequences of my failure, the western sky darkens enough to reveal lights. Huge, bright lights that can now compete with the sunset. This has got to be the border!

"There!" I point to the lights and angle us toward them. The others sense my great relief and hope, and their lighter step matches mine. "See, I told you. I *knew* we could find our way home!" And I know someone at the border will be interested to hear how we were taken and held at the "orphanage" just out of reach of their fancy lights and gates and walls. I can feel the renewed energy and sense of victory.

Yet...something strange happens to off-balance me.

My perception blurs, and somehow I'm back at the start and yet everything seems different. I can sense the boys and their desperate leader, but now I am outside the group, above them, like I had been drawn back to observe. I watch them sneak away, and then squeeze through the fence. I feel proud of them for their bravery, even though the youngest can't yet comprehend inner strength.

However, my amusement quickly sours as I watch them frolic more than they should, and then gobble down the stew without a thought for later. The leader is determined but not as careful when picking their path. They stop more than they should, and then hurry more than they should. They *must* be more careful!

As the day lengthens and they tire, the leader spends less time keeping them motivated and distracted. When at last they argue about the insanity of the escape, the leader blurts out his nightmare to them. He describes seeing the upcoming visit and how it would lead to Danny screaming in panic as he was dragged away from them forever. How Neil would be weeping from a constant pain. The leader swears that he'd not let that happen to them.

Rather than inspire them, the terror of the dream scares them, on top of the unsettling newness and strangeness of their journey. They begin to complain, first of thirst and then of hunger, and in desperation, the leader agrees to knock at a nearby home and ask for help.

Despite me wishing with all my might, yelling for them to get away, the defeated boys go inside the dingy place. Without my guidance, they flop into chairs and just wait. The big cups of water and promise of food holds them there, and when the leader stands and remembers that they must go, the smiling old woman brings out a big piece of cake.

My disheartenment is complete, because as I watch Danny tear into the cake and the rest linger because of vague assurances, I am now certain they have no chance of escape.

Chapter 17

"Okay, guys!" Cathy announced with an excited wiggle. "Guys! I've had the greatest breakthrough!" They were huddled in a corner of their favorite café, since the weather outside encouraged huddling. "Remember over winter break how I wished we had a website? I'm learning XML magic; Kris is a journalist-in-training, right? So, get this: We want to go public with our insights, as a group effort!" When she received doubtful looks instead of instant enthusiasm, she leaned forward. "We all agree this is larger than us. As we dream bigger, those dreams let us know there's so much more out there to discover. We need a bigger sample size!"

"Great way to attract nut-jobs," Nolan commented, and Will quickly pointed out with his boyish grin: "You mean *more* nut-jobs."

"No, no," Cathy said with a flip of her hand. "I can make it layered with permissions. Random browsers won't be able to see everything, but as they progress and contribute, then more of the site opens up to them, as they open up to us and we know they're legit. So, only those who participate like us can see all our dreams and discussions. Well, not *all* our discussions. But, *we* will have infinite, protected space we can keep filling up."

Kris added her voice: "We'll move information around so easily, wherever it seems to fit. I hope it will be easier to track and discuss."

"It could help us better understand the connections," Doug considered.

"As well as adding many new data points," Cathy finished excitedly for him.

"Or attract more nut-jobs," Nolan repeated deadpan, though he raised an eyebrow at Will, daring him to again up the ante.

"You know—and I know you all will find this odd—I kind of enjoy nut-jobs."

"You boys," Kris lightly scolded with a tsk. She didn't dare shift, though, because she was next to Doug, pressed shoulder-to-shoulder, and it felt so right. A cozy contact in this noisy, cozy place. With her roommate as her wingman, she was finding ways to put herself in Doug's space, and he was as warm as she had imagined he would be.

"Nut-jobs we don't like won't get past the lobby. And we can always clean the air, so to speak," Cathy added, waving her hand in front of her wrinkled nose. "We'd each be moderators, watching for new connections, and through it all, we'd have our own space for any discussions."

In her quiet, simple manner, Quani said, "I like it."

Turning his grin on her, Will blurted, "Then I'm game. Though it does sound like added work."

"We can hear more of the plan," Doug reasoned, "and always decide later. Maybe run the idea by Mark."

"Even better than that," Cathy said with renewed pep. "Give me a week and I'll show off a sample of what I'm thinking, and we can tweak it from there, or not." On impulse, she rose and held out her hands. "Come on, guys, hugs of solidarity!"

With grins and giggles, they met above the small round table to hug and talk all at once. "This reminds me to get rid of my previous coffee," Cathy said with a barked laugh, before amending, "the standing, not the hugging." Tugging at Kris' sleeve, Cathy led the girls as they wove their way toward the restrooms.

They met again over the sinks and grinned at each other in the wall mirror. "I think everyone will go for your idea," Kris said supportively, "especially when they see your sample."

"It'll be *our* sample," Cathy corrected. "Yours too, Quani, if you want to help. I already sketched a rough design from our earlier conversation and it'll only take an afternoon to lay the framework—but don't tell them that." Wearing a pleased smile, Quani nodded.

Turning her attention back to her roommate, Cathy teased, "Doug seemed mighty calm. You think he really didn't notice that I practically pushed you onto his lap?"

They laughed as Kris flushed a little. "Oh, hush now. And don't you dare ruin it!" After a pause, she relented somewhat to the unspoken question, saying, "He's warm and solid."

"He'd be more solid if—"

"Don't go there," Kris snapped a warning, motioning to Quani. "Look at her face—how dare you embarrass our friend!" Laughing again, they linked arms until the door forced them to return to a single file.

But Cathy couldn't resist a final tease, and pausing, she said over her shoulder, "What are you going to do over spring break when you have to spend an entire week apart from him?"

"I don't think that far ahead," Kris replied with a smirk and a friendly shove. But that momentary taunt by her roommate triggered an inspiration. Once they returned and resettled into their spots, she blurted out her half-formed plan. "Hey you know, spring break is only three weeks away, and my parents have a lake house..." Judging interest around the table without looking directly at Doug, Kris continued selling the idea as it came to her. "We could work on the website when we aren't floating out on the water or fishing or sleeping. Oh, and we can dream in the same space, discuss it right away, the same day, no waiting for a dream meet."

Bumping her roommate's leg with hers, Cathy responded with big eyes, "Ooo, that sounds like fun! What do you say, Doug?"

He arched an eyebrow and asked, "Didn't we just begin the semester? It's flying so fast."

"This is only my first offer," Will teased, "so I *might* consider it."

"It needs to be all of us to work," Cathy stated, playing impromptu rule maker.

"There's plenty of rooms," Kris assured them. "Three beds and two couches, and we have good quality inflatables."

"Solidarity, remember? It will only work with us all there." Nudging Quani, Cathy grinned and said, "Commit, girl, commit."

Shrinking a little, Quani could only say, "I can ask for permission."

"Even if we have to visit your home and swear to be your guardians," Cathy stated, "we'll get you there." Turning to the next, Cathy pointed both fingers at Will. "Commit."

Will snickered. "How can I say no when staring down the barrel of a gun?"

Cathy continued her antics with Nolan. "Commit." He shrugged and got the double barrels from her. "Commit, or...be a zit!" Laughing at herself and setting off a ripple of mirth, she finally got him to nod.

"And you, Mr. Group Founder." Cathy's fingers shifted to Doug. "Commit."

Smiling, he nodded and said, "I think it's a great idea—another great idea."

"You gals are on fire!" Will complimented them. "A dreaming website and a vacay on a lake... What do you do for an encore?"

"We get more coffee," Kris replied with a pleased smile. "And it's my treat."

When she returned to the group carrying a tray of steaming coffee and Quani's chai, Cathy was already into the dream they had talked about earlier, where she had been swimming, but this time it was a winding stream up a mountain.

"You were clearly looking for your spawning spot," Will joked, and Cathy gave him her sass face.

"I wasn't a fish, goof! At least, I *felt* like me."

"So many travel dreams feel like we're ourselves," Doug agreed, making room for Kris to wedge back in between them. "But the places are impossible, or distant, so is it really us or only our perspective?"

Nolan rubbed his chin. "It *bends* our perspective, so sometimes maybe we're not even ourselves."

"But not a fish," Cathy said with another titter.

Wearing his devious grin, Will added, "We can poke Mark with this idea and watch him flounder—get it, flounder?" Kris and Cathy moaned in unison, but Doug took the comment seriously.

"I keep feeling bad we don't include him, but he just isn't willing to explore like this." With a frown, Doug continued, "Which brings up the thought: do we invite him for spring break?"

"No," Kris answered like a reflex. "That'd be weird."

"No adults," Cathy agreed before catching herself. "I mean, no old people—ack!" And before Will could poke, she quickly said, "*You* know what I mean: just us."

Quani added, "Mark did say we could run with it, and we're running with it."

"That we are," Doug said, satisfaction clear in his tone.

"Or, as the case may be, swimming uphill against the current!" Cathy gestured around the table. "But my dream is exactly the kind of experience we can post in the public space to encourage participation. I *want* to put it out there and see what new angles we find. We'll save the epic ones for people who are already participating, see?" She grinned in response to Nolan's dubious look. "You'll see."

* * *

Once they settled down at the next dream meet, Cathy reached into her pack, pulled out her laptop and set it on her lap. Seeing her look of anticipation, Doug chuckled and commented, "I see you have something to show us already."

"I know I said a week to give a sample, but we were inspired, so…" With a flourish, Cathy opened the laptop and reversed it, letting the others lean in to see the screen. In bold, ever-changing colors, a banner covered much of the screen, announcing the website: The Dream Meet.

As they rose and crowded around to get a better look and began asking for details, Mark asked, "What's this? A new project?"

Cathy nodded with a big grin on her face. "In honor of this group, we're making a partially public site for our dream research—at least I think we are."

Doug turned to Mark. "I hope you don't mind that we discussed it outside this room."

"No, of course not," Mark assured them. "This is your exploration, your journey. Here: bring the chairs in closer together. And show me this next step."

With their circle tightened and knees touching, everyone watched as Cathy began unveiling her ideas. "Notice as I move the cursor to any corner, a cloud appears with embedded navigation. Obviously, the 'Project Scope' cloud will lead to an information page telling about us and this site's purpose—and feel free to help me with the titles. It's blank for now, but we'll only input the information we want shared with the public. And then clicking the cloud again takes us back to the splash screen."

She moved her cursor to the opposite upper corner. "This cloud leads to the lobby, where anyone can ask questions and post. Basic message board where we can keep focused discussions and important Q and A. I don't think it will take long to find people with serious interest."

Cathy did one of her excited wiggles before continuing. "And down here: Dream Submissions. The payoff, hopefully." She giggled and made sure everyone was still staring at the screen.

"In here, notice you either submit using this cloud, or read from the list. Later I can add browse and search functionality into the UI. Initially I wanted to use categories like 'Experience' and 'Empathy' but then I remembered our discussion of Quani's big dream and decided to leave that out. *But*, we can arrange dream submissions and link them in any way we want, including moving them back to a more private area. Which is…"

She returned to the opening screen. "…all hidden behind this last cloud for members." She clicked on it, showing them that the cloud prompt of 'Members' turned into a space to enter a name and password. Spinning the laptop around, she typed furiously for a few seconds before turning it back toward her captive audience. "*Tada!* An entirely new section with a separate message board and submission cloud."

"Nice," Doug said, nodding in approval.

"Elitist," Will accused.

"If *you* want to police this 24/7…?" Cathy eyed Will with a grin and a challenge.

"Fine," he said with mock distaste, "let's just be elitists. It's easier that way."

"This area is where we can store and analyze and discuss our truly important dreams," Cathy continued. "As you can see, Kris has already supplied us with a new dream. It's here, completely invisible to the outside, with no ability to copy the text—except by us. And this space is where we can have the serious discussions about connections and dreams' purposes and how we can travel in them.

"And *then*, behind all this, we have a board that's just for us to post and discuss. To help us administrate." Cathy sat back with a satisfied sigh, before catching herself and asking, "So, what do you think?"

"This is really *good*, Cathy," Mark praised.

"Yeah, amazing," Doug agreed, and with each compliment, Cathy's smile widened.

"Yep," Will said, "feels good to be elitist."

"Oh, you!" she said with a giggle. "I know how my girlfriends feel because we did it together, but how about you, my greatest critic?"

Nolan gave a sheepish smile while under her gaze. "If I had known...this...I would not have objected."

"*Yes!*" Cathy almost rose from her chair, caught her sliding laptop and laughed. "Yes! Your dreaded nut-jobs will have no access to our project. So, it's decided, right?" Looking at the grinning faces, she swiveled the laptop back around. "And...so..." After a few seconds more, she turned the screen back to them with a giggle. "Now our very own site is live!"

Cathy stood and put the laptop in her seat, and everyone knew what was coming. They met in a ball of excitement that showed in words and hugs.

Once they caught their breath and returned their seats closer to the original positioning, Cathy motioned to her roommate, passing her the open laptop. "Kris should read her eerie dream for us—the inaugural one posted on our new site!"

When Kris asked if that would be okay, Mark looked around and said, "As long as no one else has urgent breakthroughs to share." After a moment, he motioned to her. "All yours, Kris."

Clearing her throat, Kris said, "Not only did writing this dream help me remember the details, it helped me sort and better deal with the ick. So, I found myself at the front door of a cute cottage." Taking a moment to refocus on the laptop, Kris began reading.

"The cottage was cute, its front door made of polished wood with a distinctive grain that looked like waves rather than rings. The breeze against my back was warm, but as I entered, the cozy interior was cool in a refreshing way. And every detail of the inside was also crisp, clear. There was no hallway or entry, only a large, inviting rug in the center of the home, and around the rug were furnishings, chairs and a couch with plush, comfortable cushions.

"I slowly walked into the room and made my way to a wall to better inspect the paintings hung there. Nearby was a cute rectangular table filled with knickknacks, carved animals and a crystal bowl filled with hard candies, all sitting on a crochet of silk. At first the space held a familiar feeling, as if all this belonged to me, that each piece was exactly where it should be, as I would have left it.

"But then doubt settled in, and I wondered how this could possibly belong to me, because it felt more like how it should be rather than how it actually *is*. The room still felt safe, the small bed in the back looked soft, and the shelf above it contained a few hats and more mementos. Yet, I could not stop the growing feeling, the realization, that this space wasn't mine, that it was actually new and strange. I got a sense that I was very far away, that I was, in fact, an intruder in this cozy space.

"I didn't want the oncoming realization to spoil the moment. I struggled against it, clinging to that feeling of familiarity and welcome, and trying to convince myself that I *was* welcome. Maybe it was my heightened sensitivity that led to a new realization. I could vaguely feel someone, someone I know or could know.

"This was *their* home, even though it could just as well have been mine. I could *almost* feel that they were okay with me being inside their house—the welcome coming from them rather than from within myself or the cozy cottage. But still I could not quiet the fears of being an intruder. I knew I could get to know this someone and fit in, but I just *couldn't*. Maybe it was me who wouldn't allow it. As the dream faded, I could feel how I missed them, or maybe missed the chance to get to know them."

Looking up from her screen, Kris sighed. "I felt like I had lost an important opportunity. And that's the lingering ick that dragged on me, and yet…" She closed the laptop, patted it, and then handed it back to Cathy. "…by the time I finished collecting my thoughts or memories and writing them down, I felt fine."

"And this is a perfect example," Cathy stated, "of a deep dream we can delve into without wanting it read by anyone we don't all approve. Or it can be moved to the very back where only we can see it." Nudging her roommate, Cathy prompted, "Go on. Tell them about your thought on the dream."

Kris shrugged, unsure of herself, but she said, "Dwelling on it as I wrote it down, I realized my confusion could be evidence of what I was feeling *from* that other person, of *their* familiarity and comfort upon returning to such an inviting home. And maybe I was there with them, somehow, and it was only my own self that interposed upon that and created the conflict that made me feel so out of place."

"It's a common part of the empathy dreams," Mark reasoned, "to feel very much a part of that person or situation. In the middle of it, so to speak. How else would empathy work?"

"But she also felt distinctly like herself," Doug pointed out, "like she was there with someone—aware of someone who was clearly not her."

Mark chuckled. "Again, how else would empathy work—other than not fully? This was a poignant dream and an experience worth delving into."

"And what about my travel?" Kris asked. "I arrived in an instant, but then at a normal pace passing through the entryway into the home and looking around. And finally, the parting... It wasn't instant, but maybe the space of a few thoughts, maybe less, and I was back in my bed waking up."

"As we've talked about, scientists have done many tests monitoring sleep activity," Mark replied with the smallest hint of exasperation. "No one goes anywhere, and we can actually track the areas of the brain responsible for creating and presenting the dream."

Will waved a hand dismissively at the so-called knowledge and reiterated his perspective twist. "Except that your brain wouldn't light up differently if you're experiencing reality in a way we *could* monitor or see."

"I wonder," Kris said pensively, "since we're taught from an early age that they aren't real, we grow to ignore the finer details that actually matter…"

Mark relaxed into a smile. "Continue chasing these threads—you all know how I encourage exploration. Just continue to be careful, be safe in how you do it."

"Thanks to them," Doug said while motioning to the young women of the group, "we have a new powerful tool for doing just that."

"Oh, that reminds me!" Will leaned over to Cathy while taking out his mobile. "Let me see if I can access it from my phone now. What's the address?" With an exchange of information, Will worked intently as others looked on with amusement. "I got this. I got this. There!"

Cathy's laptop chimed, and she rolled her eyes. "Now what?" She opened her computer and a few seconds later she burst out laughing.

"What did he do this time?" asked the curious Kris.

Cathy spun her laptop around to show the group while Will just grinned. In the lobby section was a new post: "First!"

While the group cracked up and poked at Will, Cathy stated, "And this gives me the perfect opportunity to show you all just how easy it is to erase the nut-jobs from our site."

Chapter 18

Quani sat on the bed in her small dorm room, fidgeting with her phone. After a mental review of the possibilities, she glanced up to see the supportive looks of Cathy and Kris, and then nodded. "Okay, let's hope this works."

"It will," Kris encouraged, and Cathy added, "We're ready." When Quani paused once again, Cathy blurted, "Wait, wait." Drawing them both into a supportive hug, she laughed. "*Now* we're ready!"

Quani woke the phone's screen, hit speed dial, turned on the speaker, and held her breath.

"Salman." The deep voice was curt and somewhat raspy. To Quani, it was the sound of authority.

"Father, it's me."

"Ah, my baby girl! You are healthy, I trust. What's news?"

"Remember the friends I told you about?" Quani said in a rush. "They are here with me and we're hoping you will let me go on vacation with them. Over spring break."

"Why?" It wasn't a negative response; it was a simple yet loaded question.

Kris leaned in, and Quani tilted the phone her way. "Hello, sir. My name is Kristina Fawcett and it is great to meet you. We're all working on a big school project and want to continue over the break in peace and quiet at my family's lake house." So it was only a tiny white lie.

"That way we can keep making progress…" Quani added helpfully.

"Why not bring them here, Quani? Is our place not…sufficient?"

"When not working, we also want to sun and swim in the lake," Cathy explained, turning Quani's wrist so the phone angled toward her. She arched a questioning eyebrow at Quani and mouthed, "And sleep late?" Without waiting for confirmation, she told him, "And we want to sleep in. And maybe stay up late, if we're inspired. By work." Belatedly, she added, "Hi, this is Cathy."

"I see…" Quani's father said before they heard another faint voice. The girls held their collective breath as they listened to half a conversation before Salman passed the phone.

"*Chotu*, tell me," Quani's mother said. "I was wanting to see you next week."

"And me." The father now sounded as if he were talking over his wife's shoulder.

"Mama," Quani pleaded. "I will be home when the semester ends—and my studies are going smoothly. What we do is even more than expected of us." After a moment, she shifted gears taking a stab at the heart of the reluctance. "Papa, don't you trust me to be wise? We will watch out for each other and stay safe."

The moment hung in the air as she envisioned her parents staring at one another, each seeing if there was any doubt written on the other's face. She willed them to nod, to give their blessing on her newest opportunity. "Okay, sweet daughter, you earn our trust," her father relented, quickly following up with, "but we expect you to call and report each night."

Kris opened her mouth to say something, but Quani waved her off. "Thank you for your trust, Papa. I continue to make you proud." Her wingmen were already beginning to wiggle, threatening to break into full-fledged dancing, so she hurriedly said, "I just wanted to get your permission before we return to our studying. I promise to keep you from worrying. I'll call each night. I love you."

"We love you, *Chotu*," her mother said, ending the connection a fraction of a second before Cathy began cheering, and the bouncing celebration began.

*   *   *

Late in the week, Kris experienced her own burst of anxiety at their final caffeine-infused planning session in the café when Doug mentioned that his roommate was lobbying hard for him to go to Cancun. Something inside Kris seized up, while her roommate fussed, "You wouldn't *dare* abandon us! Would you?"

Grinning, he responded, "You should know me well enough by now. Between you guys and dreaming fun...or walls of people and noise and too much salt..."

Kris blew out a breath and bumped him with her shoulder. "Don't scare me like that!" Then she quickly added, "The group wouldn't be the same if we couldn't all make it."

"Yeah!" Cathy echoed the sentiment before leaning in toward her excited friends and lowering her voice in a conspiratorial fashion, saying, "Now let's *do* this!"

Once the final class ended, that last textbook slammed shut and jammed into a backpack, spring break officially began. With a flurry of texts, they launched their master plan into action. Nolan collected Doug and Will in his hand-me-down sports car, stuffing its small trunk and using the remaining room in the back seat to store their luggage. The girls packed into Kris' SUV, and then both vehicles converged on a gas station at the western edge of town.

As they refueled on gasoline and caffeine, Will snickered at the overstuffed SUV. "How can you three possibly need that much stuff? Or are there like ten more girls showing up?"

Kris eyed the small space he had crawled out of and coolly observed that he might be more comfortable clinging to the luggage rack on her roof rather than stuffed into that backseat for four hours. "Yeah," Will admitted with a dramatic sigh. "I lost the coin toss. Of course."

While waiting at the pump, Kris watched Doug squint at the sun, rocking on his heels and stretching. A fond smile welled up inside her and spread to her face. "There will be plenty of that this coming week," she called to him. "Sun and warmth and sparkling water."

"And us and our dreams," he added while enjoying the sun on his upturned face. It was an offhand comment, a sharing of general excitement, yet it set off a shiver in her and a surge of ideas.

"*Psst*," Cathy whispered, suddenly appearing at her roommate's side to nudge her and hand her a bottle of iced mocha. "You might want to be a little less obvious." The wink showed Cathy's amusement at having caught her staring. "Good thing we're keeping you two in separate cars."

"Don't make me leave you behind," Kris sassed while refocusing on the task at hand.

Despite having a pin on his GPS, Nolan had still insisted on following her, and they agreed to let neither traffic nor stoplights separate them. With a final group hug, the caravan rolled west away from the vibrant city, past patches of forest and fields of awakening flowers, which transitioned into bland farmland. But in the distance, awaiting their arrival, were vast rolling hills with a special house nestled in a lake valley.

"So..." Cathy let that hang in the air as she eyed her roommate from the passenger seat, one foot propped up on the seat with her.

Kris took a moment to shoot her a challenging look. "Okay, have your fun."

"Just saying, girl... You're going to have to be less obvious, unless you plan..." Cathy straightened, dropped her leg, and turned wide eyes on Kris. "You *are* making your move, aren't you? Tell us all about it!" Even Quani leaned forward from where she sat in the back seat.

"Yes," Kris confirmed with a nod. "I'm not waiting any longer, and after we've settled in and are enjoying the evening, I need you to run interference with the other boys. Website stuff, maybe?"

"And then?" Cathy drawled, digging for more juicy details.

"And then I'm playing it by ear—cautiously."

Cathy laughed in delight. "Oh, you got it bad, roomie!"

"He's the one for me. Positive. Well, ninety-nine-point-nine-nine-percent positive."

"Well, if I help make this possible," Cathy bargained, "I expect you to name your first daughter after me."

"Stop that!" After a moment, Kris chuckled. "And there's no way I'm naming her 'Brat'."

* * *

They were driving with the windows cracked.

"Damn, man!" Nolan repeated, alternating between waving a hand in front of his nose and imitating Doug's technique of using his shirt like a respirator.

"Pity me," Will bemoaned loudly over the sound of the wind. "I'm stuck back here with it. And blame Doug for handing me the Cheetos."

"If only you had warned me," came the muffled response.

"I hope we don't have to sleep in the same room." Nolan made a point of acting like he was recovering from a strong poisoning. "I might have to sleep outside, cold or not!"

Doug tested the air for safety before replying. "Most of the week is supposed to be warm so we're in luck."

"Okay, seriously," Will shouted. "You can roll up the windows. It's clear, for now." Once the noise was reduced, he could finally continue at his normal volume. "You know, I was really looking forward to all this, but I just had a terrible thought. I mean, what if I wake up with wood?" Over their laughs, he continued his antics, "No, I mean seriously. I bet the bathroom is on the other side of the house, and what do I do? I can't just walk around with a big tent or one of the ladies might get the wrong idea and take advantage of me!"

"Stay in bed?" Doug suggested, and Nolan snorted.

"Surely you brought some baggy sweatpants."

"Hey, that might work for you but I'm far too *gifted*, don't ya know."

While Nolan only snorted again, Doug said, "Let's just be sure to keep it PG so we don't drop into some awkward hole. Remember, group cohesion, comfortableness—if that's a word."

"Ah yeah," Nolan agreed, tapping the steering wheel. "Sweet relaxation, and much deserved! Hey, I think I'm seeing hills in the distance."

In solidarity, Will said, "The thought of chilling at the lake house has carried me through this past week. Nolan, you're going to have to share tricks on how you survived to your senior year! I'm not sure I can take the torture."

"Honestly," Nolan answered with all the wisdom of a twenty-two-year-old, "you will find a rhythm, a pattern you just make work for you. And then just grind out each semester."

"Ugh! But all that reading stuff! I just wish they'd put it in movie format."

"I'd vote for the downloadable version," Doug added to the silliness. "Jack me into higher education!"

"Huh," Will mused, "like dreaming. Imagine getting Calculus or Economics, or even your engineering courses pumped into you by dreams."

Nolan grimaced. "Civics...now that'd be one nightmare from which you'd never wake."

"Okay," Will admitted, "so a bad idea."

As they drew even with the first impressive hill, the excitement swelled within both vehicles, and they traded phone calls, and then passed the phones around so everyone could chat with everyone, just because they could. It still took almost an hour of winding between hills to reach the lake opening and then finally up to the house.

"Day-yam," Will drawled as he piled out of the car and began hobbling up the circular driveway. "Your parents must be loaded, Kris."

She had tossed her sunglasses on the dash and was beginning to unload. "Eh. They do okay, though real estate is a very successful hobby. 'Better than a bank account,' my dad would say."

"I'm guessing he has both," he said and then got fake-punched on the shoulder by Nolan.

"You going to soak in all this amazingness or stand there turning green with envy?"

"Hey, I'm just running the numbers in my head, figuring out how much I have to work to have a playpen like this." Will raised his arms to the colorful sky displaying the full majesty of a late afternoon sun. "But you better believe I'm soaking it in!"

The two-story house might have looked tiny compared to the 250-foot hill it was built near, but they could see what Kris meant when she said "plenty of room." Its simple lines and boxy structure were offset by a manicured lawn, walkways of paving stones and flower beds, large picture windows on the lake-facing side, and a double-deck pier. The top deck had loungers, while the underside boasted four kayaks tethered to the sides.

"My parents knew we were coming, of course, so they came out and set everything up for us," Kris explained. "They really are the best!" The excited impatience of her guests prompted her to stop unloading and give a tour.

"Will they adopt us?" Will asked.

More excited admiration rang out once they entered through the double doors and into a large vaulted living space. Cathy flopped onto one of the two large sectionals with a contented sigh. "Our home for the next week!"

With a sheepish look, Quani asked for an immediate tour to the nearest restroom, and Will retorted, "There's a restroom out back, that giant tub of water."

"Now, I'm thinking about *not* swimming," Cathy exclaimed with a sound of disgust aimed at Will.

Once they decided on living arrangements and settled in, they gathered on the deck to admire the view of the sun lowering toward the dark blue water and distant tree line. Quani had never been around such a large body of water before, and through her wonder, they all were soothed by the gentle waves lapping at the shore. Even Will was quiet, absorbing the fact that they were all *here* and *now* in such a place.

"Almost like a dream," Kris murmured, stirring soft agreement from the others as they let the moment bond them further.

With great reluctance, Kris stirred, rose from a lounger, and announced they needed to fire up the grill if they wanted to enjoy the feast staged in the fridge. "I'll need a helper. Doug?"

Hopping to his feet, he simply said, "Sure thing." With his back turned he didn't see Cathy give Kris a thumbs-up. Working as a team, they grilled steak and chicken while setting out several kinds of salad.

"We have ice cream in the fridge, but we also have an even fancier treat," Kris claimed before laughing lightly and adding, "though my funny mom left a sticky note on the wine fridge saying, 'This is your maturity test.'"

"So what did she mean?" Will pondered after swallowing a mouthful of potato salad. "That we shouldn't drink because we're underage?"

"Speak for yourself," Nolan teased.

Cathy giggled, waving a hand at Will. "Maybe she just meant for you to, you know, be *mature* about it."

"Oh, well then I'm screwed," Will said with a stage-grimace.

With mirth dancing like the firelight in her eyes, Kris stated, "I know my parents. They wouldn't have left the bottles here if they didn't want us to test ourselves."

"To see if we're responsible," Doug guessed, and Kris favored him with a smile.

"Okay, that settles it then," Will announced, rising to bring them a bottle of wine to complement their meal. "We sip it slow and pretend we're all grown up."

As the last sliver of sunlight was replaced by a vast tapestry of stars, they shifted from the bar top grill to the seats surrounding a stone firepit. The lengthening silences felt like a favorite comforter, and as the night air cooled, they alternated between staring into the mesmerizing fire that provided such warmth and the flickering faces of their friends who provided such amusement.

Comfortably slouched in his chair, Nolan swept an arm to include them all. "This could be our new spot to share dreams."

Kris nodded in agreement. "It's nice that our neighbors aren't in residence, so this can be as private as the living room. Though less comfortable than the couches...and no outlet or table for the laptops. I don't recommend using that ledge." She motioned to the firepit. Then turning to signal her roommate, she said, "Speaking of laptops, Cathy, don't you have something important to show them? You know, inside?"

"Oh, of course!" Cathy giggled and hopped up. "Come on, you slackers, we've got work to do! The best kind of homework!"

As her roommate led the others back inside, Kris caught Doug's sleeve and motioned with her head for him to follow her. They strolled across the grass, shoulders nearly touching. "Hey," she said softly. "I've been meaning to talk to you about something important and show you something."

"I'm all ears," Doug said amicably.

"Good," she murmured, leading him out to the deck's end. Slipping off her flats and setting them aside, she commented, "I hope your shoes are on tight. Otherwise you might want to remove them too. Hang your feet off the end of the deck." She showed him by sitting up against the railing, dangling her legs off the edge, and patting the spot next to her.

Once he settled down beside her, she told him a story. "Even as a small girl, I'd come out here, cling to the rail and hang my feet over the water. I'd listen to the soothing movements, and on nights like this I'd count the stars. On a very still night, you can even catch starry reflections on the lake surface. I'd think about my lessons and about the future and how everything fits together, or tries to. Everything is clearer when I am out here. It makes more sense."

"Yeah," Doug agreed, "it's a special place." Leaning back to look up at the countless pinpoints, he said thoughtfully, "I think...in this big, calm place, we can dream even bigger."

With the moment resonating through her, Kris placed her hand over his, leaned close, and when he returned her gaze, she kissed him. The soft exploration ended and he looked at her in bewilderment, with an expression that she knew she'd always remember and giggle about and cherish. Smiling warmly, squeezing the back of his hand in hers, she encouraged, "Dream bigger."

This time, he met her halfway, fondness blooming into so much more. When the need to breathe forced them apart, Kris giggled and tugged his arm so they lay back on the deck, arms and fingers intertwined beneath twinkling heavens.

A mind-blown Doug could only whisper, "Oh, wow."

Chapter 19

By the time Kris and Doug walked through the back patio door to rejoin the rest, it had been almost an hour. That wasn't the only evidence of their success: they each wore a huge grin, and they were still holding hands. They decided to make the obvious statement, and with this burst of sharing came the need to remain close. Neither could stand the thought of *not* touching.

"It's about time—" Will began to scold them from where he lounged in a recliner before doing a double take. "What's this?"

Cathy gave them an excited thumbs-up. "I see we have even more to talk about." Nolan merely raised an eyebrow while Quani wore a smug look from having been in the know.

But Will seemed affronted. "I suggested we send a rescue party! And so much for the 'oh, let's not do anything awkward.'" Though he mimicked Doug's statement made during the road trip, his tone was more of a playful challenge.

Doug let out a burst of happy laughter while settling next to Kris on the open couch. "I assure you I had no idea this would happen."

"His face looked even more shocked than yours," Kris informed Will while smirking at his confusion.

"Well...fan me with a brick!" Will exclaimed, much to their amusement.

Kris motioned to the laptops. "We're here to help now."

"Oh no, you're not getting off that easy," he countered, closing the laptop he had borrowed from Nolan to give this new revelation his full attention.

Giggling, Cathy imitated his motions and proclaimed, "Just for this once, I'm going to agree with Will. We need details and thrills!"

"Wait," Will said as he made quick mental adjustments and shifted his attention to Cathy. "You knew about this and brought us in here—you *planned* this!" He motioned to Quani, who was sitting next to Cathy. "And you?" Her rare and precious grin was all the proof he needed. "Why, you little sneaks! Alright, come clean."

Nolan chuckled and settled back to enjoy the show while Cathy shook her head and index finger, countering, "We're not going to give up all our secrets, Sherlock. Let's just say we knew love was in the air—" Catching herself, Cathy glanced to her roommate. "I didn't give too much away, did I?"

Kris squeezed Doug's hand, admitting, "I've known for some time but just needed the right moment."

"So, this entire lake trip...?" Will prompted.

Kris shook her head in denial. "No, nothing like that. This is all about relaxation and our dreaming."

"I know what *my* dreams will be like now." Doug's smile widened as he got a playful shoulder nudge.

"Do I need to find a new roommate?" Will asked slyly. "Are living arrangements shifting now that you two…?"

"No, goofy," Kris retorted.

Cathy said, "Look at it this way: we have all the previous wonderfulness of the group but now with added spice from our very own lovebirds." She covered her head when Kris chucked the nearest pillow at her. Giggling, she warned, "Whoa, watch the laptop!"

"Then let's get back to *using* them," her roommate sassed, "unless you want me to use this other on you—they aren't called throw pillows for nothing."

"Okay, okay, *peace*," Cathy surrendered, picking up the pillow from the floor and adding it to her collection.

Will amended, "For now." His challenging scowl promised he'd get more mileage from them. When they went to retrieve their own laptops, he called, "This time I'll send a rescue party if you're gone longer than two minutes."

Late into the night they all continued inputting their dreams onto the website, a time filled with questions and considerations and breaks to savor the joy of just *being* there. When Doug sighed happily and closed his laptop, Will teased, "I know what that sigh means. Did you get any work done?"

"Are you going to be like this constantly?" Cathy asked, and Will held up his hands.

"Hey, just an innocent question."

Cathy snorted. Then glancing at the grandfather clock against one wall, she also closed her laptop. "How did it get to be past midnight? Is that clock right?"

"Time flies…" Kris said.

"…When you're exactly where you need to be," Doug finished. This drew "awws" from the girls and "ughs" from the boys. Doug amended, "I mean for all of us."

"Right."

"Sure."

"Okay, *boys*," Cathy said with a wink, "leave the freshly love-struck alone. I, for one, need to recharge my batteries so we can have more fun tomorrow." She rose and motioned with her arms. "Come on, come on. Group hugs."

* * *

The next morning, those who weren't early birds were slowly drawn from sleep by the smell of eggs and sausage and the clinking of cooking utensils. And the slowest was treated to a giggling call of "come and get it!"

"Good morning," Doug said after emerging from the restroom assigned to the guys, still moving slowly and looking sleepy. Kris went up to him and planted a chaste kiss on his lips.

"In case you thought you dreamed about last night's kisses, this is proof it was real," she said, pulling him into a hug amidst cheers from the grinning audience.

"You make me feel like I'm dreaming," he murmured where he was sure only she could hear before raising his voice to play along. "So, it *was* real after all. The rest of my night was uneventful, as if anything could compare. Did anyone have big dreams?"

"Come and fill a plate first," Cathy called. "Then we can dive in—or *back* in. This is so cool, guys!"

Over breakfast, they alternated between talking about wisps of dreams and website progress, and planning outdoor activities. Will had the only coherent dream, but it was about a strangely dark place populated with giant flies that clung to everything. Whether activated by his run-ins with hungry flies trying to steal bites of last night's dinner or an actual foreign place, he couldn't say for sure. But they could all agree it wasn't a place any would like to visit. They were supercharged by their closeness, laughing throughout the breakfast discussions. The energy of one multiplied through each of them, until they were all antsy to go outside and enjoy the promising weather.

"By the way," Doug added as they were lining up to load their plates into the dishwasher, "thank you, whoever made the good food."

"Glad you liked it," Cathy responded in a pleased tone before adding, "because you guys are treating us tomorrow morning!"

Nudging Doug, Kris teased, "So set your alarm for a decent hour."

"Meaning noon," Will said with a confident nod.

Nolan and Will opted to explore nearby hiking trails. Quani mentioned she could use the company for a morning walk, looking to Cathy, who looked to Kris, who looked to Doug. So, they all hit the trails at their own pace, with a handholding Kris and Doug bringing up the rear. As they strolled along, nature stretched out and sang to them, wind kissed and danced between them, and the warming sun put a fine point on the experience.

After enjoying the hike, they did the next sensible activity: lounging in the deck chairs to soak in varying amounts of sun. Kris retrieved and passed around the sunscreen, most needed for the two girls who switched to swimsuits. "My God, Cathy," Will quipped while shielding his eyes, "your skin makes the sun dim!"

Snorting as she draped her towel over the chair, she sassed, "Then stop looking unless you want me to blind you! I can't help it if all my pigment went to my hair and eyes."

"But by the end of the week, we'll be more golden," Kris assured her with a smile.

"This is like waterside meditation," Cathy said, wiggling from the pleasure of the moment as she stretched out. "And here we are, under the jealous sky!"

"And here we are," repeated Kris in agreement, reclining and reaching for Doug's hand.

The first to become restless was Will, who speculated that since the sun was getting so hot, the water was bound to be pleasant.

"It's still early in the season," Kris warned.

"I know what I'm talking about," Will stated, whipping off his shirt, popping Nolan with it, and challenging him to a race into what had to be cooling water. But the yelps that drifted up to the lounging deck suggested otherwise. An amused audience listened to the antics, the taunts and dares, and in the end, both Will and Nolan had to race into the house to shower and warm up. "Loser gets only cold water!"

"Goofy boys." Cathy tsked, turning her head to watch them race across the yard.

"Yeah, but they're *our* goofs," Kris said while squeezing Doug's hand, and he shot her a wry smile.

"I'm comforted knowing you claim us, silly and all."

After showering, they reconvened over a light lunch of sandwiches and salad. "Now the day has officially begun," Will announced, wadding up his paper plate and scoring two points with a trash can dunk. Again, they drifted to the couches and recliners, using all four laptops to input more of their dreams and their connecting dots. They made a few hours of progress before Will hopped up from his chair, shaking his body and arms and blowing out his breath in a way that sounded like a temperamental horse.

Glancing up, Kris asked, "What is it this time?"

"I think he's finally lost it. I mean, lost it all," Cathy speculated.

"Yes, I have! I feel like this is becoming a second job, so I'm trying to shake off the bad voodoo."

"Ah," Kris said in understanding, also closing her laptop. "Then it's a perfect time for us to do something else. Go back outside, kayak, hike more, something. Just don't wear a hole in the floor."

For variety's sake, Kris agreed to teach them the art of kayaking, though Cathy and Quani watched the show from the safety of the upper deck. Insisting they all wear life jackets, Kris then educated them on the basics, including how to push out if they flipped. "With a water skirt attached," she explained, "you can learn to make a complete roll—they are designed to do that. But without a skirt, if you make too sharp a turn or hit a wave wrong, you'll just swamp it. So don't even try to right yourself. Just kick free and then swim with it back to the shallows."

"Man, I'd pay big money to watch you do rolls," Will stated.

Scrunching up her nose, Kris said, "But then I'd have to shower again, which would be a pain and so puts my price out of your reach."

"Hey, I have a few grand in my wallet."

Kris smirked. "Then I suggest leaving it on the shore because I'm betting you'll not stay dry."

"And let Cathy flip through my baby pics? Never!"

Hoots and splashes rang out over the water. Once they got the hang of it, they stopped wagging like drunken sailors, and their kayaks began obeying their wishes. With sunlight flashing off the spinning paddles, Kris made it look effortless, streaking out a ways before digging in a paddle and twisting at the waist to spin the kayak one-eighty.

Twirling her paddle in the air, she encouraged and then waited for them to make their way toward her before speeding off again. But by this time Doug was getting the hang of it. With increasing confidence he used more muscle to *almost* catch her. When she noticed his speed, she slacked off, letting him draw alongside so she could praise and lean over for a kiss. Of course since he didn't know to dig a paddle in the water to balance his shifting weight, he almost dumped himself in an effort to capture the promised kiss.

Kris' light laugh doubled in volume as Nolan bumped into them before spilling himself into the drink. "Push out!" she shouted, waiting for a long heartbeat before readying to go in after him.

But then he broke the surface, yelling, "Ow, my nads! Woo!"

Flushed from the exhilaration, she laughed again, observing, "This water is a harsh teacher. I remember it well! Swim for shore and I'll tow your boat."

Later that night while the others were chatting around a cozy fire, Kris and Doug were sitting at their new favorite spot, this time wrapped in blankets. Legs dangling off the dock's edge under the lightshow of stars, they held hands and smiled at each other when not softly kissing. At one point, she drew back and asked, "So if you liked me so much, why didn't you make a move or give any sign? Why make me do all the work?"

Doug chuckled as he thought about the question. "You were just too good, you know? Too…I don't know, at a higher level. Such an amazing person. And besides, I saw how you handled Nerron. I just found it safer—smarter—to admire from afar."

"Hmm… How about admiring up close?" she whispered, leaning into him.

*　*　*

The harshly bright, blinking lights, the walls and racks filled with inane junk like drinking games and "toys" of dubious uses, the smell of cheap plastic, the constant underlying roar of footsteps and a hundred blended conversations…I don't see how my sister can stand it. But here I sit on a stool in the corner behind the counter because I came to visit her and she couldn't get time off work.

"Oh, I don't work here," I would hurriedly explain whenever a grinning teenybopper would shout a question at me. And for good measure, I'd point to the other end of the counter at my sister behind the register wearing a perfectly obvious uniform of one who actually works the store. I don't see why she puts up with it all, yet at the same time I admire her strength, because she does what she has to. She remains upbeat and pure and precious to me.

"You know what I could use?" When she gets a lull in the onslaught, she asks her leading question. We've always asked each other the most random of questions as a form of amusement, but today I'm not in the mood.

"A new job?"

"No, dork!" She gently pushes at me with fingers painted in sparkles or some such nonsense. "I like my fun job. What I could really go for is a double dip ice cream, chocolate and mint—there's a shop upstairs that has the best!"

I scowl at her and in response she pouts. "Please, baby brother?" *Don't you dare...* She bats her dark eyelashes, and I give up with a sigh.

"Okay, sis, where is this magic cow byproduct?"

"Just go up the back stairs." She waves at the door marked "Employees Only" and slaps money into my upraised palm. "Can't miss it." Then she is back to work and I'm left with a fistful of dollars, but perhaps it's my ticket, a temporary relief to escape the madness.

The first place I spy across the common area is the big storefront of a bar and grill. Simple enough. I make my way into the place, waiting for my eyes to adjust, and as they do a young woman walks up smiling and hands me a folded white cloth. "There you are," she says with relief in her voice.

"Here I am?" I unfold the cloth and it's a smock, the kind worn by some of the employees.

"Throw it on and then bus the front tables. The tray—"

"Wait, wait. I'm no employee. I'm here to ask about ice cream."

"Seriously?" she asks, her face falling.

"Seriously!" I watch as she growls, grabs the smock and slings it over her neck, and then moves to do the job she was trying to pawn off on me. Weird people...

I shuffle into the customer line, wait for the floor manager to notice me, and then move to him. "You sell ice cream here, right?" To my dismay, he shakes his head. "You know where the ice cream shop is? My sister needs some and said it... No?" He's still shaking his head, so I know well enough to go elsewhere.

Retracing my steps back into the sunlit common area, I scan in all directions for a storefront that would ring the bells of success. The closest I can find is a shop with cartoon icons and candy so bright I suspect it's toxic. But there's a line of kids waiting to load up on it, so I try that line. From behind the counter, the woman catches my eye and gives me a weird look, which makes me realize I'm the only other adult in here.

No, lady, I'm not a creep, so stop with the assumptions! She only relaxes when I get a chance to ask her if this is also an ice cream shop, but of course she shakes her head and doesn't know of one. I feel a surge of annoyance rising, threatening to spoil my good mood and sunny disposition, so I force myself to thank the lady before returning to the common area and continuing my search.

The noisy space isn't open enough to handle all the people, and the run of shops is far too long for me to check them. And besides, I don't think I can take another failure. You know what? Screw it—this is pointless!

Chapter 20

As had become their pattern, they were lounging in the living room and sharing the night's dreams while the tendrils were still fresh. And for once, Will was the only one not laughing. Still affected by his dream aftermath, he could barely smile, even though his telling greatly amused the others. "No, I'm not calling my dream The Great Ice Cream Failure!" he replied to the teasing suggestion. "Seriously, if I even find that place—that mall—I'm going to track down and harass every one of those unhelpful punks."

"A shame you gave up on the simple task," joked Nolan. "Who knows what kind of shop you would have stumbled into next."

"Did it occur to you that your sister sent you on a wild goose chase to get you out of her hair?" Kris asked.

"Huh. If I ever find my sister, I'm going to give her a kick in the pants for good measure!"

Cathy snapped her fingers as she remembered. "Oh right, you're an only child. Just be happy you only have to put up with a sister in dreams. They can be awful."

"I see that now," Will said. "I'm going to have to thank my parents for stopping at me."

Turning pensive, Doug speculated, "I wonder if you could have changed the dream by steering with your focus. I mean, if you had been determined to see only the fun, in the shop, in visiting your sister, in seeing new places...or maybe it wasn't serious enough to bother."

"Not all empathy dreams need to be serious," Quani pointed out while still wearing a small smile.

"*Thank* you!" Will exclaimed, surprised at her input and immediately liking what he heard. "I agree wholeheartedly. It was still a detailed, in-depth adventure—of a sort—and it gave me all manner of new experiences."

Cathy winked at him. "And a fun story to tell."

They settled into a few breaths of amused and comfortable silence, into which Will relaxed as if shedding the last of his dream-induced irritation. Sensing this, Nolan commented, "Even without being able to steer, it's amazing the difference it can make to share and accept the craziness."

"So true." And finally, Will cracked a grin. "Find it funny, and it becomes funny. I'll still give my sister a kick in the ass if I meet her again."

Giggling and sighing happily, Cathy said, "I *knew* this vacation was the perfect idea!"

Kris leaned over to give her roommate a high-five, saying, "And check out our progress without any prompting from Mark!"

"I'm still sad he has missed all this," Doug mentioned, and Kris rolled her eyes.

"Would you *really* want him here?"

"Well, no, but still..."

"Nothing against Mark," Kris clarified in an attempt to ease Doug's inclusive sentiment, "but just look how far we've come without his help."

There seemed to be a strange tension growing, both unfamiliar and unwelcomed, so Cathy bounced out of her recliner and held open her arms, announcing, "I think we deserve a group hug. Come on, bring it in!"

As the vacationers balanced outdoor activities with in-depth conversations about their dreams, they grew even closer, more a part of each other's lives, and it seemed their dream experiences responded accordingly. Dreams became more potent, opening new possibilities. This was especially true of the group's new sweethearts.

"Then we were floating among the starry night," Doug narrated for them, though he focused on Kris while holding her hand. "Like when we're out on the dock, except we were floating, the stars all around and many were winking at us."

"Hey, hey," Cathy intoned in a sultry voice, winking comically at the couple sitting together on the couch.

"Well, except not that vocal," replied an amused Doug. "I could feel this," he continued, rubbing Kris' arm down to where they held hands, "and it was a lifeline, keeping me from floating away."

"Think I'm going to hurl," Will muttered, earning a *shush* from Quani.

When Doug just grinned in his relaxed way, Kris asked, "Do you think you were just processing us? Or perhaps a foreshadowing of our future?"

Nolan chuckled. "I doubt you guys will be floating through open space."

"Not that," she corrected with a rolling of her eyes, "but like floating *above* it all, above the bustle of mundane life?"

Doug shrugged and echoed a group-wide agreement. "All I know is this was one of those dreams that's a rule-breaker and despises being put into our tidy categories." His intensity returned when he continued, "What was amazing, Kris, was when you turned your head toward me and breathed on me. It rippled through space in a nearly invisible way and washed over me in a way I just can't describe."

Wearing a mischievous look, Kris leaned close and asked, "Like this?" She breathed softly against his neck and he visibly shivered. "Oh my!" Kris laughed and pointed to his skin. "The tiny hairs are all standing up! And goose bumps—come look, Cathy!"

A grinning Cathy hopped up and leaned in to inspect Doug while he just colored slightly and held still so they could amuse themselves. "My dream is still with me, clearly," he commented dryly as a way to handle the teasing scrutiny.

Cathy flipped her hand at them as she flopped back into her chair. "You two! You should stop showing off, making us jelly!" She laughed.

"Then you'll be relieved to know that's all I have," a blushing Doug replied.

"For now," Kris added with a smirk of a promise aimed at her roommate.

"A personalized empathy dream," Quani judged while nodding and searching for connecting dots. She opened her mouth to speak again and then snapped it closed. Then breaking from her normally quiet manner, she forced her thought out into the open. "Anyone else noticing how many empathy dreams we are having? We're sharing dreams and this togetherness, and each day we have more."

"Sounds like you have a new one to share," Doug said, happy to have her redirect the group's attention from his dream-elevated fascination of Kris.

Her eyes darted around the group. "If no one else…"

"Go, go," Cathy urged.

With a nod of acknowledgement and thanks, Quani cleared her throat. "I frequented this corner bookstore—wait, let me back up. It was more like a coffeehouse that had a college-vibe, but not really like ours. It was larger, more open. And a corner of it was reserved for a few shelves of books that patrons could browse, buy or rent, I think. Not sure about the renting part."

"More like a library?" Kris asked, and Quani considered it, searching her memory before nodding.

"It must have been. I remember books being returned because they were shelved in a random way. I did most of my reading while I was in the store, sipping my tea. I tried to mind my own business, but the worker did a bare minimum, ignoring the clutter among this collection of very good books."

Quani ducked her head in a self-deprecating way. "So, of course, I began arranging and straightening them. Each book was easy to see and in its right place." Ignoring the chuckles, she continued, "It wasn't long before I could help patrons who were browsing. I knew all the books there, and so if they wanted help, I could find what they would be interested in. I made a few good friends that way."

"A corner store librarian," Will teased.

Smiling back, Quani admitted, "It was strangely satisfying, stepping into the...role that wasn't mine. I was there more and more to read, or reread, and care for the books. At one point I even remember helping out at a register, so I guess I was adopted into that role even though I was definitely not employed. But even more satisfying was the area becoming more active, filling with people who browsed and read. One very interested and intense woman came up and asked me about the books, and I told her I had read them all so could also help her. And you know what?"

The listeners at first didn't know the question was directed toward them, and Kris was the first to respond, "What was that?"

"The lady turned out to be the store owner!" Quani tittered and played with the embroidered edge of her dress. "She turned to a hovering employee and joked to him, saying that *I* could help *her*. I remember being confused, not knowing if she meant it in jest or if she was amused or maybe accusing her employee of not offering to help. Then I worried she might make me stop doing this thing I enjoyed, and I felt the clenching of anxiety in my stomach. The employee was talking, but I woke before I could hear what he was saying."

Quani was almost pouting, so Cathy asked, "Do you feel he was going to stand up for you and help?"

"I don't know. It's so hard to pull those details with me because I'm used to waking quickly. Maybe it's just a family habit, but the quicker we are up, the quicker the new day begins." Quani shrugged.

"But you felt the satisfaction of setting things right in the dream," Doug prompted.

"Oh yes. I was definitely helping the business in my own way, and of course I wanted to continue doing that. But this strong woman... She threatened that somehow."

"At least you now know your life calling," Will teased.

Kris chided him, stating, "Not helpful," before turning back to Quani. "Maybe the woman was just amused by your dedication."

"Maybe, but I know how it feels to *belong*, and then have that threatened by someone forceful. At least, in this case." Quani ended with an awkward shrug as the group considered her experience in silence. Unable to stay quiet, she added a final, "But most importantly, I was very good at it." And with that the group's humor returned.

The days began to blur together with a level of value that can only be fully cherished once it is past and remembered. Will and Nolan tried their hand at fishing with little luck, though it didn't take long for Will to proclaim that he wasn't bored enough to be successful at it. He returned to exploring the surrounding trails and would later regale them with his attempts to startle golfers. (Fore!) Cathy tried to mix sunbathing with finishing her work on the website's layout, but it drained too much battery for the screen to stand any chance against the daylight's glare. Though she retreated to finish her work out of the direct sun, she and Kris would still compare tan lines that seemed to become more impressive with each day.

And the new love sweetened and deepened as Kris and Doug snuggled and talked and kissed every night under the majestic heavens.

One morning, Cathy announced, "I've perfected the website enough, and we're current on our stories, so I think it's time we broadcast it."

Nolan cleared his throat and coughed out a single word: "Nut-jobs!"

"Do we have to?" Will asked. "I mean, really, this is for us and posterity or whatever, and we do plenty of exploration on our own."

"But all from within our very small group," Kris countered before casting her vote. "I say the time is now."

Doug only nodded, and Nolan teased, "Of course you agree." When Kris directed a saucy stare at him, he laughed and relented. "Alright, alright. Let's throw this out there, like when we were out fishing—only I hope we don't hook a shark."

With that decision out of the way, they began to discuss where they would announce it and how, yet Kris interrupted them. "Before we get too distracted, I need to get this new dream off my chest." When the room stilled and they gave her their attention, she smiled and warned, "No, this one is nowhere near as colorful or musical as some, but this feels very connected, like... You'll see."

She took a sip of her orange juice and then settled back against Doug's side. "I was driving out west to celebrate my older brother's birthday with him and his friends."

"This is news," Doug commented with a crooked eyebrow to her knowing smile.

"My brother," she explained, "is much like Will's sister—though not in the wanting-to-ditch-me way." She spared a moment to smirk at Will before continuing her story. "I remember it being a long drive, like from here to California, but it was more of a memory or travel fatigue, because only the celebration details were crystal clear. My brother had a lively bunch of friends, and I blended right in as we gathered at his house and filled it to bursting.

"No birthday bash is complete without mixed drinks—at least this one wasn't—which helped break the ice and get everyone in the mood, all except for the few children of some of his married friends. Then we all piled into cars— who I hope had responsible drivers—and we headed out for a night on the town. I think we made a few stops on our birthday tour, but the place I remember most was some kind of dinosaur museum. Except that it had outdoor areas and even playgrounds, which we played in with the kids.

"I remember staring up at the big reassembled skeletons and even dancing around some of the statues, laughing at our silliness. It was good fun up to that point." Kris held up a hand as if to focus them on her changing scenario.

"All around were smiles and dancing couples, and kids squealing in joy as they rode the slides or swung on the swings. But, the smiles weren't of people I recognized. It's like the smiles themselves were turning bizarre, unrecognizable, like some weird bleed-through effect on my reality. Strange people, strange smiles, strange dances, even the statues seemed out of place, and at first I looked around for the children I had been watching. Finding none of them, I actively went searching for my brother, but with every turn and every face, I felt more lost. Like someone who stumbled into the wrong room, only it was the entire area—the world!" She shivered and Doug squeezed her shoulder, and yet she continued without more than a moment's pause.

"*Just like* in my cottage dream, I began to feel like the foreigner. Like the one who didn't belong. The confusion of having no brother just added onto everything else. I had no sense, no idea of what to do, because to find your way—to get anywhere—you have to be able to *recognize* something! And I didn't. Not a thing: not the people or the place or even their actions. By that point I felt a complete separation, more strongly than in my quiet cottage dream, and I was *immersed* in the bizarre with *no idea* what to do!

"That's what followed me from my dream, that having no idea what to do." This time when she shivered, Kris drew Doug's arm more tightly around her. "It's almost as powerful now as it was in my dream, the feeling of not belonging."

"Well, you belong with us," Cathy countered and Doug squeezed Kris in agreement.

"I know—I mean the memory, or whatever it is. It's so strong! That's what was so upsetting."

"Just like in our steering work," Nolan speculated, "maybe you could overcome or look past that feeling."

"Like being more open, in the moment," Doug added. "Maybe accepting is a better term. When I experience something bizarre, I just…roll with it."

"Like with the floating grumpy clouds?" Quani asked while wearing a helpful smile.

"Yep," Doug agreed. "Those were clearly foreign but I even talked with one as if I accepted the rabbit hole I'd gone down."

But rather than being mollified, Kris was shaking her head. "There's a difference. You felt *they* were different, not yourself. I felt that *I* was the one out of place."

"True, but maybe it works similarly, the acceptance? If you are the 'other' then so be it."

"Enjoy the freak show or be the freak running the show," Will injected his expert opinion with an exaggerated bouncing of his head like he was trying to imitate a jack in the box.

"Oh, you!" Kris said. Suddenly realizing she sounded exactly like her roommate, she glanced to Cathy, saw the same thought written on her face, and then they burst out laughing. Dabbing tears from the corners of her eyes, Kris said, "Oh guys, our group is so perfect."

"The right kind of crazy," Will agreed, head still wiggling.

As the group chased the amazing idea of interconnected or even reinforcing dreams, Quani speculated that perhaps Kris needed to experience her cottage dream and then hear Will's ice cream madness to be prepared for this newest one. Rather than influencing this dream, the earlier dreams *unlocked* it. The group agreed that they could only experience the powerful dreams they were having because they had worked up to them, as if they had been training.

When speculation ran its course, they returned to talk of their website logistics: how to get the rich resource of their website in front of people who would add to it. How do you entice others to take it seriously and open up to share? The remainder of the morning was spent trading ideas on how to make introductions, and Kris' lingering feelings of otherness and of being lost faded like one dream soon replaced by another.

*   *   *

"I'm going to miss being on this dock with you," Doug murmured to Kris, their faces so close that even the smallest impulse would bring their lips back together. Beneath them, little waves caressed the shoreline, and above them, bright stars went unnoticed. By some unwritten agreement, everyone had postponed talking about the end of their vacation, as if the mention would accelerate the already too quick ending. They would have to return the following day, but until then, they would squeeze every last moment from it. Every last feeling, breath, loving gaze, committed to memory.

Kris smiled happily. "Our special place." After another long moment, she promised, "We will return."

"I hope so, and we will dream even bigger."

*   *   *

Throughout their final morning routines, everyone moved slowly, even as they packed their bags and staged them by the front doors. All except for Quani, who had awoken early, quickly gathered her belongings together, and then spent the last sunrise at the water's edge as if recording the experience for all time.

When they finally all met in the foyer, looking at each other and smiling sadly, even Will was subdued. "I'm already feeling the buzzkill," he observed.

"I…" Cathy began before amending herself. "*We* will never forget this time." Her declaration brought fervent nods.

"We must take this closeness with us, no matter where we end up," Doug said.

"Hey," Kris protested, her car keys jingling in her hand when she gave him a love tap. "That sounds way too final."

Cathy laughed and sniffled, "Yeah! This is only the beginning for us." Holding out her arms, she said, "Swear it. Always this close."

"Friends for life," Kris acknowledged, and the promise was echoed by each as they joined the tight group hug.

Chapter 21

"Dude!" Doug's suitemate Tim greeted him while he was still unpacking. "You missed the best spring break ever! It was wild and wet—just the way we like it!"

Donna tucked herself under Tim's arm and added her commentary. "Oh, the warm sands and cold drinks! We had a *looong* spa session, his-and-hers side-by-side, with mud masks and hot stones and perfect massaging—I even fell asleep for a bit." She giggled until her boyfriend wryly added, "And she snored," which earned him a playful nudge.

"Oh, and I learned how to surf," Donna continued before amending, "well, kind of."

Doug calmly smiled at the pair. "I'm glad to hear you had a fun vacation."

"But we missed not having our buddy around!" Tim said, fully entering Doug's room so they could perform their ritual greeting of Klingon handshake and shoulder bump.

"Well…" Doug drawled. "If I had joined you, then I'd still be single."

Tim's big grin froze on his face. "Wait—what?"

"Wait, what?" Donna echoed, also stepping close to scrutinize Doug.

"It's true," he told them through his own amusement. "I was blinded and surprised by love."

"Oh, my, oh, my," Donna exclaimed, sliding up to Doug's other side and sitting him on the bed. "You must tell us everything!"

Doug got the opportunity to introduce his new love sooner than expected thanks to one of the many campus activities celebrating (and mourning) the semester's continued grind. Held on the intramural sports fields each year, a concert called the Spring Break Blues Festival was conveniently central and next to the large gym building. The speakers were stacked high enough that even those using the Olympic-sized swimming pool inside could still hear various bands performing. Students were drawn from all corners of campus to perform one final spring-break-related hurrah in the sun before returning to their studies.

With minimal arranging and Tim skipping his late afternoon class, the two couples met in the dorm's parking lot. Much to Doug's relief, Tim settled on a tame greeting while adding, "A pleasure to meet the one who finally caught this shy fish." And after introducing herself, Donna told Kris, "He truly is a sweetheart."

"Oh, don't I know it!" Kris replied. "And I love it when he turns this shade of red." She patted Doug's cheek while he tried to play nonchalant, which increased his friends' amusement. The group meandered around the commons areas until finding a partially shaded patch of grass far enough away from the band that they wouldn't have to yell to be heard. However, Donna was impatient, pulling Kris aside so they could "get to know each other without boys listening in."

"I would pay big money to be able to hear that," Tim said, squinting after the women as they strolled away into the sun and music pulsing through the air.

Doug stated wryly, "I'm not sure I want to know."

"You have no sense of adventure! Besides, they're just comparing endearing stories, but I'm missing out on good ammunition."

"Yeah, right. They couldn't know enough to have blackmail material."

"Well, about you," Tim offered, turning an impish look on his roommate, "I could always share stories…"

"Then we'd find out if my shoe fits up your butt."

"Does Kris know about this violent streak of yours?"

Doug traded daring grins, which reminded him of a tangential subject. "Speaking of, we should keep the gamer talk to a minimum. I think she's more like Donna and will only tolerate so much of it." When the girlfriends returned, they wore an air of secrecy and at first refused to answer any questions. Donna would only say they now had a dinner date planned for the near future.

While Kris intertwined her arm in Doug's, she said, "I was telling on you, how you made me do all the work of chasing you. Giving me *absolutely* no hint you had the same feelings, and making me anxious. Like you had planned it!"

Doug soaked in the moment, Kris' light-hearted humor and beauty, before repaying the teasing. "Now you know the pressure we're always expected to face... And besides, all's fair in love, right?"

Wiggling closer and to the backdrop of a song's swelling anthem, she murmured, "I'll remember that..." When they kissed, Tim rolled his eyes and loudly commented something about "fresh kiddie love."

*   *   *

The opening of the next dream meet was supercharged because of the group's vacation breakthroughs and their website progress. Not only did they find it convenient to add and discuss stories on their new site, they had already received a few public comments along with a posted dream. Mark's head swung from one student to another as he tried to catch up and keep up.

"You already finished the website?" Mark asked. "You guys *have* been busy. Spent your vacation time well, I see."

Cathy beamed proudly, her laptop already opened in front of her. "See for yourself. This is our first bona fide dream input." She settled further into her seat and read:

"'I stood alone in a dark, huge place. Maybe it was a field but I don't remember any grass or trees, only maybe shadows. I thought I heard nothing, but that was only because I cannot describe it. And I saw nothing, but I could feel things all around me, just beyond sight. This place wasn't alive, but it was. Does this make any sense? What does this mean? I just stood there taking it all in, but not. LOL'"

"The poster sounds hopelessly confused, a newbie," Will commented, drawing a warning look from Cathy to behave.

"Like we all would be without our study," Mark pointed out. "This is the majority of what you will find, I'd wager, because most people don't spend time analyzing their dreams nor do they train to remember enough detail to apply careful speculation or find their answers."

"But we can help them in that speculating," Cathy insisted, "which will help them the next time they have a big one." The others were nodding in support.

Scratching at the stubble on his chin, Mark said, "Maybe so, but how does that help our group? We could talk about others' dreams if we don't have enough of our own, but I doubt that's a problem, am I right?"

"We can help others without losing our progress," Quani stated, herself being a shining example of progress.

"None of us are having a shortage of dreams," Nolan answered Mark. "My latest has gotten quite a few views and some comments." He chuckled. "A couple people posted that I'm clearly a fan of superheroes—which isn't true—and one poster talked about wanting more technical details because my engineering mind was at work trying to figure out how to make power-assisted armor. In the dream, I specifically remember testing out the legs that helped me run as fast as cars—I was passing them up on city streets."

Holding up a hand to stop him, Kris said, "You should make Mark read it like we all did: on our website."

"Yeah," Cathy agreed with a decisive nod of her head, and Mark was already pulling his laptop from his bag.

"Onward with the new," Mark said as part commentary and part praise for their efforts. Once he had navigated to the site and saw the updated opening screen, he read it aloud. "'Unveiling and Exploring Hidden Realms as Real as You Allow Them to Be.' This is a new tagline, but don't you think it's a tad misleading?"

"Misleading how?" Will asked rhetorically. "Our dreams continue to become more real, more varied, richer. They *are* related, not random brain noise."

"I see we're picking up right where we left off before spring break," Mark said with patient amusement.

"Not exactly at the same place," Kris corrected him, though like most of the others, she was reluctant to discuss their vacation breakthroughs in depth.

Smiling fondly at her, Doug took that moment to repeat the saying he had first brought to the group's attention. "'All that we see or seem is but a dream within a dream.'" Turning back to Mark, he said, "Poe's quote has added meaning to us now."

The return to a scholarly angle drew Mark's attention which he focused on Doug. "An updating of perspective... That's good. That's growth in its own right. Please share what you now feel it means, Doug."

"It feels more and more possible that what we think of as reality is only a small part *within* a larger reality. Poe could very well have been pointing to his own dream experiences and the idea that while we live this fun moment, it's connected to a greater one."

"Not easy to know what Poe meant without solid context, of course," Mark said before adding, "but your working theory would sure make a grand story idea. Speaking of, show me where this newest dream is so I can read it." The group waited quietly while Mark read Nolan's short dream and summary. Once he had finished, he straightened and favored Nolan with a smile. "Nice job of recording the dream and a good summary. You guys are definitely setting positive examples of how to record and prompt discussion. In particular, I'm interested in your worry over government interference."

"That was my own addition to the dream-me," Nolan admitted with a self-conscious chortle. "The design specs were so detailed, the test so clear in my mind, that I superimposed a realistic worry on it. As one poster said, 'No way the government would let you keep such a device.' And that echoes the feeling I woke up with, even though initially I only felt joy at the accomplishment. And during my test I was passing cars—so maybe 40 or 50 miles-per-hour—which is why it was important I was wearing a helmet and leather protection like a biker would use. But the details of how to build it..." Nolan shook his head. "For a while at least, I felt capable of copying the design."

"I wonder if that's how Leonardo da Vinci felt," Quani said.

Cathy piped in, "Ooh yeah, like with his wing design."

"It's a possibility," Mark said in support. "Perhaps you should begin jotting down the designs. Try turning them into a reality."

Nolan laughed, shaking his head. "Not until after I graduate and get out from under this course load."

* * *

Days of readjusting transitioned into a steady grind, the last six-week push toward finals. But classwork was always balanced with injections of fun, and in addition to sharing vivid dreams, the tight-knit group continued to nurture their project and watch its popularity grow. The group collaborated on feedback to their first serious poster, and in turn, the enthusiasm was echoed back at them in a most gratifying way. More dream examples organized in a central place prompted more speculation, which was quickly becoming their favorite pastime.

They voted to "graduate" an enthusiastic young woman into the inner circle, the first outsider to have access to the group's more personal and meaningful dreams; this was partly aided by the fact they had to move one of her dreams behind the firewall because of its exciting significance. Despite the fact she lived half a country away, they spent time on a group call with her, meeting the mind behind the dream, as Will put it.

Together, they grew all the more certain of complex connections. There were hints and impressions that they were nearing a tipping point, a level where it would all begin making sense. A point in which the powerful ability to be *present* within a dream and exercise a measure of control would unlock deeper and more meaningful dreams. Those with keen empathy could find an extra level of meaning, which meant more training and even more opportunities. As they practiced, the group could feel how their gained experience would translate into guidance for others. And with all this budding interest, there had been only a couple of occasions where Cathy used what she called her editor's nuke button to delete bad content.

Then one evening while Cathy was checking her email before going to bed, she saw what looked like an automated notice from the website. Yet when she opened the message, it only contained a plain block of text.

> I know you strive to help-inform-free, but you delve-reveal "hidden realms" people within your society will not allow. You harm those without preparedness, and you expose you-as-you-might-become, the potentiality. Please, for your safety, remove this display and keep experiences-learning private among the closest friends. At least for current time-situation.

Turning her head this way and that, Cathy chewed her lower lip and thought, "Who writes like this?" Perhaps it was a prank—Will, probably; oh, that brat!—or one of Nolan's hypothesized nut-jobs actually showing up. She knew it was a theoretical possibility, yet the risk seemed remote from within the cozy confines of her group.

Her finger moved to and hovered over the delete command. And yet... She detected no malice or danger from the message itself. At the very least, it would make for an interesting group discussion. Only once she went to forward the message to the others did she notice it wasn't a complete email, but merely text within the body. There was no reply or forwarding options.

"Huh," she said aloud, working the command menus to find a sender path or any evidence the SMTP information was blocked to her. But she found nothing. "Okay...freaky." Making her own copy using the old school cut-and-paste, she sent the message out to her friends along with an explanation of how it wasn't a normal email. She could feel herself getting worked up over the mystery, and so she ended with a simple statement: "We have to talk about this when we next meet—the sooner the better!!!"

Chapter 22

They chose an off-hour at the café so there would be fewer people, but even still they leaned in close so their voices wouldn't carry. Upon arriving, they had greeted each other in their normal manner and talked college small-talk as they ordered their beverages. While settling around the far corner table, they chatted website progress and shared updates on various projects. Kris talked briefly of Cassie, the high school girl she had begun mentoring. Not only could she detail fascinating dreams, but the senior was planning for college and was always asking questions.

But at the first lull in normal conversation, Doug turned toward Cathy and said, "So, about your email…"

Cathy could feel the peaking of interest around the table now that the main reason they were here was drawn into the open. There was a moment of unnatural silence as they leaned together even closer. Will wore one of his looks, so Cathy accused him, "I know that grin! Are we sure this isn't just one of your tricks? That was maybe my second thought as I read it, that you decided to spice things up by playing Nolan's nut-job."

Will's impish look widened. "If only I had thought of it first!" His envious tone as he shook his head left no doubt of his sincerity. "No, I'm just thinking of all the fun we can have with this guy, who clearly doesn't know who he's messing with."

"But what does it actually mean?" Quani asked in a soft voice, concern creasing her brow.

While some of the others shrugged, Will held up a finger. "See, if you're fluent in Nut-jobish—which I happen to be—then the message makes perfect sense." Ignoring Nolan's derisive chuckle, Will interpreted, "Some dude got his imagination fired up by what we're doing, and then being his paranoid self, began projecting that onto our work."

Again, it was Quani who vocalized her doubts. "And he really expects us to hide or shut down the site?"

Cathy made a rude noise with her mouth. "As if we would!"

"And this is where we set the hook in him," Will continued smoothly, making a small gesture of rubbing his hands together. "He seems invested in 'helping' us because of course he knows what's best for us, right? But he has to understand we won't just take his word for it, so let's make him provide proof. He claims it's harmful and that the paranoid other people won't want it, well, then he has to prove this to us. Given what I read into the message, he will try his best to talk us into it, which is where we'll have our fun."

Like Quani, Nolan was wary. "I'm not so sure about this..."

"Oh, come on," Will said, turning to him. "It'll be harmless fun."

"Maybe," Doug added his tentative vote, "depending on how delicately we handle it." He received an encouraging squeeze from the hand that held his under the table, and a smile from Kris above the table.

"I agree," Cathy said, "but we can't just hit reply and say, 'Prove it to us!' As I stated, it wasn't in normal email format."

Will laid an open hand on the table and made a "gimme, gimme" gesture. "Let me have a look at the original."

"Oh, because you're so much more pro at SMTP." Despite the sarcastic reply, Cathy pulled the laptop from her bag, woke and unlocked it, and was about to move it across the table to him when she froze and frowned.

"Well?" Will prompted, his playful grin never leaving his face.

After a few more frantic keystrokes, Cathy admitted, "Well, it's not here, and I didn't close the app or anything. But the only thing showing is our emails, not the original I left open. It should have saved to drafts, at the very least!"

Will continued wiggling his fingers until, with a sigh of exasperation, she spun and slid the laptop to him. "First thing I'm going to check is your trash can," he stated with a smug air that elicited snickers from the boys and a threat of real violence from Cathy. It didn't take him long to reach the same conclusion. "Are you sure you didn't delete—"

"Don't finish that thought unless you want me coming over this table at you," she interrupted before giving up her pretense with a laugh at herself. "Of course I left it alone, because either I wanted to know how you managed the prank, or I knew you would want to double-check me."

"Am I really so predictable?" Deflated, he slid the laptop back across the table.

"Yes!" both Cathy and Kris replied in unison before giggling at each other.

Having turned pensive, Doug worked aloud through his reasoning: "We know he has seen the splash screen of the site, so maybe we leave—no, that would be too noticeable. But in the public message section we leave our response in a new post."

"Of course," Cathy agreed with a satisfied nod. "And that tells us if and when he sees it. We make it vague, of course, since it's public."

"I vote to title the message, 'Dear Nut-job,'" Will interjected with a smirk.

Glancing at her watch, Quani stated, "Whatever we decide needs to be done within 30 minutes because my first class is in an hour." Now properly focused and on a time deadline, the group worked together effectively, considering each word to craft a message that was both firm and challenging without being more than an irrelevant post to the casual viewer. And of course it was all translated into Nut-jobish by their resident expert.

To One-Concerned

On such a fun-important project and based on nothing more than your claim-opinion, we cannot agree. After giving careful consideration, we do not

see any threat-harm and feel the risk to be minimal
if any at all. If you want more from us, you must
earn trust-agreement through proof. Please advise.

With the response composed enough to suffice and time running short, Cathy posted it with a final giggle. Then closing the laptop, she called for a group hug before they went their separate ways for the day.

Time passed in fits and starts with Cathy diverting more attention to the message board and her email in hopes of a quick response, answers to the mystery that nagged. In her defense, the warning was a dose of bitter medicine, a disturbance to their happy journey, and it had set her on edge. More so, she realized, because the tone of the initial message seemed genuine enough to have gotten under her skin. Kris was annoyingly composed, reminding her they had thrown their best shot at the mystery and not to expect anything else to happen.

At that week's dream meet, Cathy bit her tongue to keep from spilling the beans and admitting her anxiety. Her only consolation came from sensing similar struggles in the others. The awkward silences were enough for Mark to notice something amiss, though he merely chuckled at the unusual distractions of the outside world. They talked a while about the college pressures leading up to finals, and Mark prompted more group participation before offering up another one of his best dreams to elicit group discussion. In the end, Cathy realized that Mark spent more time speaking of psychological possibilities and drawing responses out of them than they spent giving anything back, which was borderline bizarre!

Her heart skipped a beat when she returned home and noticed a new reply to their message. She blew out the breath she was holding when she saw it was just an inquiring post from their new high school friend they were helping. "Please ignore it," Cathy told her and any other curious innocents. "It's just a test we are running for backend purposes." On the emotional side, Cathy took ahold of herself, wiping the frown off her face and making the determination to move on. Most importantly, she needed to refocus on her studying.

Then just as she was reclaiming her routine, another message appeared in the same way as the first.

> Each of you take for granted near-impossibility. And you risk setback. Except for yourselves, none in your current time-situation accomplish more than glimpse-return. They train to forget-ignore even as they wake, and yet you would push-prod. Know the danger of forcing the frightened to face their fears. Have you not all dream-seen information-knowledge unsafe to share? Falsehood-concealment exposure-risk, open-aware to new state-of-being-joining, "power" that binds-limits-frightens, travel-shift between resonance... You know someone pushed-in-pain because she was unready-unwilling. Why not learn this lesson while safe? This is the least upsetting-disorienting method for you. Again, do not attract-involve anyone else, even one

experienced as a mentor. He will not choose the path-experience where you go. Please be patient-growing, take inspiration from quiet promise.

This time with the help of Kris' speedy taxiing, Cathy convened an emergency group meeting at their apartment, supercharged by cheap coffee and wide eyes. Though she made a back-up of the text, she didn't swap apps or close her laptop, even going so far as to disable the screensaver. So, she felt well-deserved satisfaction when Will looked up from studying the original message on her laptop and pantomimed his brain exploding, complete with sound effect. To ensure each member had a chance to soak in the message, Cathy and Kris insisted they hold any comments until everyone was finished.

Even after Quani read and reread the message, they stood around the small living room in silence until Kris quietly spoke. "I feel like we've entered The Twilight Zone."

"The what?" Doug asked.

Kris wove her arms around Doug with the need to be hugged. "An old show my parents used to watch about a place where impossible things happened. Come to think of it, that show has new significance to me now."

"*Near*-impossible, according to our nut-job," Will corrected, though even his grin was muted. "Now it's my turn to ask: are you screwing with us, Cathy?"

With an incredulous guffaw, she replied, "Would I be this freaked out if I did? I'm no actor!"

"Just had to be sure before putting on my serious hat," Will stated, also pantomiming fitting a cap snugly into place on his head.

"We did ask for proof," Quani said softly, hunching in on herself when she became the center of attention.

Will quickly countered, "But proof of what? This could be a hacker who has helped himself to our backend data."

"Or a government...?" Nolan began, shrugging away the unanswerable possibilities.

Will perked up. "Yeah, like a rogue agent saying, 'Pipe down before I flash my gadget in your eyes and make you forget all this.'"

"Is this you with your serious hat on," Cathy accused in a tone of disappointment. "Do I need to point out his reference to Mark, or to *Gabriella*? Details that aren't *on* our website at all?"

"Well, if you want to read into it. And I'm serious about not knowing what's going on."

"Guys," Cathy drawled, trying to focus them. "How is he *doing* this?" Some shifted and some scratched and one wiggled her mouth, but none of them could come up with a solid answer.

Ending the silence by taking a deep breath, Doug said, "We should take this seriously, for sure, but let's not freak out and jump to conclusions."

"Well, we know one person who has the answers," Kris reasoned, "and I say we keep pushing to get answers from him, or her, or whatever."

With a partial question in his voice, Nolan said, "Or he's just really good at fishing. Some 'fortune-tellers' are good con-artists who know how to read people and guess. Or so I hear."

"Either way we need to find out. I agree with Kris," Will decided after a moment. "It's important to try, for our exploration and our sanity, to get every answer we can."

Doug unconsciously rubbed at his chin. "Yes, I agree, but cautiously. If this is real—if *he* is for real—then we need to be careful. This opens so many possibilities…"

A fidgeting Quani suggested, "Maybe we close the site like he says, at least for now."

"But that removes our bargaining chip," Will pointed out while still considering the suggestion.

Cathy straightened her posture and added, "Not to mention ending our means of communicating." She seemed to have recovered her composure and settled back on what she knew. "This time, we put our message behind the firewall in our most secure spot. That way we can ask specific questions without anyone else seeing. He'll have to hack us, so we can learn that much at least. And while I'm at it, I'll recheck the website security."

"Okay," Doug said while glancing around at his friends to make sure they were reaching consensus. "Let's just be careful about where we take this, is all I'm saying."

Regaining a measure of his excitement, Will rubbed his hands together. "Then let's do this!"

Kris brewed another round of exam-cram coffee while Cathy supervised the rearranging of their living room. Now those squeezed together on the couch and those seated in chairs behind the couch could all share the view of Cathy's screen while they figured out what to say. Gone were the normal antics, replaced by the determination to *know*. Yet, their enthusiasm quickly returned as they considered the puzzle of drawing out answers from someone so mysterious.

> Okay, you have our complete attention. Though we still feel right in our exploring and sharing, we are willing to consider anything more you say. Clearly you know things we do not and we are eager to learn. How do you access our site, learn about us and contact us? Can you show us more that would explain why we should hide our work and our excitement? Who should we be afraid of? This doesn't seem right that we hide such inspiring dreams and not help others since we can help in our dreams. If only you would explain this without the mystery, we will do as you ask. Please show us more, and thank you for caring about us.

Doug and Nolan both seemed convinced they would never hear anything more, despite their best efforts. But in a change of heart, Will bet that the response would come and come quickly. After posting the message, they lingered together, unsure of what else to talk about, and went through two rounds of hugs before parting for the evening.

They were now hopelessly distracted. Schoolwork seemed a distant priority all of a sudden, compared to the possibilities churning through their minds. It was a good thing Doug and Nolan didn't take up Will on his bet. And it was also telling when Cathy found a new reply waiting for her the next morning as she awoke and checked her laptop.

> Understanding-smile at your attempt, though I am not immune to your charm-tactics. You being eager-hungry to learn offers hope-inspiration. Private displays are possible but risk overwhelming you, and I would not be living my own wisdom. Reverse-thought for you: What proof could you offer of being wise-sensitive as you learn, and not making your time-situation worse? How would I know the offered knowledge would support growth rather than harm? Yes, amazing-truth you can help in dreams, and yet not within your time-situation. I would save you from the pain of being pushed-back by others on a divergent-aggressive path. So, trust in my caring as I trust in my caring. When you are ready to grow-deep, I will know and come-assist.

The questers gathered again at the apartment as soon as classes would allow, quickly surrounding the open laptop sitting on the small kitchen table and then mulling over the new message in relative silence.

Unable to hold his tongue, Will turned to Nolan and then Doug with triumph radiating from him. "I told you! We've got him on the hook!"

Doug was pursing his lips, but then said in a reluctant tone, "I don't know. This feels too good to be true."

"Guys," Cathy warned, "wait for Quani to finish."

Will ignored her just long enough to declare his complete reversal from earlier in the week: "No way is this some prank. Okay, okay, I'm going silent mode now." Zipping his lips, he settled for sharing victory grins with Nolan.

Looking up from the screen, Quani said, "I think Will is right, and this…whoever is willing to give us answers. But I worry when he says we aren't ready."

"He has no idea just how prepared we are!" insisted the exuberant Will.

"Look before you leap," Doug cautioned, which only made Will counter him.

"I look *while* I leap, as we all have been doing since spring break, at least. Am I right? Have we not been training for this nearly an *entire* school year? Come on—tell me I'm wrong." Will's vibrating dance of challenge had the others grinning, and it only took moments for them to all nod in agreement.

"So," Will continued with a hurry-up motion at Cathy, "now is when we reel him in. Get him to commit information in exchange for our cooperation."

This time the group hovered over Cathy's shoulder while they plotted their final move. To individual degrees, they each sensed the nearness of answers, of dots connecting and drawing them further into the mystery. So, when the idea was floated to ask for a meeting in person, only Doug and Quani expressed doubt.

Nolan found it hard to breathe with the sudden hope blooming in his chest, and he countered their caution. "This is someone I must see for myself. I have to get answers or I will never forgive myself." And so they eventually agreed to push for this ultimate proof.

If you could meet us, you would know we are students and explorers ready for whatever you can show us. Are you able to visit here so we can meet somewhere safe and public? Please give us the chance and we will show you that we are ready AND we are able to keep secrets when needed. Caring, like you, is why we do what we do! We must know why this is important for it to make sense!

The group longed to expound, but deleted more from the message than was kept because they dared not sound too excited or too pleading or too stubborn. Consequently, this shortest version took the longest to script and required the most compromises among them. Feeling worn down from the intensity and wide range of powerful emotions, they all took turns pacing the small space or flopping onto the couch.

Once they had reached as much of an agreement as they were likely to get, Cathy sighed after a big stretch and posted the message before any could change their minds. The relief in the apartment was palpable.

Kris clung to Doug and suggested she order pizza for them since it was "past feeding time." They lounged and welcomed the diversion of more normal visiting and hot, cheesy food. As if reluctant to mention it, Quani finally said she should probably get back to her studying, and the group began to stir from their food comas. Kris had her keys in hand heading for the door when Cathy called out.

"Guys, you're not going to believe this!" She was back at the table, sliding into her chair while focusing on her laptop. Rushing to surround her, the others stared at the screen, taking turns as best they could. On it was a new message:

Would you truly choose the difficult path? Is kind concern not enough? Search-deep. Do you truly feel prepared for what I can show you? If it helps protect you from your own youth-energy-drive, then I will not deny you. Any place is possible, as long as you feel safe-wise-satisfied.

"No way," Nolan breathed in near reverence.

Will, who was stretched over Nolan's inside shoulder, replied, "Yes way! This is what we were working for. This is it!"

With a kind of focus that can only come when tired yet in the zone, the group quickly talked about logistics of a safe meeting point and ran through options before agreeing upon what they considered to be the most sensible plan. Both tense and excited at the same time, they took the leap and composed a final message.

We are bold explorers, and aren't difficult paths often the best way to grow and learn? We accept! Tomorrow night, 11 p.m., at our campus gym on the basketball court! By that time, most exercisers will be gone for the day but it will still be open. If you are truthful as we are, see you there!

Chapter 23

"I'm so nervous I think I might be sick," Quani admitted in a tone that quivered slightly as she greeted Cathy, Kris and Will. They had decided to meet in the parking lot of Doug's dorm complex so they could walk to the gym together. The unseasonably warm days had been broken by a rainy cold front that came in overnight, so now they huddled in their coats while they waited for Nolan to arrive and for Doug to come down.

"Finally, proof we've been pushing for!" Will focused them on the positive before ruining it by amending, "Well, *if* he's not a liar or a nut-job."

"I brought pepper spray," Kris said, showing them the sleek, black canister before returning it to her coat pocket. "You know, just in case." They shared muted, nervous chuckles before waiting in silence. Their plan was to arrive so early that they could watch the stranger approach and be prepared for anything. When Doug came through the dorm front doors and veered toward them, Kris told him, "Hey, you know our plan won't work if you boys are late."

Grinning and hugging her, Doug seemed to be the most at ease. "I just got off the phone with Nolan who asked if we're really doing this, so I know he's on his way. I think he wants this as much as we do. I mean, we *are* doing this, right?" With the others nodding, he teased, "Okay, then. Making sure we aren't meeting out here just for fun."

"You aren't even a little nervous?" Cathy asked.

Doug replied first with a shrug. "More like prepared. No matter what happens, we'll learn from it."

"That's the spirit!" Will exclaimed. "Though if he doesn't show—and with something good—I'm going to be plenty pissed." Once Nolan arrived, they performed their group hug and shared support. And with a final confirmation circulating among them, they cut across the commons fields toward the gym.

As they neared, Kris checked her watch and reported, "Still 47 minutes early." They slowed, approaching a propped-open side door that offered the shortest route to the basketball court by going around the pool and down a connecting hallway. Laughter echoed from inside, and when they peeked around the hallway corner, a couple of jersey-wearing athletes were slinging towels over their shoulders, grabbing duffle bags, and walking toward the main exit leading to the front parking area.

Partway up the bleachers near the center sat a man so nondescript their glances nearly slid off of him. But with focus, they could see him clutching a large book to his chest and staring off into space. When Doug led them into the court, the man's gaze swung toward them, removing any doubt this was their mysterious contact.

Since he could think of nothing else to open with once they were within hailing distance, Will blurted, "How did you know we'd come early?"

Even the man's warm smile seemed to ignore the curiosity-laden accusation. "So now we are *here* in this moment." His tone was soft, nearly a whisper, though it seemed to carry just fine. And since he seemed passive to the point of being unwilling to move, the students found themselves drawing closer. "I offer one final appeal to leave from here and ask no more questions until you are ready, to choose a path of wary-patience."

Making his answer clear, Doug began up the steps. "Might we know your name?"

"We didn't come this far to turn away," Cathy said as she followed Doug and Nolan and Will in their climb.

The man watched each approach from where he sat, still clutching the large tome to his chest as if it were a shield, or a precious gift given into his care. "We know the offer is amusing formality for I see in each of you the blazing desire-need-potential. And together..." He paused when they paused mere steps from him, spending a long moment in consideration. "Intertwined-supportive-combined...you have the energy to inspire, to reignite fallen stars."

Cathy caught herself pressing her thumbnail to the crease of her front teeth. "What do we call you?" she asked to keep from fidgeting in silence. "Is that for us?"

Smiling at her knowingly and fondly, the man replied, "You can, should, call me...Viz."

"Viz," Will mused. "Clearly an alias, your spy name?"

Pinning Will with piercing focus, Viz stated, "A true name would slip from your mind, even as you attempted to inscribe it, for you are not ready." Ignoring Will's shock of recognition, Viz continued. "It is with joy-relief that I meet you, *here*, eager ones. I offer a further exception to show your birthright-ability. Once rejected, then lost, a connection to your origin-truth.”

The tightness in Nolan’s chest—from echoed similarities most treasured, along with anxiety of the momentous—suddenly eased like a sigh of relief being blown out. So, he was the first to slide onto the bench next to Viz. While the others gathered around, Viz slowly lowered the tome from his chest to his lap, rubbing a hand over its ancient-looking, soft leather cover.

“In ages past, from a history mostly erased, your ancestors ‘walked the heavens,’ as they named their dreaming ability, gaining insights, building-cherishing bonds. Recording those fundamentals for the future to grow-evolve. The most precious-beloved of their efforts resides within this copy.” He patted the cover fondly and remained silent long enough for the dam holding back impatient questions to burst.

“What happened to the original? Why don’t we know of this?” asked Kris as she leaned around Doug.

“Did they even bind books so long ago?” Will asked.

Quani was frowning. “Why would we forget such knowledge?”

“How did you get this?” Cathy voiced her own doubt.

Unfazed and seemingly unaware of the burning questions, Viz intoned, “Truly see-expand and be joyful.” Then he carefully drew back the cover to reveal the first image, which drew a gasp from Quani.

"That—that's the panels from my dream! How…?"

Nodding serenely, Viz finally answered, "As was shown to your mother of many generations before. Once again…the Essence chooses that you feel the import-connections-purpose. What she, your mother, would have called threads."

Quani chewed on her lower lip and sniffled, blinking sudden tears from her eyes lest they prevent her from *seeing*.

"The Essence?" Nolan queried, stretching impatiently for understanding that might connect this experience to his belief. "Do you mean God?"

Instead of answering, Viz turned the first page, which had every student leaning closer. Across the top of the pages were many dots and stars, and on the first page a finely drawn woman knelt with her arms held open, face upturned toward those stars. On the facing page, the woman slept curled upon the ground, wearing tranquility as a small smile. Beneath both images were rows of intricate symbols, complex enough to make cuneiform seem like childish scribbling.

Viz trailed a finger across them. "It reads 'Pray Long for Clarity of Truth, Wisdom, Understanding. Sleep beneath Infinite-Open.' Or perhaps more like 'heavens' to you." Looking up, Viz expounded. "The preparation to live-feel the great connection between thought and *being*…it is like gaining a glimpse of the eternal from your own personal waking-place."

Will squinted and tilted his head, trying to make sense of the symbols, to match them against what they supposedly meant, but this only made them shimmer in his vision. "How can you even know this, read this? Not like it can be translated on the internet, or can it?"

"Maybe the pictures—pictograms?—gave rise to our writing," Doug speculated. Kris shushed them both while squeezing Doug's arm.

Viz merely turned the next page. On one page was an intricate swirl resembling a fractal, and on the opposite page a chaotic jumble of fine drawings. Again, Viz traced a finger along the bottom symbols. "'From the Essence, Experience All Things. Grow in Understanding, Filling your Spirit.'" Looking up again, Viz commented, "A path-progression you have already found-been-shown, even without guides."

Will scratched at his chin, still squinting occasionally. "For an instruction manual, this is very barebones. How's someone expected to learn from this?"

Surprisingly, Viz seemed to match Will in his playfulness for a moment before answering seriously. "Who thinks they can learn from a book better than experience? Early students had much help, guides-paragons from many realms. This record is more honoring-reminding of the fundamentals."

"Lucky them," Quani murmured.

Viz smiled over his shoulder at her. "Yet together, you have begun the journey as though born with training.

Take comfort-confidence what talent you show is inspiring. But we must focus on this. Our time-situation is short." He turned another page.

On the left page was a spiral, an ornamented line that rose and expanded as it circled. "'All Things Cycle to Improve,'" Viz continued to read. On the other page were more lines, spiraling and intersecting as if they grew in an intricate interaction. And beneath were a jumble of symbols.

"'Even Dreams Cycle. One Step Before the Next. Preparation Dreams...'" At that point, Viz paused and turned to make eye contact with each. "Experiencing even brief-brushing glimpses of what can be possible is vital to prepare for deepening-elevating into what this refers to as 'Opening-Embracing-Knowing,' which is like a heart-key. You would use the term *empathy*."

Will was fidgeting. "Again, how can you *know* that type of stuff about us?"

"Instead of asking this of me," Viz instructed in his soft, calm cadence, "open further toward the possibilities and apply your dreaming experiences. When you reflect upon your own question, the answer will move through you. And with that one answer, you will connect to more question-opportunities."

The group analyst and connector was already following the line of thought. "You're not..." Quani struggled with herself to form the words and pass beyond her final barriers of doubt. "Not from *here*."

"How could I be?" The soft tone and straightforward logic triggered widening eyes and instinctive distancing, even if that was quickly amended.

Cathy was shaking her head as if to clear it. "Wait, wait! You're not...like us?"

And nearly at the same time she asked, Viz was answering, "In some ways, I am just like you: a student-explorer. As you now glimpse, learning offers gifts-without-end."

Cathy sputtered, "But *who are you*?" With a smile, Viz used a finger to trace one of the spirals in the book.

"This is about you, precious-bursting-eager ones, not of me. So please let me help you while I can." They could hear a new urgency in his voice, and they hung on his every word. His once measured words came in a rush: "So much you are not prepared for, but my heart-mind-wish is for your success in this opening-deepening you have begun."

Viz laid his hand upon the picture. "Note this drawing shows six travel-paths, intertwining, and in this I see more than coincidence. These reinforcing cycles cannot be skipped, so learn and relearn even as you grow-push into deeper knowledge. Roll each mistake-setback into your next cycle, and support-inspire each other. In a better time, your ancestors could display such affinity-empathy others would spend lifetimes to acquire, as if you were born-chosen to travel and serve the Great Role."

"Like knights," Will interjected softly.

"Knights?" Viz seemed to shift his head to the side in consideration. "Only in the best of meanings, and yet...yes, this is potentiality. In each of you, when together. This talent and hope..."

The book slammed shut with a suddenness that made those crowded around Viz jump. Instantly alert, he stood in a single fluid motion. "You have so much history to overcome-reject, but too-soon-they-come. We must leave," Viz said in a rush while the group followed him down the steps and onto the court.

"But who are 'they'?" asked Quani in a pleading voice as she struggled to keep up.

"I warned you of this path, though I promise to return when you are prepared."

As if on cue, a pair of well-dressed men dashed into the main entrance. "Found them!" one of the pair called out.

Again hugging the precious book to his chest, Viz turned a final time to them. "Flee-return the way you came. Do-not-be-caught. *GO!*" That final word was like a whisper rolling through every adrenaline-charged fiber of their being, and the group turned for the far exit.

"You, kids, stop!" called one of the intruders.

Nolan's chest tightened again, fiercely, like he would hyperventilate. He didn't have to imagine what an entire crowd's worth of this man would sound like, for he had been there. Upon dusty streets, he had pushed through the fear-hate and directed aggression.

Heads down and arms pumping, the girls were sprinting into the hallway and rounding the first corner. Yet Nolan found himself compelled to linger. What could he do? With that driving urge in him, he looked back.

"You cannot have what you reject!" Viz called, presenting himself as a distraction by performing a dramatic whirl. The book rolled out of his straightening arms and spun across the polished court, toward a darkened corner.

"Grab that!" one man commanded to others who were racing onto the court and then veering to retrieve it. The closest pair were spreading out, drawing weapons as they approached Viz, who was now standing still. Nolan dared to stop at the hallway, laying a hand upon the tiled corner toward freedom, yet unable to move away.

"This is not the path." It was a simple statement from Viz, spoken at the men yet also echoing through Nolan as he held his breath and clenched his teeth.

The men were wary, but Viz was passive, even as one reached for a back holster and whipped out an odd-shaped gun. In a swift arc, the man brought the strange gun to bear and fired. Needles and leads spread through the air with a *foomp*.

But Viz was simply no longer there.

And so too vanished Nolan's anxiety. He released his breath while twisting and racing down the hallway toward the others. He knew without any doubt he could outrun the men and catch the others, no matter how fast they might run. He could outrun the dark, he could outrun thought.

A *whoop* burst from his lungs as he cleared the doorway into the night. Will turned at the noise and so it was an easy thing to catch and sling an arm around him. While trotting toward the safety of the dorm complex, Nolan laughed and told him, "Yes, my friend, we are knights!"

297

Chapter 24

I'm near a city, foreign and yet familiar, from there and yet not *of* there. This affects me with a kind of disorientation, so instead I focus on the immediate.

My younger brother is a gangly teen on the cusp of adulthood who pours over books as though they hold the sum of his enlightenment. I hang out with him, humoring and even lightly teasing as I encourage him to look up and out. There is only so much preparatory understanding he can gain from study. Inspired by memories of my own time, I regale him with stories most playful and informative, of how the world *can* be for him too. But of course that would require him leaving behind his books.

Despite my bold example he remains hesitant, so with a sigh of disappointment, I give detailed directions for him to take the next steps. I promise he won't regret it. "You have to *do* to feel right," I offer as a final encouragement before leaving to begin my adventurous stroll.

With anticipation, I cut through the small park and onto familiar trails, toward the dense cluster of buildings rising tall above the tree line. The musing that these paths are well worn by others offers comfort. Yet while I move across yards that should be cared for, I notice signs of neglect—tell-tale signs that actually worsen as I near the hustle and bustle.

Soft grass becomes offensive weeds, high and threatening to strangle the paths I once again tread. Homes become eyesores, testaments to the no-longer-caring, down times of the spirit. I swing wide to avoid a structure that emanates more than just disrepair, but something more insidious.

Trading earthen paths for the paved, I turn the corner to my vague destination. But I pause and balk, feeling the vibe of the dingy. Seediness has replaced any brightness of progress. Now I worry a bit, recalling that my directions would take my younger brother through this. For the first time, I hope he is *not* following my instruction. He isn't prepared to experience this—*no* one is. Nor should they have to be.

Feeling bummed, I veer toward cleaner areas. Following another vague urge, I search for comfort. I need to feel and share the zest for life, the anticipating and savoring and *adventure*. I find myself in a house crowded with many generations: high-pitched giggles of delight, amusement and cooed encouragement of the elderly, the impatient bustle of teenagers. And in the midst, I soak in the gaiety and feel a moment of contentment.

"Hey," says a man with a stern frown. "You don't belong in my house, do you? Who are you—why are you here?"

I feel the urge to answer and mollify while the realization washes over me that I am an interruption to his daily process of overseeing this successful family. And with dawning discomfort, I find nothing to say, no justification. When he points toward the door and orders me out, I am only left with the need to comply, though it saddens me to leave this sanctuary so soon. I find the hallway leading to the front door, a path I have no memory of previously walking, which is again very disorienting. I manage to make my way outside, away from the shelter and once more into the sounds of city hyper-activity.

In the front yard is a young girl who has just unhooked her bike from the fence and secured her backpack. She glances back to the house, notices me, my sorry state, and smiles warmly at me. After winking as if to tell me it'll be alright, to regroup and get back out there, she performs a run-hop that mounts her onto her bike and sends them through the gate and off into the world. Watching her go and remembering that knowing wink, I feel a little better about doing the same. But only a little bit.

*   *   *

"I also had an upsetting dream," Kris admitted to Doug while lending her comfort after he finished relaying the disturbing sequence.

The previous night while regrouping outside Doug's dorm, Cathy had admitted she wouldn't be able to sleep at all if they separated. Kris quickly followed up with the idea that they cram into their apartment with the guys sleeping on the couch and on blankets in the living room. Will joked that she just wanted them to be first in the line of fire when men burst through the door; unsurprisingly, his humor fell flat since it only inflamed their imaginations.

Despite Nolan's exciting revelation about Viz, the unknown men and unseen pressure loomed large over them. So they quickly piled into their cars and caravanned to the apartment. Some had wanted to discuss every angle and idea, but others had just wanted the calm and quiet of sleep. They compromised, settling on group comforts like, "It will be alright," and, "We'll figure it out," before turning in.

Now, they sat in momentary silence huddled over cups of coffee, still struggling through a whirlwind of emotions. No one knew quite what to make of the tumultuous events. It was clear neither Cathy nor Will got much sleep, and Quani admitted with tears threatening that she spent much of the time trying not to cry.

"I don't know what I will do if they come for us," she said. Just the admission started her softly weeping, and the other girls moved to flank and comfort.

In earnest, Nolan leaned toward her. "I don't think Viz would allow that. I mean if we were truly in danger." Will made a derisive noise but it seemed to help Quani, and so Nolan continued, "I'm not saying I know how. I'm just saying I saw him *control* that situation last night."

"It has occurred to me," Doug mused agreeably, "how he managed everything just as we might do in our best dreams."

Nolan was nodding, excitement back in his tone. "I think he's been doing this longer than we've been alive!"

Again, Will interjected. "Like this was all just a bad dream for him..." Despite his playful mocking, Will's tone betrayed his interest, and they were all perking up.

"Think about it," Nolan encouraged. "He knew exactly when and where to be, despite us being early. He knew exactly what to say, and acted like he knew the moment they had arrived and when to move. And I swear to you, he stayed just long enough to protect us. By the time he went poof, there was *no way* those men could have caught us!"

Quani sniffled and smiled an apology, wiping her eyes and asking, "Do you really think he was dreaming? It all...he seemed solid to me."

Nolan leaned back enough to make the chair creak. "Maybe, maybe not. In the message, he mentioned my travel dream, so maybe like that? All I know is it was fast, faster than their weapons, faster than I could blink." After chewing at his lip, he said, "Still, I know this much: he's right that we have so much to learn. He made a promise to return, and I believe that as much as anything."

Into the easing tension, Will rubbed his hands and adopted his boyish grin. "I wonder if we could ever get that good. Just show up or poof whenever."

"Like your contagious superpowers dream?" Quani reminded him, amused at his comical pole-axed expression.

"Oh, snap, you're right! It had G-man problems in it and everything—do you think I was dreaming of the future?" In a rarity for Will, he was instantly and completely somber. "It was very much a hide-what-you-got thing, not because it was bad or wrong, but because of *other people*! Just like Viz was trying to get us to do!"

While Will was busy being dumbstruck, Doug made the next connection. "I guess we should take down the dream site. Not sure how we should go about it..."

"No way am I putting more dreams out there for those assholes to read!" Will said with fiery conviction. "I say we delete the lot."

Wincing, Cathy complained, "But all our work and connections—I don't think I can do the same without it!"

"No way is it secure or safe," Nolan pointed out.

Fanning herself with a hand, Cathy said, "But guys…" And then she began to cry. "I *love* what we do with it," she stated while weeping. "It's *good*!"

Doug closed the distance to the couch and knelt, enfolding her in his arms, and as others joined in, Cathy tucked her head and bawled. "I love what we do," she repeated.

"We do too," Kris assured her while rubbing her back and searching for the right thing to say. "We'll find a way…maybe save all the data offline."

"Yeah," Doug said in a conciliatory tone. "We can maintain it on our personal laptops. Share new dreams by swapping jump drives, or just, I don't know, hide the sensitive stuff better."

Will broke the group huddle so he could pace. "But it's still not *private*! I'd totally call out these guys, expose and get them royally screwed over if I could think of a way. News or campus police or something like a coordinated blast of information they cannot suppress."

"But that's the bad kind," Quani countered in a soothing voice. "Aggression."

"Hey, it's not aggression to make them pay for doing this to us!" Relenting, he said, "I know, I know. I'm just frustrated."

"If you go after them," Nolan predicted as he disengaged and returned to his seat, "that'd only make things worse. And I think Viz was right. If we hadn't posted what we did or had removed it when he asked, then they never would've shown up. He implied as much in what he said to us."

Still gently rubbing Cathy's back, Kris stated, "I don't think we should delete anything, and maybe only temporarily take the site offline. We can make up something for Cassie and our other followers—tell them we're doing internal review and making adjustments or upgrades."

Doug could feel Cathy nod against his shoulder and so he added his agreement. "Yeah, it should stop the attention, and we have to at least keep our word to Viz. Maybe we'll make a separate and totally private space just for us. Can we do that?"

Cathy straightened, sniffled, and rubbed at her eyes. "Maybe. Yeah, I think so."

"And we will never lose this, what we have." Doug's confirmation made Cathy cry again, but this was a cleansing cry supported by lots of affirming nods and hugs. And they continued to support her as a group while she opened her laptop, took deep, calming breaths, and began making the necessary changes.

After a while, Quani cleared her throat before saying, "I hate to bring this up, but I should head back to my dorm and get ready. My first class is in less than an hour, but... I don't want to leave."

Will gave her a knowing grin. "So be a rebel and skip class like I'm doing." Doug let out an amused chuckle yet shook his head.

"Not the right way to handle this. We can't just hide out, and I refuse to."

"He'd not want that for us, I think," Nolan speculated, and everyone knew who he meant.

In agreement, Kris rose to collect her car keys. "We need to push through this," she added her resolve, "and figure out how to carry on doing our thing."

Even Will caught the renewed determination. "And acing the upcoming finals."

"Can we hang out more often?" Quani asked.

While Kris nodded, Cathy said, "Oh, definitely! And I'm sticking to crowds for a while."

"Yeah, stick to crowds and if they approach you, play dumb and scared," Will suggested. Then raising his hands, he began a comic playacting. "Huh, what? I don't know anything about your so-called dreams."

Cathy shook her head and sent a *tsk* his way. "I don't have to *fake* being scared. Anyone *not* scared has no sense!" Turning to Nolan, she gave him a sheepish smile.

"With that out there hanging in the air, would you mind not leaving until my roomie returns from dropping them off?" He readily agreed, settling across the table from her.

Keys jingling as they dangled from her hand, Kris held up her phone, saying, "And we'll keep in touch."

The two staying behind watched the others pile out the door with Will saying, "How much can they even monitor? Maybe they have satellites on us."

Kris' sassy response came as the door was being closed: "Then just don't say anything incriminating, goof."

* * *

Each day of normal activity lessened the students' worst fears. Even their dreams were muted. By the beginning of the next school week, they began transforming their worry into a caution that wouldn't interrupt their classwork. Emotionally, they helped each other renew their shared determination for adventure and learning, though this new push was tempered with a newfound wariness. They felt how their dreaming had both warned and prepared them for this balancing act.

Since they had spent so much time together working through their own issues, the pre-meet at the coffeehouse was dominated by the upcoming problem of Mark. Viz's warnings now carried exceptional weight, and so they all agreed on the importance of hiding both the inspiring and distressing revelations. But this was far easier said than done. The previous dream meet had been strained when all they were withholding was Viz's initial contact.

"I will only speak for myself," Quani said in a way they knew she was confirming for them all. "I see no way to keep this from him while still discussing our dreams."

"Even if we were successful at ignoring the elephant in the room," Kris agreed with slow nods, "we would spend more time pretending dreams don't mean what they mean than making progress on them."

Will made a dismissive motion. "Mark would see through the pretense."

"Exactly my point." Kris settled back in her chair with a sigh, and Doug squeezed her hand in support. "But how? We can't just *not* show up to something that's been so important to us all this time!"

"No way are we treating Mark like that," Cathy said with a determined set of her jaw, ready to argue with anyone who would dare mistreat their first guide and counselor. All she received were nods and a couple of resigned shrugs.

"I don't know...maybe," Nolan began, "we make our own reasons for ending the weekly meetings. I can say that I'm focusing on my upcoming graduation and have to commit extra time."

Will asked, "How do you even know that's not the truth?"

"I don't," Nolan replied with a grimace. "And I probably should find out."

"But that doesn't help us," Quani pointed out. "Remember he's still our freshman mentor."

Will joked in a singsong tone, *"Awkward."*

Kris was quick to respond: "I don't think so, if we're talking about classes and finals and normal stuff. I just wish we could pretend for the last few weeks."

"But I can't sit there and lie to him." With a furrowed brow, Cathy shook her head. "I just don't think I can pull it off, and you know he will start prying."

"Agreed," Doug said while leaning forward. "We cannot skip the meetings, and yet we can't pretend. It'll be tough on us and maybe on Mark, but that's not as bad as the alternative. Let's keep that firmly in mind. Drawing him into this would be bad for *him*." Amid nods, he continued, "If we need to focus on our finals, and Nolan on his graduation, then it makes perfect sense for us to cut back on dreaming, which was the reason for the meetings."

Will made like he was dusting off his hands. "Yeah, simple. And anyway, I wouldn't want to continue unless we could all make it."

Of course, the reality was never going to be that simple. They met outside the building and confirmed to each other that they could manage this: cancelling the dream meets and saying their goodbyes to Mark. Yet still they delayed until the last possible minute. When they arrived, Mark was already settled on his couch and smiling up at them. What washed over them was the sudden realization they would lose all this wonderfulness, the kernel—the joy—that had allowed dreams to grow within them.

Before they were more than three steps inside the room, the group staggered to a halt. "I see you have more news," Mark commented easily, though his smile faded a bit.

"Well, it's kind of bad news," Doug began.

Cathy quickly added, "For the group—our group."

Mark motioned around to the empty seats. "So settle in and tell me about it. This is what I'm here for."

Still frozen with her backpack clutched to her chest, Cathy said, "I'm so sorry but we can't keep up these meetings with finals approaching."

"And I need more *normal*, to focus on my upcoming graduation," Nolan mumbled. "Wish I had more time."

"And if we can't all make it..." Will shrugged.

"I see," Mark said amicably. "Saddening, though I was getting some sense of this at the last meeting. I'm sure we'll all miss this, but we can always chat about grounded stuff, finals and graduation."

Fighting back her tears, Cathy set her pack on the ground and held out her arms. Mark had just enough time to stand before she embraced him. In a shaking voice, she said, "We're all *so* grateful to you, for this."

"You helped make this group special," Kris added, joining in the hug, quickly followed by the others.

Doug reached over Kris to squeeze Mark's shoulder, saying, "We'll never forget this time and how you helped us."

Recovering slightly from his surprise, Mark said, "Thank you. I'm deeply moved, truly. Thanks to each of you for being such amazing students." Then Cathy began crying and squeezing him tight, but she bit her lip and kept her promise to herself so Mark could remain safe.

Chapter 25

"So…" Once again the totem pole of heads was peeking at Doug from around the adjoining door's frame. When Tim hesitated, Donna nudged him and then finished the sentence when he took too long.

"We've noticed you're kind of down," she said to Doug. "Is everything okay? Want to talk about it?"

Doug closed his notebook and leaned back in his chair. Though touched that they would notice, he realized he wasn't doing a good enough job at hiding his distress. "Just added stuff on top of exams, trying not to get distracted so I can finish strong. Maybe a little tired."

Nodding sagely, Tim said, "Oh yeah, you will adjust as she whips you into shape—maybe literally. *Whippow!*" In time with the whipping sound, he spanked his girlfriend, who in turn smacked his chest.

"No, you horndog. He's obviously just stressed and needs to blow off steam. Dancing tonight—come with us, and bring your cutie!"

Tim added, "Yeah, it's been like a week or more since we've partied."

"That does sound nice," Doug admitted with relief that they bought his story. "I'll ask her, but remember this is her first time dealing with finals, and she's pulling an eighteen-hour load."

"Yikes!" Tim grimaced in imagined pain. "If I had to deal with more than nine hours, I'd never get to *live*!"

Doug poked at his roommate: "Which is why you'll be living here for many more years."

"Living the *good* life!" Tim countered. "So, hurry up with that studying nonsense and let's get rolling!" He began strutting and scooting in the doorway before wrapping an arm around his giggling girlfriend and disappearing from sight.

Kris declined the offer not only because she was struggling to maintain top grades, but also because she didn't enjoy dancing. The Senior Ball in high school was enough for her; it was a noisy, messy jumble, and dancing made her feel too exposed. Like putting only one part of herself on display for leering boys and competitive girls. She knew some people just found it fun, but what was the use in pretending?

Besides, that particular night she was helping Cathy carefully word a response—now well aware that anything they sent might be monitored—to the always inquisitive high school senior, Cassie. The budding dreamer had been perceptive enough to note that while the older girls still offered life advice and tales of college fun and trials, they had gone silent about their dreaming exploration. Rightfully so since the site had been taken offline, Cassie had asked why they had turned evasive, and there was no easy answer to satisfy her. The roommates had agreed that in some ways, Cassie needed just as much protecting as Mark did.

Cathy was still suffering about Mark, who had casually inquired about their dreaming progress during two separate freshman meetings. It was clear he missed their dream meets, perhaps even more than they did. This made Cathy feel sick all over again about the whole situation, with its uncomfortable revelations and increased unknowns and the need to feel so closed off. This was *not* in her nature, and it felt too much like a betrayal of self. She hadn't trusted herself to have an in-depth conversation about it with him, and so had been more flippant than she wanted to be.

At one of their final coffee meets, Cathy vented to the group about it as well as her lack of interesting dreams. "It's like going back to square one!" she stressed, her normally cheerful countenance held in check by a look of simmering frustration.

"Yeah, I got nothing," Nolan also admitted.

Will leaned forward, saying, "It's as if the dreams have also gone into hiding. My style is *so* cramped—I'm actually catching up on my sleep!"

"Let's remain patient," Doug counseled. "Look at it as a needed break while we deal with school and let the dust settle. I think it's significant that we're all dreaming less."

"Except you've had some," Will countered, stubbornly refusing to see the point.

"Only a few, cautionary—I think—and certainly not much fun."

Cathy grumped, "How long must we hang in this...limbo? Everything is so slow and boring without them!"

"You mean 'normal'?" Will teased, though everyone could tell his heart wasn't in it. They huddled in silence for a while, stirring over-stirred coffee, or sipping lukewarm remnants.

"Yep," Nolan said just to have something to say. "I miss them...and I miss us picking them apart."

"When it was only a game," Will added.

Kris brushed the air with her hand. "But would you really give up knowing there's more to it? To go back, rather than going forward?"

"But where *is* forward?" Cathy asked.

"We'll know that when we push toward it, right?" Doug's tone was loaded with encouragement. "I know the good dreams will return when we're ready for them, and maybe that's just it: now we need to take them seriously in some way that opens us to more...depth, meaning, something."

Nolan was nodding. "Yeah. Just as Viz promised to return, so will the dreams."

Will arched an eyebrow. "And when he does, he'll be drowned beneath our tidal wave of questions."

"Shh," Cathy hushed, letting the group playfulness ease her tension, "don't let him hear that or he might delay his visit."

Quani caught their attention and their mirth with her single addition. "We can prepare by making many lists of questions."

* * *

"I wasn't walking or riding through the field, but I was moving...somehow." Kris was in the middle of recounting a dream that had prompted an additional group meeting amid the stress and anxiety of finals week. "It was flat and featureless, or so I thought, like going through a uniform field of wheat for the umpteenth time. But in the distance, on the horizon... It was a city of gleaming towers and ornamental bridges and buildings, so beautiful that I literally have no words."

With intensity, she leaned in toward the others. "But here's the thing: even if I could describe it in exact detail, it wouldn't matter, because—amazingly—I knew the city could be anything or look like anything. Like I could mold it or influence it, but even that isn't right because it had nothing to do with *me*, personally. But I know for a fact that the vision could and would change *as needed*."

When she was clearly done, and in an attempt to help, Doug asked, "Like it could change for you, based on your need?"

"Or perhaps that you were there because it was what you needed?" Will speculated.

315

With tears forming, Kris said in an emotional voice, "Yes, and yes, and...more. I don't know, but it was promise and stimulation and *relief*!"

Cathy stood with arms held open. "Oh, how I missed this!" she exclaimed while they hugged. After lingering in that shared moment, they returned to their seats, trading contented smiles. No one else had a dream worth mentioning, but now they felt the truth of their convictions, that when they were ready and hungered for them and reached for them and opened to them, dreams would return like a bright spring day after an unseasonable stretch of gloomy weather.

As the group talked about what the city alluded to and what that feeling of promise meant, whether intellectual or spiritual or some balance of both, or something altogether different, Doug looked around at their rebound of enthusiasm. "And we can now view these with newly opened eyes."

With a giggle, Cathy added, "Even if we're still lost."

"Exploring," Will corrected with a finger in the air to say, This Is Important. "Explorers are never lost."

Not to be outdone, Nolan said, "Or maybe they are always lost, by design."

"A quibble." Will tapped his nose at the perspective shift before grinning again. "The important thing is that we search without ever feeling at a loss."

Doug agreed. "The searching is part of the gift, this treasure we've discovered."

"And here's to treasure," Will crowed in a slight pirate-y tone while holding aloft his now-empty coffee cup. Though some rolled their eyes, all participated in the toast before heading for refills.

While enjoying another round of caffeine and with all their spirits lifted, Nolan found the right opportunity to address what was on his mind. "So, my graduation is six days from today. I have all the details now, and even have my cap and gown ready for pickup."

"You sure you're going to pass?" Will teased, and Nolan chuckled.

"I could skip my last final and still be fine. So, are you all able to make it?" He didn't even have time to hold his breath in anticipation before getting confirmations from each of them.

"I received permission to stay until then," Quani said quickly.

With a warm smile, Doug answered, "I wouldn't miss it, buddy. Summer classes don't begin for about three weeks, so I just need details."

So pleased that they could all attend, Nolan joked, "I can show you how it's done, the proper strut and all."

"Oh, you're definitely tripping over your hem now," Cathy predicted with a laugh, and Will added, "And none of us would dare miss that!"

The group support was the last piece he needed to finalize his decision. "As for after graduation," Nolan continued, "a career can wait. I've decided to find a job here locally, at least until you all graduate. For what we do, being long distance would suck."

"Oh, that's great news," Kris said amid similar sentiments from the others. "Find a job for Doug while you're at it."

"I know it's against the odds," Nolan said, "but I hope we can stay in the same area."

*   *   *

Since their parents lived in opposite directions, Doug and Kris spent as much time together as possible. Sunny days meant time for strolling hand-in-hand around the campus or through the local parks. Rainy days just meant more time cuddling together on the couch, sharing and learning from each other.

Despite not wanting to be separated, Doug had firm plans to gain six more credit-hours at the local college. In addition, he would return to a part-time job to help his parents pay for his education. He had confirmed both of these plans before he had any clue of the romance that would have him wishing he could obsolete his previous schedule. And since it was her first year away from home, Kris' parents would want her to spend the majority of the break with them. Through a family friend, they had arranged an internship at the local newspaper.

So, the lovebirds savored every moment together, even if they only gazed and smiled and let the larger-than-words pass between them. The only promise they could make was to look for ways to bridge the twelve-plus-hour-drive between them so they wouldn't have to be apart all summer.

When Nolan's big day arrived, Kris showed up early at Doug's dorm so she could rummage through his clothes and pick out what he should wear. Amused, Doug asked if this was how it would be from now on. She grabbed the front of his shirt and pulled him in for a quick kiss before answering with a smirk, "No, of course not...because you will learn to read my mind. Now let me have my fun."

The commencement ceremony was everything that people like to forget: lengthy and droning, a final test of endurance for those who desire to have their diplomas handed to them by a longsuffering professor. The group sat near the back, huddled together for this final day, and tried not to titter when Will quietly added his own flavor to the speaker's overly serious elocution. And when at last Nolan crossed the stage, they (just barely) observed the request to refrain from cheering until the end. Though when Nolan looked out across the audience wearing a proud smile, placeholder diploma now in hand, he spied a cluster of waving arms.

Once the caps were tossed by those who survived the ordeal, the group quickly converged. "Thanks so much for coming," Nolan told them before gesturing to the lady at his side. "Everyone, this is my mother, Gamon. Mother, these are the great friends I told you about."

"We figured as much," Will said while wearing his goofy grin, "since we know you aren't into hugging strangers."

"See what I warned you about?" Nolan told his mother as she chuckled and held out her hand, only to be given five more hugs.

The group clung to each other, affirming their friendship and already wishing for the time when the fall semester would bring them all back together.

Cathy fanned herself with a hand. "I won't cry, I won't cry," she said and was then struck by a random thought. "You know, I've cried more in these past few weeks than in all the rest of my adult life."

Will snorted. "Which has only been for what, like nine or ten months now?"

"Technicalities!" she defended her thought. "My point is this has been a stressful time, but we've been together, had each other. And now…"

"Don't dwell on it, roomie," Kris said with another hug for her anxious friend. "Just enjoy your summer activities, and it will pass soon enough. If Doug and I can survive it, then you all can."

They lingered as long as they could, but Nolan needed to spend time with his mother, Doug had an evening flight to catch, and Quani's father would soon be arriving to take her home. One by one, they gave their final hugs and then went their separate ways.

Cathy

When she spied who was waiting for her at the airport, Cathy had the momentary wish her flight had been canceled rather than merely delayed.

"Aww, little sis!" Tina crowed at a cringe-worthy volume while holding out her arms. "Bring it in, bring it home." When Cathy only rolled her eyes, the older sibling insisted. "Come on. Let's give onlookers something to dream about."

"Seriously, Tina," Cathy grumped while letting herself be bear-hugged. "I thought Mom was meeting me."

Tina pouted. "Am I not fancy enough for you?"

"Don't start that again."

Keeping one arm slung over her shoulder, Tina flipped her other hand dismissively. "When we found out your flight would be late, I suggested coming instead—pity me! I'm starved for fun that isn't fit for babies, ya know? Even if all I get is driving you around and living vicariously through your college adventures. Now come on before you have to pay my parking ticket!"

Though her sister did most of the talking, Cathy managed to share a few stories about vibrant college environments and quirky professor behavior. While getting bombarded with questions and other prompts, she steered clear of anything that would bring up her dream group and their trials. She already missed her friends, and it had been less than two days since those final hugs at Nolan's graduation!

Once they reached the modest, cozy home, Cathy was greeted by her mother's proud smile and a cheering four-year-old nephew. Both demanded hugs and attention, so each got double the hugs and tailored information: to her mother she told of the tough yet successful year, digging through her purse to find and present the printed report card, and to her wide-eyed nephew, Devin, she told of friends full of fun ideas and laughter.

"You wouldn't believe how big the playgrounds are!" she told him, making him giggle with a few well-placed tickles. "Giant pools and slides and things to climb on—oh, and lots of music!"

"Oh! Like Barney?"

Cathy laughed and said, "I'm sure somewhere they play Barney music." To her sister, she made an I-don't-really-know face and shrugged.

"Then I should go there, too!" Devin stated with that amusing child logic.

"You can when you get to be my age." Unable to resist, Cathy smirked at her sister. "I'm sure by that time your mother will have saved up enough."

"Anyhoo," Tina drawled, changing the subject. "You should get settled in before we go eat."

Their mother chimed in, "Yes, your father is meeting us at the steakhouse to celebrate."

* * *

It had only been two weeks and Cathy was already bored of summer break, falling asleep reading books that barely held her interest, amusing her nephew and yet struggling to minimize the times her sister dragged her on some mindless errand, and wishing she could do more than see her friends on a screen. She began toying with the idea of building a new website just for them. But how to ensure their work was private without selling her soul to the dark side?

She knew just enough to understand the complexity required to VPN-host and hide a webserver, a level of sophistication she did not have nor *want* to have. A few hours of searching also told her that the blog scene was even worse than what they had; it invited exposure in a way that would clearly be another mistake. Managing a private message group seemed to be as low profile as they could get without being physically near each other, and yet it meant almost no control over their own material and what happened to it. Besides, she wanted it to be more than a basic messaging setup, except now she was scared that any web work they did would have too large of a public footprint. The only thing she knew for sure was the loss of their site itched and pained her like a phantom limb.

She was lounging in bed, humming and considering various options when she heard the chime of a new email notification. The humming died in her clenched throat when she tabbed to her mail and saw an official-looking seal with the words ringing it: Department of Justice, Federal Bureau of Investigation.

Hello, Cathy. My name is Julie. My partner, Daniel, and I are with the public relations department of the FBI. We would like to offer our sincerest apologies for what happened on your campus, and need to find out more about the actions taken by one of our field teams. We would like to understand what led up to this, about the stranger, and how we can better protect you in the future. I will be in your area for the next several days so you can help us answer these questions. Please let me know where you would be most comfortable meeting to discuss this sensitive subject.

Sincerely, Julie Trival, Office of Public Affairs, Federal Bureau of Investigation

"Oh, dookie!" Cathy breathed to herself and then chewed on her lower lip while rereading the message. Those men at the basketball court didn't act like FBI—at least not from any show she had seen! She was tempted to hit the delete button.

But that wouldn't really make the problem go away. The anxiety they were all feeling might get worse. She looked around her room, safe in her parents' home, in her small town with its four stoplights and as many decent restaurants. This was safe heartland America, right? And if she refused to see them, who would they turn to next? Doug? Nolan? Or Kris? It had been her idea to make the website and buy the hosting, after all. Could she put on a brave face and meet the ones Viz had warned them about?

She shivered and felt a tinge of nausea.

Regardless of her misgivings, she pursed her lips in determination and wrote a courteous reply, setting a midmorning time for tomorrow. Her father knew the owners and staff at the steakhouse in town, and her family regularly ate there. So if she went missing, someone would surely avenge her.

As an afterthought, she forwarded the email thread to Kris, adding, "If you don't hear from me by tomorrow afternoon, hire protection and publish this!" She chuckled with dark humor and had to admit this would be the most excitement she was likely get all summer. Predictably, Kris called her that afternoon.

"Goodness, girl! What have you gotten yourself into?"

Cathy shrugged, even though it was unlikely that the close phone camera would relay the motion. "Now you know as much as I do—except for a short confirmation that this is happening. I just wanted to share my nervousness because I knew you'd understand."

"You don't have to go."

Cathy let out a barked laugh and exclaimed, "That was my first instinct, too! But of course I have to. If this had come to you, would you hide?"

After a moment's thought, Kris shook her head. "You're right. I'd go, even if it was only to pacify them. Be sure to make them give you more than you give them. Don't be afraid to question them about how they knew and why they barged in like that."

"I know." Cathy sighed before continuing, "Of course, that's easy to *say*..."

"Yeah, but you'll do great, roomie."

"Thanks, I needed to hear that. And I need a hug badly!" Cathy laughed at herself, but her understanding roommate just nodded soberly.

"You call me as soon as it's over, okay? Even if I have to burn my lunch break—which I rarely have time to take!—I'll stop everything for your call. You can tell me all about it then."

"Right." Cathy took a deep breath while nodding. "I look forward to this being over. Now I think I need to go flop in front of the television and distract myself."

The next day, Cathy made excuses to her mother and then drove to the steakhouse right as they were opening. Since they didn't serve breakfast, the best way to assure elbow room was to show up before the early lunch crowd. She reserved a table along the back wall so it was away from the general traffic areas, settled in to wait, and concentrated on not chewing her fingernails.

The moment they walked in the door, Cathy knew it was them. The tall blonde was scanning the inside before her sunglasses were hooked onto her blouse, and the duo's sharp suits screamed official business—especially in an area where ninety-nine percent of the population wore blue jeans. Cathy stood and gave a small wave, though she need not have bothered because they were already heading toward her.

"Cathy," Julie greeted in a friendly tone to match her bright smile and extended hand. "It's really good to meet you." Then Julie motioned to the man hovering at her shoulder tight enough to be a bodyguard. "This is my partner, Daniel."

After the firm handshake and courteous nod from Daniel, they settled around the table and ordered coffee. "I hope they make it strong here," Julie said with another one of her bright smiles. "We're still feeling the jet lag." Cathy saw nothing but alertness and confidence with no strand of hair out of place.

"You…" Cathy began and then tried to swallow her anxiety, "didn't need to fly out here. Did you?"

Julie touched her chest above her heart with manicured fingernails. "This big of an apology cannot be done via email or a phone call, don't you agree?"

"I guess…" Cathy caught herself fidgeting with her napkin's edge and made her hands go still. They remained quiet while a waiter poured their coffee and inquired about lunch.

"Nothing for us, thanks, but, Cathy, you can order anything you want."

"No, thanks," she mumbled.

"You sure? Our treat."

Leaning forward and arching an eyebrow, Daniel stated, "We'll order if you order."

Cathy shook her head, already feeling what would happen if she were to eat. "Not sure that's a good idea."

Julie released the waiter before showing a face full of empathy. "Please, don't be nervous. We are the ones who mishandled the situation. If I had been alerted and in charge, it could have been a pleasant meeting, as long as all of you were safe."

"Please, accept our deepest apology," echoed her partner. Cathy could only nod as she glanced at each of them and then down at the table. The vibe she felt seemed conflicted, at odds between the calming words and their alert postures, between the cozy, familiar restaurant and her memories of the gym.

After a titter, she blurted, "You're not what I was expecting."

Julie's brow arched in amusement. "Oh? You expected the FBI to be all lawyer cops? It's as huge and diverse an organization as any." Placing a ringed hand flat on the table, she explained, "We're in the Public Affairs department for the very reason that we're involved, caring...you know, in public affairs."

They let the moment stretch, taking the first tentative sips of their coffee. "Mm, good coffee," Julie noted. "This hits the spot."

Cathy admitted, "Yeah. Not at all like the stuff we buy at school."

Flashing her bright smile, Julie said, "I remember those days well. Wasn't so long ago—did you know the FBI recruited me directly from college? They often do that with promising students. From my junior year onward, I was getting twice the education."

Remembering Kris' admonition to her, Cathy glanced to Daniel. "And you? Same?"

"I took a different route," he replied with a slight twitch of his lips, "but I also remember plenty of cheap coffee."

They seemed content to let another silence stretch, so Cathy took a sip, a firm swallow, and then asked, "So why me? Why come to me?"

At ease with the opener, Julie casually extended an open palm. "It was your website that first alerted us something might be wrong. But don't worry—it simply makes you the best person to begin building a picture of what happened."

"Tell us about the visitor." Daniel leaned forward. "What was he like?"

Cathy noticed Julie cutting her eyes toward her partner and then perhaps catching herself. Did she disapprove of his eager impatience, or was this how they traded off? Cathy settled for the view of the cup in her hands and shrugged. The cup turned a complete circle in her fidgeting fingers before she answered aloud. "We don't know much about him—he was very mysterious, strange."

"But you met him," he insisted. "What did he seem like?"

"Well, definitely strange. But it was short, less time than this." Cathy's laugh was weak and nervous. "To be honest, we kind of tricked him into showing. We were just having fun, but now I feel bad about it."

"I know you're a perceptive young woman," Julie said in an encouraging tone. "What were your impressions? Of his character, of his motives?"

Cathy shrugged again. "He wanted us to stop, to remove some of the things we posted—well, at least to make them private. He seemed concerned for us, gentle, kind."

"What did he ask you to remove, and do you know why?" Julie pressed lightly.

"Some of our travel dreams and speculation about them." Cathy straightened. "Look, we were exploring and having fun. We just wanted to see what others found and add that to our own experiences. Honestly, we had no idea of the *mess* this would cause!"

She was about to say more, driven now by her misery and regret, but she caught a flash of sauntering cowboy boots out of the corner of her eye a second before she heard: "Are you two bothering this young lady?"

Mortified beyond words, she slowly turned her head to look up at her ex-boyfriend, with his thumbs hooked into his belt, striking a pose and probably thinking himself the hero.

Wearing a look that was a cross between amusement and annoyance, Julie pointedly ignored him and asked Cathy, "A friend of yours?"

"Gary," Cathy said, voice low from the effort to keep from grinding her teeth, "what are you doing here?"

"On lunch break with my compadres. You know, like *normal* people. Then I noticed you over here looking all distressed. Are they bothering you?"

Daniel seemed relaxed, but his glare was unwavering. "Did it occur to you that you might be interrupting? An interview?"

"For what job?" Gary shot back, shifting his weight as a way of broadcasting his machismo.

Julie held up hands in either direction. "Please, sir, we're trying to have a private conversation, and it's clear Cathy doesn't appreciate the interruption. Please." She made a gesture which asked him to back off.

"I'm just over here, Cathy. Remember Jeff's a deputy now and only a speed-dial away." When no one said more and Cathy just remained with her head in her hands, Gary backed away a couple steps before spinning on his booted heel.

"Oh my god," Cathy murmured.

"Boyfriend?"

Cathy lifted her head to see that the chagrin on Julie's face matched her tone. "Ex, and for good reason, though I think he's worse now than he was in high school. I'm so sorry. I can't guarantee he'll leave us alone."

"That's okay," Julie said with grace, rising and shouldering a thin purse in one smooth motion while her partner flipped a crisp twenty onto the table. "If you can think of anything else that would help us, please contact me on my email. By the way, did your school counselor know anything about this?" When Cathy only shook her head, Julie continued, "If only I had been there… Again, on behalf of the agency, please accept our apology."

Cathy nodded mutely, and couldn't move to follow them outside. There was no clear way to grasp onto what had just happened.

"You're welcome. And if you spin that cup any more you're gonna drill a hole in the table."

Standing near her again was the smirking motivation to rise and leave. She wanted to show her fangs, to tell him to drive in the opposite direction—or off a cliff. Maybe threaten to tell his wife of the unwanted attention. But instead, she could only manage to huff, "Gary, you're truly hopeless!"

Cathy sat in silence in the car for a while, and then drove slowly back to her parent's house. As nice as Julie and Daniel were to her, she had no doubt they didn't get all the information they wanted. Would they try to meet again or just move onto the others? Did she owe them any other information? She needed to hear from her roommate, and possibly from the entire group on this.

When she pulled into the driveway, she adopted an everything-is-fine face before hurrying to her room, closing the door and collapsing onto her bed. She spent a leisurely moment enjoying the serenity of her small space before dragging her phone from a deep hip pocket and calling Kris.

"That was fast," came Kris' quick answer. "Are you safe?"

"Yeah. They were less of a deal than Gary was."

"Uh oh. Look, let me call you back in about 30 minutes when I can go on break—they are working me like a dog!"

"I'll be here, trying not to pace—or cry."

"Chin up, girlfriend. I'll call soon and you can tell me the juicy details!"

Will

Will was spending his summer practicing what he had learned from his mother over the course of his childhood: making money owning and managing properties while claiming financial losses on them, all within a system that encouraged ownership. As he had grown from elementary to junior high to high school age, his mother had transitioned from successful realtor to broker to land owner. Because of her constant example, Will possessed insider knowledge on the process that made it all seem simple.

He still planned to finish his biology degree, even if it felt like more of a hobby than following his mother's path to financial independence. In reviewing his first year of college with its comfortably average grades for minimal effort, he knew the true value of this stage of his life was in meeting his new friends with their shared greater purpose. Biology was amusing, interesting, and all around him, a fine study in its own right, yet dreaming was *woven through all of it* in a way that made life something gloriously greater than accidental. So to his way of thinking, making easy money merely gave him the flexibility to pursue what was most important.

While he was still a minor, his mother had seeded his bank account with plenty of funds, so that as an adult he could buy a starter property from her. It was a low, long building on a quaint neighborhood street stuffed with four units which could not decide if they were apartments or condos in style. Among other minor upgrades, he planned to fence off the backyard area into individual garden plots while also using new landscaping in the front to further distinguish the units—or rather, to hide the fact they were all cut from the same cloth. Once he sufficiently blurred the line between apartment and condo, he could attract great tenants who acted more like owners than renters, and enjoy a steady stream of income for the foreseeable future.

And of course, his savvy mother used the sale to benefit them both. Her strategy allowed her to officially walk him through the paperwork cycle while still making more profit (and commission) from the previously seeded money and then reinvest that into other projects. During school years, she would help him lease and manage it once the remodeling was complete.

He was at his new property overseeing the fencing and landscaping crew when he got his email from Julie-of-the-FBI. In it, she explaining they had just met with his friend, Cathy, and were driving into his area next to be available for his earliest convenience. Will scrunched up his face in consternation, let out a "huh," and then tucked his phone back into his pocket. To be dealt with later. Whatever it was they had to say to him could wait until he got Cathy's side of the story.

He didn't have long to wait before getting a group message from Cathy briefly describing the meeting and asking to talk. "The sooner the better," Will responded with his own text, "because they are headed my way." And then because he couldn't wait, he ducked into an empty room, shut the door, and called her.

"I didn't mean right away, silly," Cathy said by way of an answer, and he matched her tone.

"Yeah, well I might not have enough time. You said your meeting was this morning, and I got an email from them more than an hour ago. And since we live only about two hours apart, you do the math."

"Yeah, well…" She gave a short laugh. "I'm just relieved they're done with me."

"So what did they want?"

"Like I said, they apologized for the gym disaster—"

"Those weren't FBI guys at the gym."

He could hear Cathy sigh. "That's what I thought, but then how does the FBI know, and why send their own?"

"A ruse, or some spy shit. Are you sure this Julie is FBI?"

"Why wouldn't she be? Her and her partner seemed legit to me. They seemed like nice people, so don't be a total jerk! Anyway, they were also digging for info on Viz, what was he like and so on. I only told them we were just playing around and kind of tricked him into showing up. Then my ex-boyfriend rudely interrupted so we didn't get further, though I guess that was for the best."

"Well, if they expect information out of me, they're going to be sad-faced."

"The less they learn about us the better, I agree, but at least be pleasant."

"Eh, you know me…"

"Yeah, I do." There was the tint of humoring in this laugh. "Which is why I encourage you to at least *try* to be nice."

"Yes, Mother."

He could hear the verbal equivalent of her tongue being stuck out at him. "Goodbye, brat. Don't get us in trouble. Remember our promise to Viz." He disconnected with a grin on his face, already making plans of how he would turn the tables on the supposed FBI agents.

The expected follow-up email came an hour later, informing him they had settled into a hotel and were anxious to meet wherever he felt most comfortable. Will let that email also sit until late afternoon, imagining them pacing—hoping they were pacing—before giving a casual reply to prove to them he wasn't rattled.

> Hello. I am finishing my business for the day and so am available. Any place is fine. Perhaps at the bar or restaurant in your hotel?

They chose to meet in the small restaurant across the street because it was likely to be quieter than their hotel's lounge. When he arrived and casually strolled in, the tall blonde who rose to shake his hand was prettier than she had any right to be—for someone into that hyper-prissy, sharp-and-cleverly-deceptive type—and Will was instantly wary from being thrown off balance by the warm visage and handshake.

"Thank you for agreeing to meet on such short notice," she said, broadcasting her bright smile. "I know we presume, so thank you for taking the time." As they sat down, she motioned to the man who had not offered a hand or bothered to introduce himself. "This is my partner, Daniel. On behalf of the department, please accept our sincere apology—"

Will interrupted though used his polite tone, "Might I see some ID?"

Julie looked annoyed for just an instant before reaching inside her jacket for her badge and handing it to him. Will detected a slight, amused smile as Daniel did the same. Regardless of whether or not Daniel had anticipated his move, Will was pleased with himself as he studied the badges, pausing to scrutinize each face and official seals before passing them back. Teach them to presume so much.

"You say you're here to apologize for the madness that happened at our gym," Will carefully prefaced his question, "but what exactly is the FBI's interest in this?"

"We want to make sure you understand how wrong our team was to behave like that, hence the personal visit to each of you. If I had been there, it would have been different." Her shrug seemed a little tired and much rehearsed.

"But you weren't there, because those goons who barged in on us were not FBI."

"Oh?" Exchanging glances with her partner, she replied showing a light touch of sarcasm, "Well now, that's certainly news to us."

"Let's put it this way: they didn't *act* like FBI."

Julie leaned forward. "Which is why we are here, and I assure you they are one of our field teams or, as you implied, we would not be here."

"There was no identifying—or wearing clear identification," Will said, trying to keep his anger at the memories carefully in check. "And then the drawing guns…"

"Terrible misjudgment."

"I'm certain there are laws, or you just end up being our Secret Police."

Daniel quirked an eyebrow and spoke for the first time. "Perhaps you watch too many dramas."

Julie let out a sigh of concession. "Would it ease your mind to know there is an ongoing, formal inquiry of all involved, with careers on the line? Please believe me when I say we don't take errors like that lightly."

Will felt he had them against the ropes, and searched for a way to keep them there. "You mentioned had you been there… How do you think it should have gone?"

Instead of being put off, Julie jumped at the opportunity to shift focus. "That's simple. No guns being drawn, for starters." Her bright smile was back. "I would have conversed with him, made certain he was not a danger to you. Could you sense any aggressiveness in him, get any hint of danger?"

"Not until your not-so-FBI guys showed up."

Julie leaned back in her chair. "It's been a really long day—twenty-four hours ago we were in D.C.—so please help us out just a little."

Will had no intention of letting her shift in tactics work on him. "In truth, you guys probably know more about him than we do. Our meeting was too short and too interrupted. To us, he remains a mystery." He shrugged as if it didn't really bother him much. "What do you know about him? I mean, why fly all the way out here to dig for answers we simply don't have?"

Julie worked her mouth like she was trying to suppress her agitation, to hold in a sigh of exasperation, or perhaps she was considering and rejecting what she should tell him. What she finally settled on was this: "The last *reported* manifestation by his kind happened long before any of us were born, so you might pardon us for our curiosity. I don't know more, so honestly, anything you can remember or feel might be significant."

Will couldn't help himself and cracked a grin. "Cue the X-Files music, right?"

"I told you they never should have made that show," her partner commented into the easing tension when Julie gave a muted laugh of surprise.

"To be quite fair to the show—which I liked, by the way," Julie responded to them both, "there's no evidence to rule out a connection with some of the unsolvable disappearances. And yes, we actually have teams of investigators trying to solve them."

"Sounds like plain old paranoia to me," Will commented lightheartedly. "I assume you recovered the book...?" Before the question was fully out of his mouth, he knew he had made a big mistake.

"Ah, that's right," Julie said, renewing her focus in an instant. "I remember reading he brought a book. What was it like?"

"You mean you didn't recover it?" Once it became clear they had no intention of answering, Will shrugged and measured his words. "It seemed ancient, but it was also bound. So, maybe not?"

"Describe it for us, please."

"Leather, I think—none of us touched it. Old, thick paper, parchment maybe? We just figured you guys had it." He continued to hang that question between them, hoping she would supply an answer.

Instead, she asked, "What was on the pages?"

Will stretched and stifled a yawn to buy himself time. "Excuse me." He found himself wanting to back away from the loaded questioning because answering or speculating would only buy him more scrutiny. The best he could manage was sounding vague. "He barely had the chance to open the book before your guys burst in. If only you had given us more time, because we were tossing around questions at a frantic pace." He knew that wouldn't satisfy them, and they would keep pushing, so he snorted flippantly. "I thought he was just a paranoid mental case, but at least in the mental part, I was happy to be proven wrong."

"Why is that?"

"Because we stumbled upon and drew out something truly bizarre. Which does explain why you're really here," Will added, letting them know he was onto their game. "But it doesn't make me happy I was wrong about the paranoid part. Look... If we had known it wasn't just fun and games, we'd have never made the website—or at least we would have removed the sensitive speculation. Who knew bold exploring could be so dangerous?"

With a casual gesture that wasn't at all casual in tone, Daniel chided, "Bold exploring is always dangerous."

Will had to beat back the rebel in him and swallow a couple of responses before he huffed, "Well, you should be satisfied now that the website is down. And by the way, Cathy was really torn up about that, but did it anyway out of fear of *your* goons."

Julie frowned. "We didn't know. As I said, it never should have happened that way."

"Yeah, I get that," Will grumbled, feeling like the wind was knocked out of him, "but it *did* happen and it sucked."

"And we're working to make sure it never happens again," she repeated smoothly. "Please, let us buy you dinner. We can call over the waitress. Maybe talk about something pleasant like summer plans."

Will looked up to see her apparently genuine concern, which bothered him almost as much as the partner's intense scrutiny, and he had a feeling this was one conversation he would never regain control over. Which also pissed him off. "I don't have much of an appetite."

Julie sighed in resignation, clearly seeing she could get little more from the stone wall. "I empathize, and can see your mind is already out the door. One final thing, I promise: tell us about your freshman counselor, Mark. How much does he know of this?"

"Why pry into his life, too?" Will's tone turned accusing. "We were asked to keep him completely in the dark about our explorations, and that advice, at least, we managed to keep."

With obvious satisfaction, she said, "Good advice, since I doubt he would understand, right?"

"Yep, advice from the same source who warned us about you guys. You know... I think we're done here." With that declaration, before he could let anything else slip, Will stood and walked out without looking back.

Kris

Kris was lying on her stomach in her bedroom, fluffy-slippered feet gently swaying back and forth while she considered her latest composition to Doug. What had begun as a witty one-sided conversation quickly devolved into a sappy love letter—oh, how she missed him! In such a short time, she had grown used to feeling him against her, *with* her, in a way that now made the surrounding air seem empty. In her head, she knew she needed to express herself in the safety of an unsent email, but she would have to redraft the entire thing, and sleep-time was fast approaching.

This is how epics become short blurbs, she mused to herself. *Our time runs out before we find the perfect way to say what is in our hearts*. She stifled a yawn, finger hovering over the delete key.

Then again, he *needed* to know how she felt for him. Perhaps just in a more lighthearted tone that wouldn't scare him off. Kris pursed her lips, moving them from side to side as she considered how to transform her pitiful prose into the cleverly romantic.

It was true enough that she felt the distance from him was making her heart wither, but ugh! No. How about instead the cheeky "I need my *you* fix, my withdrawal feels worse each day"? Also true—when she wasn't distracted by the stress of her frantic internship—and maybe less sappy than her first draft. As a bonus, the new wording transitioned smoothly into her wish: could he create enough of an opening in his packed schedule to visit, even for two or three days…even though that would mean more driving than visiting? It felt unfair yet vital to *them*.

She skimmed down until her mourning turned almost fatalistic. "How are we ever going to survive when so much of summer remains?" No need for both of them to wallow in the obvious. Perhaps replace the desperation with the need for a long phone call tomorrow evening when he finished doing homework. "At least call me," she summed up the thought, "so we can *sound* closer together. And plan for a long call. That way we can eat up more of the summer so it passes quicker!"

The following day, it seemed Kris' longing for Doug acted like blood in the water for sharks. First it was Curt, whose eyes lingered far too long on her body while complimenting her sharp dress. Then nearing the lunch break, Evan practically cornered her in the narrow copy room, diverting her attention from her paperwork to focus on him.

During her first day of introductions, she had been reminded so forcibly of Doug's detailed young-woman-new-job dream that Kris felt forewarned. She more easily avoided traps being set for her because of her group's discussions on the pitfalls and complex dynamics in that dream. After the initial lunch "party" where Evan and Curt bookended her in a booth, pressing their confident male auras into her personal space, she made sure to have a ready supply of excuses.

Now in those tight confines, Evan was using his tradecraft to subtly probe her. "I don't understand. Help me understand why you would snub our group when we get along so well." After getting nothing but dead air between them, he again filled the space. "It's just lunch—well, it is lunch at an amazing restaurant where *living* tops the menu! How can you say no to that? Many of the reporters are going. Come socialize, network. You know you're curious."

Their persistence finally forced Kris to show her fangs. "Look, Evan," she said, exasperated tone accompanied by a sigh. "You *really* have to pick someone else. You already know I have a boyfriend, and even if I didn't, I'd tell you I had one anyway."

Evan flinched in the face of her sudden scolding, yet he was smooth and practiced. While pressing a hand to his heart and grinning, he replied, "Don't do me like that, Kris." Relaxing against a wall, he gestured back and forth in the space between them. "No one said anything about a boyfriend/girlfriend—we're all too busy for something so quaint. But *serious* fun, blowing off steam, gaining experiences of a lifetime...this is how we cope. You'll see. You either have your outlets to make this all worth it, or you break. In this pressure cooker, there's no other option."

Kris shook her head to firmly reject his rationale. "Next time I won't ask politely; I'll report you. I'll use my father's connections if you make me." Everyone knew her father had gone to school with the managing editor, their direct boss. "Professional only from now on..." She was already pushing past him while the threat hung in the air between them. For the moment, she had made it crystal clear she wasn't a conquest-in-progress, and hoped fervently that it was enough to make both of them back off. She would be prepared regardless of whether or not they respected her wishes.

That evening after dinner while lounging on the back deck with her parents, she described her latest trials. They often shared daily events during their comfortable end-of-day family time. And true to their calling as teachers, Kris' parents understood and added to their previous good advice.

"You were right to take the next step," her mother, Barbara, counseled. "It seems stern warning looks weren't enough to curb their flirtation, and so at the risk of causing a scene, it becomes important to throw them to the mat…figuratively." She wore a small smile as she recognized the reference to her favorite sport, Judo. "Continue to be consistent. Don't even give them a smile or any toehold they can interpret wrong." Kris often found inspiration in her mother's blend of caring and firmness. Barbara could be kind yet at the same time show her strength of character as if hers was a steel backbone wrapped in velvet. Or perhaps what people sensed was her black belt in Judo and the associated, hard-earned confidence.

"*If* they were decent men, you wouldn't have to go this far, so be watchful," Dave, her calm yet always supportive father, added his warning. "If they even *seem* prepared to push, report them. As much as it pains me to acknowledge, there are men who will only stop if their way of life is threatened. So, don't let it come to that."

Kris nodded. "Yes, but *only* if they push… As you can imagine, the office relationships are very complicated, in a way that feels good-ol'-boy-like." She shrugged it off and mused, "It's so hectic there I don't see where they get the energy. In between the manic pace and constant loud conversations, phones ringing, keyboards frantically clicking... How can they find the single quiet moment to pester me? They are driven, I'll give them that."

Barbara tsked in general disapproval of pushy men. "There's letting someone know you're interested, and then there's trying to bowl them over and dominate them. Remember, if they do anything more, then they *deserve* to get in trouble. That reflects poorly on them, not you."

"If only they could be as timid as this Doug-fellow we keep hearing about," teased her father.

"Hey, he's not timid!" Kris then laughed at the realization that her father had successfully baited her. They shared a grin, before Kris settled back into her lounger to stare up at the starry night. "He *is* polite, and you know me: pushy enough for the both of us. As busy as I am, I keep wishing he'd skip class and his work to come meet you. I miss him being beside me, and that." She pointed to their joined hands.

Barbara held aloft her glass of wine as if making a toast and said, "It's a good sign that distance is making your heart grow fonder, as the saying goes. With any luck, you can figure out something before the end of summer, and we can meet this mystery man."

* * *

Once FBI Agent Julie contacted her, Kris had more urgent news to share. Her parents already knew of the group's adventures, their experimenting and bonding, as well as the scare at the gym and now these visits. The only thing Kris didn't volunteer was the speculation about Viz, mainly because it was wild fancy which unsettled her deeply. Her parents could be trusted to guard the information as well as show empathy, and like Kris figured, they were equal parts curious and cautious.

"It seems the FBI have me next on their list," Kris informed her mother while walking in the door and tossing her keys on the kitchen counter. "They're coming into the area and want to meet. The email mentions dinner 'as part of an apology,' much like what they offered Cathy and Will."

Barbara looked up from the cookbook she had been browsing and removed her reading glasses. "And what did you tell them?"

"Nothing yet—it was a typical crazy day at the paper." Kris shifted her weight to lean against the counter next to her mother. "I was thinking... Would it be okay if they came here instead? It might keep them off balance with you two around." She tapped a finger on the open cookbook. "Maybe turn the tables and invite them for dinner."

"That's my girl, the tactician," her mother praised. "Change their plan and see what they do." Barbara smiled and wrapped an arm around her daughter, sliding the cutting board in front of her. "Let's discuss it this evening."

During a dinner of spicy Chicken Jalfrezi stir fry, Kris reread the reports from Cathy's and Will's encounters with the public relations team.

"That makes them sound like two different sets of agents," Dave commented.

"Yeah." Kris nodded and added, "My roommate is easy going, and Will is anything but. So, we're seeing very different viewpoints. Their accounts both show questions the FBI is likely to ask: about Mark and the book and Viz. Though, I wonder what they really want."

Barbara pointed her fork at the open laptop as if she could get at them through the email. "That makes me curious to quiz these agents about their ulterior motives. They might just be fishing for anything new, even if they know more than you."

"Oh!" Kris said, perking up. "That gives me an idea. You are both used to critical thinking on the fly. What about inviting them over and you be the ones quizzing *them*? We could have a prepared list of questions. They would think they are coming to talk to me, but instead…"

Her parents looked at each other, passing silent notes and seeming to warm to the idea. They knew their natural authority would be like a protective shield for their daughter, which would be the main motivation behind their agreement. "We're here for you," Dave told his daughter, "so of course we'll help you figure this out."

Armed with a satisfying plan, Kris and her parents began discussing potential questions while she composed a response to the agents. At first, Julie resisted the change, replying that, "It would be best for everyone to find a public yet quiet space."

In a politely worded refusal, Kris said she did not feel comfortable meeting anywhere but her home. Then she reconsidered with an amused chuckle, altering her reply to add that they could always meet during a lunch break at her workplace. "If they know where I work," Kris said, "it'll get my point across about all this secrecy nonsense."

Shortly after, Julie returned, "Then your parent's home will be fine, though it wouldn't feel proper to stay for dinner. We won't need to take up much of your time. Would tomorrow around 6:30 p.m. work for you?"

*　*　*

Kris felt the change in the air when the moment arrived and their doorbell rang. They had been sitting quietly in the living room, as prepared as they could be, and now her father rose to answer the door. His greeting was good-mannered, but he lingered in the doorway even after they introduced themselves and produced their identification. He was like a barrier reminding them that they would have to deal with him before talking to his daughter. Dave might not have been as physically imposing as the male agent, but he stood as an intellectual and emotional bastion.

Once they had all been introduced and settled into the temporarily arranged chairs, her parents let the silence stretch—a tactic Kris made a mental note of—until Julie cleared her throat and said, "We appreciate the invitation to stay for dinner. However, we must catch a flight back to D.C. this evening and feel it is best to keep this short." Focusing on Kris, she leaned forward in her chair. "We are spending the time and travel because we recognize how badly our organization messed up. We want each of you to know we are working to correct and prevent any future errors—including, I was just informed today, an overhaul of our training in how we handle these unexpected situations. Basically, a reeducation."

Crossing his arms in a way that drew their attention back to him, Dave stated, "Help us understand why this was necessary: the actions in the gym of a major United States of America university, the lengthy silence immediately following, and then the need to personally visit each student involved."

Julie promptly replied, "Our primary goal has always been to shield and protect people, which is why we also investigate. The more we learn of each situation, the better we are prepared in the event it happens again."

"But at the gym..." Barbara prompted.

"It's true we were caught unprepared by the suddenness. Analysis, confirmation, authorization, response...all of this happened in less than twenty-four hours." Making sure to leave no one out, Julie turned back to Kris. "As we told your friend Will, the last documented incident we are aware of occurred before any of us were born. So in that sense, we are also students trying to learn."

Julie's partner placed a hand on her arm so he could speak. "Are we correct in assuming you know everything Kris does?" Seeing the nods, he continued, "Then we also trust in your discretion. It's vital none of this incident spreads further."

"Of course we can be discrete if it makes sense," Dave answered the agents agreeably.

Yet Barbara held up a finger as if teaching in a lecture hall. "It can be a fine balance between safety of information and suppression for an ulterior motive. Information that aids in understanding, education, is never right to withhold. Is this what played out at the gym?"

The agents exchanged glances before Julie stated grimly, "We believed the students were in grave danger."

"Wait…" Kris felt the conversation suddenly twist in a way that made her dizzy. "Danger?"

"Why not just warn the kids beforehand?" Dave added, also perplexed.

Leaning forward and showing a flash of zeal, Daniel urged, "Not only can that type of information be harmful, but the kind of visitation it prompted can be *disastrous*."

"Again," Julie added smoothly, "our job is to protect. The evidence seems to point to an unwitting summoning—"

"Hold on…" On the couch beside Kris, her mother shifted to the edge of her seat, looking ready to spar, or to pounce. "Are you suggesting the FBI gained knowledge about something harmful, which you could neither warn about nor avoid, yet instead felt the need to burst in and draw weapons? Show me what I'm not understanding."

The agents remained still for a moment, and then Julie made a mollifying gesture. "It was mishandled, as I said. We take this seriously and are determined to do better, I assure you."

Kris shook her head, trying to clear what seemed like darkness at the edge of her vision. Her father, always the calming influence, merely pointed out, "We have yet to hear why discussing and writing about dreams, posting them, meeting someone, is dangerous—or any more so than normality—that it would *summon* the FBI." His subtle emphasis seemed lost on them as they again traded glances.

"I'll answer as best I can," Julie pronounced while making an effort to seem relaxed, "but the information is protected with good reason. Trust that we have many generations of documentation, millennia of reasons why we reacted so."

When nothing else seemed forthcoming, Barbara's response was crisp and curt. "If that's the case, the best way to avoid future problems would be to educate."

Julie grimaced while shaking her head vigorously. "I wish we could, but it's already bad enough with rumor and lore. Terribly foolish urges to 'contact the spirit world,' hold a séance, talk to the dead, the *vulnerability* to influences…"

"If published truth were to legitimize their fancies," Daniel added with intensity, "it would lead to more disasters. We humans have more than our fair share already." As if catching himself, he eased his posture though his expression remained grim. "The rarity of this kind of situation might frustrate our efforts, but it is also a blessing."

Barbara held up her lecturing finger. "One can offer information *about* danger without putting people *in* danger. That is where the proper distinction lies."

"In this case, it is not that simple," Julie replied, rejecting the rebuke. "The information we protect against might seem...*unreal* or harmless precisely *because* we have guarded against it for so long."

There was an awkward space growing between them, with one side not wanting to say more, and the other side processing while waiting to hear more. Into this space, Daniel glanced at his watch and tapped it so his partner would notice. "Please trust that we are tasked to protect you," Julie said in nearly a pleading tone, "to monitor and react in a way that might prevent the next big disaster." She stood, which prompted the others to do so, and the common movement made the tension drain away. "We appreciate the time and the dinner offer, but tonight we must eat in the air."

As they shook hands, Barbara was courteous but still pressed gently: "Trust wouldn't be necessary if we had connecting information. We would love to believe in the goodwill of others, and yet asking someone to take your word for it isn't what I would expect from the FBI."

Julie paused at the front door, glancing at her partner with a furrowing of her brow. "If Daniel will allow, I'll leave you with a concrete example near to my heart, because we've both seen the proof in his own handwriting." When Daniel merely shrugged, she turned to them and continued, "But promise me this stays here, or I could get in serious trouble. I believe you will understand why this cannot be repeated. Not even to your friends, Kris."

Julie waited just a moment to see nods of agreement. "When we first began our careers, we were taken to the archives. Its quiet halls store documents and analyses spanning many generations, along with fragments telling about much older information. Among them is a personal journal of a...dedicated man: well educated, open-minded, full of empathy for suffering. And I was allowed to read the direct translation where he documented his struggle to help his people, to educate and bring order in a war-torn area. In his own words, he was 'driven to help all peoples.'"

Lowering her voice while increasing the intensity, she said, "What follows is a nightmarish account as he begs for answers, opens himself up for guidance from his dreams, then *experiments*, and is slowly warped by them. People only know the monster he became rather than who he began as. As far as we can tell, the later concepts of racial purity and cleansing were not his own, but came from those darkest of places.

"But the *consequences* of Hitler's experiments and mental imbalance will forever haunt people. Historians will blame the corruption of power or claim he was always insane. We *know* better because we have seen the seemingly impossible become reality. And so, we must learn and always stay vigilant against that kind of warping influence."

When they had said their goodbyes and the door shut between them, the remaining three looked at each other. "Well, that was…something," Dave observed in his understated style.

Barbara quirked an eyebrow and said matter-of-factly, "Quite the performance."

"You mean you guys don't believe them?" Kris shuddered. "Sounds nightmarish to me."

Her mother flipped a hand. "I mainly see how they steered the topic, and we didn't get to ask the questions we wanted to."

Now that they were alone, her father relaxed into his playful tone. "Just be your cautious self when you go poking about. We'll be sure to let you know if you start going insane and trying to take over the world."

Overcome by a burst of emotions, Kris laughed and gave each a squeezing hug. "Thanks for your help tonight. That could have really been stressful… More freak-out stress isn't what I need!"

"We just enjoy seeing something new every once in a while," Barbara said with a wink.

Back in her room, Kris kicked off her shoes, flopped onto her bed and blew out her breath. Her ceiling with its ten-years-old sparkles, the cute, curvy blonde wood desk and antique chair, the dresser with its colorful stickers and worn handles, the beanbag in the corner with her old teddy bear lounging in it…these were cozy sights to sooth her racing mind. Her parents were flippant, but she suspected that was for her benefit.

What deeply disturbed her was this idea claiming some knowledge is dangerous and should be hidden—this was completely opposite of what she had always felt! She picked a nail and then chewed on it. The very idea upset her, even made her angry at… She didn't have a direction, and knew it wasn't fair to blame the messengers.

She stretched, straining her arm so she could retrieve her laptop off the desk without having to get up. With it open and ready to report her meeting to the others, she found herself pausing then revising what she should tell them, and feeling annoyed all over again. A scared voice in her said it was important not to tell them about the revelations and the example Julie gave, and that thought seemed to betray her and reinforce the agents' contention that the knowledge should remain secret. And yet, what could she report if she censored herself?

After wrestling with this new reality and losing at least an hour of sleep she could never get back, all she had to show for it was a bland email. She noticed that she talked more about the agents than what they said. Yes, she thought the FBI agents were decent and believed in their job. Yes, she confirmed that they didn't know much and were digging for information, but didn't get much from her, mostly thanks to her parents being superheroes. Yes…there wasn't much else she could say about the whole thing.

Disgusted with herself, she gave a final growl, hit the send button, and prepared for sleep. Nothing in her message even hinted at the Hitler story.

Nolan

He wasn't normally an impulsive person, but Nolan didn't second-guess his choice as he pulled open the local company's main door and strode through it.

After graduation, his mother had seemed distressed when she learned he intended to stay in the area rather than come home. That weighed heavily on him, and he had taken some "me-time" to play video games, watch shows, and consider the emerging priority conflict between his friends and his mother. Those few days had threatened to stretch into a week.

But then his mother had called and apologized for not being supportive. His father, who had died of cancer two years before, had been in the military, and so she was a victim of constant change. A part of her had hoped that would all settle once Nolan moved back. In the culture she came from, families tended to remain together or very close for their entire lives, with multiple generations sharing space. Realizing the expectation she'd placed upon her son, she made sure to give her blessing for him to forge his own way. Her change of heart dissolved the unwinnable struggle inside of him, emotionally setting him free.

Now all Nolan had to do was stabilize his life here while waiting for his friends to come back from their summer break—something he would never again experience. He set out immediately to do just that, spending a pleasant Sunday morning and afternoon at a local church's monthly celebration, where a spunky young woman named Teressa took a shine to him. They had spent much of the afternoon lounging in the acorn-speckled shade, chatting about themselves.

Then the following morning, Nolan combed an internet job site as well as browsing the local paper. When nothing caught his eye, he simply set the paper aside, got in his car, and drove to the local power company's offices.

"Pardon me," he said to the receptionist. "I'd like to speak to whoever is in charge of hiring."

"For?"

This made him blink a couple times at the studied disinterest. "For work, for me. I'm a recent engineering grad from the university here."

"Oh," she said while picking up the phone, "then you'll want to speak with Mr. Hewitt." After a moment's pause: "Mr. Hewitt, there's someone from the school's Engineering here to see you."

Nolan followed the prompts: around the lobby, down the hallway, last door on the left. When he tapped on the door, a brisk voice said, "Enter," and Nolan stepped inside.

Mr. Hewitt was a man seasoned with gray, and the wrinkled work shirt lying beneath the hastily tightened tie was still mostly clean. And to complete the bespectacled engineer look, his blue jeans were there to prove he wasn't all business. He stood and came around the desk with an extended hand. "I didn't know you were coming, Mr...."

Nolan returned the handshake and replied hesitantly, "Just Nolan, sir. Nolan Banyen." Motioning with his head back toward the open doorway, he said, "I told your receptionist I was a recent graduate."

"Oh!" Mr. Hewitt made the mental adjustment and motioned to a chair before heading back to his own. "Well, that's much different, and I admit it's a relief since I haven't finished the analysis they want."

Nolan mildly suggested, "I suspect we're all the same to your secretary."

"Ha! You got that right: techies, hard hats, socket-pokers. She just sees us all as wanting something from her." Now comfortably settled back in his chair, he made an open-armed gesture. "So what can I do for you, Nolan?"

"I'm looking for a job that can take advantage of my education."

"Well, normally new hires are posted and handled online."

Nolan felt a pang of uncertainty, pushed through it, and leaned forward in earnest. "I realize that, sir, but I wanted to see systems and equipment, the works, and meet the people."

"Admirable, in an old school way. Like me." Mr. Hewitt spared a moment for his amusement before switching gears. "Electrical?"

"No, Civil, though I also made A's in my electrical and chemicals classes. They all relate to how we build better, smarter."

"Ah." Mr. Hewitt nodded, considering. "We engineers usually do what's needed rather than what we actually schooled to do. Perhaps you'd find a good fit at one of the building companies. An ol' friend of mine works for Brown & Root, which has a fantastic, extensive training program. I might be able to get you an application there."

"I appreciate the offer," Nolan said, showing his gratitude. "However, my priority is staying near my friends who have yet to graduate. I won't abandon them because without solid friendships..." Nolan shrugged rather than finishing the thought, and instead considered begging. "If you give me a chance you'll find I'm a fast learner, which I think counts for more than the degree."

"I like your style, and might be able to test your claim, adaptability and all. Though," he added with a chuckle, "it might involve pushing around a low-tech broom and bouncing around with us seniors while we find a spot for you. We're pretty small for a municipal, mostly because we share *loads* with the campus." Detecting nothing but willingness from Nolan, Mr. Hewitt came to a decision. "You know..." He reached back, scooped up one of the hard hats sitting on the shelf behind his desk and settled it onto his head in one swift, practiced motion before tossing another one into Nolan's arms. "Follow me outside, and let's see what we can see."

* * *

By the time the FBI emailed Nolan and asked to meet, not only was he well informed about them, he was comfortably settled at his new job with an initial week of long hours yet smooth adjustments under his belt. And unlike the others, he maintained a peaceful feeling concerning the gym incident, partly because he saw what Viz could do, but mostly because of his familiarity with a spiritual kind of trust often called faith. Nothing in his experience or journey or imagination could upset his beliefs, only inform and enrich them.

When the FBI agents sat down with him at the restaurant he recommended, Nolan gave them an easy-going smile while they went through their formal apology opener. "Apology accepted," he assured them. "And we're all glad to have some explanation after what happened."

His congenial nature was contagious, and the agents eased into a pleasant conversation that lasted until they had placed their food orders. "We figured—or hoped—that you would be more understanding," Julie said after their waiter was out of earshot. "Would you mind talking about the encounter?"

"Sure. I mean, even with the disruption, it was an amazing experience."

Julie leaned forward, opening her palm like a supplicant. "Please, describe your experience to us."

Nolan shrugged yet did as she asked. "It only happened because we told the mystery guy we wouldn't change our website—as he had begged us to do—unless he showed us proof. So, I cannot regret our...assertiveness."

Daniel asked, "This *being* made no attempt to influence your meeting?" When Nolan shook his head, Daniel pressed, "Are you certain? Could there have been any subtle manipulating on his part?"

Nolan replied mildly, "As sure as I am of anything. The forcing came from us. He had warned against it multiple times. Yet when we met, he showed happiness at seeing us—that's the best way I can describe it. Like we'd made his day. Of course, he ended up making ours."

When he remained silent after that, Julie prompted, "And he showed you an artifact?"

"Yeah, the proof we had demanded of him."

"Please tell us whatever you can about it," she urged.

Nolan scrunched up his brow, rubbing his chin. "You really didn't recover it? He tossed it across the gym in order to give us time to run away."

Julie seemed hesitant in answering, and when she did, it was evasive. "We're more interested in your impressions of it."

"Everything about it said 'ancient' even though, now that I think about it, it seemed to be in perfect shape." Nolan shrugged as if to say, "But what do I know?"

"And its contents?" asked Julie, her tone hinting at the struggle to show patience.

"Pictures—drawings, really—and some form of writing none of us had seen. More intricate than any script I have researched on the web. Believe me; I tried to find a match to fill in that part of the mystery. But he could read it and said it told the story of our ancient ancestors' dreaming, more of a tribute than an instruction manual. I think the term he used was an 'honoring'." Nolan saw they were hungry for more from him, but he shook his head. "He had just begun explaining it when we were interrupted."

Julie sighed. "If only *we* had been informed, been there..."

Strangely, Nolan felt the need to ease her frustration, and he leaned forward earnestly. "That interruption, your men barging in, was part of the experience, I believe, just like our pushing despite his warning. He somehow knew your men would interrupt and scare us, and I think he knew down to the second when to close the book and tell us to flee. I'm not sure you being there would have changed anything."

"But it could have changed *everything*," she replied before smoothing out her scowl.

Into the lull, her partner tossed his questions. "Besides wanting you to remove content, was there anything else he wanted from you? Even the smallest hint of purpose?"

Nolan didn't have to think about it longer than a heartbeat. "No," he replied with certainty. "He was there because we made him, and he did nothing but give to us, even with throwing away the book and standing in the way to protect us."

"Like a guardian angel?" Julie prompted.

"Exactly like one."

"And yet," countered Daniel with conviction that was blatantly *not* FBI in tone, "we know well the dangers of angels who have fallen…millennia of struggles with them."

Like a flash of insight, an idea made Nolan blurt, "If anything, the fallen angels are *us*. We who used to *travel* and *help* others."

To this, Daniel reprimanded, "Be wary of twisting doctrine and confusing yourself."

This admonishment highlighted just how far the topic had drifted, so Nolan blinked a couple of times, asking, "Anyway, what does this have to do with the FBI? That has baffled us."

"Simple," Julie said with a disarming smile, as if what she was admitting was anything but simple, "we're devout Christians just like you. We're FBI, and yet also belong to our faith and guardianship against immaterial dangers. Of course, our task is much older than the FBI, older than our country."

Her partner added, "Protection does not stop at manmade law."

Nolan didn't know what else to say or think, so he used his noncommittal, "Okay."

Julie smiled. "We know you understand the need for vigilance and wisdom, *especially* in matters of the soul."

In among those admissions was a glimmer of insight for Nolan. "You have nothing to fear on that account from us or *him*."

"Let us be the judge of that," Daniel stated.

Julie leaned forward as if collaborating with a kindred spirit. "Would there be a chance you could summon this entity again—in a controlled environment? We would love to visit and question and understand the purpose: why here, why now after so long?"

Nolan struggled to hide his discomfort. "I don't...think it works that way."

"How else would it work?" Julie asked rhetorically. "Your activity led him here, and your group somehow made him manifest."

Daniel joined his partner in leaning toward Nolan. "There could be an incredible, *meaningful*, career opportunity for you in cooperating with us..."

"Okay," Nolan said in a guarded tone.

Julie quickly amended, "Not that we have recruiting authority, mind you, but someone with your skills and maturity and *understanding* would be a valuable teammate. I believe that."

Nolan knew they needed something, some agreement or acknowledgement, but he was having a hard time framing any response. Finally, he said, "You guys seem focused on the darkest of possibilities. But if you saw what I saw, you'd be in awe, not fearful of it."

"It's not fear," Daniel countered, while Julie set a restraining hand on his arm.

"You also have a valuable perspective that could teach us," she urged. "It could be that your good perspective is what attracted your 'mystery guy'." Giving a dainty shrug, she added, "We know so little, which makes our mission all the more difficult."

Daniel also added a justification: "Being innocent, naïve, is fine and safe *as long as* there are people like us to safeguard that innocence."

Again, Nolan had nothing to say and so he held his tongue. Perhaps sensing his discomfort, Julie changed the subject. "Speaking of safe and innocent, I confirmed with my superiors that as long as your group amends the website to not *publish* secrets of the places you explore, you are welcome to continue using it. In fact, they encourage it as a healthy outlet. Consider the good will as a part of our apology."

Her partner qualified the offer: "It should be more of a personal tool for study, rather than trying to broadcast ideas, especially those that can be so dangerous."

To this, Julie added, "As soon as we're sure you're safe, you won't hear from us about it again."

Considering all the implications of this offer, Nolan gave them a pleasant smile. "I'm certain we'll feel much

better with your approval. Cathy will be especially happy.
I'll let them know." As if on cue, their dinner finally arrived,
and they could enjoy their meal while letting the
conversation drift back toward the normal.

* * *

One evening after church as they were chatting,
Teressa stated, "You're cute." When all he did was smile
serenely, she said, "If you invite me to dinner, I'll say yes."

"Okay." Nolan looked as if he were processing and
making adjustments. "How about dinner sometime?"

"No, no, not like that." Teressa laughed. "But like
this." She pushed her voice as deep as it would go and
frowned intently, pretending to be him. "I really like you,
Teressa, and would like to take you to dinner."

"Okay. That." He chuckled when she arched a sassy
eyebrow at him. "I *do* enjoy our chats. Let's do more over a
nice dinner, say, tomorrow around 8?"

"Why, Nolan," she said with staged surprise, "you
come up with the best ideas! But how about tonight?"

Quani

She loved all her family, her two younger siblings and her parents, but it was her father's parents she treasured most of all. Quani would give or do anything for them, and only partly because they would do the same. Her grandparents had been the guiding force behind their immigration from a northern province of India. Their openness, even enthusiasm, was the key to their blended culture of strong family values and nurtured independence, all woven together by the force of their love.

Once Quani had become old enough, her grandparents—with sparkling eyes and fond looks cast toward each other—had told her their tale of forbidden love. How they came from families on opposite sides of religious conflict, how they had used wits and caution and no small amount of luck to withstand the pressures from both groups while beginning their own family. All the while, they had been slowly saving up enough to escape the entrenched expectations and choose a third, unexpected option. They had set their sights on that giant statue of the lady with torch held high.

Quani figured nothing her grandparents had encountered while moving to the U.S.A. and adapting to life here could compare to the pressures they left behind. "The only way to be on the winning side," her grandmother had revealed to her, "was to be on *no* side." That wisdom had stuck with Quani, such was its resonance within her.

After another pleasant day spent visiting and helping with chores, she gathered around the gaming table with her grandparents, slowly but surely fitting together the colorful 5000-piece puzzle laid out before them. That was when her phone chimed, notifying her of the dreaded event. The FBI agents had arrived in the city and wanted to meet. Even with days to prepare, Quani could see no good way to deflect them. So with hands that trembled slightly, she quickly replied, "I don't think it's a good idea."

"What was that?" Her perceptive grandmother was examining her with curiosity.

Quani ducked her head as she slipped the phone back into a pocket. "Just another friend thing."

"Hmm," her grandmother said with a challenging look. "Must be good friends to keep in touch this often. Any boys?"

Quani's cheeks felt hot at the teasing—and this from her grandmother!—but the answer was simple and away from her underlying anxiety. "No, none for me. I'm too busy." Returning the smile, she added, "Dadi, I'll let you know when the perfect one comes along."

Then early that evening, her father, Salman, answered a knock at the door and she heard her name mentioned. Quani came around the corner as he was asking what this was regarding, and instead of answering, the two agents looked toward her as she set comforting hands on his arm. "It's okay, Papa," she said, even though it was very much *not* okay. "I will speak to them just outside."

The agents eyed her curiously as she slipped past and motioned them down the front yard's walkway. She dared not look back at her father.

As they neared the street by the parked rental car, she took a deep breath and said, "Please make this quick."

Julie studied her. "I hope we don't get you in trouble. Would you like us to intercede for you with your father?"

Quani shook her head emphatically. "Anything you might say would only make it worse. He is not like Kris' parents."

Moving on to the topic at hand, Julie said, "As you know, we came to apologize, and we must be thorough or we're not doing our job. I hope you understand."

In a soft voice, Quani repeated, "Just please make it quick." They might mean well, but their intrusion could upend her quaint little existence further.

"Anything you can tell us about the visitor or the book he showed you would be helpful."

"I don't know what I could tell you that the others haven't already."

"Please help us do our job," Julie insisted. "Even the smallest detail you remember."

As they stood in the heat, one agent with her hands in her pockets and the other agent leaned against the car with his arms crossed, Quani tried desperately to give them what they wanted as quickly as she could manage without being rude enough to rush them. She was highly conscious that anything she might try in desperation could only make it worse. And the clock was ticking, questions forming in her family's minds.

Finally, her anxiety made her say, "I'm sorry I don't have more, but I really should get back to my family before they worry." Of course, the moment these agents showed up unannounced at her home it was too late!

To her relief, they nodded, with Julie shaking her hand before they loaded into the car and pulled away. Then her heart seized up when Quani turned to find her father still standing in the doorway and wearing a scowl that broadcasted, "This is something I should have been told about!"

She knew he was strict because he cared for his family and felt a huge burden upon his shoulders, and she also knew she was about to feel the full weight of that burden. He didn't say a word as he closed the door and led them to the living room, but then his arms folded in preparation. "What have you been keeping from me?"

The rest of the household was still, all eyes on her. Slouching her shoulders, Quani mumbled, "Nothing."

Her father jabbed a finger toward the front door. "Officials coming to our home isn't 'nothing'! Who were they? Police?"

Shaking her head, Quani feared this, though she had to answer truthfully. "FBI."

"FB… As in *Feds*, from *the capitol*?" When she merely nodded, her father exploded with indignation. "And this *nothing* you kept from me?"

"Salman, please, let the girl explain." The calm voice of reason from his mother, Quani's loving grandmother, gave her the strength to respond.

"They are going around to all of us, my friends. It doesn't mean anything. It's just about something from school."

"Then you cannot go back!" He gestured toward his wife and back to his eldest daughter, sputtering. "See? This is the reason you marry them off first thing. Before they can cause so much trouble."

"What a terrible thing to say," his wife gently chided, but she too was frowning at Quani.

"This is how I am repaid! All my work, all my love!" Salman was nearly apoplectic from situations real and imagined, betrayals and mischief most dramatic. Yet into this tense moment, Quani struck upon a saving insight, even if it was only a partial truth.

"Please don't, Papa. It's just that they considered hiring—recruiting—some of my friends, and so they have to interview everyone. I didn't want you to worry because it won't mean anything. And I didn't know they would just show up here!" She clung to his arm with both of hers. "Please, Papa, I'm sorry I didn't tell you earlier."

Even with his fears abating, he scowled at her. "Unexpected visits, complications, this is what makes rumors fly."

"I'm sorry, Papa," she repeated, wrapping her arms around him, and this time he reciprocated.

"You had me worried for you, I imagined..."

"I'm sorry." Tensions were draining, and her grandfather was even returning to the puzzle after trading bewildered looks with his wife.

Quani's mother had approached, and now she hugged them both, instructing, "*Chotu*, just be sure to inform us of anything like this, even if you think it's nothing. It is our *responsibility* to worry." She was rubbing her husband's back in a mollifying, peacemaking way.

Salman's wife might have soothed the outburst, but his parents weren't so forgiving. When Quani went back to the puzzle table, her grandfather winked at her. In a volume meant to be heard across the house, he commented to his wife, "Our son is going to need one of those pacemakers before we do."

"Not helping," Salman retorted from where he was settling back into his recliner.

Quani knew then the danger and uncertainty of her returning to school was past, and only when she relaxed did she realize everything in her body had been tensed. But she could go back to savoring the small activities with her family, determined to show constant gratitude. Then she could return to her new life at college with her friends. Assuming, the FBI didn't blunder further.

At some point in the near future, she would have to figure out what to tell her family, how to explain her interest in a way that wouldn't backfire. But for now she couldn't even think of what to tell her best friend from high school, much less her overprotective parents! She would need some kind of inspiration to meet that impossible challenge.

Doug

Doug realized early on that summer would not be restful. The research and extension center he had previously worked at was understaffed, and so he was welcomed back with big smiles, back-pats, and loads of interesting work to consume his energy even before his next class began. And hearing that many summer courses were like full time jobs didn't prepare him for the strain.

Four days a week, he would wake at 6am to be at class by 7:30, so he could be back at work by noon. He'd often help the research teams beyond dinner time before rushing home to study for the next day. The professor seemed to punish his students with a condensed schedule that had tests coming in rapid-fire mode. Doug found himself constantly struggling not to fall behind.

The only thing keeping him going was the knowledge that these back-to-back summer courses would allow him to graduate on schedule next spring rather than coming up 6 credit-hours short or having to squeeze them into an already packed senior year. His parents understood because they saw the results of the strain. Even his snarky little brother, who had just finished his first year in high school, noticed enough to comment that Doug was becoming an old man.

However, his new love didn't understand. Not only did he hear it in her tone, he felt it in his heart: the disappointment that they might not see each other until fall semester reunited them. They had just enough time to long for each other without enough to actually do anything about it, since there was now a full day's drive between them.

Despite the extra notice and the back-and-forth chatter of his friends, Doug had no time to settle on a plan for his meeting with the FBI agents, or even to fret much about it. So, he just showed up with a smile and a hope for the best. True to their pattern, the FBI agents offered to buy him dinner while they interviewed him, which, from the standpoint of his busy schedule, helped him shoehorn them in. And as had been reported, Julie wore her bright smile, leading with a warm greeting and sincere-sounding apology. Daniel was more frugal with his words, preferring to observe Doug in a way that brought to mind a stalking lion.

Tacking on an extension to her practiced apology, Julie said, "And please tell Quani that we didn't mean to be disruptive to her. We hope she didn't get in trouble on our account."

"She'll be able to return to school, if that's what you mean," Doug said with unguarded disapproval before moderating his tone. "I'll make certain she knows next time we talk."

"And the website?" Julie prompted while hunting for more common ground. "Are you guys going to continue with it?"

Doug nodded. "Cathy is stoked about it. Thanks. I take it you put in a good word for us. No way do I have the time to help right now, but I know the others are already working on revisions." He paused while considering broaching the point of contention being discussed among his friends, and decided to just throw it out into the open. "There has been the question of whether you plan on monitoring it still. I mean, what *is* your interest, exactly?"

"That question from Will, no doubt," Julie guessed with a suppressed smile. "I assure you our interest is only in being certain you don't trip into danger and then spread that. We want to be clear: as long as you guys are careful about what you post publicly, we see no reason to take any steps."

"As far as content," Daniel spoke up for the first time since his greeting, while motioning back and forth between them with a finger, "we prefer to get our information this way, not by snooping."

Using that lead-in, they began inquiring about Doug's involvement and impressions of the visitor. The questions they asked seemed more perfunctory, as if they knew they weren't going to get satisfactory answers and were simply completing their assignment to interview each of the witnesses.

When they mentioned the tome, Doug countered with a question of his own. "We've had a running discussion about the book, and Nolan figures you didn't get access to it for some reason. Would the men who burst into the gym have kept it from you?"

Julie shook her head, but it was her partner who spoke up with a slight smirk on his face. "We thought you would have figured it out by now."

"Figured what out? Why ask us about the book if you have it?"

"That it's not real. We didn't recover it because there *is* no book."

Doug was taken back as much by Daniel's casual tone as the implication. "*What?*"

"It was a trick," the agent replied, "an illusion of sorts."

Doug shook his head in denial. "But we *saw* it, the cover, each page that was turned… Nolan saw it being thrown across the floor!"

Quirking a heavy eyebrow, Daniel replied, "But did he hear it hit the floor or make a sliding sound?" He gave Doug only a moment for the implication to settle in before adding a teasing, "Nothing?"

"I don't know," was all Doug could manage.

With sympathy in her voice, Julie said, "We thought you guys would come to this realization on your own. You are right: had it been real, we would be studying it. One of the reasons we want to hear about it is to gain insights into what the artifact actually represented."

Unsettled, Doug was still shaking his head. "That's… But it *told* about our human dreaming, our abilities. Detailed drawings, fancy writing… There's no way we hallucinated it. Are you saying it was made up?"

"If an illusionist holds up a flower for you to see and then makes it disappear before your very eyes," Daniel asked in a hypothetical, "was it real?"

"But it's just hidden," Doug sputtered, "sleight of hand."

Julie simply shook her head, but her partner wasn't finished. "And yet it's as though it were never there, for you will never be able to find it or hold it or smell it. See what I mean?"

Doug sat at the table looking dumbfounded.

"But there *are* elements of the spirit world that are dangerous," Julie continued softly while leaning toward him, "especially to your mental state, so promise me you will be very careful."

"Or better yet," Daniel interjected, "just return to your studies and your social life and be happy."

With a glance at her partner as if to warn him to stop while he was ahead, Julie turned back to Doug, insisting, "At least promise me you will help keep the website safe and warn your friends. This will make us feel better if you truly understand the danger and are guarded."

Hesitantly, Doug nodded, and feeling that more was being asked of him, said, "I'll talk with the others and make sure we're careful not to spread any speculation."

Julie was looking satisfied by his answer, and perhaps by his off-balance. "Now we feel confident you guys know the risk and will be more...reserved."

"And so our work here is finished," her partner added.

When their food arrived, Doug didn't feel like eating with them, but he forced himself out of courtesy. They never mentioned a job offer like they had done with Nolan, and Doug couldn't decide whether to be disappointed or relieved. Then as the food began settling and normalcy brought back his tiredness in spades, he decided while stifling a yawn not to care either way. Once they were gone and he had discussed this with his friends, he vowed to forget it all.

But of course it wasn't that simple. The agents' implication that what they'd felt and witnessed had been something less than magical bothered Doug on a level that just wouldn't go away. Even as the days and then weeks passed and he struggled to keep from drowning, his mind kept returning to the nagging discouragement.

His support group of friends would assure each other that they were still onto something amazing, and the agents were just being deceitful. There was a spike of excitement when Nolan agreed to become his roommate and promised to find them a cool rent house, now that he was "rolling in the dough." But, then the worry that it was all for nothing would return.

The dreaming, the limitless *beyond* of possibilities, the *ability* to be a helpful force wherever that might take them...all nothing? Doug's frantic routine seemed to threaten him with a sense of disconnection from everything else in his life.

One night into his second summer semester as the exhaustion and sadness threatened to overwhelm him, he lay in his bed trying not to cry, feeling the need for sleep warring with the need for something greater. Even as he closed his eyes and sank, he *reached* for a lifeline. Stretching out like a needy supplicant, opening and drifting and *becoming* that cry for help...

Viz sat upon an indistinct ground facing him with a bemused smile that softened his bland features. "I sense you are ready for my help-comfort."

"Oh, you have *no* idea!" Doug felt a laugh slip out as the wave of relief swept through him. "I could have used your help much earlier."

Viz approximated a shrug. "This meet-timing is yours. Much sooner than expected, though I should not be surprised by your potential."

"The *always* being tired—and those FBI agents—they made me doubt *this*!" As if swimming slowly through the essence of the real-in-the-making, Doug gestured around them.

Viz seemed to tilt his head, understanding. "Those types would have you forget everything again. Who, in wrongness, would sever you from that which encouraged-nurtured your conscience out of mindlessness." It was his turn to gesture around them. "Despite their efforts, you are here-ready. *Present*."

"I should have never questioned it."

"Worry not over questioning, for it is questioning which forms answers." With a touch of a smile, Viz added, "*This* can survive your doubt."

Doug grinned for a miniature eternity, savoring the *present*. Swirls ebbed and flowed around them, both indistinct and achingly unique. Everything held in a state of potential, the breath before the song.

Yet inevitably, Doug urged himself forward. "Where are we? What now?" Even as he turned to look around, to explore more, he felt the insubstantiality. He heard Viz as if through an elongating tunnel. "Do not rush your journey, for it is wonderful and long." And again as a fading whisper. "Savor each step."

Then Doug was awake, relaxed and energized and excited once more, hearing the memory of Viz's encouragement. *Savor each step.*

Chapter 26

Intertwining emotions filled the modest living room of the rental house to bursting. Relief like the bright sun emerging after a long storm; fondness rediscovered and multiplied by each interconnection; excitement at a yearned-for reunion finally realized.

Kris and Doug seemed glued together, sitting on a single couch cushion. Nolan lounged next to his new roommate, having the rest of the couch to himself. Even now he still glowed from the group's compliments about the rent house, which they all agreed would be their best meeting space for the foreseeable future. Across from him on a folding chair, Will leaned in and chattered on overdrive. Next to Will, Quani was settled onto her chair, relishing each detail. And across from Kris, wiggling atop the padded bar stool, Cathy just finished telling them the latest drama with her ex-boyfriend.

As the initial welcoming surge subsided, Cathy shared her joy with those around her. "Guys…" When she held up spread hands, they were already coming together for yet another hug. "Oh," she exclaimed as she squeezed as many of them as she could get her arms around, "how I missed you guys so very much!"

"I thought summer would be my break," Will commented, "but *this* is."

Kris steered the moment back into the comical: "That better be Doug's hand on my butt and not yours, Will." They laughed, separated and wiped at their eyes while settling back into their seats. And now with their burst of happiness satisfied, they could get down to business.

"So…" Kris prompted her love, marveling at the fact that the distance had indeed made them grow fonder. "We're finally all back together!" This brought about a new burst of cheers from the group.

Into the happy noises, Will asked of Doug, "What's this secret spy stuff you couldn't mention over the phone?"

Doug arched an eyebrow while clearly enjoying the attention. "I'm not sure I should say just yet, since we haven't swept the room for listening devices."

"Oh, come *on*!" Cathy exclaimed, slapping the air in his direction, a move that was completed by her roommate separating just enough to smack Doug on the arm.

In earnest, he leaned forward. "Ready to have your minds blown?" He made them wait only one long breath before dropping the bomb. "For the last six weeks, I've been meeting with Viz. Inside the dream realm."

"*What?*" several exclaimed in unison.

Nolan laughed. "I *knew* it was something huge because he wouldn't say anything until you all arrived. But…wow!"

Doug admitted, "Only four times so far, and he keeps urging patience."

"What about *our* visits?" Will demanded.

"It's a careful process, this introduction," Doug answered in a less-than-confident tone. "I'm guessing too much at once can mess us up. Though, I have plenty to report."

Kris pressed back close to him, saying, "Please share."

"Do tell!" echoed Will while leaning forward eagerly.

"First of all, I was tempted to think of the place I meet Viz like a waiting room, or a visiting room, but of course that isn't right at all. Here, we separate rooms from each other," Doug explained while gesturing to the walls, "but there's no distinguishing—or rather, there's a separation only when you *need* it to be. Driven by need, not structure." Doug laughed, clearly remembering a fun moment. "Of course, it's not even a *place* as we think of it. Viz was actually amused at me, urging me to instead think of it as our shared moment. But it also feels like something much greater than that. I don't know." He ended with a shrug.

"Maybe his understanding of the 'moment' means more than it does to us," Nolan speculated.

Doug said, "Yeah, maybe. Probably. I don't mind admitting how in awe I am, of his...gentle way, his patience, his control. Its subtle but I think he's more experienced and skillful than we can imagine."

Furrowing his brow, Nolan asked, "Could the FBI guys be right at all about needing to be wary of him?"

Will snorted. "Don't let their paranoia infect you."

"I doubt it," Doug answered with more consideration, shaking his head just slightly. "In a way Viz is a perfect teacher, also a dreamer and yet much older and certainly more skilled. But he basically acts like he's just one of us."

"Just making sure," Nolan said as if justifying his question to the group.

Quani made an uncharacteristically impatient gesture to pull them back on track. "So what did the moment *look* like?"

They watched him anxiously while he struggled to find the right description. "Like swirls of smoke, but with substance, always moving, *living*."

"Like in my dream," Quani confirmed, almost moved to tears by her powerful remembrance, "with the shifting, dream-like puzzle! It was maybe tan or all colors around that, without being bright."

Doug agreed. "It's muted, I think is the best way to describe it, but it doesn't *have* to be. Viz called it 'the potential of everything.'"

Beside Doug, Kris murmured, "That's beautiful."

"There's no getting enough of that!" Cathy exclaimed with a giggle.

"Or getting bored with it," Will added.

Doug cautioned, "But it's far more than just for our amusement."

To which, Will immediately qualified, "Which is part of what makes it *so awesome*! We can learn much more than we can here." He gestured to the floor, but everyone knew he meant at the university, or even within their world, for once they had a glimpse of the *greater*, their perspective was forever opened.

Smiling, Doug broke the momentary silence. "Viz knew you would be impatient, of course. He can visit each of you when you're ready. He also said there's only so much he can help with, and that we must continue pushing ourselves. He told me something to the effect that true learning comes from within your own efforts. Some details of our chats become hazy once I awake, but I swear each time gets clearer, which he says is a function of practice—I remember now him using the word 'attuning'."

"Well, I'm ready to start *now*," Will declared. "Load me up with sleeping pills and give me a pillow! I'm *kidding*," he made sure to add when Cathy turned a disapproving glare on him.

"I doubt that's the patience Viz was talking about," Nolan said with his dry humor.

"Yeah, yeah," Will sassed, "I'll have the patience to wait until tonight then. So, how'd you do it?"

Doug looked sheepish. "The first time, I was really in the dumps. After the FBI guys and the huge load of other stress, I doubted everything, which made me feel worse. I just kind of cried and opened up and reached out as I was falling into sleep. And let me tell you, the relief I felt at seeing him again and hearing his comfort was more than I can describe!"

"If that's all there is to it, I think we'd all have had visits by now," Kris said with a frown.

"It's hard to explain." Doug wore an apologetic look. "For me, maybe it was the desperate need that triggered it. Now, I think it kind of just *happens* whenever Viz is available." With a self-deprecating chuckle, Doug added, "I'm sure you don't have to sink to the low levels I was at to connect. It might be different for each of you. Viz basically hinted as much."

"That's not very helpful," Will fussed at Doug with a raised eyebrow.

"Sorry. I noticed no one has been adding new dreams to our site. Has there been none?"

They looked around at each other and shook their heads. "Still not much since the FBI disruption," Kris admitted.

"Which might have been their intent," Will said with residual sourness.

"Well, let's get dreaming again," Doug encouraged. "That's the best place to start. Get back on our roll before the gym disaster."

"Or even better—deeper—than that," Cathy stated with a firm nod, "armed with our new knowledge."

"Speaking of the website," Will said, "it is *such* a relief to be here together where they can't snoop and just come out and say it: there's no way they're not still spying on us. The only reason they'd okay our website is they gain something."

Kris cast a worried glance to see how that impacted Cathy while arguing, "It's still more than that to *us*, but yeah, we've been smart to assume they're still monitoring it."

Cathy flipped her hand in the air. "We play their game to get what we want, right? We all know now that putting certain things out there is a bad idea. Things like Viz meetings stay here, between us. What's the harm in dumping the rest on our site?"

"I don't want to give those fake FBI guys *anything*," Will stated. "They can all drop into a black hole!"

Doug was shaking his head. "But then they'd definitely know we were up to something. Like Cathy said, it's best to keep up the more normal stuff for them to follow whenever they see fit."

"Our 'creative outlet' cover story," Kris agreed with a conspiratorial grin.

"Then how will we keep a record of the most important things?" Quani asked.

"Here, and in your perfectly kept notebook," Doug stated simply before being struck by an idea that made his eyes twinkle. "Or better yet, when we meet in the dream realm, a *real* dream-meet!"

Will sputtered, "We can do that?"

"Viz said it's possible for us to do what he does, so why not? His comment and encouragement is also why I think he's an advanced dreamer, like we can be. Imagine being able to play within pure imagination—or tag-team on helper dreams!"

Kris turned to Doug and whispered in a stage voice, "I want to see you in my dreams."

"Music to my ears," he replied, to groans and hoots from the rest of the group. After a fierce hug with Kris, he said while still grinning, "The things we all can accomplish...well, no telling what waits for us."

Nolan mused, "It's like Viz—from the very start—knew there'd be things we would have to learn to keep to ourselves."

"That one dream of mine also said so," Will emphasized with a nod. "Now if only I can harness my prescience to keep us out of trouble!"

Cathy snorted at Will before turning her attention back to Doug. "So what else did Viz have for us? I am *so* ready to get started again!"

"It was pretty much that encouragement. So far."

"Man, you didn't ask him about the book?" Nolan stated with a shake of his head, "It would've been the first thing out of my mouth."

"Well, now that you remind me…" Doug's impish grin had returned. "I did happen to get an answer from him about that. He actually admitted to being amused at the thought of them chasing an echo."

Quani frowned. "So it wasn't real after all?"

"Oh, it was real but destroyed long ago, just as he implied to us. He told me nothing created is truly gone. I have no clue how, but echoes are like copies, I guess, and Viz said that with enough skill and need, they can be brought forth again. Recreated, maybe?"

With slow emphasis of a mind blown, Will said, "Like fricken magic!"

"Yep," Doug responded to his silly friend, "like fricken magic. Are you ready to learn how to become a conjurer?"

"You know it! Maximum level!"

After catching herself at the start of a giggle, Kris instead tsked and intoned, "You boys…"

Turning earnest again, Doug said, "By the way, I found out a very interesting tidbit about Viz."

Cathy perked up. "Oh?"

"If you draw this out again," Kris warned him playfully, "I'm going to really smack you."

Shoulder-hugging his girlfriend to prevent her abuse, Doug continued, "When I asked about why he chose us, what his interest was, he said some confusing things, but basically admitted it was more likely *he* was chosen for us or *by us*. Partly because in his waking world, he is some version of a teacher—which confirmed my impression, though I can't remember the complex phrase he used. I think they take teaching much more seriously than we do. And also, he said, because we fascinate him." Chuckling, he confessed, "That's a rough translation, anyway. So it's kind of a perfect match: we're avid students and he is some ideal mentor."

Looking around at his friends, Doug leaned forward. "And I can *feel* the truth of that in how he affects me, encourages me. I hope that soon each of you will feel what I feel, because I'm inspired."

"Me, too," Cathy said with a little wiggle in her chair, "just by hearing about it!"

"And by us actually being together again," Nolan added.

"Yes!" Cathy exclaimed, hopping up to instigate another giant group hug. Even if they had more news to talk about, they were too charged and anxious to focus on anything but the promise of upcoming dreams and who would be the next to, according to Will, "break the Viz-barrier."

While they were milling about deciding what to do next, Kris grabbed Doug's hand, tugging him toward the hallway. "I don't think you gave me the complete tour of the house earlier." The suggestive tone was not lost on Cathy, who let out a funny *meow!* and then a whistle while a grinning Doug let himself be led away. After all, they had months of lost time to make up for.

* * *

Cathy was drifting without paying attention when she felt a tinge of familiarity. Glancing up, she thought she spied a lone man, higher up, clutching something to his chest. Recognition increased even as he began to drift away.

Focus, FOCUS.

He became instantly closer, clutching a tome to his chest, looking up to catch her eye. "Viz?!" The image of him solidified, even as she felt herself gain substance. And then she could *feel* his recognition, as well as his growing smile.

"And so you found me."

"Oh, thank goodness! I have so many burning questions."

He chuckled, becoming as solid as that night in the gym. "No need to inquire about readiness—" She wrapped him in a hug fierce enough to cause a strange ripple, and she could feel his surprise and his adjustment. "Precious One, you must learn to control your potent emotion-surge-broadcasts. You almost knocked me from your moment."

She let go, embarrassed, and gave him a bit of respectful distance. "Sorry. Oops…sorry."

"In little, right-measured amounts." Then she could feel his teasing exaggeration as he added, "Lest you create a storm where none should be." She could only giggle in her embarrassment, but he praised her. "Your *presence* astonishes. So, too, will need to be the responsibility to use it with thoughtful wisdom."

"I'm so happy to learn," she gushed, feeling dizzy in her excitement until she remembered his admonition to control herself. "I...need practice, I guess."

Viz seemed to gaze through her before nodding. "Your new understanding of this reality has inspired-elevated you." Again, she felt his relaxed amusement—which was so unlike how awkward he had seemed that night in the gym—when he next stated, "I hear...*whispers* that you will have practice-exposure enough to satisfy even you. Just...be careful of yourself."

"Okay, I will. I promise!" This time her laugh was from relief and anxiousness. "When do we begin?"

Viz answered simply, "We have already."

"Oh!" All she seemed to be able to give was nervous anxiety, but she could only feel warm acceptance from him. In searching around for one of her now-missing burning questions, she blurted, "So why didn't you *warn* us about those FBI agents?"

Amusement. "When did you give me the chance? And yet you have found-learned everything you need to be *here*. Explain to the others what you are learning, how to *focus*, how to *feel*, so they can apply their own to it. As I knew from the first time I saw you together, much of your potential comes from each other. And your deep caring is much of your success. Nurture these advantages."

"I will, I will," she promised fervently, even as she felt the all-too-brief meeting coming to a close. "When can I see you again, learn more?"

Wonder. "Apparently whenever you desire, so please take care not to abuse your gift."

"That was *me*?"

Viz held up what was still in his hands as if showing her proof. "It was you who recalled the book-echo." She was awed and baffled and overwhelmed by the possibilities. She was filled with hope and promise and *purpose*, and another urgent need to *hug*.

And the next thing she knew, she was instead hugging her pillow.

Chapter 27

It was a magnificent day. After certain mid-fall storms, local nature lovers were treated to blue skies and cooler breezes to offset the sunshine's heat. And today seemed like the best of the best, where in shorts and t-shirts, people could feel warm or cool but never too much of either. The first round of fallen leaves rustled and drifted across grassy fields. Birds sang brightly as if performing one last celebration of summer's success—or perhaps, using the happy weather to play mating games. And in a slightly more sophisticated sense, this was also true of the humans at the park.

Deflecting Doug's old roommate's invitation to go clubbing, Kris instead steered Tim and Donna toward the idea of a long, leisurely picnic. They could soak in some of the best rays, work on tans, and get to know each other much better than they could while dancing. If the urge overtook them, well, they could always break out their happy dances on the soft grass. Doug enticed Nolan into coming with talk of reliving their glory days tossing about the football, and Nolan thought it would be the perfect opportunity to introduce Teressa. When questioned by a teasing Kris, Nolan said he could neither confirm nor deny that they were getting serious.

Of course, Cathy wanted to come, but refused to feel like the only single person on the planet, so she cajoled the ever-safe Will into being her non-date. He was happy to show up if only for the promise of free food, and was assured there would be plenty of goodies. In the end, only

Quani declined because she had a semester full of study-intensive classes which threatened to overwhelm her.

The group exchanged energetic introductions before setting out to explore the park and find their ideal spot. Once they settled upon a grassy knoll with a nice buffer from other sun worshippers, the students spread out four large blankets, weighted down with coolers and other picnic necessities. Almost immediately—after pecks or fond pats of loved ones—the former teammates set out with the football to test their skills.

When Cathy settled onto their shared blanket, she traced an imaginary line across its middle. With a smug look and a taunting tone, she told Will she was establishing their boundaries. "It's not that I don't trust you, but you *are* a boy!"

"*Pffeh*," he retorted, "I don't think that blanket is big enough for the both of us." With a grin and a clumsy flip of the Frisbee, he continued, "Besides, we'll be too busy playing to care about such trivialities. Or wasting a perfect day being lazy—unless you're *scared*…" This had her hopping up to prove him wrong.

When Kris and Teressa and Donna lounged alone together, they talked of hometowns and classes and plans and "their men." "Nolan is so passive, or maybe just secretive," Teressa complained lightly. "I mean, it took him all this time to introduce me to his friends."

"He's just a careful guy," Kris answered, feeling the need to defend him, "and hey, you are here, so let's enjoy every moment."

Once the boys returned for drinks, they snitched brownies despite warnings to save those for dessert. As penance, they were tasked with applying suntan lotion to their girlfriends, and accepted the "punishment" with good humor. Donna's giggles hinted that at least one of them was taking advantage of freshly exposed ticklish spots.

During the Frisbee tossing contest, Cathy's phone chimed. She glanced at it as the disk sailed past her and Will chirped his annoyance. Then returning immediately to the blankets, she showed the screen to Kris with an arched eyebrow.

"It's from Mark," she explained, impatient to get input from her roommate.

"Who?" asked Teressa, always eager to be a part of the conversation.

"Our counselor—freshmen counselor," Kris quickly corrected herself while skimming the email.

"It's how we all met, only one short year ago when we were *so* young," Cathy mused. Before Teressa could ask further questions, Kris handed the phone back to Cathy and said they should talk about it later, when they weren't busy enjoying the day.

*   *   *

They decided to discuss Mark over a conference call since the hour was late and Will was already complaining how he managed to get a sunburn that made him "radiate like a nuke reactor."

"So you should have kept your shirt on, and saved us the blinding," Cathy sassed him, feeling a fleeting sense of symmetry.

He snorted. "It would've been *more* of a crime to hide my magnificent body."

"*Anyway…*" Cathy rolled her eyes from where she and Kris huddled over her phone. "Mark sent this while we were at the park." And promptly, she read the email from her laptop. "'Hello, Cathy. I hope you are doing great with the new semester and life, and especially with your dreaming experiments. Please tell the others hello from me, because I know you will still be in touch. And I have a big favor to ask of you. I've picked my dissertation topic covering some of the dream experiences we've shared, both from my original group and from yours, and to that end I am sending a detailed questionnaire to each of you (I might need a couple of email addresses from you to manage this).'"

"Oh, shit," Will interrupted when Cathy paused for breath.

"Oh shit is right," she agreed. "He finishes by saying, 'Please encourage the others to complete this as thoroughly and quickly as possible since it will be vital to my research section. And please stay in touch. Let me know how you are doing.'"

After a momentary silence, Kris bemoaned, "Oh, Mark. I feel bad all over again, like the first time we had to keep this from him."

"But it's still clear, right?" Doug insisted in his prompting manner. "We cannot confide in him without getting him in trouble." There were murmurs of agreement, and Doug continued thinking aloud. "Yet, don't we need to do this questionnaire for him as a courtesy, at least partly?"

"It's for his degree and maybe his career," Nolan reasoned. "We owe him at least this much."

Cathy made a gesture in the air that only her roommate could see. "For sure. Just not exposure to our thing."

Kris added, "We'll just need to carefully edit ourselves, and double check each other. Even more than with the FBI, we need to play dumb. And yes, I hate myself for saying that."

They could almost hear Will fidgeting. "But...how do we give him something valuable enough to be worth writing about *without* exposing him? This is right back to our previous problem."

"Not quite," Doug corrected, "because now we can prevent a face-to-face, keep it in writing, which should be much easier to pull off. Mark deserves our protection. And we have yet to see his questions."

"Maybe, maybe," Will said, "but what if he pushes or insists?"

Nolan offered his advice: "There needs to be a line we don't cross no matter what, and this exercise will help us find out where it is so we can stay far away from it."

"I wish we didn't have to tell him anything," Quani said quietly. "He could stumble into the same problem we did, and then you know who those FBI will blame." That implication hung in the air between them, further dampening their spirits.

Refusing to be daunted, Cathy shook herself and said, "Remember what Viz told me. These skills we practice and what we experience and all we will learn… Sure, there's a little danger, but what we share is *so* worth it!" She could feel the effects of their redirecting.

"Yeah!" Will said, the delight back in his tone. "Always diving deeper! I just wish Viz would hurry and come visit me! And this school business needs to stop cramping my style."

"Oh, it gets easier," Nolan promised with a short laugh. "By comparison, work is a no-brainer, just lots of doing that's still interesting in its own way. Especially when we test and roll out new equipment. In the meantime, we keep the lights on, which is gratifying."

Quani said, "I just hope we can all find good jobs like yours. What are we going to do once more of us graduate?"

Doug reassured her, "Well, I'm next and not going anywhere far, even if my buddy has to find me a job at his work. After that…we play it by ear, right?"

"We'll do the best we can to stay close," Cathy agreed.

"And take plenty of vacations!" Will added.

Riding the wave of amusement washing away their worries, Kris said, "I know a sweet, sweet lake house that should fit us perfectly."

They shared laughter, and Doug said in a low voice, "I'm missing those nights on the dock."

"Don't want to hear it," Will stated.

"Well, come on over then, lover boy," Kris said in a matching sultry tone.

Will squeaked, "Ack, my ears...my mind!" They laughed at the antics before wishing each other a good night and ending the chain call.

*   *   *

Serene as a distant mountain peak, smooth as the calmest mountain lake, flexible as the tall grasses which always straighten after a breeze...

"And as lovely as the brightest of mountain flowers," Viz added to her thoughts from where he sat cross-legged beside her in imitation of her pose. Quani wasn't sure if he was talking about her or the gentle swirling movements of the dream potential she was admiring. But she turned to find him looking at her with kind eyes that she couldn't believe she ever thought were expressionless. In this realm, she couldn't/wouldn't blush.

Simply, she said, "Thank you for visiting me."

"It is my joy to see you growing, understanding. Embracing." As it seemed they had been doing before the soft spoken exchange, they returned to contemplating the intricate weave within this intimate moment. In the shared experience, even *time* was part of an artistic design. The thought settled upon her like another comforting layer.

"I love this," she admitted, though she had not consciously chosen to say it aloud.

"And it loves you, Weaver."

"Weaver?"

Viz turned again to face her. "This term *belongs* to you, does it not?"

Quani thought it over, savored it, and nodded. "What does this mean for me here? That I see the connections and patterns?"

"See-realize what *is* your hand," he said.

Without thought, she held up her primary—her left—hand, and marveled. Within her palm a microcosm of *this* moved in similar patterning. Or perhaps the patterns *were*, in fact, her hand. In this moment, the distinction seemed irrelevant.

"And now your other," Viz again prompted.

When she lifted her right hand, it was almost as surprising, because it was merely a hand, creases and soft tan skin and familiar fingers.

"Once they become the same, joined to each other through you and because you *are*, connections can-will-have-been made."

"My doing?"

"It can be," he affirmed. "You experience intricacies that already *are*, and yet you are also connecting them so there is no separation-apartness."

This resonated with her in a way that made her want to weep. "And so they can *belong*."

"Yes, Bright Mountain Flower." To emphasize the importance, Viz repeated, "In one way, they always do, and in another sense, they *will* because of you."

"Thank you."

"It is my joy." In hearing this phrasing again, Quani understood it must have been how he said "you're welcome." She made a mental note to adopt the sweet essence of it.

Then in a rare instance of Viz volunteering information, he continued, "There is risk in the pattern-weaving for you, so be wary. Risks which not all your mothers have avoided. You reach-strain to see too much, too soon, and become overwhelmed."

Quani grunted and admitted, "I have experienced that before."

"You will make peace with what you cannot see, and let it be for someone else. Be confident: if you need to see it, then you will, and you must be ready to understand-connect its context."

"Easier said than done."

Viz smiled fondly at her. "As is the struggle against ignorance, but wisdom is a well-earned benefit you can forever rely upon. Unlike *not* seeing."

Quani returned his smile. "I understand." After a moment she recalled a question. "You mentioned my mothers; do you mean my ancestors, my lineage?"

Viz sat for long enough that she almost repeated the question. "They are connecting echoes to you, within you."

"So my lineage, a bloodline?"

In a first, Viz shrugged in confusion. "I see-understand no distinction. They are a part of your existence here, and that is all I see-need-to-see. Should a distinction matter to you?"

Surprised by the outside perspective, Quani turned the question over in her mind before shaking her head. "No, it does not. I will honor them regardless. Thank you."

"It is my joy."

They returned to savoring their moment, and by placing her palm against her chest, she connected their moment to her heart. This was her gift and her joy.

Chapter 28

I'm floating along with her, as if hovering upon her shoulder—but am I the little angel or little devil? I feel professional discipline blended with the willingness to take personal responsibility mixed with worry for her students; I already like what I see. She takes a calming breath, lowers the handle, and steps into a bright room.

As one, the men and women in decorated uniforms look up when she enters. "Good, Dr. Ramsey," says one as he motions to the chair at the end of the oval table, "have a seat and let's begin." There are no pleasantries, no small talk or even a, "Hello, Anne, how are you?" The strain in the room is almost a solid presence, and before she fully settles, she finds out why.

"Your kids have closed off all communications."

Not a good sign these are suddenly not our kids, Anne is thinking while she adjusts and asks, "An accident, a problem with the equipment? I was there only three days ago and all was proceeding—"

"No accident," one interrupts with a dismissive wave of her hand and a matching scowl. "They don't trust you nearly as much as you claimed they do if you have no knowledge of this."

Biting down on her annoyance, Anne states once she releases her tongue from between her teeth, "I cannot answer productively unless I understand more. Why not begin with consecutive facts? Step at a time."

After a pointed silence, the ranking admiral in the room raises a printout from where it lay in front of him. "At 12:12 yesterday a single communiqué went out through our monitoring stations…" He raises an eyebrow at the appointed program administrator before quoting, "'Paging Professor Anne Ramsey.' And then every system went silent."

"But there are redundant systems—"

"All of them," he confirms rather than waiting on her to state the obvious that it shouldn't have been possible. "Within the hour we had verified all physical components are operational on our end. The facility is most likely unharmed but now sealed to us."

"And the staff?" To this question, she only gets a few heads shaking and a shrug. "Then I must return at once."

"And how do you plan on dealing with the barrier?"

"What barrier?"

Rather than answering, the top admiral leans forward to pin her beneath his glare. "We will not accept any more rebellious foolishness from them—no more nonsense, no more insurrection."

She feels compelled to add the missing element in the room. "But these are *our children* we're talking about, our best and brightest and most driven and most *loyal*. So there must be an unexpected problem."

The scowling woman again: "Then why the antiquated taunt, as if our high tech equipment were only a paging system for them to play with?"

"There must be a valid reason."

"Which we intend to hear from you A.S.A.P. Carry on."

Anne wants to add that the trust the students placed in them and the staff must be returned, that she must be given the time to handle the situation as delicately as needed, but again she bites her tongue and stands as she is dismissed. "Yes, sirs. I will report as soon as I know more."

Two years earlier, the object first appeared as a sudden burst of static on military channels, a *ping* on all nearby radar-sonar equipment, and it caused a modest swell along all local beaches. That made it simple to track back to its source. Near the ocean shelf's edge off the western coast, military search patterns located a large crate similar in size to what might have fallen off a shipping vessel sailing into port.

But closer scans from the dive team they sent down revealed it was anything but ordinary. Suspecting an extraterrestrial origin, the military machine kicked into high gear, first constructing a containment housing around it, and then a fully equipped laboratory around that. There had been brief discussions of moving it to a land facility already equipped to handle such investigations, but the fact it seemed fused into the sea floor, and that they didn't know how deep it went, decided them on the extraordinary expense of building a new underwater facility.

The chosen military scientists wasted their first six months ignoring the initial message. They tested and poked and theorized, all of which failed to get them any closer to a workaround. Then the military investigators spent another six months profiling and monitoring the message's subject, until they were faced with the choice of either destroying the apparent container to break it open or following the baffling instructions. Reluctantly, they chose the latter by summoning specifically one Professor Anne Ramsey, who held dual doctorates in wildlife biology and child psychology (regarded in some circles as closely related subjects).

Once Dr. Ramsey was equipped with the appropriate security clearances and read in, momentum made the rest as inevitable as if it had already happened. Military decision-makers watched via remotes as the baffled young professor circled and queried and touched the object. They saw it respond as if a living thing, shy yet very particular. They were committed enough to follow the next set of instructions to form a special school. Especially when a pensive Anne had told them she felt as if the prompts from the container already knew her answers, her *needs*, better than she did until the moment it revealed she needed to accept the administrative role, to be a major part of what made the school special. Then there were also enticements: advanced design schematics for the school, a list of candidates for the charter class, and the molecular structure for a previously unknown—and some began to suspect, not-yet-invented—material.

The implication was clear: there were more breakthroughs where that came from.

While military contractors were building the underwater facilities, Anne engaged with each kid, testing and evaluating them, then offering a personal invitation to a new school that promised to revolutionize education (and therefore, in the humble opinion of Professor Ramsey, the world). She had to tailor her approach with each child and adapt to each new situation, but none of the students could resist the invitation. And the entire time, Anne knew she was doing her life's work, firmly within the sweet spot of her abilities and desires.

It took less than six weeks at the school—despite the frantic pace of multiple overlapping learning techniques—for the students to begin asking inconvenient questions. Why this location? Why all the extravagance for a school on the ocean floor? What did they want in return? The nearby military base and frequent patrols couldn't be hidden, even if many of the school staff successfully concealed their military backgrounds. Then there was the windowless area and heavily secured doors that obviously led somewhere important.

Dr. Ramsey had planned to spend at least a semester for acclimation before opening Pandora's Box, as she now thought of the mystery object. Instinct, however, told her that any delay would damage their trust levels, and so she unlocked the doors to the warehouse laboratory and introduced them to their newest fascination: the world's most sophisticated puzzle. "This package was specially delivered for us," she had explained to the gawking kids.

"What it is and who sent it…well, this is our ultimate test and field study." As the space filled with excited speculation, she smiled and noted, "This might be our ultimate goal, but it's also *extracurricular*, so schoolwork first." Over groans, she continued, "Remember that your studies are your foundation, and could even be the key to success with the mystery and with our future."

Back then, she had no idea just how accurate she was.

I experience the unfolding scene from both inside and outside the high-tech, pressurized suit that Anne is standing in. She stares in wonder at the new addition to her school: an encompassing barrier that seems made of water yet is impenetrable to everything—so her military escort assures her. Absently, she nods and then takes another calming breath before moving away from the transport sub toward the dome. Her escort remains a respectful distance away, though I feel certain they were ordered to stay at her side.

The wall in front of her glows as if reflecting the lights of her suit at odd angles, yet when she switches off her lights, the glow remains. She raises a hand toward the luminous water. "Be careful, Doctor," one of her escorts says from his safe distance. "That's new."

And then all at once, dozens of gallons of water push her through—or rather, the water around her is sucked inside from the sudden pressure difference. She staggers and almost falls as the water cascades away from her and rapidly seeps into the soggy ground. Unable to see through the running droplets, she wipes frantically at her faceplate before it dawns on her: the sudden inability to see isn't because of the water, but from the *lack of water*!

An amused laugh comes to her muted through thick pressure-resistant glass, and she looks up, steadying herself to barely make out one of the students, James, waiting for her, hands in his slacks pockets, wearing a thin knit sweater—and no wetsuit. Smiling, he gestures to his head. "You can take it off, unless you like the look."

With a mind still screaming that this shouldn't be possible, she reaches for the latches, pops them, and hesitates another moment before lifting her helmet free from the suit. And takes a long breath of air, clean and damp and crisp. Dr. Ramsey looks around to see several of the students in chairs or "sunning" on beach towels even though they were on the ocean floor.

"So how do you like our air?" James asks pleasantly as he strolls up to her. One nearby lounger smirks and states, "I know it's chilly, but it's still an improvement now that we removed most of the humidity."

"This shouldn't be possible," she echoes her internal thoughts.

"Oh of course it is," James replies, "that is, once you know how to maintain a gravity wall."

Anne glances behind her at the shimmering curved wall of water and shivers from the cold. "A gravity wall."

"Well, it's really a vacuum-interspaced, intertwining-dual-sided gravity wave, but I doubt that name will catch on."

Another student quips, "The makers of your fancy suit will be bummed. We just obsoleted it."

"And something you found in the box made this?" the administrator prompts, reminded of her duties.

"Nah." James makes a flippant gesture. "We designed it with a little help from us."

"Mrs. P!" Anne knows who it is even before she feels the awkward hug against her suit and the tug on her hand, because there was only one student who bothered finding out and using her middle name. "So glad you came!" Tammy exclaims. "Come and make yourself comfortable! Ignore James—he's just showing off." Tammy sticks out her tongue at James as she pulls the director past like she would a best friend who is making her late for class.

"We need to talk about this, so gather everyone," is all Dr. Ramsey can manage to tell James before she is stepping through the open and currently pointless airlocks.

When Dr. Ramsey first met and interviewed Tammy, it didn't take long to figure the girl to be an elevated level of social genius, with no detail too tiny or unimportant to be left unused in the grand game of human relationship management. And while the trained counselor sometimes worried about the potential sociopathic tendencies inherent in that extreme level of skill, she rarely observed or heard of Tammy using her talents poorly.

Now, the girl is chattering, "I told the boys this was a bad idea, springing it on them. Not only would it seem we're ungrateful, they would react like getting an ultimatum."

"They are somewhat upset," Anne Ramsey admits mildly, wary of being probed for information she isn't yet ready to divulge. Though she always felt drawn to trust this playful and kind girl, it was part of her training to be careful.

"Yeah, and now we have an additional hole to dig our way out of, though I can't say I'm unhappy about the challenges awaiting us."

Dr. Ramsey tugged back to slow the girl down. "What about the other staff? Cletus, Steve, Mark—?"

"Oh, they're still here if we can trust them."

"And if not?"

Tammy looks at her with a twinkle, but there is perhaps a look of disappointment there too. "Would you think we'd shove them out the airlock, our bubble? They got recalled back to the base. And I see what you're thinking, and yes, that was me, but I swear it was the best way." Resuming her march toward the living quarters, Tammy continues, "I was really bummed I couldn't vet Josh, but he also had a call from base. Never try to play the player, you know?" That would be one of their science lab tutors and perhaps one of her love interests.

"I see." Anne remains cautious while receiving the subtext and deciding to change the subject. "So everyone is safe? No one hurt?" When Tammy nods her head, Dr. Ramsey feels a relief that also reveals how tired she is.

"Good to know, and I hope to make sure it stays that way. I'm still baffled—in shock maybe—about why you did this, and all of a sudden."

Tammy smiles at her once they slow outside of the living space Anne uses when staying at the school. "It will all make sense, I promise. Trust that we have good reasons."

"I do," Anne replies without hesitation.

"Good." Tammy goes up on tiptoes to peck her on the lips, saying, "We love you too. Freshen up, change, take a nap if you want. Just let us know when you want to meet in the lab—the intercom works, but the gravity bubble bends all waves back on themselves." Meaning, it is impossible to send outgoing communications.

Anne needs rest, downtime to let events settle on her, time to consider what little she knows. She forces herself to remove the wetsuit and change clothes, and then stares at the wall before admitting her responsibility is to at least try to send communication to the military, if only to stall them. She goes over to her desk, knowing the console will be useless, fiddles with the controls, and then muses when she notices the apple on her desk. *Her kids.*

Resigned and yet slightly renewed, she walks to the intercom. "Please gather in the lab," she says through it. "I'm ready to see what kind of craziness you've gotten us into." That should set them to giggling and confirm she is in their corner. She gives them just enough time to gather before making her way down to the original building, noting immediately that the container now sports an opening folded back like dragonfly wings at rest.

"So you cracked it," she notes, glancing around at the grinning faces. "And inside? Who's going to fill me in?"

"More secrets in another box," James states, grinning at his evasiveness, "once we prove ready for them. Feels like we're learning at an exponential rate to keep up with what was in the first layer."

"This couldn't have all happened in the last three days, so why keep it from me?"

"Information given too early can be truly damaging," Tammy says in a consoling tone. "Lack of deniability and all. But now that we have a protective layer and you, our champion, we can tell you and *only* you."

"Why keep this from our people who found and funded all this?" Dr. Ramsey motions around the lab and notices for the first time several of the remaining staff members standing against the wall as if afraid of the spotlight.

"Oh, we already tried giving them the technology," answers one student.

"At least once," amends another student.

Tammy sighs dramatically and finishes, "Apparently, the results were disastrous, though I'm unsure of the details. But we *believe* it was, like, world-ending bad."

"We were told as much by ourselves, along with the promise of more details to come," James corrects her.

"Which we chose to *believe*, as I already stated," Tammy counters.

"Wait…" Anne shakes her head. "You…sent this back…to yourself?"

"Well," James says wearing his boyish grin, "in a way, we actually sent it to you, Professor Ramsey, because that was the first lock."

"And the first test to see if the military would relinquish control," one student adds while casually twirling a pen through his fingers as if this were the most normal of conversations.

Anne looks around and tries to seem calm but suddenly needs to sit down.

"You're having trouble believing this," Tammy says, full of keen empathy. "I understand, but we're here, inside a barrier made of shaped and bound *gravity*." She holds up a hand when others go to speak. "Give her another minute to process."

"I'm okay," Dr. Ramsey says, straightening and knowing she should show authority. "Well, what I'm not okay with is the method, the lack of trust in your mentors, in your country."

James shakes his head, and asks rhetorically, "The piece of tech we already offered to our *financiers*…did they begin designing incredible home appliances, or did they design wartime applications?"

"You are not winning any points by treating me like a simpleton."

"My apologies," James mutters, still capable of being scolded.

And Tammy is there again to smooth the relations. "We simply need you to understand each step to see the *inevitable* failures that lead to disaster if we give them all they want. What we have uncovered and hidden in the past weeks is a tiny bit of what is in store for us, and we *must* be ready for it." She repeats her earlier sentiment, "Too soon, too dangerous."

"This container, for example," states a student as if he is the one giving the lecture, "is made of *programmable* material, half of which is now in the hands of military warmongers. And it apparently can survive the insane forces of time distortion."

Anne has to clear her throat twice before speaking again. "Right, so time travel..."

"Nothing will blow your mind quite like talking to an older you," James states with a subdued grin before perking up. "Better yet, you should already suspect who first contacted you and had you contact us."

"Tell me." Though Anne suspects what she is going to hear, she still needs to have it dragged into the open.

"*You* did," Tammy emphasizes softly, letting that sit between them for the length of a skipped heartbeat, then a held breath, before continuing, "which is probably why you agreed to do what you did. And why I also know you will help us. Because you already did, or *will*."

James adds in an additive, unhelpful way, "Or *would* have, if that future happened to play out."

This resonates on an undeniable level and makes Anne need to cry. The way the message said each perfect thing she needed to hear, how each piece was set in place... If *she* were to craft something for herself, that would be how she would do it—*especially* if she were protecting information and people, her students.

Dr. Ramsey looks up to find all eyes on her, and she rubs at her face lest tears escape. "So, that bad, if we tell them?"

James nods. "Apparently disastrous enough that we—they—potentially destroy themselves somehow instigating and manipulating a singularity to send this warning back. We are assured more details will follow once we unlock the next."

"Along with the tech to protect ourselves and the future," adds another student, "and the names of those 'leaders' who are going to drag us into that hell."

Still, strangely, Anne is torn or perhaps only overwhelmed, and I also realize I have been holding my breath this entire time, if I had breath to hold while existing in the silent spaces between her thoughts. Slowly as if from being inactive too long, I uncurl, focus, and gently nudge her forward.

This is the way. Trust in your students. Trust in yourself.

Taking a steadying breath, Professor Anne Ramsey looks around at her kids and then nods. "Okay," she says firmly, "where do we begin? How do we prevent this awful future?"

Chapter 29

The stillness of Will's room was shattered by his gasp. "Holy—!" He gulped a breath, eyes flying wide in the dark. "Oh my *god*!" Sitting up, he laughed, feet already dropping to the floor. "Amazing! *Insanely cool!*"

With a swing of his arm, he threw on the light switch and slid into his desk. Even the pain from striking his knee didn't distract him from his mission—or continued mission—as he grabbed notebook and pen and began writing like a madman. Or a visionary prophet. Or mad visionary prophet—on a mission!

"Don't lose it," Will muttered to himself. Then to the dream wisps that he chased, he begged, "Don't you lose me!" If he didn't record fast enough, the thread of experience, of *understanding*, would drift away, and he knew he would lose something immensely valuable. He didn't pause to ponder or select words or consider implications; he did all that while scribbling frantically.

Only once he became confident in his ability to capture it all did the adrenalized tension begin to ebb. He snatched his phone and used the favorites list. When it reached the fourth ring, threatening to go to voicemail, he hung up and redialed.

"Will?" Doug's voice came through too groggy to be upset or even baffled.

"Dude! You will not *believe* the epic dream I just had!"

"At…5:12 A.M.?"

Will could hear Doug's mind beginning to stir. "Nah, it's already 5:15—your clock is slow. I gotta talk about it or my brain's gonna bust. You know how it is."

"Yeah," Doug said slowly, then more briskly, "yeah, I do. So lay it on me." Judging Doug to be mostly coherent, Will did exactly that, launching into the how and the when and the why of it.

"I've had some powerful stuff, but *never* like this," he concluded, "like a grand sense of accomplishment—even though my urging was a tiny, minor part, and yet…it was *exactly* what was needed! And I can tell you with all confidence that wherever or whenever this was, the future will be fixed, will work out. I mean, I knew even before I was conscious in bed that *I* had done my part. Maybe even my observing it was enough, you know?"

"I think I do," Doug said when given a chance to respond, and Will could hear the grin. "Quite the victory."

"*Yes!*"

"So when are you going to tell the others?"

"We should meet now—it feels that important."

Doug chuckled. "I highly recommend waiting the whole—what? 12 hours?—until our next meeting, as long as you're certain you have all the details. Besides, it's always good to let it bounce around inside your head."

"Yeah, okay. You're right," Will said, adding, "thanks and sorry about this."

"No, no, it's fine. You just owe me. You must wake up immediately to hear my next breakthrough."

Will laughed. "It's a deal, bud. Damn, I'm *so* pumped!"

"I know exactly how you feel," Doug assured him. "We all do, which is one of the reasons we're so close. Now go spend some quiet time with those feelings, if you can manage it. I still have some sleep to get and maybe some dreams to catch."

*　*　*

As the students' dreams gained in momentum and importance, they began meeting twice a week, with an occasional extra meeting wedged in between when the dreams called for it and they could manage their schedules. This instance was opened and driven by Will's excitement. His zest for the dream set the tone that they tossed between them like playing a game of catch.

"It's *incredible* how the smallest nudge can have *such* a great effect!" Will was recapping the dream. "For the most part I was watching, even during the background events, so much that I could forget I was even there!"

"Oh, I know how that feels," Kris assured him with a smile.

Will leaned back in his chair with a satisfied sigh. "I'm addicted! Might have to drop a class to make more time for the real stuff."

Cathy cleared her throat, hesitated, and then speculated, "I wonder if we can make terrible mistakes just as easily. I mean, I'd hate to think it was so easy to slip up and have that *negatively* affect so much. Like if you had told your professor-leader-gal to turn the kids in—I don't know— like they were doing it all wrong, and reporting to the military was the right thing to do."

"Interesting," Doug said before Will quickly responded.

"I'm not sure I could have. No, it doesn't feel possible."

"So then it's not really up to us?" Cathy asked. "Does it all play out regardless of what we do?"

Doug was slowly shaking his head. "I think it's more than that. Like, we are shown things and given opportunities or insights based on what we can handle. Not that we *couldn't* mess things up, but that we won't—that's just not who we are. Or who we're training to be."

Kris sensed her roommate's insecurity and added, "We need enough confidence in ourselves and our learning to keep from feeling scared, or timid. Together, we *will* handle it."

"Which isn't the same as being cocky," Will clarified, quirking an eyebrow and amusing Cathy enough that she barked a laugh.

"Good thing *you* said that."

"Hey," Will retorted, following her into their typical banter, "I see what you're implying, that it takes one to know one. Seriously though, these dream lessons fill me with this grand feeling, which has nothing to do with cockiness."

"We stride forward," Nolan said with his own confidence, "with our hearts in the right place. If we mess up, we will keep improving and making up for it, but like Will, I also trust we're given everything we need to be successful.

"However," he continued, "I could really use help—advice—with a real life thing." Once he checked they were all attentive, he began. "You know I've been dating Teressa—it's been like over five months now."

"Then congratulations are in order," Will teased.

"The point is, even though she's met everyone but you, Quani, she knows nothing about these meetings. What happens when—if—we get more serious and committed to each other? I've been thinking about it a lot and just don't think it's right to sneak around or be deceptive, but..."

"But we've been told specifically and have agreed to keep this secret," Doug finished for him.

"Could she be content with a simple statement, like we meet as friends?" Cathy began before laughing at herself. "Of course she wouldn't—I wouldn't."

"Good topic. This goes for each of us," Quani pointed out while briefly removing her pen's cap from between her teeth. "Future relationships, marriage…"

"A no-brainer," Will said with a dismissive wave. "This is a *secret* society, *our* secret society."

"That's simple for acquaintances and random people," Kris responded to him with a frown of consideration, "not for our dearest loved ones, those we trust and share most everything with."

Nolan nodded. "And so you see my issue. Teressa is nothing if not curious and…bold. She wonders what else we do, and so far I say things like you guys are always studying or just hanging out to blow off steam. But every time I shrug it off like it's nothing, I feel more like the liar."

"I'm not sure we should take that risk," Doug said but he had no conviction in his statement, only uncertainty. "Maybe if you get to the stage of…" He snapped his mouth closed when he noticed Kris' scowl.

She pointed out, "I told my parents and knew they would both understand. They kept the secret just fine, and I'm not sure I could have gotten through that FBI meeting without their support."

"Not the same," Will argued. "You've known them all your life, and besides, that was before we fully understood how important secrecy is. None of *our* parents know, nor will they!"

"It must be on an individual case basis," Quani spoke up. "No way could I hide something like this from my husband. He would have to be able to understand." For a long moment, they sat in silence, considering as many ramifications as they could think of, worrying what this could mean for their group.

"Well, no way I would tell a boyfriend," Cathy said, thinking about her disruptive, nosey ex and shaking her head, instinct screaming that telling significant others was a Bad Idea. "This is *ours*, at least for now."

Nolan leaned forward plaintively. "No offense, Cathy, but you don't have a serious boyfriend who will be pressing for details or wanting to join in. How can I handle that without being a complete phony?"

In an attempt to lighten the mood, Will stated, "Spies do it all the time."

"Which we aren't," Nolan said with annoyance in his tone.

"But maybe it's time for us to create elaborate backstories. You know, secret-society-like." Will could tell his lightheartedness wasn't working, yet he felt inspired. "No, hear me out; I'm being serious. Having a cover is super important, and we've already done so with those FBI jerks."

Kris arched a challenging eyebrow. "What, like a knitting circle?"

"Or a 'hunting' lodge," he said by way of agreement. "Just enough cover to satisfy everyone except those few who are so close that they eventually get inducted into the group."

"So..." Doug scratched his chin, trying to piece the puzzle together. "Long, careful consideration, and even more careful introduction."

"Careful only gets you so far," Will pressed. "Once the secret is gone, it's *gone*, out of our hands but on our heads... That's what the good cover is for, to make it easier until we are considering adding someone. Then we swear them to secrecy, or something."

While Nolan had relaxed into the couch, he was still frowning. "I *hate* lying to her—having to lie."

Doug reached behind his girlfriend to set a comforting hand on his roommate's shoulder. "But it is for the best and you know that. There's an overriding reason to be careful, even for *her* sake."

"Yeah, maybe," Nolan mumbled, "but it won't be long before she's asking or demanding to come."

With a wide grin, Will said, "And those are the times we bring out the knitting stuff."

"Oh, you *can't* be serious!" Cathy exclaimed while snorting.

The joking created space for them to realize that no solution would be forthcoming or easy. Kris remained supportive of Nolan and his feelings, optimistic that Teressa could eventually be trusted. Will insisted it could just as easily be a train wreck. As a comfortable middle ground, they all agreed to dwell on it and discuss options later.

As a distraction from the previous intensity, they talked about the upcoming Thanksgiving holiday with Kris being unable to hide her anticipation.

"It will be like an extravaganza: finally meeting both sets of parents over two different Thanksgiving holidays compressed into one!"

Doug agreed, "An epic journey worthy of song. Maybe a few songs."

"If you're not flying, that has to be one insane drive," Will stated, adding, "though I'm guessing at this time of year, flying might take just as long."

Reciting like it was a badge of honor, Kris told of their tight schedule: "At my parents for Thursday meal, then eleven or twelve more hours of drive time to dine with his parents on Saturday and then back here almost immediately. So I figure at least twenty-four hours of the break—like, a quarter of it—will be spent in the car."

Cathy leaned toward her roommate, grinned wide, and spoke in a stage whisper, "If you can still stand each other after that, then you'll *know* it's true love."

* * *

Nolan thought it and therefore said it: "I'm so happy to see you again." He went to shake hands with Viz and felt nothing, yet was still satisfied by shared feelings of friendliness.

"You all are a joy to see," Viz replied, rotating to gesture at the intricate patterns' many dances. "Safer than the last time we met."

Nolan smiled and let the patterns *speak* to the marvel in his soul, and infuse him with excited wonder. This was creation and *creationing*, super-cosmic and yet intimate. "This place and what it means...so overwhelming and beautiful and heavenly!"

Viz tapped the front of his head. "As it is for us all. Though be wary of impatience in your drive to know-experience it. This is more than you were taught by your upbringing-stories, so allow time for the truth to work on you and through you. Learn the many realities of *Here*."

"I will be as patient as I must," Nolan promised, sensing the reflexive rewards of patience and openness on his character development.

However, two urgent questioning thoughts interrupted his musing, and he chose the one for his friend first. "Cathy was worried about the possibility that we might accidently do wrong inside our dreams, hurting instead of helping. In essence, I said to trust in this place and our ability. I hope that was the right thing to say."

"You are nurtured-watched-loved, true. Each of you would have to betray yourselves to bring harm-without-benefit." Viz then became still, either to give understanding time to grow, or to await Nolan's next question.

Turning to study his mentor, Nolan broached what was bothering him most: "I also have a dilemma..."

"This drew me to you," Viz stated simply into the hesitation.

"Teressa."

Viz already knew in the way dreams let you *know*. "You struggle-consider telling her about this, about us, as though you could convince her of worth. Certain life-aspects are individualized and should remain so, even in a pairing."

"I doubt she would accept that, and besides, I feel terrible about lying."

"Consider: if you give someone a gift they cannot accept, is it truly a gift?"

"Couldn't I help her accept it? Love her in a way that she accepts? I don't know...*show* her?"

Viz shook his head, and just when Nolan thought he would remain silent, said, "She would shrink from this, as would her love for you." Viz's image vibrated in a subtle way that Nolan intuited as signifying a *vision*, a view of what might become. "She would talk, her mother would gossip, Reverend Patterson would insist you denounce-erase the possibility, and still your church-group would turn away from you and from your truth."

For Nolan, hope was a most fragile thread. "But what does that mean for *us*?"

"I share your distress yet cannot give you answers. Except to state what I see, that Teressa can never find one as benevolent as you."

"But in time...given time for growth and deepening, slowly earning her trust..." Nolan could sense Viz sharing— reflecting—his mounting angst.

Gently yet firmly, Viz explained, "You cannot *see* for others, cannot heal what they will not acknowledge-understand. Even in this awareness, the cost is challenging to bear. Please do not allow your sorrow to corrupt-transform into bitterness."

Nolan needed to weep, but the peace of the dream wouldn't give in to his urge. Viz only shimmered in grief and waited for him, helpless but supportive. *Even the greatest of truths bears a high cost.*

Teressa would never accept this realm, or how he must live. Nolan had trouble breathing. He could ask of his friends to help him deceive her, to protect her from her lack of *understanding*. And they would, but that didn't mean he should. *Even the greatest of truths bears a high cost.*

They could live blissfully as long as she remained ignorant. They *could*, if he dedicated enough willpower to it. For her love, he could make it happen. *Even the greatest of truths bears a high cost.*

Nolan awoke with a large gasp, choking on his own spit, and released a weak cry. Then the floodgates of misery opened. He didn't deserve this. Teressa didn't deserve this! Yet, he *knew* he could not keep lying or thinking she might be the right one for him.

Chapter 30

The sun dominated a clear sky and yet the wind was crisp, a perfect combination for their road trip. Risking the hazard of suicidal bugs, Kris let both sun and wind flow over her, eyes closed, head leaned out the window, long hair glistening and flowing like the finest spun gold. Doug tried not to stare since it was his turn at the wheel, but couldn't help the occasional—or rather, frequent—glances.

Kris' smile became a grin as she pulled her head back inside and began closing the window. "I see you peeking at me." As the wind noise subsided, her amusement fully shifted to him. Busted. And the only proper way to handle it was with a full confession.

"How can I resist? You are glowing!" Though his focus remained mostly on the highway stretched out in front of them, he added, "Makes me want to pull over and kiss you."

She quirked a playful eyebrow and reached for his hand. "Hmm, we should have allowed more time. But impatient parents await."

"Perhaps," he suggested as a compromise, "at the next stop...just a little."

Miles flowed past smoothly as they listened to music, shared jokes and stories, and then comfortable silences. After relieving stiff joints and swapping roles at a gas station, Kris countered the drone of road noise with a rare bit of gossiping. "Did you notice how tired Will seemed yesterday?"

Doug considered it for a moment. "No, I didn't. Maybe I was too busy enjoying a calmer Will."

"Cathy said he will most likely drop a class to make more room."

"Oh, boy. I didn't think he was serious." Doug shook his head before adding, "Not good. Maybe we should talk with him once we return, if he hasn't already done something rash."

"Yeah," Kris agreed with a chuckle. "That goof!"

After another pause, Doug rubbed his chin and said, "Huh. Now that you mention it, Nolan was acting different, too. Even quieter than his normal self. And all this morning before you came over...kind of dragging, I guess, but I didn't think to ask. Did you sense anything?"

"Nothing noticeable, but," she teased, "you were pretty distracting."

He shrugged it off. "Maybe they both need to take a break from dreaming to recover."

*　*　*

The front door was flung open before they could set aside their bags and knock. "My prodigal daughter returns, and this time with her mystery man," Barbara exclaimed, holding out her arms to give a fierce hug.

"Now you have proof I didn't make him up," Kris said as she returned the embrace, glancing over her mother's shoulder to her smiling father. "So, don't chase him away."

Answering her warning with a cocked eyebrow, her father replied, "He'll have to be made of stronger stuff than that to be worthy." He stepped forward and extended a hand. "I'm Dave, generally responsible for my daughter being spoiled." This earned him a grin and a firm handshake, a *tsk* from the mother, and a swat from Kris. "In the most excellent way, I mean."

The disarmed young man said, "Doug—though I guess you already know that."

"And you have probably been warned about us," Dave speculated.

"Enough to be excited about meeting you."

"Oh, a charmer! Come here." Barbara had disengaged so she could also hug the boyfriend who had enchanted her highly selective daughter.

After sharing fondness with her father, Kris went to gather her bags only to be beaten to it by him. "Let's get you guys settled in and take the grand tour," he prompted.

Kris rolled her eyes, reaching for Doug's free hand. "All seven rooms of it."

"Eight," her mother corrected. "We also count our screened-in porch as a room—and don't forget the space around the dinner table!"

"Size isn't what makes it grand," Dave pointed out while holding the door open for the others to pass through.

"Funny enough," Kris said while motioning Doug into the room closest to the front door, "this is the smallest house they own. You can put your stuff in here, the 'grand' guest room."

To their amusement, Dave insisted, "And it's only for *grand* guests."

Doug set his bag on the bed, glanced around the cozy space, and quipped, "It has a place to sleep, so that's fine by me."

"If you're wondering why we have multiple homes," Dave said conspiratorially, "clearly, we take bribes in exchange for passing grades."

Barbara snorted at her husband's antics. "Our inheritance," she corrected. "It's how we invest. Nothing safer than a charming property at an ideal spot."

"I totally get that, especially with your amazing lake house," Doug blurted, remembering in a flash all his mind-blowing experiences there. He was saved from his embarrassment by them entering the next room.

"And this is where I grew up," Kris informed him, gesturing like a tour guide at the stickered desk and dresser, the sparkly ceiling, and her childhood teddy bear still resting on his beanbag throne.

"And in a manner of speaking," her father pointed out, "so did we."

After transferring luggage to the bed, she snatched up her bear and gave it an appropriate squeeze. "And this is my most loyal childhood friend, Teddy. I was very shy back then."

Barbara commented, "We all have to start somewhere, and from such humble beginnings…"

Her father intoned, "We hope you have returned to us both smarter and wiser."

"You know it!" Kris stated before giving Doug a wink and saying, "This is our ritual, just roll with it."

Ending their tour of the modest house in the living room, they settled onto cozy furniture to begin the serious visiting. The parents politely asked about school progress and aspirations and how they met, before leading into the obvious subject.

"So…" Barbara prompted, "dreaming. We hear you began all this."

Doug shifted in his spot next to Kris, and she squeezed his hand, perhaps reminding him that they agreed they could talk about anything but Viz. "Not really. Cathy was the one who pulled us all together. I guess I was just the first to post a dream."

"Well," Dave added playfully, "we hear it's more than an occasional amusement for you guys."

Doug hesitated out of a now-ingrained habit before responding, "I'm not sure how much you want to hear about our explorations and discoveries. You're the only parents who know anything at all."

"We aren't working with the FBI, if that's what you're asking."

Doug barked a laugh. "I sure hope not! Ever since that night in the gym and all the warnings, we've made a point to not involve anyone else."

"Sounds sensible," Barbara commented. "We took a careful measure of them when they visited here. While they might be a bit loopy, they certainly take it seriously. Keeping your heads down should, hopefully, minimize any future messes. And if that's to tell no one else of your experiments, then it's for the best."

As a way to catch them up and give an example, Kris mentioned, "You know we couldn't even tell our freshman counselor, Mark, without endangering him. We recently filled out surveys—very carefully, to not give away too much—to help him with his doctoral research. And let me tell you, that was a chore!"

Her father nodded in understanding and approval. "Well, if you even *think* they are becoming unreasonable, tell us right away."

Barbara promised in her fierce tone, "We'll add all of our leverage to the problem if they become one."

With that support shown, Dave shifted his focus back to the boyfriend. "We're curious about your take on the dreaming, and what it means to you."

Doug took a long drink of water from the glass he had been offered during the kitchen tour before answering. "For starters, the more we learn about them, the more amazing they become. More immersive. There seems to be endless opportunities to learn." Doug shrugged in his inability to properly express the wondrous, mind-opening transformation dreams offered without broaching the subject of their mysterious mentor. "We found that some special dreams allow us to influence and *help* in a way that reflects positively here in the waking world, whether we gain empathy, understanding, confidence… If we didn't need to rest from them so often, we could effectively double our rate of learning."

"Oh, if only the education field could tap into that market," Dave quipped, "we'd turn out 18-year-old doctors."

Making a face, Kris exclaimed, "Sounds like a nightmare, Dad, having to do homework in your sleep!"

Laughing, he agreed. "Okay, maybe it *is* best if we keep the secret."

They could have comfortably talked for the rest of the day and into the night, sharing stories to learn more about each other. But, they had Thanksgiving dinner reservations at one of the highest rated restaurants in the area, and an even longer drive the following day. By the time the young couple actually left, Barbara and Dave knew the visit had been successful, because the young man already began to feel like family.

* * *

By comparison, Doug's homecoming was quite mellow. The traveling pair had dragged their feet at Kris' parents, enjoying breakfast and savoring the last bit of visiting before beginning the most demanding stretch of their journey. They had to travel almost as much north as east across most of the time zone, so it was dark by the time Doug navigated into the hushed suburb and onto the driveway.

For the final hours of the drive, they had been so worn down they couldn't find much to talk about. Kris bravely fought off the nods, even when Doug insisted he was fine and she could sneak in some sleep to take the edge off. But she had to prove she was also a trooper, and so they used smiles and hand-squeezes and the occasional oddball comment to keep themselves awake. In those grueling hours, Doug felt it was the bizarre comments they tossed back and forth that bonded them the most. They had shared their crazy-tired-goofy selves, and in a way, that *heightened* their compatibility.

The outside lights in the vestibule and above the open garage were the only signs anyone expected them. With audible relief and the kind of loud silence that came from tortured ear drums, they exited the car, grabbed their bags, and entered through the garage door. Doug's parents were on the couch watching their usual fare, Hallmark Channel sappiness, though one would have to ignore that his father looked comatose to claim he was actually watching.

"Ah, finally here." His mother paused the show and rose to greet them while tapping her husband on the leg to get his attention.

Doug sighed, dropping his bag on the floor to give her a hug. "As we suspected, it was a brutal drive. Dear Mother, this is Kris. Kris, this is Stephanie."

"Glad to meet you," his mother warmly greeted, waiting courteously until Kris made the move to also receive a hug.

"And this sleepy man is my father, Evan."

He blinked sheepishly, claiming, "I was just resting my eyes."

"It's great to meet you both," Kris said while shaking the father's hand. "Thank you for delaying your Thanksgiving meal for us."

"Oh." Stephanie brushed away the comment. "It has given me extra days to prepare." Gesturing toward the open kitchen and island with covered pans piled on top, she said, "As you can probably smell, I just finished the baked goods." After a moment's reflection, she added, "You must feel like sleeping late in the morning, so if you want, we can time the meal to count as your breakfast."

Kissing her cheek, Doug replied with a grin, "Just be sure not to let us sleep through it."

"I'd be happy to help with anything left to do," Kris offered, but again, Doug's mother waved it away.

"I have it well in hand, but thank you. Just make yourself at home."

After depositing their bags in the guest room, they stood in the space and clung together. "Feels so nice just to be standing still," Kris murmured against Doug's chest.

"Yeah," he agreed while gently rubbing her back. "But before we crash, there's one other you must meet." Hand in hand, he led her around the corner to another door, tapping twice before opening it.

The boy wore a gaming headset, intent on his screen until the motion caught his eye. There was a flash of annoyance before he registered who stood in his doorway, and then a smile covered that, followed by practiced nonchalance. This was a new phase for him.

Lowering his headset to his neck, he droned, "Aren't you a little young to be bringing strange women home at night?"

"I see you're learning dry humor, little brother."

"Actually, I'm practicing my fatherly disapproval skills."

"Nice. By the way, this 'strange woman' is Kris." Doug turned slightly to his girlfriend while gesturing to his sibling. "And this dork is Jason."

Kris gave him a small wave and teased, "Will you be needing those fatherly skills anytime soon?"

"Can never be too prepared, I say." And with that, Jason cracked his first genuinely boyish grin, inviting them to join him and watch his digital dominance.

"We're really tired, little bro. We just needed to make sure you were still alive."

"So, tomorrow, then?" the boy asked.

"Tomorrow, then," Kris promised, waving goodnight and noting with amusement that his attention was already turning back toward the screen.

The traditional Thanksgiving meal was beyond pleasant, in that it seemed to highlight all the things worth keeping for all time: warm company, amusing conversation, and excellent food made with that extra spice of love.

All too soon, it was time to think about getting back on the road. They had originally planned to use the last day of the holiday weekend to regain their equilibrium before Monday classes. But as they hung out with the parents on their living room's twin couches, they decided they could just as easily sleep there, which had the added benefit of putting off that final eight hours of driving.

*   *   *

At long last and with great relief, they were parked in front of Doug's rental. They kissed tenderly as if in celebration, basking in the success of a wonderful trip being over.

"We made it," Doug whispered into the sudden quiet after Kris switched off the engine. "Mission successful, right? I think the parents love us."

In answer, Kris turned more fully to him, touching his face and shoulders before resting her palm against his chest.

"Yes," she finally vocalized, her eyes radiating her intensity. "And now I don't want to let you go."

With an understated smile, he said, "That's fine by me."

Kris giggled. "Now that I've met your parents, I see where you get your cool-customer aura."

He had an immediate response for her: "And I see where you get your brilliance and passion. Kris, I love everything about you."

Doug hesitated and Kris waited. An expectant quality grew heavy in the air; the confines of the car suddenly became more intimate. He drew in a large breath. "I know this isn't the right place—"

"It is."

"—or the right time—"

"It most definitely is!" Kris took and squeezed both his hands in hers.

"I would do better if—"

She gave a joyous laugh. "There *is* no better, and *yes*!"

"Will you marry me?"

Tears forming in her eyes and a shaky smile on her lips, Kris sassed, "I just gave you your answer, silly."

"Are you sure?"

"Oh, *yes!*" With the force of her passion, in the thrill of the moment, she said yes in a manner more potent than any words. When she caught her breath, her tone was deeper, softer, sensual. "I'm suddenly energized, and *definitely* not letting you go." With that hanging in the air, she started the engine and began driving to her place. "I know we should rest, but some things we need more. And, besides, my shower is bigger."

* * *

Will seemed always tired. He had begun skipping classes to relieve the pressure. And yet still he pushed with a hunger unsated. Even when his ability to clearly remember dreams started to falter, he pushed.

"You are exposing yourself to out-of-balance. To damage." Viz was gazing sadly at him while dull surroundings swirled sluggishly, ever so slightly out of focus.

"*Viz!*" Will exclaimed in recognition. "How you been? I'm learning faster and faster, more and more." Was his speech slightly slurred?

Viz shimmered as he shook his head. "You neglecting other parts of life is the same effect as limiting your own growth, for you need all-together. One in-balance-part aiding another, inter-supportive."

"But there are only so many hours in the day—night—and this feels so...*liberating!*"

"It is known, if you push too hard to learn, you close yourself to learning. Pushing always narrows focus.

Learning has cost-requirements, including being open and patient."

Will objected. "That makes no sense, because it's willpower, *drive*, which speeds up learning."

"Only when joined with the realization-acceptance that you do not yet know what it *is* you must learn. This process is on-purpose-exploratory, not a race to be won. Determination has no speed setting." Viz settled in beside Will, who was now seated more calmly, yet struggling to comprehend that which was at conflict with his *mission*, or so he felt.

"Consider," Viz continued earnestly, "the most ancient are still learning as if new-fresh, such is the endlessness of exploration. How damaged might they become if they were impatient. With the infinite."

Will mused, "No rushing infinity, is there?"

With a hint of playfulness and an encouraging smile: "Not to my knowledge."

"Speaking of knowledge, tell me about this place— what is it, exactly?"

"*Exactly*?" Viz's surprise grew into humor. "You ask the wildest-boldest of things! No wonder 'this place' loves-protects you." Viz raised one ethereal eyebrow. "It could-in-theory force you away until you rested. I suspect I too could do this benefit-service for you. But then, you would not learn-understand-resonate what has become so vital for you. Trust in this *Here*." Viz swept an arm to include their murky-sleepy surroundings. "It wants the best *you*. It does not want you harmed by your own impatience-joy. You *must* absorb-savor each aspect in order to prepare for the next."

Will was thinking in deep breaths, anxiousness ebbing. "I have the time to wait for that?"

"Yes. As much time as you need, dear student, it will offer."

"Okay—it's just that I don't want to miss a *single* bit of it!"

"Yet if you hurry, that is exactly what will happen: you will miss what you should take the time to learn."

Feeling more himself, Will grinned at Viz. "Are you avoiding my 'boldest' question? What is this place?"

"You expect a simple answer to the infinitely complex, a question no one can answer for anyone else. Begin by seeing this as your learning-proving ground. Your life-love-gift. It *wants* you to succeed on your own, to grow in such a fulfilling way that your own question will be answered to your satisfaction *by you*.

"Yet, I will offer more, sharing hints of my journey flowing from me, in joy. To my experience, *Here* is the Essence of all past-and-future hope-potential, complete genius-of-awareness, giver-host of attunement, the timeless-boundless growth-space of the new-to-come."

"Well, you lost me at 'Here is the...past-and-future...'"

For a moment, Viz wore what seemed to be a teasing smile. "You are the one who asked." Straightening, he admitted, "Much more is beyond my comprehension, for current-now. What you can measure *This* by, reliably in all journey-steps, is your growth-of-self. Which is perfectly within its defining. And this is why I have come-been-brought to you now, when you most threaten to hurt yourself."

"So…" Will struggled, yearned, to make the final connection. "Are you linked to here, somehow?"

Viz held up a single finger to emphasize his point. "Simply, I am here-now because I accept the need to be here. There is no force in our visit, no pushing-hurry, but *all* of my learning-being."

With a form of relief he had never experienced, in the presence of such benevolence and wisdom, Will could only manage to say, "I understand, I understand," even as he was fading into a deep sleep.

Chapter 31

Nolan's house was abuzz with pre-meeting chatter and laughter, quips and hugs. And then there was the comforting and promising sound and smell of coffee brewing. Nolan smiled sadly, resting his hands on the counter as he stared at the coffeemaker. Everything still felt painful to him, but the hyper-sensitivity was beginning to fade as his acceptance firmed and set. His understanding and resolve, like the chemical process of concrete, took the right mix of ingredients and time to achieve. This was his chosen life, and these were his friends and fellow explorers. He only needed more time—

"Hey you, all quiet in here." Cathy gave him a gentle nudge with her shoulder. Catching a glimpse of the raw, she softened her voice. "You okay?"

Nolan nodded, not feeling quite ready to share. "Us," he explained instead while scooping her into a hug. "Our fellowship, our *warmth*…"

"Yeah," she agreed, "we're special—and in a good way." She giggled at herself. "At least *most* of the time."

"Yeah. Sometimes I just get overwhelmed."

At that moment, Will made his grand entrance: "I *have arrived*, lovelies!" And then it was time to start passing out cups of coffee or tea. "I finally had my first one-on-one with Viz. It only took me nearly destroying myself!" Will looked energized, refreshed, more than he had been in weeks, and the others recognized the kind of momentum in him that had to be released immediately, even as they were getting their preferred beverages and settling in.

"Do tell!" Cathy encouraged, as she carried two cups of coffee into the living room, handing one to her roommate with a wink that said, "You need this." The lovebirds had hardly left Kris' room since their commitment to each other.

Without even bothering to grab coffee, Will settled onto his usual seat. "So, of course I was getting too obsessed, and it was hurting my balance."

"We could have told you that," Kris sassed from where she leaned against Doug's side, cupping her mug in both hands and casually swaying her crossed legs.

"And I would have ignored you." Will cocked a defiant eyebrow before shifting gears again. "But Viz *showed* me how it was dangerous, my push for more and more dreaming. Because each piece of our life is intertwined, dependent, on the others. So if something isn't supporting and helping the others, then it is damaging you, or something to that effect."

Will rubbed his hands together, leaning forward. "And I can now *see* that if I push too hard to learn, being impatient and whatever—trying to skip steps—then I actually don't gain what I need to reach that next level. And reaching the next level unprepared...well, then you just 'F'. Big flop. Oops-fail!" The group chuckled at his antics even while they were nodding.

"I could easily *know* that, of course," Will continued, still on his roll, "but I couldn't *feel* it, the extreme importance to me, and the trap I was sliding into. Until, that is, Viz spent the time with me. The dude really is amazing!”

“So, you’re saying Viz solved all your problems, huh?” Doug teased.

Will made a face at Doug but played along for a moment. “Even Viz isn’t *that* good. No, he didn’t press or force, either. He only offered insight until I felt the truth of it.” Will roughly tapped the side of his head as if it would help him remember a point. “He said something to the effect that all of *him* was there, to support or teach or whatever. He even said that the dream realm could probably kick me out and force me to rest, but then I *wouldn’t learn*. A-and it all came together for me: that great advice meant nothing if I didn’t feel it deep down, understanding it in a way that *changed* my thinking and pattern!”

Will sat back and relaxed with a smile growing on his face, finishing with the simple confirmation: “And it did.”

Cathy began the clapping, which prompted Will to rise and take a stage-bow. Then she instigated their group hug so they could properly celebrate Will’s breakthrough.

“Another interesting thing,” Will continued while they were returning to their seats, “is when I asked Viz about the dream realm. He almost laughed at me, called me bold, said I should look at it like a training ground. That I’ll grow enough to answer my own questions about it. And the weird thing is he volunteered more, defining what it meant to him, but the details just kind of...” He swept his hand over his head while making a jet noise.

"Though I got the basics, I think, something like the past and future of everything—only more. According to Viz, it's definitely alive and loves us, wants the best for us."

Doug spoke for the rest in saying, "I think that makes perfect sense to anyone experiencing it."

"Without any doubt," Will summarized, "there's *incredible* stuff to learn, endless things. And Viz promised I have plenty of time." He held up a hand. "But the main reason I'm no longer in a hurry is *because* I don't want to miss any of it."

Kris complimented him with a bright smile, "Which shows you learned a fine lesson."

"And shared it with us," Quani added. "Thank you."

"I also had a meeting with Viz," Nolan mumbled into the savoring pause, and the attention in the room swung to him, "but wasn't nearly as nice."

"Oh?" his roommate asked. "When was this?"

Nolan considered blowing it off, but then changed his mind. "Last week, but I've had to work through many things first." Taking a steadying breath, he said, "Viz confirmed what we suspected about Teressa, that it'd be wrong to tell her. Even a disaster of sorts."

"Oh, no," Kris said, already stretching out with her empathy.

"He... Viz seemed to be able to glimpse a future where I told Teressa about our dreaming, and it wasn't good for anyone. He said that to give someone a gift they couldn't accept wasn't giving a gift at all. And it took me a while to really understand what he meant. That she would never be able to accept *this*, and it'd become a burden or even a danger to us all." Nolan looked around their circle, and they all seemed to be holding their breaths. "Insightful, but painful. But as necessary, I guess, as what you needed, Will."

"Man!" Will responded. "That sucks it has to be that way. So...breaking up with her?"

Nolan nodded and looked down at the cheap carpet. "I did it this weekend. Not the best timing, but..." He shrugged, and Cathy's arms were then encircling him.

"We're here for you," Kris comforted, rubbing his shoulder.

"I know," he said, trying desperately not to weep again. "Being here with you helps so much. Getting it out. I'll be okay."

"Of course you will," Cathy said softly, settling lightly onto his lap so she could maintain the embrace. Each of the others in the room stated their support, salving over the grief.

"It sucked," Nolan murmured, and then more firmly, reiterated, "but it *was* necessary. Like the FBI guys said. I think she was in shock or something, because she took it pretty well. Objected, pouted, you know, but she didn't scream or strangle me."

"Obviously," Will teased ever so gently, "or you'd not be alive to tell us about it."

"And after that, I couldn't stay. I won't be going back to that church. I'll find a new one, or, you know..." Nolan shrugged, and Cathy straightened, slowly disengaging and returning to her chair.

"Or you get what you need with us," Quani suggested. "With our dream realm."

And for the first time in days, Nolan smiled. "Yeah. Maybe I can."

Everyone seemed to breathe easier, and Cathy cleared her throat. "In better news..." She let that hang in the air until she saw Nolan look up and nod. "I have a new roommate, of sorts."

Kris hissed, "Cathy!"

"You expect me to keep a secret, from *them*?" The saucy roommate smirked. "Then *you* tell them."

Kris glanced to Doug, who just smiled lovingly in return. So, she turned to the group and announced, "We're now engaged!"

"Ooo!" Quani said with widened eyes while Will let out a *whoop*.

Cathy sassed, "*Engaged* is one way to put it, sure. This is like the first time they've left her room."

Uncharacteristically, Doug laughed, and Kris turned back to see him trying to contain his mirth.

"What's so funny?" his fiancé asked.

"I just realized something," he said, feeling only giddiness when recalling his previous roommate Tim, and all the times *he* felt like he had a third roommate. "I've now become Donna, my last roommate's girlfriend!"

Laughter and congratulations mixed with demands to hear details, and it was clear that this news deserved to take up the remainder of their time together.

*　*　*

The swirling-shifting patterns of potential were now dancing, sparkling as if creating-composed of a billion-billion crystals, or star-hearts glowing in gentle brilliance. There existed a resonance like a hum of the exultant, and a playfulness? A...celebration? Something fundamental had-changed-was-changing.

Viz marveled-absorbed the surroundings. "I have never seen such."

In front of him waited a smiling-glowing Kris, hands clasped in front of her, a mysterious out-of-focus in her center-being. "Hello, Viz. It's been a long time."

"Is *this*...you? Kris, love-of-Doug?" Adjusting to his shock, he opened himself more to the newness-of-experience, attuning to the surrounding shimmer.

Kris shrugged demurely before answering, "Everything in me *sings* in joy, even more here than in my world." Her eyes glistened in symmetry to the billions. "My love *pours* from me."

Viz bowed his head-mind in awe. "So it does, most-precious."

"Doug and I have become engaged," she informed him happily. "Finally, completely."

"Engaged?" Viz stretched out for the taste-experience of the foreign concept. "You are already sharing-intertwined."

Kris sensed his confusion. "This is how we proclaim to everyone, not just those who know us."

"And such joy-of-proclamation!" He understood, motioning at their now-surroundings. Though, curiosity of the not-quite-completely-correct drew him closer to her. "Please, tell me of it."

Kris spread delicate hands and fingers, like ethereal wings of the Long-Silent, and then she began dancing-swirling-floating to the timing-tuning of *Here*. "We visited those who love each of us," she recounted for him while drifting in total harmony, "who now love us *both*.

"And I only *thought* we truly connected before, but now it is...beyond description. I don't understand why or how, but I fascinate my Doug more than ever, and he *fills* me with this joy!"

Viz repeated in amazement of the experience: "I have never seen such."

Kris giggled in a purest harmonic, joyful poetry-in-motion. "I never imagined seeing you surprised, Viz. Does my happiness confuse you? I thought you had seen it all."

"*Love*, I now-know," Viz expressed his truth-resonance, "will always amaze us, no matter how much else we understand. I, too, celebrate you and Doug-friend, and this moment, and glorious *Here*." And in that instant of acknowledgment-learning, a veil lifted from his mind-eyes, and he *saw*!

Viz cried-pulsed-emoted: "Newest-precious-divine spark! *Rebirth* of potential!" Kris' previously blurred center-being radiated in a way that made all pieces of the mystery come into time-place.

She slowed and then stopped her spinning, now the one being confused. "What do you mean? Viz, I'm ready to *learn*." Could she not truly know? *Here* most certainly celebrated the future-hope.

"This is why you feel such joy," he explained carefully, containing his own awe-joy. "Your deepening with Doug and within yourself is *also* a deepening of the New."

With that emphasis, he witnessed intuition replace her confusion. Kris slowly brought her hands to her belly, which to Viz' mind-eyes seemed rounder, full-in-potential. "But," she said, oddly confused-combating her knowledge, "I am on birth control. I told him... We didn't plan..." With each statement, her glow dimmed in a way alarming to Viz, and then he *knew* his truth-helper-moment.

"Dearest Kris," Viz pleaded, drawing even closer and projecting support, "do not close yourself off out of fear-shock, but *open*. Learn-feel-learn." He performed a familiar-to-them version of kneeling in front of her, before the blazing potential so clear within her. He raised spread arms to the dancing *Here*, which now was slowing as well. *"This* and you and Doug and your New…this is your *complete* joy. Life-who-wants-to-be asks for *you*, calls to you, *yearns* for you. *Mother."*

Kris had closed her eyes, beginning to drift again, to feel the joy-truth once again. Considering-journeying through murky complexity-conflict.

Mother. This seemed to be a gentle, tiny breath both from the surrounding billion-billions and from within Kris, from under the hands which remained over her womb.

Almost as an afterthought, elsewhere-distracted, Kris spoke, "I guess I should stop taking… Should talk to…" She opened her eyes to look directly at Viz. "I will remember all of this, right?"

"Of course, Kris. Now, you can feel-understand the joyous of the New. A choice both yours, and *so* much more."

"Potential," she murmured his term, as if seeking confirmation. Viz refocused and concentrated on his vision-need. He gazed into one potentiality, a future baby bump, and then beyond, to see a true gift from *Here*.

So, again in amazement, he replied, "Yes, *she* will-be, more than we can now-know." Then Kris nodded, to him and to acknowledge his truth-telling, and was gone.

Chapter 32

"Pick up, pick up, pick up," Kris murmured while counting the rings. It was still dark outside, and she was in her bathroom, door shut and locked, sitting on a towel in the corner near the toilet. In case the roiling confusion within her made her throw up. She hung up and dialed again, and knew she would repeat until—

"Kris?" her mother's sleepy voice queried.

Oh thank god! "Mom, I have to talk—I'm sorry, but I have to talk to you."

"Okay, okay," said Barbara, her voice now gentle and urging, her motherly voice. "What's on your mind?"

"I just found out I'm pregnant! I thought it couldn't happen right away *and* while I'm on the pill, and well, we haven't even told you we got engaged!"

"Oh. That's sudden but great news."

"About us getting engaged?"

Kris could hear her mother's humor as she adjusted to her surprise. "That, too. I have to say it *is* a strange way to find out."

"Oh, *god*, I'm so sorry, Mom. I'm just…"

Soothingly: "I know, I know."

"We've only *just* made the commitment and…celebrated."

"Then I'm confused," said Barbara. "How can you know you're pregnant?"

"It was shown to me tonight, by my...you know."

"Hmm. Sure it wasn't just a dream? We know how powerful they can be."

Without humor, Kris laugh-cried quietly into her hand. "Quite sure, Mom. I'm still resonating like a plucked string. *Everything* about me knows."

"Okay, okay, well...that certainly has its advantages, I guess. You know, I haven't had the chance to tell you this, but..." Barbara paused dramatically. "I've only seen love like you and Doug share once before. And *you*, my dearest daughter, are a result of that love."

Kris' stomach and mind did a few flips. She desperately needed to be hugged by her mother and to have these unexpected knots removed from her, to be held until they at least eased. But that need was sidelined by a thought. "Wait, wait... Are you saying *I* was unplanned?"

"Oh, I would never say that. You were *always* planned. And besides..." Kris could again hear the playfulness in her mother's tone. "A mother has to keep *some* of her secrets." Then, Barbara refocused on her daughter, asking, "So, what are you thinking?"

"I don't know yet, Mom," Kris answered while attempting to keep the frantic from her tone. "I don't know. I still have so much I want to do."

Her mother snorted. "We're living proof living doesn't stop."

"I didn't mean it like that."

"I know it's a major adjustment."

"And confusing," Kris added, struggling to keep from being overwhelmed. "I'm a little terrified, but also happy—I think. Shockingly happy, maybe even."

There came a gentle tapping on the door. "Kris?" Doug asked. "Are you okay?"

Kris cleared her throat and emotions. "Be right out," she said in a raised voice before hugging her phone again. "Mom, I need to go. Doug's up, but...thank you."

"I'm always here," her mother replied. "Keep us informed."

"I know, Mom," Kris said and cried lightly. "I love you."

"We both love you so much," Barbara responded before adding in good humor, "and now I'm going to go celebrate this news with your father."

After disconnecting the call, Kris rose, straightened her nightie, and checked in the mirror to see how badly her anxiety reflected on her face. Fortunately, she thought while wiping at her eyes, Doug hadn't turned on the bedroom light. She collected herself as best she could and opened the door to see her love sitting on the end of the bed.

"Hi," he said softly as she shut the door behind her so only the light escaping from under the door acted like a nightlight. "What's going on?"

"That was my mother," Kris explained instead, holding up the phone in case it needed clarification why she was holding it. "They now know we're engaged, which I guess we should have called them right away."

"We've been a little distracted," he replied.

Even in the dimness, she could see his grin, his loving grin, and that helped ease her tension, so she plopped down beside him with a sigh. "I had other sudden news that I had to…you know, get advice on." Subtlety had never been Kris' preference; she turned so she could fully see him and said, "I'm pregnant. Viz told me—though actually, the entire dream realm told me."

She could see the whites of his eyes. "Really?"

"Please don't be upset." And by blurting that, Kris realized her deepest worry. She desperately needed him not to be upset.

"I'm not," he said hastily yet unable to get in another word.

"I had no idea it could happen! So quickly, despite birth control! I'm maybe freaking out, and I need you to not be. Please don't be."

"Hey…" He gathered her into the hug she so urgently needed and squeezed. "I'm just surprised, not upset." She could almost feel him casting about for something more to say. "I bet…you are probably the only one to find out from within a dream."

Kris giggled and clutched him even tighter. "I bet not, but maybe not since that long, long ago."

"Hmm true, but then you are like an awakening of it."

That resonated with her so much she burst out crying. "Yes!" she laugh-cried. "Viz was shocked—you should have seen him! It's funny how he was…and maybe that's what he meant…by 'rebirth'."

"Rebirth," Doug repeated while cupping her crying face and kissing her lightly. "I like it."

She smiled through tears and guided his lips from damp cheeks to her lips. "Rebirth of Potential, he called my pregnancy and what he saw."

She felt him shudder. "That gave me goosebumps," he whispered between deepening kisses. "I like that even more." He laid her back onto the bed and then bent to kiss her belly. "Hello, little Rebirth of Potential."

She giggled at the delightful silliness of it all, but then he parted the thin cloth and touched her with his kisses in a way that transferred his goosebumps into her. "Oh," she breathed deep in her throat, and then it didn't seem so silly.

* * *

Viz waited expectantly, legs slightly apart, hands clasped in front of him. The slight smile on his face grew while Doug adjusted and realized he had been summoned. The expectant quality permeated every swirl of their meeting space. Yet, Doug still could feel the echo of Kris in his arms, of her great relief and joy and love.

"Focus on here-now," Viz instructed, standing close before his student. "Now is not the time to fade."

Doug frowned even while concentrating on Viz. "But Kris might need me."

His mentor gently shook his head. "You were there, perfect for her. She can recover-adjust. Now you are *Here*, for *us*. This is *your* balance."

"Did you have to *worry* her so much?"

Instead of being defensive over Doug's implication, Viz replied, "I feel the resonance of your protection-barrier encompassing your love. This is good." His amusement transitioned into the earnestness of a teaching moment. "Would you blame inevitability for its life-purpose? If *you* had seen-been-shown the importance of her needing to know in that instant, would you have delayed?"

"No, I guess... No."

"You *feel* this: choice is dependent upon knowledge-understanding. Without awareness, all that remains are missed opportunities. Instead, you accept the need to help because you are in-place and embrace *responsibility*." Viz' gaze was piercing. "I *see* you, Doug, opening to what you must understand, evolving your role-potential. Reaching out to *help*, and to continuously explore what that *means*. You are ready to see...a greater view. Come, *Dream Knight*."

The closeness of their surrounding seemed to fall away, though to Doug's recollection it felt more like an instantaneous vanishing of an artificial barrier in space. As his mind caught up to the revelation, he saw vastness beyond comprehension. Yet somehow it felt layered, filled. "Viz," Doug breathed in a way that felt like he had no breath. He grasped for support, and Viz was there with a steadying arm to cling to.

"Open yourself in awe-acceptance," Viz urged him, covering the desperately gripping hand in his own. "Each and every being...connected and connecting. Greatness incarnate, consciousness." With a free arm, Viz swept around, a gesture so small it highlighted the lack of any boundary, horizon-less. Calmly, he continued, "Worry not, Doug-friend. Stand firm, stand ready. I am with you and *for* you."

Doug could only whisper, "I don't understand." What his struggling mind registered as vastness became...*busy*.

Viz provided the needed confidence while images continued to materialize. "From *Here*, any can see us, can learn of you."

Now, there were countless distinct forms, moving, milling, perhaps curious, but never pressing close. Except for an immense presence that resolved like clouds being revealed by the first hints of sunrise. And Doug could feel reverence radiating from his mentor.

Viz acknowledged softly, a tiny sound compared to the rumbled resonance which filled their surrounding: "Ancient. Allow me to present New-Which-Isn't-New. Doug."

Doug felt the vibrations within everything that made him. It tested and discerned and judged: "***Revival***."

"Yes, Ancient," Viz agreed. "What-could-have-been now can-be.

It lingered in a timeless way conveyed by its mere presence, though the moment had been the length of Doug's held breath. In its final statement, Doug felt...benediction. "***At last***."

Doug trembled, overwhelmed while watching the awe-inspiring being recede. Multitudes around them, above and below, gently swayed as if waves lapping upon his shore during the most unforgettable of sunrises.

Then from the waves rose the sun. A light such as Doug would never forget! Yet before he could squint, it was dimming into focus. At first, Doug grasped a wild thought that the emerging woman was Kris. His heart fluttered in recognition, but then he noticed the maturity in the unhurried walk, the confidence in her sway, and the timelessness in her delicate features.

His mentor raised his palm, calling to her. "First Mother." As she drew close, Viz motioned to Doug. "Yes, you see true, Mother: a son to mend your broken heart. One to prove all is not lost to you."

"It cannot be," she stated, softly enough to carry only within the vacuum of held breaths. "My children left me." There was no recognition in her face as she looked past Doug and focused on Viz.

Doug perceived her long-held sorrow, *generations* of disheartenment from squandered potential drawn into herself, contained within her great burden of love. And that empathy stirred him to action. "I am here." He stepped up to her, his hands held out like an offering. Swinging her gaze back to him, he could tell that she was prepared to give him love, as she would for any who called upon it. He repeated with tenderness, "I am here for you."

Recognition dawned slowly within her as she placed her hands in his. Hesitantly, she dared to believe. "Son?"

In a declaration: "I am here."

Her eyes glistened with rekindling hope. "It has been *so* long... I feared...forever closed off."

Doug wanted to mourn with her, but more strongly, he needed to protect and assure her. He urged her to embrace him, proving him real. "I'm sorry we left you," he whispered. Even while ethereal in a sense, he felt her shake with the release of grief, with the *righting* of her existence, and he squeezed with every measure of his love and understanding. "I will make you proud!"

She drew back to better *see* him, to savor the sight and point out, "You already do."

Sensing her increasing joy, Doug blurted, "I have friends—also your children—who would love to meet you."

Still standing beside them, Viz chuckled and promised, "When they are ready. And one day, Mother, your people *can* return to you."

The First Mother raised hands in celebration, radiant in her newfound hope, lifting her voice to those countless watchers to proudly proclaim, "My people can return!" Gazing at Doug, she gave her blessing, bringing his bowed head to her lips, which, through her great love, seemed to touch his very core.

And then Doug was waking to the dim light of early morning, lying next to Kris, breathing deeply, and yet feeling the motivation to make up for lost generations. *Please let me never forget this* gift *of a dream!* He had so much to share with his friends about their future!

Kris stirred when he wrapped his arms around her and buried his face in her hair. "Kris, my love," Doug whispered when she rolled over and gave him a sleepy smile. "I met our *first* mother." In the hush and smallness of the room, he searched for ways to explain. "She has been cut off from us for so long." Yet gazing at his love, he felt certainty. "Now, *we* can change that."

An End

Afterword

And so concludes this story arc that I have been faithful to—and to the wonderful students of life-consciousness: Cathy, Will, Kris, Nolan, Quani, and Doug. Just like in my dream of the mysterious box and underwater academy, I feel as if all the right pieces are set in place and a better future awaits. The overarching message is one of awakened potential and purpose, and true to this, I encourage those with curious imagination to explore the numerous future potentialities: that-which-might-happen.

I aimed this challenging story at young adults, not only because that age group are the superstars of my dreams, but because more than ever they seem to be tricked by the superficiality of modern success into thinking they have no purpose left to them, which couldn't be further from the truth. So if more who languish in self-worth limbo are motivated to explore the subtle depths of true purpose, chasing the multi-layered, increasing potential of an ever-shifting future, then this story has done more than merely entertain. And entertainment that focuses rather than distracts...well, this is as it should be: the complete picture, the glimpses of life possibilities within *both* of her palms, not just the obvious one.

Acknowledgements

I'd like to express my deepest gratitude to Sharon and Leigh Ann and Ken and Darrell for all their help and support. And I must thank a bright young woman who helped me when things were at their worst, bolstering the motivation to finish for her and others like her. In the eyes of the cosmos, may they forever outweigh the destructive types who, it seems, only live to criticize. Finally and with a certain amount of cheekiness, I must appreciate whatever mysterious force(s) fed these wild dreams to me—including much of the plot itself. This novel is clearly a work of fiction, as it's meant to be. But in the interest of objectivity, I must report that in all my experiences or research I have seen nothing that proves dreams are merely random brain function. Such is the delightfully complex and mysterious existence we are born into.